continued . . .

FRIDAY NIGHT BITES

CHLOE NEILL

A ROC BOOK

ROC
Published by the Penguin Group
Penguin Group (USA) LLC, 375 Hudson Street,
New York, New York 10014

USA I Canada I UK I Ireland I Australia I New Zealand I India I South Africa I China
penguin.com
A Penguin Random House Company

Published by Roc, an imprint of New American Library, a division of Penguin Group
(USA) LLC. Previously published in a New American Library edition.

First Roc Printing, July 2014

 REGISTERED TRADEMARK—MARCA REGISTRADA

ISBN 978-0-451-46996-0

Printed in the United States of America
10 9 8 7 6 5 4 3 2 1

"First get the facts.
Then you can distort them all you want."

—Mark Twain

movin' out

Late May
Chicago, Illinois

"Higher, Merit. Bring up that kick. Mmm-hmm. Better."

I kicked again, this time higher, trying to remember to point my toes, squeeze my core, and flutter my fingers in the "jazz hands" our instructor ceaselessly demanded.

Next to me, and considerably less enthused, my best friend and soon-to-be-ex-roommate, Mallory, growled and executed another kick. The growl was an odd accompaniment to the bob of blue hair and classically pretty face, but she was irritated enough to carry it off.

"Remind me why you dragged me into this?" she asked.

Our instructor, a busty blonde with bright pink nails and impossibly sharp cheekbones, clapped her hands together. Her breasts joggled in syncopation. It was impossible to look away.

"Fiercer, ladies! We want every eye in the club on our bodies! Let's *work* it!"

Mallory glared daggers at the instructor we'd named Aerobics Barbie. Mal's fists curled and she took a menacing step forward, but I wrapped an arm around her waist before she could pummel the woman we'd paid to grapevine us into skinny jeans.

"Ixnay on the ighting-fay," I warned, using a little of my two-month-old vampire strength to keep her in place despite her bobbing fists. Mallory grumbled, but finally stopped struggling.

Score one for the newbie vampire, I thought.

"How about a little civilized beat-down?" she asked, blowing a lock of sweaty blue hair from her forehead.

I shook my head, but let her go. "Beating down the teacher's gonna get you more attention than you need, Mal. Remember what Catcher said."

Catcher was Mallory's gruff boyfriend. And while my comment didn't merit a growl, I got a nasty, narrow-eyed snarl. Catcher loved Mallory, and Mallory loved Catcher. But that didn't mean she liked him all the time, especially since she was dealing with a supernatural perfect storm centered over our Chicago brownstone. In the span of a week, I'd been unwillingly made a vampire, and we'd learned that Mallory was a still-developing sorceress. As in, magical powers, black cats and the major and minor Keys—the divisions of magic.

So, yeah. My first few weeks as a vampire had been inordinately busy. Like *The Young and the Restless*, but with slightly dead people.

Mal was still getting used to the idea that she had paranormal drama of her own, and Catcher, already in trouble with the Order (the sorcerers' governing union), was keeping a pretty tight lid on her magical demonstrations. So Mallory was supernaturally frustrated.

Hell, we were both supernaturally frustrated, and Mallory didn't have fangs or a pretentious Master vampire to deal with.

So, given that unfortunate state of affairs, why were we letting Aerobics Barbie guilt us into using jazz hands?

Simply put, this was supposed to be quality time, bonding time, for me and Mallory.

Because I was moving out.

"Okay," Barbie continued, "let's add that combination we learned last week. One, two and three and four, and five, six and seven and eight." The music reached a pounding cre-scendo as she pivoted and thrusted to the bass-heavy beat. We followed as best we could, Mallory having a little harder time of not stepping on her own feet. My years of ballet classes—and the quickstep speed that vampirism gave me—were actually serving me pretty well, the humiliation of a twenty-eight-year-old vampire doing jazz hands notwith-standing.

Barbie's enthusiasm aside, the fact that we were doing jazz hands in a hip-hop dance class didn't say much for her credentials. But the class was still an improvement over my usual training. My workouts were usually *très* intense, be-cause only a couple of months ago I'd been named Sentinel for my House.

To make a long story slightly shorter, American vampires were divided into Houses. Chicago had three, and I'd been initiated into the second oldest of those—Cadogan. Much to everyone's surprise given my background (think grad school and medieval romantic literature), I'd been named Sentinel. Although I was still learning the ropes, being Sentinel meant I was supposed to act as a kind of vampire guard. (Turns out that while I was a pretty geeky human, I was a pretty strong vampire.) Being Sentinel also meant training, and while American vampires had traded in the black velvet and lace for Armani and iPhones, they were pretty old school on a lot of issues—feudal on a lot of issues—including weapons. Put all that together, and it meant I was learning to wield the antique katana I'd been given to defend Cadogan and its vampires.

Coincidentally enough, Catcher was an expert in the Sec-ond of the Four Keys—weapons—so he'd been tasked with prepping me for vampire combat. As a newbie vampire, hav-ing Catcher as a sparring partner wasn't exactly great for the confidence.

Aerobics Barbie whipped herself into a hip-hop frenzy, leading the class in a final multistep combination that ended with the lot of us staring sassily at the mirrors that lined the dance studio. Session concluded, she applauded and made some announcements about future classes that Mallory and I would have to be dragged, kicking and screaming, to attend.

"Never again, Merit," she said, walking to the corner of the room where she'd deposited her bag and water bottle before class started. I couldn't have agreed more. Although I loved to dance, hip thrusting under Barbie's bubbly instruction and ever-bouncing bosom involved too little actual dance and too much cleavage. I needed to respect my dance master. Respect wasn't exactly the emotion Barbie inspired.

We sat down on the floor to prep for our return to the real world.

"So, Ms. Vampire," Mallory asked me, "are you nervous about moving into the House?"

I glanced around, not entirely sure how much chatting I should be doing about my vampire business. The Chicagoland Vampires had announced their existence to Chicago roughly ten months ago, and as you might guess, humans weren't thrilled to learn that we existed. Riots. Panic. Congressional investigations. And then Chicago's three Houses became wrapped up in the investigation of two murders— murders supposedly perpetrated by vampires from Cadogan and Grey, the youngest Chicago House. The Masters of those Houses, Ethan Sullivan and Scott Grey, dreaded the attention.

But the Master of the third House (that was Navarre) was conniving, manipulative, and the one that actually planned the murders. She was also drop-dead gorgeous, no pun intended. She might as well have leaped from an editorial spread in *Vogue*. Dark hair and blue eyes (just like me), but with an arrogance that put celebrities and cult leaders to shame.

Humans were entranced, *fascinated*, by Celina Desaulniers.

Her beauty, her style, and her ability to psychically manipulate those around her were an irresistible combination. Humans wanted to learn more about her, to see more, to hear more.

That she'd been responsible for the deaths of two

humans—murders she'd planned and confessed to—hadn't minimized their fascination. Nor had the fact that she'd been captured (BTW, by Ethan and me) and extradited to London for incarceration by the Greenwich Presidium, the council that ruled Western European and North American vampires. And in her place, the rest of us—the exonerated majority who hadn't helped her commit those heinous crimes— became that much more interesting. Celina got her wish— she got to play the bad little martyred vampire—and we got an early Christmas present: We got to step into the vacuum of her celebrity.

T-shirts, caps, and pennants for Grey and Cadogan (and for the more morbid, Navarre) were available for sale in shops around Chicago. There were House fan sites, "I ♥ Cadogan" bumper stickers, and news updates on the city's vampires.

Still, notorious or not, I tried not to spread too many deets about the Houses around town. As Sentinel, I was part of the House's security corps, after all. So I took a look around the gym and made sure we were alone, that prying human ears weren't slipping a listen.

"If you're debating how much you can say," Mallory said, unscrewing the top of her water bottle, "I've sent out a magical pulse so that none of our little human friends can hear this conversation."

"Really?" I turned my head to look at her so quickly my neck popped, the shock of pain squinting my eyes.

She snorted. "Right. Like he'd let me use M-A-G-I-C around people," she muttered, then took a big gulp of her water.

I ignored the shot at Catcher—we'd never have a decent conversation if I took the time to react to all of them—and answered her question about the Big Move.

"I'm a little nervous. Ethan and I, you know, tend to grate on each other's nerves."

Mallory swallowed her water, then wiped her forehead with the back of her hand. "Oh, whatever. You two are BFFs."

"Just because we've managed to play Master and Sentinel

for two weeks without tearing each other's throat out doesn't mean we're BFFs."

As a matter of fact, I'd had minimum contact with Cadogan's Master—and the vampire who made me—during those last two weeks, by design. I kept my head down and my fangs to the grindstone as I watched and learned how things worked in the House. The truth was, I'd had trouble with Ethan at first—I'd been made a vampire without my consent, my human life taken away because Celina planned on me being her second victim. Her minions weren't successful in killing me, but Ethan had been successful at changing me—in order to save my life.

Frankly, the transition sucked. The adjustment from human grad student to vampire guard was, to say the least, awkward. As a result, I'd pushed a lot of vitriol in Ethan's direction. I'd eventually made the decision to accept my new life as a member of Chicago's fanged community. Although I still wasn't sure I had fully come to terms with being a vampire, I was dealing.

Ethan, though, was more complicated. We shared some kind of connection, some pretty strong chemistry, and some mutual irritation toward each other. He acted like he thought I was beneath him; I generally thought he was a pretentious stick-in-the-mud. That "generally" should clue you in to my mixed feelings—Ethan was ridiculously handsome and a grade-A kisser. While I hadn't completely reconciled my feelings for him, I didn't think I hated him anymore.

Avoidance helped settle the emotions. Considerably.

"No," Mallory agreed, "but the fact that the room heats up by ten degrees every time you two get near each other says something."

"Shut up," I said, extending my legs in front of me and lowering my nose to my knees to stretch out. "I admit nothing."

"You don't have to. I've seen your eyes silver just being around him. There's your admission."

"Not necessarily," I said, pulling one foot toward me and bending into another stretch. Vampires' eyes silvered when they experienced strong emotions—hunger, anger, or, in my case, proximity to the blond cupcake that was Ethan Sullivan. "But I'll admit that he's kind of offensively delicious."

"Like salt-and-vinegar potato chips."

"Exactly," I said, then sat up again. "Here I am, an uptight vampire who owes my allegiance to a liege lord I can't stand. And it turns out you're some kind of latent sorceress who can make things happen just by wishing them. We're the free-will outliers—I have none, and you have too much."

She looked at me, then blinked and put her hand over her heart. "You, and I'm saying this with love, Mer, are really a geek." She rose and pulled the strap of her bag across one shoulder. I followed suit, and we walked to the door.

"You know," she said, "you and Ethan should get one of those necklaces, where half the heart says 'best' and the other half says 'friend.' You could wear them as a sign of your eternal devotion to each other."

I threw my sweaty towel at her. She made a yakking sound beneath it, then threw it off, her features screwed into an expression of abject girly horror. "You're so immature."

"Blue hair. That's all I'm saying."

"Bite me, dead girl."

I showed fang and winked at her. "Don't tempt me, witch."

An hour later, I'd showered and changed back into my Cadogan House uniform—a fitted black suit jacket, black tank, and black slim-fit pants—and was in my soon-to-be-former Wicker Park bedroom, stuffing clothes into a duffel bag. A glass of blood from one of the medical-grade plastic bags in our refrigerator—promptly delivered by Blood4You, the fanged equivalent of milkmen—sat on the nightstand beside my bed, my post-workout snack. Mallory stood in the doorway behind me, blue hair framing her face, the rest of her body covered by boxers and an oversized T-shirt, probably Catcher's, that read ONE KEY AT A TIME.

"You don't have to do this," she said. "You don't have to leave."

I shook my head. "I do have to do this. I need to do it to

be Sentinel. And you two need room." To be precise, Catcher and Mallory needed *rooms*. Lots of them. Frequently, with lots of noise, and usually naked, although that wasn't a requirement. They hadn't known each other long and were smitten within days of meeting. But what they lacked in time they made up for in unmitigated, bare-assed enthusiasm. Like rabbits. Ridiculously energetic, completely unself-conscious, supernatural rabbits.

Mallory grabbed a second empty bag from the chair next to my bedroom door, dropped it onto the bed, and pulled three pair of cherished shoes—Mihara Pumas (sneakers that I adored, much to Ethan's chagrin), red ballet-style flats, and a pair of black Mary Janes she'd given me—from my closet. She raised them for my approval and, at my nod, stuffed them in. Two more pairs followed before she settled on the bed next to the bag and crossed her legs, one foot swinging impatiently.

"I can't believe you're leaving me here with him. What am I going to do without you?"

I gave her a flat stare.

She rolled her eyes. "You only caught us the one time."

"I only caught you in the *kitchen* the one time, Mallory. I eat in there. I drink in there. I could have lived a contented, happy eternity without ever catching a glimpse of Catcher's bare ass on the kitchen floor." I faked a dramatic shiver. Faked, because the boy was gorgeous—a broad-shouldered, perfectly muscled, shaved-headed, green-eyed, tattooed, bad-boy magician who'd swept my roommate off her feet (and onto her back, as it turned out).

"Not that it isn't a fine ass," she said.

I folded a pair of pants and put them into my bag. "It's a great ass, and I'm very happy for you. I just didn't need to see it naked again. Ever. For real."

She chuckled. "For realsies, even?"

"For realsies, even." My stomach twinged with hunger. I glanced at Mallory, then lifted brows toward the glass of blood on my nightstand. She rolled her eyes, then waved her hands at it.

"Drink, drink," she said. "Pretend I'm some *Buffy* fan with a wicked attraction to the paranormal."

I managed to both lift the glass and give her a sardonic look. "That's exactly what you are."

"I didn't say you had to pretend very *hard*," she pointed out.

I smiled, then sipped from my glass of slightly microwaved blood, which I'd seasoned up with Tabasco and tomato juice. I mean, it was still blood, with the weird iron tang and plastic aftertaste, but the extras perked it up. I licked an errant drop from my upper lip, then returned the glass to the nightstand.

Empty.

I must have been hungrier than I thought. I blamed Aerobics Barbie. Regardless, in order to make sure that I had future snacks (thinking a stash of actual food would increase the odds that my fangs and Ethan's neck stayed unacquainted), I stuffed a dozen granola bars into my bag.

"And speaking of Catcher," I began, since I'd cut the edge off my hunger, "where is Mr. Romance this evening?"

"Work," she said. "Your grandfather is quite the taskmaster."

Did I mention that Catcher worked for my grandfather? During that one big week when all the supernatural drama went down, I also discovered that my grandfather, Chuck Merit, the man who'd practically raised me, wasn't retired from his service with the Chicago Police Department as we'd been led to believe. Instead, four years ago he'd been asked to serve as an Ombudsman, a liaison, between the city administration—led by darkly handsome Mayor Seth Tate—and the city's supernatural population. Sups of every kind—vampires, sorcerers, shapeshifters, water nymphs, fairies, and demons— all depended on my grandfather for help. Well, him and his trio of assistants, including one Catcher Bell. I'd visited my grandfather's South Side office shortly after becoming a vamp; I'd met Catcher, then Mallory met Catcher, and the rest was naked history.

Mallory was quiet for a moment, and when I looked up, I

caught her brushing a tear from her cheek. "You know I'll miss you, right?"

"Please. You'll miss the fact that I can afford to pay rent now. You were getting used to spending Ethan's money." The Cadogan stipend was one of the upshots of having been made a vampire.

"The blood money, such as it was, was a perk. It was nice not to be the only one slaving away for the man." Given her glassy office overlooking Michigan Avenue, she was exaggerating by a large degree. While I'd been in grad school reading medieval texts, Mallory had been working as an ad executive. We'd only recently discovered that her job had been her first success as an adolescent sorceress: She'd actually *willed* herself into it, which wasn't the salve to her ego that a hire based on her creativity and skills might have been. She was taking a break from the job now, using up weeks of saved vacation time to figure out how she was going to deal with her newfound magic.

I added some journals and pens to the duffel. "Think about it this way—no more bags of blood in the refrigerator, and you'll have a muscley, sexy guy to cuddle with at night. Much better deal for you."

"He's still a narcissistic ass."

"Who you're crazy about," I pointed out while scanning my bookshelf. I grabbed a couple of reference books, a worn, leather-bound book of fairy tales I'd had since childhood, and the most important recent addition to my collection, the *Canon of the North American Houses, Desk Reference*. It had been given to me by Helen, the Cadogan Liaison burdened with the task of escorting me home after my change, and was required reading for newbie vampires. I'd read a lot of the four solid inches of text, and skimmed a good chunk of the rest. The bookmark was stuck somewhere in *chapter eight: "Going All Night."* (The chapter titles had apparently been drafted by a seventeen-year-old boy.)

"And he's your narcissistic ass," I reminded her.

"Yay, me!" she dryly replied, spinning a finger in the air like a party favor.

"You two will be fine. I'm sure you can manage to keep each other entertained," I said, plucking a bobble-headed Ryne Sandberg figurine from the shelf and placing it carefully in my bag. Although my new sunlight allergy kept me from enjoying sunny days at Wrigley Field, even vampirism wouldn't diminish my love for the Cubs.

I scanned my room, thinking about all the things—Cubs-related or otherwise—I'd be leaving behind. I wasn't taking everything with me to Cadogan, partly out of concern that I'd strangle Ethan and be banished from the House, and partly because leaving some of my stuff here meant that I still had a home base, a place to crash if living amongst vampires—living near Ethan—became too much to bear. Besides, it's not like her new roommate was going to need the space; Catcher had already stashed his boy stuff in Mal's bedroom.

I zipped up the bags and, hands on my hips, looked over at Mallory. "I think I'm ready."

She offered me a supportive smile, and I managed to keep the tears that suddenly brimmed at my lashes from spilling over. Silently, she stood up and wrapped her arms around me. I hugged her back—my best friend, my sister.

"I love you, you know," she said.

"I love you, too."

She released me, and we both swiped at tears. "You'll call me, right? Let me know you're okay?"

"Of course I will. And I'm only moving across town. It's not like I'm leaving for Miami." I hefted one of the bags onto my shoulder. "You know, I always figured if I moved out it would be because I got a kick-ass teaching job in some small town where everyone is super smart and quirky."

"Eureka?" she asked.

"Or Stars Hollow."

Mallory made a sound of agreement and picked up the second bag. "I assumed you'd leave after you got knocked up by a twenty-one-year-old classics major and the two of you ran away to Bora-Bora to raise your baby in the islands."

I stopped halfway to the door and glanced back at her. "That's pretty specific, Mal."

"You studied a lot," she said, edging past me into the hall-way. "I had the time."

I heard her trot down the stairs, but paused in the doorway of the bedroom that had been mine since I'd returned to Chicago three years ago. I took a last look around at the old furniture, the faded comforter, the cabbage rose wallpaper, and flipped off the light.

CHAPTER TWO

HOME IS WHERE THE HEART IS . . .

NOT NECESSARILY WHERE YOU SLEEP

Okay, so I was procrastinating. My bags were stuffed in the backseat of my boxy orange Volvo, but instead of heading directly to Cadogan House, I passed my future Hyde Park home and kept driving south. I wasn't quite ready to cross the threshold of Cadogan as an official resident. And, more importantly, I hadn't seen my grandfather in nearly a week, so I opted to do the granddaughterly thing and pay a visit to his South Side office. My grandparents had all but raised me while my social-climbing parents, Joshua and Meredith Merit, were gala-ing their way across Chicago. So paying my grandfather a visit was really the least I could do.

The Ombud's office wasn't glamorous; it was a squat brick building that sat in the midst of a working-class neighborhood of small, squarish houses, tidy yards, and chain-link fences. I parked the Volvo on the street in front, got out of my car and belted on my katana. I doubted I'd need it in my grandfather's office, but word that I hadn't been diligently armed was just the kind of talk that Catcher would pass along to Ethan. It's not that they were buddies, exactly, but chatting about me seemed like the kind of thing they'd do.

It was nearly eleven o'clock, but the few windows in the office were ablaze with light. The Ombud's office, or so my grandfather figured, served creatures of the night. That meant third-shift hours for my grandfather, his admin Marjorie, Catcher, and Jeff Christopher, my grandfather's second right-hand man, an undefined shapeshifter and computer whiz kid. Who also had a giant crush on yours truly.

I knocked on the locked front door and waited for some-one to let me in. Jeff turned a corner and headed down the hallway toward me, a grin breaking across his face. He was all lean appendages and floppy brown hair, and tonight he wore his usual uniform—pressed khakis and a long-sleeved button-up shirt, the sleeves rolled halfway up his forearms.

When he reached the door, he typed an alarm code into a keypad beside it, then turned a lock and opened it.

"Couldn't stand being away from me?"

"I was hurting a little," I said, then stepped inside as he held the door open. "It's been, what, almost a week?"

"Six days, twenty-three hours, and about twelve minutes." He recoded and locked the door, then grinned over at me. "Not that I'm counting."

"Oh, of course not," I agreed as he escorted me down the hallway to the office he shared with Catcher. "You're much too suave for that kind of thing."

"Much," he agreed, then entered the room and moved be-hind one of the four metal, atomic-era desks that sat in two rows in the tiny room. The top of Jeff's desk was taken up by a Frankenstein-esque collection of keyboards and monitors, upon which sat a stuffed toy I'd learned was a model of H. P. Lovecraft's Cthulhu.

"How was tap class?" asked a sardonic voice on the other side of the room. I glanced over, found Catcher at the desk opposite Jeff's, hands crossed over his skull-cut head, an open laptop on the desk before him. One brow was arched over his green eyes, his curvy lips slightly tipped up in amusement. I had to admit it—Catcher was irritating, gruff, a demanding trainer . . . and ridiculously pretty. Mal defi-nitely had her hands full.

"Hip-hop," I corrected, "not tap. And it was just fancy. Your girl nearly coldcocked the instructor, but it was pretty uneventful other than that." I edged a hip onto one of the two empty metal desks. I wasn't entirely sure why there were four desks in all. Catcher and Jeff were the only two in this office; my grandfather and Marjorie had desks in other rooms. My grandfather had reached out to a vampire source since Catcher and Jeff represented Chicago's sorcery and shapeshifting communities, but the secret vamp avoided the office in order to avoid House drama, so no desk for him. Or her. Or it, I suppose. I was still trying to work that one out.

Catcher glanced over at me. "She nearly coldcocked the instructor?"

"Well, she wanted to, not that I blame her. Aerobics Barbie is hard to stomach for more than five minutes at a time. But thanks to my excellent mediation and negotiation skills, no punches were actually thrown." The pad of footsteps echoed through the hall, and I looked over at the door to find my grandfather in his usual plaid flannel shirt and sensible pants, his feet in thick-soled shoes.

"And speaking of excellent mediation and negotiation skills," I said, hopping off the desk. My grandfather extended his arms and beckoned me into a hug. I walked into his embrace and squeezed, careful not to inadvertently break ribs with my increased vampire strength. "Hi, Grandpa."

"Baby girl," he said, then pressed a kiss to the top of my forehead. "How's my favorite supernatural citizen doing this fine spring evening?"

"That hurts, Chuck," Catcher said, crossing his arms over his chest. "I thought I was your favorite sup." His voice could hardly have been dryer.

"Seriously," Jeff said, his gaze shifting between computer monitors. "Here we are, slaving night and day—"

"Technically," Catcher interrupted, "just night."

"Night." Jeff smoothly adjusted. "Trying to keep everyone in the Windy City happy, trying to keep the nymphs in line." He bobbed his head up toward the posters of scantily clad women that lined the walls of the office. They were river nymphs—tiny, busty, doe-eyed, and long-haired women who controlled the branches of the Chicago River. They were also, as I'd seen on the night of my twenty-eighth birthday, pretty dramatic. They'd shown up en masse at my grandfather's house, all atwitter because one of the beauties' beaus had cheated on her with another nymph. It was a catfight of monumental proportions, complete with tears, swearing, and raking nails. And it'd been stopped, surprisingly enough, by our Jeff. (My reticence notwithstanding, Jeff had a way with the ladies.)

"And we all know how difficult that can be," I said, giving Jeff a wink. He blushed, crimson rising high on his cheekbones.

"What brings you by?" my grandfather asked me.

"Wait, wait, I got this one," Catcher said, grabbing an envelope from his desk and pressing it to his forehead, eyes closed, the perfect Carnac. "Merit will be undergoing a change . . . of zip code." He opened his eyes and flipped the envelope back onto his desk. "If you were trying to get to Hyde Park, you've gone a little too far south."

"I'm procrastinating," I admitted. I'd done the same thing the night before my Commendation into the House, seeking solace among friends and the only family that mattered before I became part of something that I knew would change my life forever. Ditto tonight.

Catcher's expression softened. "You're all packed?"

I nodded. "Everything's in the car."

"She'll miss you, you know."

I nodded at him. I had no doubt of that, but I appreciated that he'd said it. He wasn't one for the mushy-gushy emotional stuff, which made the sentiment that much more meaningful.

My grandfather put a hand on my shoulder. "You'll be fine, baby girl. I know you—how capable you are and how stubborn—and those are qualities that Ethan will come to appreciate."

"Given time," Catcher muttered. "Lots and lots and lots of time."

"Eons," Jeff agreed.

"Immortal," I reminded them, using a finger to point at

myself. "We have the time. Besides, I wouldn't want to make it too easy on him."

"I don't think that will be a problem," my grandfather said, then winked at me. "Could you do your Pop-Pop a favor and give him something for us?"

My own cheeks flushed at the reminder of the name I'd given my grandfather as a kid. "Grandpa" was much too hard for me to say.

"Sure," I said. "I'd be happy to."

Grandpa gave Catcher a nod. Catcher opened a squeaky desk drawer, then pulled out a thick manila envelope tied with a loop of red twine. There was no addressee, but the words CONFIDENTIAL and LEVEL ONE were stamped in capital black letters across one side. "Level One" was the Ombud version of "Top Secret." It was the only category of information that my grandfather wasn't willing to let me see.

Catcher extended the envelope. "Handle this with care."

I nodded and plucked it from his hand. It was heavier than I would have guessed, and held a good inch-thick sheaf of papers. "I'm assuming there's no free sneak peek for the delivery girl?"

"We'd appreciate it if you didn't," Grandpa said.

"That way," Catcher put in, "we won't have to resort to physical violence, which would make things really awkward between us, you being Chuck's granddaughter."

"I think we can trust her," my grandfather said, his voice as dry as toast, "but I appreciate your dedication."

"Just a day in the life, Chuck. Just a day in the life."

Task in hand, I figured now was as good a time as any to quit procrastinating and actually make my way to the House. I did have a first glance at my new digs to look forward to.

"On that note," I said, "I'm going to leave you three to it." I glanced back at my grandfather and held up the envelope. "I'll make the drop, but I'm probably going to need a little somethin'-somethin' for my efforts."

He smiled indulgently. "Meat loaf?"

He knew me so well.

*   *   *

They called it "losing your name." In order to become a vampire, to join a House, to gain membership into one of the oldest organized (and previously secret) societies in the world, you had to first give up your identity, surrender yourself to the whole. You gave up your last name to symbolize your commitment to your brothers and sisters. Your House affiliation stood in for your former surname, the hallmark of your new family. I suppose I was a weird exception to that rule: Merit was actually my last name, but I'd gone by "Merit" for years, so I kept the name post-Commendation.

According to the *Canon* (*chapter four: "Vampires—Who's on Top?"*), by giving up your name, you began to learn the communitarian values of vampire society. Shared sacrifice. Leadership. Accountability—not to your previous human family, but to your new fanged one. Master vampires, of course, got to take their names back. That's why it was Ethan Sullivan—not just Ethan—who held the reins of Cadogan House.

And speaking of Sullivan, that brings us to the most important communitarian value—kissing the asses of higher-ranked vampires.

I was on just such an ass-kissing mission now.

Well, I was on a delivery mission. But given the intended recipient, ass kissing went along with the territory.

Ethan's office was on the first floor of Cadogan House. The door was closed when I arrived, bags in hand, post-procrastination. I paused a moment before knocking, ever delaying the inevitable. When I finally managed to do it, a simple "Come" echoed from the office. I opened the door and went in.

Ethan's office, like the rest of Cadogan House, was elegantly decorated to just this side of pretentious, as befit the Hyde Park address. There was a desk on the right, a seating area on the left, and at the far end, in front of a bank of velvet-curtained windows, a gigantic conference table. The walls were covered by built-in bookshelves, which were stocked with antiques and mementos of Ethan's 394 years of existence.

Ethan Sullivan, head of Cadogan House and the Master who'd made me a vampire, sat behind his desk, a sliver of cell phone at his ear, eyes on a spread of papers before him. There always seemed to be papers before him; Masterdom was evidently heavy on the paperwork.

Ethan wore an impeccably tailored black suit with a pristine white shirt beneath, the top button undone to reveal the gold medal that vampires wore to indicate their House affiliation. His hair, golden blond and shoulder length, was down today, tucked behind his ears.

Although it bugged me to admit it, Ethan was beautiful. Perfectly handsome face, ridiculous cheekbones, chiseled jaw, shockingly emerald eyes. The face complemented the body, the majority of which I'd inadvertently seen while Ethan entertained Amber, the former Cadogan House Consort. Unfortunately, we'd discovered shortly thereafter that Amber had been assisting Celina in her attempt to take over Chicago's Houses.

He glanced down at the bags in my hands. "You're moving in?"

"I am."

Ethan nodded. "Good. It's a good move." The tone wasn't laudatory, but condescending, as if he was disappointed it had taken me as long as it did—not even two months—to make Cadogan House home. It wasn't an unexpected reaction.

I nodded, holding back the snark in light of his grumpiness. I knew the limits of pissing off a four-hundred-year-old Master vampire, even if I pushed them sometimes.

I dropped the bags, unzipped the duffel, pulled out the confidential envelope, and held it out to him. "The Ombud asked that I deliver this to you."

Ethan arched a brow, then took the envelope from my hands. He uncoiled the twine from its plastic disk, slipped a finger beneath the tab, and peeked inside. Something in his face relaxed. I wasn't sure what the Ombud's office had delivered, but Ethan seemed to like it.

"If there's nothing else," I said, bobbing my head at the bags on the floor.

I didn't merit so much as a glance. "Dismissed," he absently said, pulling the papers from the envelope and thumbing through them.

I hadn't seen much of Ethan in the first few weeks. As reunions went, this one was pretty undramatic. I could deal with that.

Having done my familial duty, I headed to the suite of first-floor offices reserved for Cadogan staff. Helen was behind her desk when I arrived. She wore a tidy pink suit, apparently having been granted an exception from Cadogan's all-black dress code. Her office was just as pink. Materials were stored in colored binders along neat wooden shelves, and her desk was carefully set with a blotter, pen cup, and calendar, events and appointments neatly penned in colored inks.

She was on the phone, the earpiece of a princess-style handset tucked next to her perfect bob of silver hair, the fingers wrapped around the phone carefully manicured.

"Thank you, Priscilla. I appreciate it. Goodbye." She placed the phone carefully back on her receiver, clasped her hands, and smiled at me. "That was Priscilla," she explained. "Liaison for Navarre House. We're planning a summer event between the Houses." She cast a wary glance toward the open door, then leaned toward me. "Frankly," she confided, "this relationship between you and Morgan has done wonders for inter-House relations."

Morgan Greer was my would-be boyfriend and the new Master of Navarre House. He'd assumed the position when Celina had been captured, rising to the ranks of Master from his former position of Second. From what I'd seen, Second was a kind of vampire Vice President. A man named Malik served as Second of Cadogan House. He seemed to mostly work behind the scenes, but it was clear that Ethan relied on him, confided in him.

Thinking I owed it to Helen to be polite, I smiled and didn't correct her assessment of our "relationship."

"Glad I could help," I said, bobbing my head toward the bags in my hands. "I've got my bags, if you'll show me my room?"

She smiled brightly. "Of course. Your room is on the second floor, in the back wing."

Luggage notwithstanding, my shoulders slumped in relief. The second floor of Cadogan House held the library, the dining room, and a formal ballroom, among other rooms. Those other rooms did *not* include Ethan's apartments, which were on the third floor. That meant an entire floor would separate me and Ethan. I wanted to jump for joy. But given where I was standing, I silently screamed my happiness.

Helen handed me a navy blue binder bearing the round, Cadogan House seal. "These are the residency rules, maps, parking information, cafeteria menus, etc. Most of the information is online now, of course, but we like to have something for the Novitiate vampires to hold on to." She rose and glanced at me expectantly. "Shall we?"

I nodded, resituating my bags and following her down the hall, then up a narrow back staircase. When we reached the second floor, we turned, then turned again, and were soon before a door of dark wood, a small bulletin board hanging from it.

MERIT, SENTINEL, read a nameplate just above the bulletin board.

Helen reached into a pocket of her jacket, pulled out a key, and inserted it into the lock. She twisted the doorknob, opened the door, and stood aside.

"Welcome home, Sentinel."

CHAPTER THREE

AMERICA'S NEXT TOP MONSTER

I stepped inside, put down my bags, and looked around. The room was small, square, and simply furnished. Wood paneling rose to chair-rail height, its color the same dark shade as the gleaming wood floors. Immediately facing the door was a window covered by a folding shutter. On the left side of the room was a bed with a wrought-iron frame. A small nightstand stood next to it, and an armchair sat beneath the window. On the right side of the room were two doors. A full-length mirror was attached to one. A bureau stood between them, and a bookshelf took up the wall to the right of the hallway door.

It was basically a dorm room.

For a twenty-eight-year-old vampire.

"Is there anything else you need?"

I smiled back at Helen. "No, thank you. I appreciate your arranging a room so quickly." My retinas, already singed by the images of Catcher and Mallory's liaisons, were also appreciative.

"No problem, dear. Meals are served in the cafeteria at dusk, midnight, and two hours before dawn." She glanced down at her watch. "You're a little past second meal now, and a little early for third. Can I find you something to eat?"

"No, thank you. I grabbed something on the way over." Not just something—the best homemade meat loaf this side of Chicago. *Heaven.*

"Well, if you find you need anything, the kitchens on each floor are always stocked, and there's blood in the refrigerators. If you need something that you can't find in the kitchens, tell the waitstaff."

"Sure. Thanks again."

Helen left and closed the door behind her. I laughed out loud at what she'd revealed. On the back of the door hung a poster for Navarre House, a life-sized image of Morgan in jeans and a snug black thermal shirt, black boots on his feet, his arms crossed, leather bands around his wrists. He'd been letting his hair grow, and it was wild in the picture, waving around his starkly handsome face, cut cheekbones, and cleft chin, his bedroomy navy blue eyes staring out beneath long, dark brows and ridiculously long lashes.

Apparently Helen had been coordinating with the Navarre Liaison on more than just a summer picnic. This required serious teasing, so I pulled the cell phone from my pocket and punched in Morgan's number.

"Morgan," he answered.

"Yes," I said, "I'd like to speak to someone about ordering some Navarre porn, please. Maybe a six-foot-tall poster of that gorgeous Master vampire, the one with the dreamy eyes?"

He chuckled. "Found my welcome gift, did you?"

"Isn't it a little weird for a Navarre vamp to leave a welcome gift for a Cadogan vamp?" I asked, while checking out the doors on the right side of the room. The first door opened to a small closet, inside of which hung a dozen wooden hangers. The second opened to a small bathroom—claw-foot tub with shower, pedestal sink.

"Not if she's the prettiest Cadogan vamp."

I snorted and closed the door again, then moved my bags to the bed. "You can't think that line's gonna work."

"Did we finish off a deep-dish pie Saturday night?"

"That's my recollection."

"Then my lines work."

I made a sarcastic sound, but the boy had a point.

"I need to go. I've got a meeting in a few," he said, and the Master around here is a real administrative bastard."

"Mmm-hmm. I bet he is. You enjoy that meeting."

"I always do. And on behalf of Navarre House and the North American Vampire Registry, we hope your days in Cadogan House are many and fruitful. Peace be with you. Live long and prosper—"

"Goodbye, Morgan," I said with a laugh, flipping my phone shut and sliding it back into my pocket.

It was fairly debatable whether Morgan had manipulated me into our first date, which was the result of a political compromise (in front of fifty other vampires, no less). But we'd passed that official first date a few weeks ago, and as he'd pointed out, we'd shared a pizza or two since then. I clearly hadn't done anything to quell his interest; on the other hand, I hadn't really tried to encourage it. I liked Morgan, sure. He was funny, charming, intelligent, and ridiculously pretty. But I couldn't shake the feeling that I was dating him from behind a wall of detachment, that I hadn't fully let my guard down.

Maybe it was chemistry. Maybe it was a security issue, the fact that he was from Navarre and that, as Sentinel, I was supposed to be always on guard, always on call, for Cadogan House. Maybe it was the fact that he'd gotten date number one because he'd forced my hand in front of Ethan, Scott Grey, Noah Beck (the leader of Chicago's independent vampires), and half of Cadogan House.

Yeah, that could be it.

Or maybe it was something even more fundamental: However ironic, the thought of dating a vampire—with all the political and emotional complications that entailed—didn't thrill me.

I guess any of those could have been the reason it felt strange, the reason I enjoyed his company but couldn't seem to just sink it, Morgan's enthusiasm notwithstanding.

Since I wasn't going to find resolution today, I shook the thought from my head and headed back to my bags, still zipped atop the small bed. I opened them and set to work.

I began by pulling out books, writing supplies, and knickknacks, then organized them on the bookshelf. Toiletries went into the bathroom's medicine cabinet, and foldable clothes went into the bureau. Shirts and pants were hung from the wooden hangers in the closet, beneath which I unceremoniously dumped my shoes.

When I'd emptied the bags, I began zipping them up again, but stopped when I felt something in an interior side pocket of my duffel. I reached in and found a small package wrapped in brown paper. Curious, I slipped the tape and unfolded the wrapping. Inside was a framed piece of cross-stitched linen that read: VAMPIRES ARE PEOPLE, TOO.

Although I wasn't sure I believed the message, as surprise housewarming presents went, it wasn't bad. I certainly appreciated the thought, and made a mental note to thank Mal the next time I saw her.

I'd just folded the empty bags into the bottom bureau drawer when the beeper at my waist began to vibrate. Beepers were required gear for Cadogan guards, intended to ensure that we could quickly respond to fanged emergencies. Now that I was an official resident of the House—instead of twenty minutes north—I could respond in record time.

I unclipped the beeper and scanned the screen. It read: OPS RM. 911.

Not much for poetry, but the message was clear enough. There was some kind of emergency, so we were to mobilize in the House's Operations Room, the guards' HQ in the basement of Cadogan House. I reclipped my beeper, grabbed my sheathed katana, and headed downstairs.

"I don't care if they're taking your picture, asking for your autograph, or buying your drinks! This. Is. *Completely*. Unacceptable."

Luc, the head of Cadogan House's guard corps, growled at us. As it turned out, the emergency, although arguably of our own making, had passed during the daylight hours. This lecture was the unfortunate fallout.

There we were, sitting around a high-tech conference table in the equally high-tech, movie-ready Ops Room—Peter, Juliet, Lindsey, Kelley, and me, the guards (and Sentinel) responsible for ensuring the health and welfare of Cadogan's Novitiate vampires.

All of us were mid-upbraiding by a blondish, tousle-haired cowboy-turned-vampire who was berating us for the "lacka-daisical attitude" our newfound popularity had spawned.

So, yeah. We weren't exactly feeling the love.

"We're doing the best we can," pointed out Juliet, a fey-like redhead who had more years as a vampire under her belt than I had years of life. "Reporters followed Lindsey around last week," she said, pointing at another guard. Lindsey was blond, sassy, and, thankfully, in my corner.

"Yes," Luc said, lifting a copy of the *Chicago World Weekly* from the conference table, "we have evidence of that." He turned it so we could all get a glimpse of Lindsey, who'd been honored with a full-page photograph on the cover. She was decked out in her traditional blond ponytail, as well as a pair of designer jeans, stiletto heels, and oversized sunglasses, her body in motion as she smiled at someone off camera. I happened to know that the individual she'd been smiling at was, like me, one of Cadogan's newest vampires. Lindsey, much to Luc's dismay, had started seeing Connor just after the ceremony initiating us both into the House.

"This isn't exactly the approved Cadogan uniform," Luc pointed out.

"But those jeans are sweet," I whispered.

"I know, right?" She grinned back at me. "Seriously on sale."

"Seeing your tiny ass on the cover of the *Weekly* isn't the way to my heart, Blondie," Luc said.

"Then my plan worked."

Luc growled, his patience obviously thinning. "Is this truly the best you can do for your House?"

Lindsey's chronic irritation with Luc was equaled only by what I imagined was her deep-seated passion for him, although you wouldn't know it from the menace in her glare. She popped up her index finger and began counting.

"First of all, I didn't ask to be photographed. Second of all, I didn't ask to be photographed. Third, I didn't ask to be photographed." She raised brows at Luc. "Are we getting the point here? I mean, really. That not-showing-up-in-photographs deal is a total myth."

Luc muttered something about insubordination and ran a hand through his hair. "Folks, we're at a crossroads here. We've been outed, we've been investigated by Congress, and now we've got the paparazzi breathing down our necks. We've also learned that in a few weeks' time, the head of the North American Central, Gabriel Keene himself, will be visiting our fine city."

"Keene's coming here?" Peter asked. "To Chicago?" Peter leaned forward, elbows on the conference table. Peter was tall, brown-haired, and thin, and looked to be thirty. He also had the just-so clothing and serene attitude of a man who'd seen a lot of money in his lifetime (human or otherwise).

"To Chicago," Luc confirmed. "Humans may not know shapeshifters exist, but we do, unfortunately for everyone."

There were a couple of snickers among the guards. Vampires and shifters weren't exactly friendly, and those tensions were increasing—I'd heard Gabriel was coming to town to scope out the city as a future conference site for his shifters. News related to that visit, and the possibility that shifters would assemble en masse in Chicago, had made the dailies— daily news updates for the Cadogan guards—more than once.

"Look, let's not be naïve and pretend this celebrity deal is going to last forever, all right? Humans, and no offense to you, Sentinel, since you're the recently fanged, are a fickle bunch. We've seen what happens when they get pissy about us."

Luc meant the Clearings, the vampire version of witch hunts. There'd been two in Europe, the First in Germany in 1611, and the Second in France in 1789. Thousands of vampires, a big chunk of our European population, were lost between the two—staked, burned, gutted and left to die. Shifters had known about the Second Clearing but hadn't stepped in; thus the animosity between the tribes.

"And here's the punch line," Luc said. "We've learned that the *Weekly* is planning a multipart, in-depth exposé on underground vamp activities."

"Underground?" Kelley asked. "What do we do that's so underground?"

"That's exactly what I'm about to find out," Luc said, pointing up at the ceiling. "I'm meeting your Master and mine in a matter of minutes. But until I've had a chance to liaise with the big man on campus, let me remind you of some things you apparently need reminding of.

"We are here," Luc continued, "to make our Master happy, not to increase the weight on his shoulders. Henceforth, because you were apparently not doing so in the first place, you will consider yourselves representatives of Cadogan House within the human world. You will conduct yourself accordingly, as befitting Cadogan vampires." He narrowed his gaze in Lindsey's direction. "And if that means no carousing into the early-morning hours with newbie vamps, so be it."

She gave him a look that was both evil and pouty, but managed not to comment.

Apparently believing that he'd made his point to her, he returned his gaze to the rest of us. "Any action that you take out there, outside the House, reflects on all of us, especially now that our asses are, apparently, news. That means you may be called upon to discuss House or vampire matters."

He opened a folder in front of him, slid out a sheaf of papers, then passed the stack to Lindsey, who sat closest to him. She took one, then passed the remainder along.

"'Talking Points'?" Kelley asked, repeating the title that spanned the top of the document. Kelley had a kind of exotic beauty—pale skin, coal black hair, slightly uptilted eyes. Eyes that looked decidedly unimpressed with the paper she held gingerly between the tips of her fingers.

"Talking points," Luc said with a nod. "These are answers you are authorized—and when I say 'authorized,' I mean 'required'—to give if a reporter tries to engage you in a politically sensitive dialogue. Read this, memorize this, and verbalize appropriately. Is that understood?"

"Yes, sir," we answered, a chorus of obedience.

Luc didn't bother with a response, but stood up and began shuffling the rest of the materials that were spread on the table before him. Taking the hint—meeting adjourned—we pushed back our chairs. I rose, folded the talking points sheet, and was preparing to head out when Luc called my name.

He stood, moved to the door, and beckoned me to follow with two crooked fingers.

Damn. I knew what was coming, and twice in one day, too.

"Sentinel, you're with me," he said, and I blew out a slow breath, the beginning of my mental preparation for interacting with the world's most stubborn vampire.

"Sir," I said, stuffing the talking points into a pocket of my suit and straightening the katana belted at my waist. Lindsey gave me a sympathetic smile, which I accepted with a nod, then followed him. We took the stairs back to the first floor, headed down the hallway to Ethan's office, and found the door shut. Luc, without preliminaries, opened it. I tugged at the bottom of my black suit jacket, and followed him in.

Ethan was on the phone. He nodded at Luc, then me, and raised his index finger as if to signal the call wouldn't take long.

"Of course," he said. "I understand completely." He pointed at the two chairs in front of his desk. Obediently, Luc took the one on the right. I took the one on the left.

"Yes, sire," he said. "The information is before me as we speak." As Master of Cadogan House, Ethan got the honorific "liege," but "sire" was a mystery. I looked at Luc.

He leaned toward me. "Darius," he whispered, and I nodded my understanding. That would be Darius West, head of the Greenwich Presidium.

"We've considered that," Ethan said, nodding his head and scribbling something on a tablet on his desk, "but you know the risks. Personally, I advise against it." There was more nodding, then Ethan's shoulders stiffened and he looked up.

And looked directly at me.

"Yes," Ethan said, hauntingly green eyes on mine, "we can certainly explore that route."

I swallowed reflexively, not comforted by the possibility that I was a "route" to "explore."

"Whatever this is," Luc said, leaning over again, "you're not going to like it."

"I'm really not going to like it," I quietly agreed. There were a few more minutes of nodding and validating before Ethan said his goodbyes. He replaced the receiver in its cradle and then looked at us, a tiny line between his eyes. I'd seen that tiny line before. Generally, it wasn't a good sign.

"The *Chicago World Weekly*," he began, "with its apparent interest in vampire activities, will be investigating the raves. They'll publish a three-part series, one story per week, beginning next Friday."

"Damn," Luc said, before sharing a weighty look with Ethan that suggested he knew why that was a problem.

I guessed these were the "underground" details Luc had been waiting for. Unfortunately, they didn't mean much to me. I'd heard a reference to vampire raves before; Catcher had mentioned them once, then refused to give me any details. My subsequent research in the *Canon* was equally unproductive. Whatever they were, vamps weren't chatty about them.

I raised a hand. "Raves? They're investigating parties?"

"Not parties," Luc said. "Humans actually borrowed the term from us. Raves in the supernatural world are definitely gatherings, but they're much . . ." He trailed off, shifted uncomfortably in his chair, and looked at Ethan, who then looked at me.

"Bloodier," Ethan matter-of-factly said. "They're bloodier."

Raves, Ethan explained, were the vampire version of flash mobs. They were, essentially, mass feedings. Vampires were informed (electronically, of course) where and when to meet, and awaiting them would be a group of humans. Humans who believed in us, even before we announced our existence to the world. Humans who wanted to be near us, to savor the element of the darkly forbidden.

Of course, given the bumper stickers and pennants and

Lindsey's new position as reigning vampire cover girl, I wasn't sure how "darkly forbidden" we were.

"They want to be part of our world, to see and be seen," Ethan said, "but they didn't necessarily want our fangs in or near their carotids. But that's what happens. Drinking."

"Feasting," Luc added.

"Surely some humans do consent to the drinking," I suggested, glancing from Luc to Ethan. "I mean, they walk willingly into some kind of vampire feeding. It's not like they're heading out for a garden party. And we've all seen *Underworld*. I'm sure there are humans who find that kind of thing . . . appealing."

Ethan nodded. "Some humans consent because they want to ingratiate themselves to vampires, because they believe they're positioning themselves to serve as Renfields—servants—or because they find an erotic appeal."

"They think it's hot," Luc simplified.

"They believe that dabbling in our *world* is hot," Ethan sardonically corrected. "But raves take place outside the oversight of these vampires' Masters. Agreeing to spend time in the company of vampires may indicate consent for a sip or two. But if a vampire is willing to participate in activities of this nature—activities forbidden by the Houses—he or she is unlikely to abide by the request of a human to stop drinking." He gazed solemnly at me. "And we know how crucial consent is when human blood is at stake."

I knew about consent, largely because I hadn't been able to give any. Because Ethan had given me immortality in order to save me from Celina's flunkies, and that split-second decision hadn't allowed him time for deliberation. I understood the sense of violation that came with the unrequested bite . . . especially when the vampire wasn't interested in just a sip or two.

"After they're relieved of a few pints of blood," Luc said, "to add insult to injury, the vamps often attempt to glamour the humans to make them forget what happened. To forget the supernatural assault and battery. And let's be frank—

raving vampires aren't usually at the top of the vampire food chain. That means they usually aren't very good at the glamouring."

The ability to glamour a human—to bring a human under the vampire's control—was an indicator of a vampire's psychic power, which was one of the three measures of a vampire's strength, Strat (alliances) and Phys (physical strength) being the other two. I couldn't glamour worth a damn, at least not the couple of times I'd tried to make it happen. But I seemed to have some kind of resistance to *being* glamoured, which was one of the many reasons Celina Desaulniers was none too fond of me. She was a queen of glamouring, and it must have gotten under her skin to know that I wasn't susceptible to her control.

So, to review, not only were humans made unwitting vampire snacks, the perps weren't even very *good* vampires. None of that added up to a scenario that many humans would find comfortable. I didn't find it comfortable, and I hadn't been human in nearly two months. Humans had agreed to live with us on the understanding that most vampires no longer drank from people but utilized blood that was donated, sold, or delivered in sterile plastic by businesses like Blood4You. Only four of the twelve American Houses, including Cadogan, still participated in the ritual of drinking straight from the tap. But those that drank did so in an officially sanctioned way—inside the House, after careful screening and after consent forms had been signed and notarized. In triplicate. (Personally, I was far from mentally or emotionally prepared to sip from anything other than plastic.)

Unfortunately, vampires who drank from humans were considered out of sync, or at least that was the image perpetuated by Celina when she'd organized the vampire coming-out. Vamps drinking en masse and without oversight, even if the humans had consented to a sip, was a PR nightmare waiting to happen.

Since vampires who chose to drink from humans were supposed to follow those cover-your-ass safeguards, this blossoming PR nightmare begged a question: "Which Houses participate in the raves?" I asked.

"None of them, theoretically," Luc muttered, prompting a sympathetic nod from Ethan.

"As you know, a handful of the Houses remain pro-drinking," Ethan answered. "But none of the Houses condones raves."

"Could be sneaky Housed vamps or Rogues," Luc added, referring to the few vampires who lived outside the House system. "Maybe wandering vamps from other cities, other countries. Add those groups together and you've got a hornet's nest of thirsty vampires and naïve, wannabe humans. Bad combination."

I crossed my arms and glanced at Ethan. "I understand your concerns, but is there a reason the House Sentinel is only hearing about these raves now?"

"We don't exactly advertise them," Ethan mildly replied. "However, now that you are in the know, we believe there are services you can provide." He pulled a gray folder to the top of the stack of papers on his desk, then flipped it open, revealing paper-clipped documents that were topped by a small color photograph.

"We understand the reporter is currently doing his background research." Ethan lifted the picture and flipped it around to show me. "And I believe you two are acquainted."

I reached out, gingerly took the picture from Ethan, and stared at the familiar image. "Hello, Jamie."

CHAPTER FOUR

THE PRE-PARTY PLANNING COMMITTEE

"He's the youngest Breckenridge," I told Ethan and Luc, who'd swiveled in his seat to watch me pace the length of Ethan's office and back. "The youngest of four boys." I stopped pacing, stared down at the photograph between my fingers, and tried to recall the math. "Nicholas is three years older. Then Finley, and Michael's the oldest."

"Nicholas is your age?" Ethan asked.

I glanced back at him. "Yes. Twenty-eight."

"And how long did you two see each other?"

I resisted the urge to ask how he knew Nicholas and I had been an item, realizing that Ethan was at least as well connected as my money-hungry father and was equally keen a purveyor of information. I'd wondered if Ethan was my grandfather's secret source. At the very least, his access to information was as deep.

"Nearly two years while we were in high school," I told him.

Nicholas Etherell Arbuckle Breckenridge (and yes, his brothers and mine had tortured him about the name) had been totally dreamy—wavy brown hair, blue eyes, Romeo in our junior production of Shakespeare, editor of the school paper. He was funny, confident, and heir, if you didn't count Michael and Finley, to the fortune that was Breckenridge Industries. Started by their great-great-great-grandfather, the con-

glomerate manufactured steel components for the construction industry. That meant the Breckenridges were reported to
own a good chunk of the Loop. But while the Breck boys
lacked for nothing, they were brought up with a very commonsensical attitude toward their money. Public school, high
school jobs, paying their own way through college. After
college, Michael and Finley headed for the family business,
while Nick skipped B-school and law school for a master's
in journalism from Northwestern, followed by a trek across
sub-Saharan Africa to study the impact of Western medical
relief efforts. When he returned to the States with a Pulitzer
to his credit, he joined the *New York Times* as a bureau reporter.

Jamie, on the other hand, was the family black sheep—
although even sheep were productive from a wool-making
perspective. From what I'd heard, word having passed from
Mrs. Breckenridge to my mother during a meeting of one of
their ubiquitous clubs—golf club, book club, cotillion club,
travel club, heirloom asparagus club, etc.—Jamie mooched
off his parents, occasionally dabbling in a get-rich-quick
scheme, Internet start-up, or "surefire invention," most of
which fizzled as quickly as his temporary interest in working.
That Ethan and Luc believed it was Jamie, not Nick, who'd
taken up the reins of a vampire investigation was a surprise.

I leaned back against the conference table and checked out
the picture of Jamie. Tall and brown-haired like his brothers,
he had been photographed walking down the street in jeans
and a T-shirt, cell phone in his hand. The picture was taken in
front of what looked like a neighborhood bar, although I
didn't recognize the location. Whatever the setting, the expression on his face was unmistakable—he looked, and this
was a first as far as I was aware, *determined*.

I glanced over at Ethan. "How did he go from slacker to
pounding the pavement for the journalistic equivalent of *The
Jerry Springer Show*?"

"Luc," Ethan prompted.

"First of all, was that really such a leap?" Luc asked. He
rose from the desk, went to the section of the bookshelves

that I knew held a built-in liquor cabinet, and after a nod from Ethan, poured amber liquid—Scotch, maybe—into a chubby glass. He raised his glass to Ethan, who looked vaguely amused by the gesture, and took a sip.

"We've heard Jamie is feeling some pressure from Mr. Breckenridge about making something of his life," Luc said. "Apparently, Daddy referred to Nicholas as a model of how to flourish outside the family fold, and young Jamie took offense. Our guess is he figured that if big brother could make a living as a journalist, he'd take a stab at it, too."

I frowned. "I guess," I said. "But that really doesn't sound like Jamie. He wanted to outpace Nicholas, so he hired on with a tabloid? And no offense, but to investigate vampires?"

"Not just vampires," Ethan noted, relaxing back into his chair. "Celebrity vampires."

"Or even better, bloodsucking vampires taking advantage of poor defenseless humans." Luc lowered himself onto the buttery leather couch on the left-hand side of the room and cradled his drink in his hands. "Not the kind of headline we want inked across the city, but exactly the kind of headline that could make a name for young Breckenridge."

"Especially if he's the one to break the second-biggest story since our coming-out—if he gets to spill the beans about the inherent evilness of vampires," Ethan said, rising and making his own trip to the liquor cabinet. But instead of pouring a stash of undoubtedly expensive alcohol, he opened a small refrigerator and pulled out what looked like a juice box. As Ethan was the type to use fine china and silverware to eat a hot dog, I had a feeling it didn't contain juice. Blood4You usually sent its wares in plastic medical bags. I guess it had upgraded to convenience products.

"Not Nicholas with his Pulitzer," he continued, "but Jamie. The youngest Breckenridge, and a man who has little, academically or professionally, to his credit." Having offered his theory, Ethan poked in the plastic straw attached to his "juice" box.

"Cocktail," he said, his tongue flicking the edge of one

suddenly extended canine. My heart skipped a disconcerting beat. His eyes stayed emerald green as he sipped, a sign of his ability to control his emotions, his hunger.

Ethan drank the blood in seconds, then crushed the packaging in his hand and threw it into a silver trash can. Apparently refreshed, he slipped his hands into the pockets of his trousers and leaned back against the cabinet. "We won't be popular forever," he said. "We got lucky with regard to the murders—lucky that most humans were willing to direct their ire toward Celina while embracing the rest of us. The idea of magic, of there being more to the world than meets the eye, remains very attractive to many."

Ethan's expression darkened. "But people fear what they don't understand. We may not be able to avoid that fear forever. And popularity invites criticism, fuels jealousy. It is, for better or worse, human nature." That's when his head lifted, and he looked at me. His eyes sparkled, orbs of emerald green ice, and I knew he was about to make his pitch.

Voice low, grave, he said, "We maintain alliances, Merit, form connections, in order to protect ourselves. To give ourselves what advantages we can—advantages that we need in order to survive, to safeguard ourselves, our Houses." He paused. "You have these connections."

"Shit," I muttered, squeezing my eyes closed, already knowing what he wanted me to do.

"You grew up with the Breckenridges. Your families are friends. You are, for better or worse, part of that world."

I felt my hackles rising, my heart beginning to beat faster. I was already beginning to sweat, and he hadn't even gotten to the meat of it yet. "You know I'm not like them."

He raised a single blond eyebrow. "Not *like* them? You *are* them, Merit. You're Joshua and Meredith Merit's daughter, Nicholas Breckenridge's ex-girlfriend. You had your cotillion, your debut. You were introduced to that world."

"Introduced to it, and walked right out of it. I didn't belong there," I reminded him, holding up a finger in protest. "I'm a graduate student. Was one, anyway, before your trip

to campus." His face tightened at the comment, but I pushed
forward. "I don't waltz. I hate wine and creepy little appetizers. And as you damn well know, I don't care if I'm wearing
the latest designer shoes." His expression was still bland, my
tantrum being apparently ineffective, so I switched tactics,
went for commonsensical strategy. "I don't fit in with them,
Ethan, and they know it. They know my parents and I aren't
close. The socialites won't give me any information, and they
won't help me get closer to Jamie."

Ethan watched me quietly for a minute, then pushed off
the bar and walked toward me. When he was a foot away, he
crossed his arms and looked down at me from his six feet and
change.

"You are no longer a graduate student. Whoever you were
back then, you're different now."

I began to object, but he lifted his brows in warning. New
vampire I might be, but I'd sworn two oaths to serve him and
the House. More importantly, I'd seen him fight. I was willing to test the boundaries of my obligations, but I knew
where the lines were drawn. And when he spoke, I was reminded why he was head of Cadogan House, why he had
been chosen to lead and protect this band of vampires. Whatever personal issues I had with Ethan, he knew how to coach.

"You are not merely his daughter. You are a Cadogan
vampire. You are Sentinel of this House. When you walk into
a room filled with those people, you will know that you are
not one of them—you are more than they are. You are a vampire, of an historic house, in an historic position. You are
powerful and well connected, if not because of your father,
then because of your grandfather. You are nothing more, and
nothing less, Merit, than exactly who you are. The question
is not *can* you do it, but will you *choose* to do it?"

I lifted my gaze, looked up at him. He arched a single
eyebrow, a challenge, and kept talking. "You have accused
me of not believing in you. If this story goes to press, and
Chicago's vampires are demonized as manipulative predators, we all lose. Who knows what we'll face then—another

Clearing? Perhaps not. But registration? Incarceration? Suspicion and regulation? Undoubtedly. But if you can get close to Jamie, become a source for Jamie, help him see who we really are, or, better yet, convince him to drop the story altogether, then we stand to fare better. If nothing else, we can put off the vitriol for a little while longer. I'm coming to you, Merit, because you have the connections to do this. Because Jamie knew you before, and he'll be able to see that your goodness, your decency are still there, even though you've become one of us."

"Christine has the connections to do this," I noted, recalling one of my fellow Novitiate vampires, who'd taken the Cadogan House oaths on the same night as me. She was the daughter of Chicago attorney Dash Dupree, and while like every Novitiate vampire she'd lost the privilege of using her last name, she was still a Dupree, still a member of that family, which stood in the highest echelon of Chicago society.

"Christine cannot do this. You have the strength to defend yourself. She does not." Arms still crossed over his chest, Ethan bent over, whispered in my ear. "I can order you to do it, to fulfill the role you accepted when I Commended you into this House, or you can accept the job willingly."

He stood straight again, offered me a look that made clear exactly how much choice I had. He was allowing me the perception of choice, but he was right—I had given my oaths in front of him and Luc and the others to protect the House, even if it meant wearing Dolce & Gabbana and attending society dinners.

Ugh. Society dinners. Prissy people. Uncomfortable shoes. Butlers, and not even the monkey kind. But I said goodbye to my Friday nights, and I sucked it up. "Fine. I'll do it."

"I knew I could count on you. And there is an upside, you know."

I looked back at him, brows lifted in silent question.

"You get to take me with you."

I nearly growled at him, kicking myself mentally for not

guessing that was coming. What better way for Ethan to ingratiate his way into Chicago's (human) social scene than to
use me as his entry ticket?

"Clever," I commented, giving him a dry look.

"A boy learns a thing or two in four hundred years," he
smartly said, then clapped his hands together. "Let's strategize, shall we?"

We convened in the sitting area of Ethan's office over a plate
of vegetables and hummus I'd ordered from the kitchen.
Ethan turned up his nose at the vegetables, but I was starving,
and he found me petulant enough on a full stomach to avoid
low-blood-sugar grouchiness. So I munched on celery sticks
and carrots as we plotted over a map of Chicago locations
believed to host raves. They included a club in Urbana, an
expensive suburban home in Schaumburg, and a bar in Lincoln Park. Any spot would do for a bloodletting, apparently.

As we leaned over the spread of information, I wondered
aloud, "If you had all this information about the raves, why
not stop them?"

"We didn't have all the information," Luc said, flipping
through some documents.

"So how do you have it now?" I asked.

The look of mild distaste that pinched Ethan's features
gave away the answer. Well, that and the fact that as Luc
pored through the scattered documents, he revealed a manila
folder that bore a tail of red twine. I could just make out the
phrase LEVEL ONE stamped across the front. Bingo.

"You called the Ombud's office," I concluded. "They had
the info on file, or they did the research. That's the stuff I
brought you earlier."

Silence. Then, "We did." Ethan's answer was as clipped
as his tone. Although he apparently wasn't too proud to beg
for information, and despite the fact that he and Catcher were
friends (of their peculiar sort), Ethan wasn't a big fan of the
Ombud's office. He thought they were tied a little too closely
to Mayor Tate, whose position regarding "the vampire problem" was less than clear. Tate had all but refused to talk to the

House Masters even after we became public, despite the fact that the city administration had known about our existence for decades.

The Celina fiasco hadn't helped Cadogan-Ombud relations. The Greenwich Presidium didn't recognize Chicago's authority over Celina, no matter how heinous her acts. Since she was a member of the GP, the GP believed she was entitled to certain accommodations, including not serving an eternal sentence in the Cook County jail. It had taken no little diplomacy on my grandfather's part to secure the administration's support for her extradition to Europe. That meant my grandfather, who'd made his own oath to serve and protect Chicago, had been forced to release the vampire who'd tried to have his granddaughter killed. Needless to say, he felt a little conflicted. Ethan, on the other hand, was bound by his loyalties to the GP. Awkwardness, thy name is vampire.

"Whatever the source, Sentinel, we have the information now. Let's use it, shall we?"

I bit back a grin, amused that I'd reverted back to "Sentinel." I was "Merit" when Ethan needed something, "Sentinel" when he was responding to my snark. Admittedly, that was frequently.

"They're going to be suspicious that Merit wants back in," Luc pointed out. "Which means she's going to need a cover story."

"And not just a cover story," Ethan said, "but a cover story that can make it past her father."

We pondered that one silently. As head of Merit Properties, one of the city's biggest real estate management companies, my father was enough of a salesman to know when he was being conned.

"How about a little familial gloating?" Luc finally asked.

Ethan and I both looked at him. "Explain," Ethan ordered.

Luc frowned, scratched absently at his cheek, and relaxed back into the sofa. "Well, I think you laid it out earlier. She's a member of a key Chicago family, and now Sentinel of one of the oldest American Houses. So she plays the youngest daughter making her triumphant return to the society that once scorned her. You start with her father—approach him first. She plays cool, confident, standoffish, like she's finally come into that famed Merit attitude." He clapped, apparently for emphasis. "Boom. The patriarch welcomes her back into the fold."

Ethan opened his mouth, closed it, then opened it again. "That's an interesting analysis."

"*Dynasty* reruns have been rolling nonstop on cable," Luc said.

Huh.

That was an interesting bit of information about our guard captain.

Ethan stared at him for a moment before offering, "Pop culture notwithstanding, your plan would require some considerable acting on Merit's part." He slid me an appraising (and none too flattering) glance. "I'm not sure she's equipped."

"Hey." With a chuckle, and without thinking of who he was or the authority he held over me, I punched Ethan lightly on the arm. Fortunately he didn't jump out of his seat and pound me, although he did stare at the spot on his tidy black suit jacket where I'd made contact.

"Look, I know acting isn't exactly my background, but I'm pretty sure I can fake being pretentious." I did have one hell of a teacher. "But I actually have a better idea."

Ethan arched his eyebrows. "We're all ears, Sentinel."

"Robert," I said. "He's our cover story."

Despite our ongoing estrangement, or maybe because of it, my father had approached me a few weeks ago, on the evening of my twenty-eighth birthday no less, to ask that I help my brother Robert, who was poised to take over Merit Properties, make inroads with the city's supernaturally endowed population. I'd declined for a number of reasons, the speed with which Ethan would punish what he imagined to be my pro-human treachery first among them. My dislike for my father, though, ran a real close second.

I'd corrected my father's assumptions about what I "owed" my family in strong enough terms that he would wonder why I was coming back. But if he thought I was willing to help Robert make connections with sups, my guess was that he'd bypass wondering and move right into gloating.

"That's not bad," Ethan said. "And when you secure an audience with your father, which you can work on this evening, you'll be delivering him one hell of a connection."

It was my turn to lift sardonic brows. "And that would be?"

"Me, of course."

Yeah. That was exactly the pretension I was referring to earlier.

Luc looked at me. "You'll want to call the family as soon as you have a chance. Let them know you want to return to the fold. Ask them if there's anything on the social calendar that looks interesting."

"Aye, aye, Captain."

"Well, now that we've arranged a strategy," Ethan said, slapping his knees and rising from his seat, "you're dismissed. Luc, make the arrangements we discussed."

The arrangements they'd *discussed*? As in, past tense?

"Wait a minute," I said, lifting a finger as Ethan walked back to his desk. "How much of this little plan had you two already decided on before I walked in?"

He offered Luc a thoughtful look. "What, Lucas, all of it?"

"Pretty much," Luc said, nodding.

"Never underestimate the power of staff buy-in," Ethan said, glowing with Gordon Gecko–worthy smugness. I humphed.

Luc, the traitor, grabbed a celery stick from our spread, then rose from the couch, patting my shoulder as he walked past, a gesture that was equal parts camaraderie and condescension. "But thanks for coming to the party, Sentinel. We appreciate you sparing us some of your time."

Ethan's chair squeaking, he situated himself behind his desk, then ran hands through his hair and squinted at his computer monitor.

"If we're done," I said, "I'm going back upstairs."

Luc settled into the chair in front of Ethan's desk while Ethan attended to his e-mail, or whatever business electronically preoccupied him. He poised his fingers above the keyboard, and like a pianist's, they flew across the keys. "Do that, Sentinel. Do that."

Luc munched the end of his celery stick, then waved the stalk of it at me. "Have a great evening, Sunshine."

I left them to their gloating.

CHAPTER FIVE

TALKIN' 'BOUT FREEDOM

I'd never been much for chatting on the phone. I'd been obsessed with books and ballet growing up and wasn't the kind of teenager who spent an evening at home, cordless pressed to my ear. That meant I'd never really gotten used to it. Sure, I occasionally called my older brother and sister, Robert and Charlotte, to check in, and when I was still in school, I called Mallory to arrange lunch dates in the Loop, but chatting up Joshua and Meredith Merit was a bird of an altogether different feather. Of course, it was nearly midnight, so there was at least a chance that my parents were asleep, prepping for another day in the upper echelon of Chicago society.

That debate—were they asleep, or weren't they—was why I spent the first hour after returning to my room with a granola bar and book in hand. It was only when I didn't think I could put it off any longer that I sat cross-legged on my bed, staring at the phone in my hand, cursing the loyalty oaths I'd sworn to one Ethan Sullivan.

I took a breath, steeled myself, dialed my parents' number, and was pleasantly surprised to get a crisp and carefully scripted answering machine message.

"You have reached the residence of Mr. and Mrs. Joshua Merit," my mother said. "I'm afraid we're unable to take your call at this time. Please leave a message following the tone."

There was a digital beep. I closed my eyes and faked the nonchalant self-confidence that Ethan, Luc, and I had discussed. "Hello, it's Merit. I wanted to talk to you both. In short, now that things have . . . changed, now that *I've* changed, I think it's a good idea that I rebuild some relationships." I cringed, and continued. "That I start spending time with the *right* kinds of people—"

I was interrupted by a clicking sound—the sound of a phone receiver being picked up. I silently cursed. I'd been *so* close.

"Well, darling," my mother said, apparently awake regardless of the time, "your call couldn't be more timely. The Breckenridges are hosting an event Friday night—cocktails for the Harvest Coalition—in Loring Park." The Breckenridge estate was located in Loring Park, a suburb in the Illinois countryside. "I won't be there," she continued. "I have an auxiliary meeting. But your father will. And, of course, the Breckenridges. You should come, say hello to the Breck boys."

The Harvest Coalition was a Chicago food bank. And while the cause was obviously laudable, I wasn't thrilled about being in the same house with my father. On the other hand, my first gala out the door and I was headed right into the Breckenridges' backyard. Or maybe more accurately, right into the Breckenridge henhouse, a vampire in tow. God forgive me.

"That sounds great, Mom."

"Wonderful. Black tie, cocktails at eight o'clock," she said, repeating the stats of the rich and famous. "I'll have Pennebaker"—that was my parents' fusty butler—"call the Breckenridges and messenger over an invitation. You're still living with that Carmichael girl, I take it?"

If only. "Actually, Mom, I moved into Cadogan House today. With the rest of the vampires," I added, in case that wasn't obvious.

"Well," my mother said, intrigue in her voice. "Isn't that quite the development? I'll be sure to pass that along to your father." I had no doubt she would, my father being a dealer of information—and the connections that this specific information would signal.

"Thank you, Mom."

"Of course, dear."

That's when I had a brainstorm. I might not have my grandfather's secret source, but I had a Meredith Merit. "Mom, one thing before you go. I hear Jamie's working now. Maybe at a newspaper?"

"Newspaper, newspaper," she absently repeated. "No, I don't recall anything about a newspaper. Everyone knows Nick is the journalist in the Breck family, anyway. Unless you've heard something different?" Her voice had dropped an octave; she'd moved directly into gossip mode and was waiting for me to pass along some juicy detail. But my job was to investigate, not fan the flames.

"Nope," I said. "Just thought I remembered hearing something."

"Oh, well. God willing, he'll find a place of his own at some point. Something to keep him occupied."

She paused, then asked, a little too loudly, "What, dear?" Silence again, then, "Darling, your father's calling me. I'll arrange for an invitation. You enjoy your Cadogan House."

"Sure, Mom. Thanks."

I pressed the END CALL button and snapped the phone shut in my palm.

"Damn," I muttered. I'd made headway on Ethan's assignment, and I'd gotten us an in at the Breckenridge estate. My ego swollen by my minor success, however questionable (I had just signed to hang out with my father), I decided to attend to my remaining House business for the evening—filling Ethan in on the phone call.

I rebelted my katana, then made my way down to his office. When I reached the first floor, I passed Malik, Ethan's vice president, as he walked away from Ethan's office. Malik's expression was grave, and he made no move to acknowledge me as we passed.

That did not bode well.

This time, Ethan's door was open. That was strange, but

worse was the fact that he stood in the middle of the room, arms crossed, gaze on the floor, that line of worry between his eyes. And he'd changed clothes, too—his tidy black suit jacket was gone. He was in shirtsleeves, no tie, only the glint of the gold Cadogan medal around his neck breaking the expanse of pristine white shirt that hugged his torso. He'd even changed his hair; it was now pulled back into a short ponytail at the nape of his neck. The kind of move a girl might make when she had to get down to business.

My stomach knotted uncomfortably. In the time that I'd gone up to my room and returned to the first floor again, something had happened.

I rapped my knuckles against the threshold.

Ethan glanced up. "I was about to page you," he said. "Come in and shut the door."

I did as ordered, then figured I might as well get the good news out first. "I called my mother. There's a charity cocktail thing at the Breckenridge estate Friday night. She's going to messenger over an invitation."

Ethan lifted approving brows. "Well done. Two birds with one stone, and all that."

"FYI, she also said she hasn't heard about Jamie being involved in any kind of journalism work. I didn't tell her anything," I added, when Ethan's gaze snapped up. "I just asked a very vague question. If he was working, especially in Nick's field, she'd have heard. Mrs. Breck would have been thrilled. She wouldn't have kept that kind of thing from my mom."

He paused, looking perplexed. "Hmm. Well, be that as it may," he said, walking around his desk and taking a seat, "given the nature of the damage a story could cause, we're going to err on the side of caution on this one. There's undoubtedly some kernel of truth to the information we've received, specific as it is." He gazed down at his desktop for a moment before lifting clouded eyes to me. "Have a seat, Merit."

There was concern in his tone. My heart thumped disconcertingly, but I did as directed, holding my katana aside and slipping into one of the chairs in front of Ethan's desk.

"The Presidium has released Celina."

"Oh, my God." I knew my eyes had gone silver, maybe with anger, maybe with fear, maybe with the adrenaline that was beginning to rush my limbs. "How—when? When did this happen?"

"Three days ago. Darius just called. I spoke briefly with Luc; he'll update the dailies and inform RDI and the other Chicago Houses." In Cadogan speak, that meant Luc would update our security reports, inform the mercenary fairies (yup—fairies) who worked for RDI, the company that oversaw security at the House during daylight hours and who stood guard at the front gate, and call Morgan and Scott Grey.

"He *just* called?" I repeated. "You only talked to him a few hours ago. He didn't mention then that they were releasing crazy into the world?"

"He didn't know. He wasn't there when the vote was taken, probably by design. The Presidium is a majoritarian body, and she's in the majority, as this should demonstrate. The Presidium"—he paused and shook his head—"they're vampires, Merit. Predators, who were born at a time when that meant more than it does today. When it wasn't flash, but substance. When humans were . . ."

I could tell that my being newly and somewhat controversially changed, he was looking for a polite way to explain something that could be easily summed up in a single word. "Food," I finished for him. "They were food."

"And little else. The politics of it aside"—was it disturbing that the perception that humans were upright cattle was mere "politics" to Ethan?—"the other members could have been glamoured, and yet be completely unaware of it. She's that powerful."

Having felt the slow sink of her glamour, her ability to pour herself into your psyche and manipulate it at will, I understood. I'd been able to resist it, but that was a personal skill, apparently. Some weird quirk of my makeup.

"As we've discussed, I expected that Celina would be confined for her crimes. That was the agreement your grandfather negotiated between Tate, the district attorney, and the GP. The

Presidium has a short memory for Clearings. Although I didn't doubt that she would receive four-star treatment, I expected she would lose her House, which she did, and would remain confined in London." He shook his head, then closed his eyes in apparent exhaustion. "At least humans aren't aware of her release. *Yet.*"

Whether humans found out or not, Celina's release still threatened to make a liar out of Mayor Tate and everyone else in Chicago who had attested to the justness of her extradition, including Ethan and my grandfather.

Jeez. And I'd thought relations with the Ombud's office were awkward *before*.

"How could they do something so politically stupid?" I wondered aloud.

Ethan leaned back in his chair and steepled his fingers together over his chest.

"GP members tend to be polarized on issues like this," he said. "Many credit their longevity to staying under the radar, living as humans, assimilating. They're happy to stay that way. Others feel they've spent centuries in hiding, and they hold no little bitterness about that. They want out, and Celina offers them an option. She has given them life among humans. She offers them a new kind of leadership. Besides— their strength aside, you've seen Celina, Merit. You know she has certain . . . charms."

I nodded. Her dark-haired beauty was undeniable. *Still.* Since when was hotness an excuse for irrational decision making? "Okay, but we're talking the *Presidium* here. The strongest vampires. The best. The *deciders*. Hot or not, how could they not have known what she was doing?"

"They're strong, but not necessarily the strongest. Amit Patel is, by all accounts, the strongest vampire in the world, and he avoids politics altogether. He has successfully avoided membership on the Sabha for many, many years."

There was a change of tone in his voice, from fear to noticeable admiration, something Ethan wasn't generous with. His voice held that same note of reverence that human men used when talking about Michael Jordan or Joe Namath.

"You have a man crush on Amit Patel," I said, mouth lifting into a smile. "A bromance. That's almost charming." And humanizing, I thought, but didn't say it aloud, knowing he wouldn't consider that a compliment.

Ethan rolled his eyes disdainfully. "You are much too young to be as strong as you are." I took that not to be a reference to chronology, but some Ethan-sense of vampire maturity.

I *hmphed*, but frowned back at him for a different reason. "She'll come to Chicago," I predicted. She'd tried to have me killed as part of her plan to take Chicago's Houses, and she'd been thwarted in killing Ethan by a stake I'd thrown. Whatever her other motivations, her other reasons, she would come to Chicago to find me . . . assuming she wasn't here already.

"It's not unlikely," Ethan agreed. He opened his mouth to speak again, but paused, seemed to think better of it. Then, with a frown that pulled down both eyebrows, he crossed his arms over his chest. "I expect that any information you gather from other Houses regarding Celina will be passed on to me."

It wasn't a question, or an "expectation," regardless of his phrasing. It was an order. And since there was only one House source from whom I even could arguably gather information, it was a pretty obnoxious order. Avoiding conversations like this at four in the morning was *exactly* why I hadn't wanted to move into the House.

"I'm not spying on Morgan," I told him. While I wasn't sure how far I wanted my relationship with Morgan to go, I was pretty damn sure "far" didn't include espionage. Besides, I'd already gone too far in mixing the personal and the professional by agreeing to help Ethan with the rave issue. I was, at least symbolically, bringing Ethan home; that was as far as I was willing to go.

Predictably, given my challenge to his sovereign authority, he tensed, his shoulders squaring. "You will report the information that you are instructed to report." His voice was crisp, chill.

The hairs on the back of my neck stood on end, a reaction

to the spill of magic that vampires leaked as our emotions rose—magic that was currently spilling into the room as our discussion heated. Vampires weren't able to perform magic, but we were magical beings, magical predators. Add that dust of magic to the silvering eyes and the fangs, and you had a pretty good survey of vampire defense mechanisms—defense mechanisms that were beginning to fire up.

I clenched my hands into fists and tried to slow my breathing. I assumed my eyes had silvered, but I was trying to keep my fangs from descending. *She* wanted something else, though . . .

I'd noticed over the last couple of months that when I was stressed or afraid, when the fight-or-flight instinct was triggered and my fangs dropped down, I could *feel* the vampire inside me, something *separate* inside me, like we hadn't quite fused together. My three-day genetic change was supposed to turn me—fully and completely—into a vampire, fangs and silvering eyes and all. I didn't understand it, how I could be vampire—the craving for blood, the nocturnal schedule, the fangs and heightened senses—and still feel the separateness of the vampire, a ghost in my machine. But that's what it felt like.

I'd mentioned it to Catcher once; his lack of recognition, of reassurance, had shaken me. If he didn't know what was going on, how was I supposed to know? How was I supposed to deal with it?

More important, what was I supposed to be?

A part of me wondered, whispered, something I could hardly stand to acknowledge—that this wasn't normal. That as a vampire, I was broken.

I could feel her now, a tiger beginning to pace. I could feel her moving, shifting beneath my bones, my muscles beginning to vibrate with it. She wanted my eyes fully silver, my fangs fully descended, my magic spilling through the room. She wanted to take Ethan's words and throw them back, to challenge him with steel.

Or she wanted to throw him down and have her way with him.

Either act would have been violent, primal, incredibly satisfying. And a truly bad idea.

I gripped the handle of the katana, pressing my nails into the cording around the grip to maintain my control. After my failed attempt at warning Catcher, I'd decided to keep the problem to myself. That meant Ethan didn't know, and I wasn't about to announce to a Master vampire who already had trust issues that I thought I was broken.

That she was waiting.

It took seconds for me to push her down, to breathe through her again, seconds during which the magic rose in eddies through the room.

Welcome to Cadogan House, I thought, and with some burst of strength, I willed her back down, lifted my chin and stared back at him. His eyes were wide crystal pools of green.

"I am Sentinel of this House," I said, my voice sultrier than usual, "and I recognize as well as you the responsibility that entails. I have agreed to get you into the places where you need access. I have agreed to help you investigate the raves, and you'll be the first person on my contact list if I learn that Celina is in town. But my love life is off limits."

"Remember who you're talking to, Sentinel."

"I never forget, Sullivan."

Nearly a minute passed, during which neither of us moved, even as the weight of our collective stubbornness thickened the air.

But then, miracle of miracles, he relented. The tension and magic diffused. A single stiff nod was all he gave me, but I relished it, savored it, resolved to commit the moment to memory—the moment he'd tapped out. I managed not to scream, "I won!" but couldn't help the grin that lifted a corner of my mouth.

I should have known the celebration was premature.

"Regardless, you'll check in with me if you bring Morgan to Cadogan House," Ethan said, his tone self-satisfied enough to deflate my smile.

Of course he wanted me to tell him. He wanted to savor the victory of my delivering the new head of Navarre

House—and the possibility of a Cadogan-Navarre alliance—
to his doorstep. Given his previous doubts about my
loyalties—spurred by my controversial change from human
to vampire—what better way for Ethan to ensure that I
wasn't leaking information in the halls of Navarre House
than to keep me safe and secure in Cadogan, Morgan in tow?

I wasn't sure how much I cared about Morgan. It was
early; the relationship was young. But in comparison with
the man Mallory had aptly nicknamed "Darth Sullivan,"
Morgan was Prince Charming in Diesel jeans. I took the
comment, inflammatory as it was, as my cue to exit. There
was no point in pretending we were going to just laugh this
off, and the longer I stayed in the room with him, the more I
risked my vampire surfacing. And if she gained control, God
only knew what she'd do. That was a risk I couldn't take—
not without risking my own death by aspen stake. So, without meeting the glare I could feel boring into my skin, I rose
from my chair and moved toward the door, reaching for the
handle.

"And lest you forget," he added, "my interest in your personal life is wholly Cadogan-motivated."

Oh, right in the numbers with that one.

"My concern is about alliances," he said, "about the potential of putting Navarre alliance insignia over our door.
Don't mistake it for anything else."

"I wouldn't dare make that mistake, Sullivan." Hard to
mistake it when he'd admitted that he was attracted to me,
but only begrudgingly. When he'd practically handed me to
Morgan. Of course, that was right after he'd offered to make
me his newest consort. His live-in, go-to girl. (Needless to
say, I'd declined.)

But here he was, raising the issue. Maybe Ethan Sullivan,
despite his crystalline facade of control, didn't really know
what he wanted after all.

"Watch your tone," he said.

"Watch your implication." I was toeing the line of insubordination, but couldn't let him get in the last word. Not on
this.

His jaw clenched. "Just do your job."

I nearly growled at him. I'd done my job. I'd done my job when there were a million reasons why I shouldn't risk my life to defend his. I'd done my job, despite his lack of faith, despite my better judgment, because there'd been nothing else to do but to do my job. I'd accepted my life as a vampire, I'd defended him before Morgan, and I'd defended him before Celina.

My frustration rose again, and with it the threat of her breaking through. I could have let her loose, could have allowed her to test her mettle against Ethan . . . but I'd sworn two oaths to him, one to defend him against all enemies, dead or alive.

My vampire probably counted as one or the other.

So instead, calling up the willpower of a saint, I forced my lips into a smile and gazed at him beneath half-hooded lashes. "*Liege*," I said crisply, an allowance of his authority, and a reminder of exactly what our respective positions were. If he could put me in my place, I could remind him of his.

Ethan watched me for a moment, nostrils flaring, but if he was angry, he resisted the urge to push back. Instead he bobbed his head and looked down at the spread of papers on his desk. I walked out and, with a decisive *click*, shut the door behind me.

It's not like I hadn't known it was coming, that he'd work that "I'm the boss" tone and attempt to meddle in my social life. Moving into the House was necessary to quickly respond as Sentinel, to help out my fellow guards, standing by their side instead of cruising down from Wicker Park at the whim of Chicago traffic.

But there was a cost. Being near Ethan was just . . . incendiary. Part animosity, part ridiculous chemistry, neither conducive to a peaceful home environment. And this was only my first night under his thumb. Not a good sign of things to come.

I returned to my room and worried the end of my ponytail as I looked around. Although the sun's rising would knock me out pretty quickly, I had an hour yet to go before dawn, and my encounter with Ethan had done a pretty good job of winding me up. I figured I could head down to the gym in the Cadogan basement, maybe put a few miles on the treadmill, or check out the Cadogan cafeteria's pre-sunrise offerings. I wasn't going to go that one alone—I was still the new girl, after all. So I took the stairs to the third floor and set about finding Lindsey.

Turns out, it wasn't difficult: a picture of Brad and Angelina was pinned to her bulletin board, a tiny cutout of Lindsey's face glued over Angelina's. "Bradsey," maybe?

The door opened before I had a chance to knock. Lindsey stood in the doorway, her gaze on the magazine in her hands. Her hair was in a low ponytail, and she was out of her Cadogan suit, having exchanged it for a fitted, short-sleeved T-shirt and jeans.

"I was waiting for you," she said.

I blinked at her. "What?"

"I'm psychic, remember?" She grinned up at me and waved one hand in the air. "Woo-woo," she said, apparently mocking the supernatural quality of it. "I sensed you were coming, and I know you're hungry."

"You can psychically tell that I'm hungry?"

She *hmphed.* "I can tell because you're Merit. When are you *not* hungry?"

She had a point.

I only got a peek of Lindsey's room before she threw the magazine inside and shut the door. The layout and furniture scheme were the same as mine—basic vampire dorm—but her room was riotous with color. The walls were crimson red, loud posters and pictures and album covers papering a good portion of them. Directly above her bed hung a giant New York Yankees flag. Lindsey was born in Iowa, but she'd done some time in New York. Apparently, it took. While I loved the Big Apple as much as the next girl, I was a Cubs fan through and through. She couldn't seem to shake her pro-Yankees affliction.

When the door was shut, she glanced at me, then clapped

her hands together. "All right, Hot-shit Sentinel. Let's go downstairs so you can get your feed on and share your live-in goodness with the rest of your brothers and sisters, yes?"

I scratched absently at my biceps. "The thing is . . ."

"They don't hate you."

"You have really got to stop doing that."

Lindsey held up both her hands. "That one was written on your face, chica. Seriously, they don't hate you. Now, shush so we can chow."

I obediently shushed, then followed her down the hall to the main staircase and down again to the first floor.

At this time of night, the main floor was all but empty of vampires. One or two sat around in conversation or with a book in hand, but the House was beginning to quiet as vampires settled in for sunrise.

We walked through the main hallway to the cafeteria, where a handful of Novitiates carried trays through a U-shaped line around glass-shielded, stainless-steel bulwarks of food. We joined the end of the line, grabbed our own trays, and began to follow the route.

The food was largely breakfasty—sweet rolls and bacon and eggs. It didn't seem like a typical dinner spread; on the other hand, it was nearly five o'clock in the morning.

I plucked a box of organic chocolate milk from an array of drinks, then snatched a cherry Danish and a pile of bacon. I probably didn't need a heavy pre-sleep breakfast, but I figured the protein would do me good. And, seriously, when you wave a plate of bacon at a vampire, is she really gonna say no?

My tray full, I sidled behind Lindsey, waiting for her and the vamps in front of us to make their selections. She squeezed honey from a plastic bear onto a bowl of oatmeal, then lifted her tray and walked toward an empty table. I followed, taking the seat across from hers.

"Do I want to ask what's going on downstairs?"

I glanced up at her. "Downstairs?"

She dipped her spoon into her oatmeal, then nibbled a bit off the end. "Again," she said, "I'm psychic. There are vampires wigging out all across Cadogan House tonight. There's a kind of nervous energy. Preparations, maybe?"

There was little doubt that Lindsey, as a guard, wouldn't ultimately hear about Celina. "Celina's been released," I whispered, tearing a corner from my cherry Danish.

"Oh, shit," she said, surprise and worry in her voice. "That explains why your energy's all over the place."

When I glanced up at her, her head was tilted to the side, an expression of curiosity on her face. "And there's something else there, too. A different kind of energy." After a pause, she grinned. "Ooooh," she said. "I got it now."

I lifted a brow. "Got what?"

"Nope," she said, shaking her head. "If you don't want to talk about Celina, I'm not going to talk about why you're all hot and bothered." She closed her eyes and put her fingertips against her temples. "Although I'm seeing someone—yep, definitely someone there. Someone with blond hair. Green eyes." She dropped her hands and gave me a flat stare.

"Shut it," I warned her with a pointed finger, a little embarrassed that she knew Ethan was the one who'd gotten me "all hot and bothered," but glad she thought it was lust-related—and not because I might have been biologically amiss. Well, vampirically amiss, anyway.

I glanced around, noting the curious looks of the vamps who sat at the wooden tables around us. They sipped at mugs and forked through bowls of fruit, their eyes on me.

They didn't look too impressed with their Sentinel.

I leaned toward Lindsey. "Have you noticed that everyone is staring at me?"

"You're a novelty," she said. "You challenged their Master before you even took the oaths, you were named Sentinel, you threw down at the Commendation ceremony, and our beloved leader still covered for your skinny ass."

That made me smile sheepishly. "I got thrown down. Not exactly the same thing."

"Did you know that I've been in this House one hundred and fifteen years? In all that time, Ethan's only nominated one other Master."

I tore at a corner of my pastry, popped it into my mouth. "I'm not a Master."

"Yet," she said, pointing at me with her spoon. "But that's only an issue of time. Of course, you could have inherent magic, be able to work some of that Mallory Carmichael juju—she's going to be good, you know—and you still wouldn't measure up to the Golden Child."

"I know she's going to be good," I agreed. "It scares me on a daily basis. Who's the Golden Child?"

"Lacey Sheridan."

I'd heard that name but couldn't place it. "Who's Lacey Sheridan?"

"The Master Ethan nominated. Master of Sheridan House."

"Ah," I said, understanding dawning. I remembered seeing the House name in the *Canon*. There were twelve vampire Houses in the United States. Sheridan was the newest.

"Lacey was in Cadogan for twenty-five years before Ethan nominated her for Testing. She passed, and Ethan Apprenticed her before she took the Rites. Then she moved to San Diego, opened Sheridan House. They were close, he and Lacey."

"Business partner close or . . . ?"

"Touchy-feely close," Lindsey said. "And that was unfortunate."

I didn't disagree. Something twinged in my chest at the thought of Ethan being touchy-feely with anyone, and that was despite the fact that I'd been a firsthand witness to the act. Nevertheless, I asked, "Why unfortunate?"

Linds frowned, seemed to consider the question as she stirred her oatmeal.

"Because Lacey Sheridan was picture-perfect," she finally said. "Tall, thin, blond hair, blue eyes. Always respectful, always acquiescent. 'Yes, Liege,' 'No, Liege.' She always wore the right thing, looked like she'd stepped out of an Ann Taylor catalog. Always said the right thing. It was unnatural. She was probably barely human even when she was one."

"Ethan must have been crazy about her," I said, thinking

she was the kind of woman he'd prefer to prefer. Elegant. Classy. And, I thought, as I nipped the end of a strip of bacon, acquiescent.

Lindsey nodded. " 'Crazy' is the word for it. He loved her, I think. In his way."

I looked up at her, bacon halfway toward its vampiric end. "You're serious?"

I couldn't imagine Ethan in love, Ethan letting his guard down. I wouldn't have figured him capable of trusting someone enough to let the man inside him peek through.

Well, except for those weird few moments with me, and he never seemed happy about those.

"Aspen-stake serious," Lindsey said. "When he realized how strong she was—she's rated a Very Strong Psych—he took her under his wing. After that, they were constantly together." She ate another spoonful of oatmeal. "They were like . . . arctic bookends, like some Nordic fairy couple. They were beautiful together, but"—Lindsey shook her head— "she was all wrong for him."

"Why's that?"

"Ethan needs someone different from that. He needs a girl who'll stand up to him, who'll challenge him. Someone to make him better, more. Not someone who'll kiss his ass twenty-four/seven and bow to every little suggestion he makes."

She eyed me speculatively.

I caught the glimmer in her eyes, shook my head. "Don't even think it. He hates me, I hate him, and acknowledging that's the only way we stand to work together."

Lindsey snorted and grabbed a strip of my bacon. "If you hate him, I'll eat my napkin. And he may hate you, but that's only skin-deep. That's only the surface." She took a bite, shook her head, and waved at me with the rest of it. "No. There's more to him than meets the eye, Merit. I know it. There's heat beneath the chill. He just needs . . . reforming."

I made an impatient gesture. "So tell me more about Lacey."

"She had friends here, still does, but I thought she was

cold. Arrogant. She's a Weak Physical, but a Very Strong Strat. She's political through and through. Maneuvering. She always came off as vaguely friendly, but like she was a politician on a campaign stop, like she was going through the motions." Lindsey paused, looked contemplative, and her voice softened. "She wasn't kind, Merit. The guards hated her."

"Because of her attitude?"

"Well, yeah, in part. Look, Ethan rules the House, so he's kind of . . . separate from the rest of us. And honestly, I'd say the same thing about you. Folks are suspicious about how you made the Sentinel short list, about your family. You're completely naïve about vamps, and yet you've got this historically important position, and although you're kind of a guard, you're closer to him than the rest of Luc's corps."

I grumbled at that, downed the bacon.

"It's not like I think you two are doing it," she said, but she paused, apparently waiting for confirmation.

"We are not 'doing it,'" I said dryly and jammed the little plastic straw into my chocolate milk box. It bore the brunt of the aggression that question always aroused. Tasty, though.

"Just checking," Lindsey said, hands raised in détente. "And if it helps, they'll get over it once they get to know you." She grinned at me, winged up her eyebrows. "I did. Of course, I have excellent taste in friends, but whatever. Not the point. The point is, Lacey was different. Not like us. She was the classic teacher's pet—wanted to be near Luc, near Ethan, near Malik, constantly near the source of authority. She didn't hang with us, didn't work well with us. But," she said, bobbing her head, "even if she was fake, she was really, really good. Always analyzing. Strategizing. She was a guard, and while she couldn't have fought off a wet cat, she had the mind for it. Planning. Long-term ramifications. Future steps."

My next question probably belied my feigned lack of interest. "Why did they break up?"

"He and Lacey? They stopped seeing each other after Testing, when she came back to Cadogan to Apprentice, to get ready for her own House. Word was, it was important to him that they stay professional while she trained. Too much at stake, ha ha, to spend time gazing into each other's eyes."

"He wouldn't care for the emotional interruption," I agreed.

"I've heard he flies out to San Diego occasionally to, what, copulate?" She nodded, grinned. "Yeah. I bet he'd put it like that. Very formal. He and Lacey probably mapped out a contract, probably negotiated terms."

"Hmm." I spared myself the embarrassment of considering, exactly, the terms they'd negotiated.

I glanced up, noticed that Malik had walked into the cafeteria. He nodded at me, then made for the buffet line.

Malik—tall, caramel-skinned, handsome, and quiet—was a mystery. In the two months I'd been a member of Cadogan House, I'd had approximately three conversations with him. As Ethan's Second they shared the bond of House leadership, but they rarely ventured off campus together in order to protect the line of succession should someone make an attempt on Ethan's life. I had the sense he played the part of CEO and understudy, learning how the House worked, how to manage it, administering the details while Ethan played Chairman of the Board. But I still hadn't gotten a feel for Malik as a vampire. As a man. The vamps who were obviously well-intentioned—Luc and Lindsey came to mind—were easy to spot, as were the overtly strategic ones—Ethan and Celina. But Malik was so reserved that I wasn't sure where he fit in. Where his allegiances lay.

Of course, he and Ethan did have one thing in common—excellent taste in Armani. Malik wore a suit as crisp and pristine as Ethan's usually were.

I watched him move through the line, but his eyes were on the vampires around him. He was all business around Ethan—at least when I'd seen them together—but he was downright friendly with the other Cadogan vamps. They approached him as he selected his breakfast, said hello, chatted. Interestingly, while the other Cadogan vamps tended to give Ethan a kind of respectful distance, they went to Malik. Talked to him, joked with him, shared a camaraderie they didn't afford their Master.

"How long has Malik been Second?" I asked Lindsey.

She swallowed bacon, then lifted her gaze to where he stood in line, chatting with a vampire I didn't know. "Malik? Right after the House was moved to Chicago. '83."

That's 1883, not 1983, for those of you following along at home.

"Ethan picked Chicago, you know. Once Peter Cadogan died, he wanted the House out of Wales, out of Europe. Malik lived in Chicago. He was an orphan."

"He lost his parents?" I asked. "How awful."

"Wrong kind of orphan. He was a Rogue. Houseless. A vampire orphan. His Master wasn't strong enough to keep her House together, and she was ix-nayed by a rival." Lindsey held her fist to her chest, mimicking a staking. "Then he and Ethan met, and the rest is history."

"Do you know him? Well, I mean?"

"Malik? Sure. Malik's great." Lindsey checked her watch, then finished a glass of water before rising and picking up her tray. "So, there's three hundred and nineteen other vampires affiliated with Cadogan House. Suggestion?"

I looked up at her, nodded.

"Consider the possibility that they'd like to get to know you if you gave them a chance."

"That's why I'm here," I said, and followed her out.

CHAPTER SIX

THE RETURN OF THE PRINCE

I woke bright and early—or maybe more accurately, dark and late—the next night. It was my turn on guard duty, patrolling the blocks-wide grounds around Cadogan House, keeping an eye out for breaches of the ten-foot-high wrought-iron fence that kept intruders out and vampires in.

In a city of supernatural weirdos, one had to stay alert.

I got up and showered in the tiny bathroom, completed the few girly tasks in my repertoire, then climbed into my Cadogan suit, complete with belted katana and my own Cadogan medal, given to me by Ethan during my Commendation into the House. I brushed my long, dark hair until it shone, pulled it into a high ponytail and combed through my bangs. Vampirism added a new glow to my complexion, so I added only a little blush and lip gloss for shine.

Once I was prettied up and well armed, I headed for my door, then glanced down as colors caught my eye.

Mail lay in a pile in front of the door. Figuring it had been delivered while I was in the shower, I leaned down to pick up a J.Crew catalog forwarded from Mallory's and an envelope of thick linen paper. The stock was heavy and nubby, and undoubtedly expensive. I slipped open the flap and peeked inside. It was the promised invite to the Brecks', probably messengered by my mom while the sun was still above the horizon.

I guessed the Breckenridge gala was a done deal, unfortunately. I dropped the catalog on the bed, pocketed the invite, and was about to head downstairs when my cell phone rang. I slipped it from my pocket, then glanced at the screen. Morgan.

"Good evening," he said, when I flipped open the phone.

Cell at my ear, I headed into the hallway, then closed the door behind me. "Good evening back," I replied. "What's new in Navarre House?"

"In Navarre, not much yet. Still early. We try not to start the dramatics until closer to midnight."

"I see," I said with a chuckle, as I took the hallway to the main stairs.

"The thing is, I'm not actually at Navarre House. I took a field trip south. I'm actually a little more in the vicinity of Cadogan House."

I stopped at the staircase, hand on the railing. "How much in the vicinity of Cadogan House?"

"Come outside," he said, voice playful. Invitational. Curiosity piqued, I closed the phone and slipped it into my pocket, then took the stairs at a trot. The first floor was still quiet, vamps not quite up from their midday naps. I headed for the front door, then opened it and stepped outside onto the small stone portico.

He stood on the sidewalk, halfway between the front door and the gate. He was dressed in his typical style—runway rebel. Designer jeans, square-toed shoes, a short-sleeved T-shirt that hugged his lean form, and a wide leather watch on his left wrist.

I always seemed to forget the soul-stealing grin and those baleful bedroom eyes when I was away from Morgan, my mind usually preoccupied with other vampire antics. My heart tripped at the remembrance of exactly how pretty he was.

And in his hand, a vase of flowers. The vase was slender, a milky-colored glass. The flowers were puffs of color, peonies or ranunculus or some other explosion of petals on slender green stems. They were beautiful. And a little unexpected.

"Hi," he said when I went to him, smiling slyly. "I'm not sure I've seen you in your Cadogan black." He tugged at the lapel of my coat, then wet his lips in obvious appreciation. "You look very . . . official."

I rolled my eyes at the flirtation, but could feel the heat rise on my cheeks. "Thank you," I said, then bobbed my head toward the flowers. "I assume those aren't for Ethan?"

"You would be correct. I know I didn't call, and I have to get going—I've got a meeting—but wanted to bring you something." He looked down at them, his grin a bit sheepish. A little goofy. A little heartrending. "I decided you needed a housewarming gift."

I grinned back at him. "You mean other than the life-sized poster of you that you already gave me?"

"Well, not that that wasn't a fantastic present, but I had something a little more . . . feminine in mind." With that, he handed over the vase, then leaned in and pressed his lips to my cheek. "Welcome to the life of vampires, Merit." When he leaned back again, the smile on his face made it clear he meant the welcome sincerely. Morgan was a vampire's vampire, a believer. By moving into the House, I'd made a new commitment to the fraternal order of vampires, and that obviously meant something to him.

"Thank you," I said, the vase warm beneath my fingers, the heat of his touch—and the slightest tingle of magic—still lingering there.

He gazed at me for a moment, heartfelt emotion in his eyes, then shook it off as his cell phone rang. He pulled it from his jeans pocket, then glanced at the screen. "Gotta take this," he said, "and gotta run." He leaned forward and—ever so softly—pressed his lips to mine. "Goodbye, Merit," he said, then turned and trotted back down the sidewalk and disappeared through the gate.

I stood there for a moment, playing emotional catch-up. He drove down from Navarre House just to surprise me with flowers. *Flowers.* And not, It's-Valentine's-Day-and-I-feel-obligated flowers. These were just-because flowers.

I had to give him props—the boy was good.

Interestingly, as Morgan walked out, Kelley walked in in full Cadogan attire, katana in one hand, a slender clutch purse in the other. It was interesting because Kelley, like the rest of the guards, lived in Cadogan House. Since the sun had fallen beneath the horizon only an hour ago, I had to wonder where—or with whom—she'd spent the daylight hours.

"Nice flowers," she said as she reached me on the side-walk. "A gift from the new Master of Navarre?"

"Apparently so," I said, turning to follow her into the House.

Those few words were all I got, as she immediately pulled out her own cell phone and slid open the keyboard, keys clicking as she walked. Kelley wasn't much for chatting.

"Good day?" I asked her, as we took the stairs to the base-ment.

She paused as we reached the landing between the floors and tilted her head thoughtfully, inky dark hair falling over her shoulder as she moved. "You'd be amazed," she said throatily, then continued her trot to the basement.

I stood on the stairs for a moment, watching her descend, curiosity killing my cat, then made myself get to work. Even though it was only just past dawn, the Ops Room was already abuzz with activity. Lindsey and Juliet were already at their respective stations, Juliet perusing the Web, probably doing research. Lindsey was on environs duty, staring intently at a bank of closed-circuit monitors while speaking quietly but steadily into the earpiece-and-microphone duo that curled around her ear.

I put the flowers on the conference table, then went to the hanging wall of folders that held instructions, announce-ments, dossiers, and anything else Luc felt we needed to know. Inside was a single sheet of daffodil-colored paper. It bore two simple, ominous sentences: "Celina Desaulniers released. Expect Chicago infiltration."

I glanced at the rest of the folders; each held the same yellow sheet. Ethan must have spread the news. The word was out, and so was the warning. Celina was probably on her way . . . if she wasn't here already.

With that motivation in mind, I decided it was time to do my Sentinel duty. I started with my homework, handing the Breck invitation to Luc. "For Ethan," I told him. "Friday night with the Breckenridges."

He peeked inside the envelope, then nodded. "Fast work, Sentinel."

"I'm a goddess among vampires, Boss." That bit done, I grabbed a slim earpiece-and-microphone set from a rack, slipped it over my ponytail, and walked to Lindsey's monitor.

"Hot shit on duty," Lindsey said, and my earpiece crackled to life.

"Sentinel," acknowledged a gravelly voice from the earpiece. That gravelly voice belonged to one of the RDI fairies at the Cadogan gate. They kept watch on the grounds while we slept (or not, in Kelley's case) and stood point at the gate twenty-four/seven. The earpieces kept us all in contact in the event of a supernatural catastrophe. As I'd once told Mallory, you never knew when giant winged nasties were going to swoop down from the sky and snatch up a vampire.

Did I have a great job, or what?

Sucking in a breath, I adjusted my earpiece, tweaked Lindsey's blond ponytail, and headed for the door. "I'm on my way up," I said into the tiny jaw mic. "Be there in two."

"Pack your lipstick," Luc threw out.

Like Lindsey, Juliet, and Kelley, I looked back at him. "Lipstick?"

"Paparazzi," he said. "RDI herded them together, but they're standing at the corner." He half smiled. "And they've got cameras."

Kelley glanced back from her computer monitor. "I saw them on the way in. Maybe a dozen." She turned back to her computer. "All eager for images of Chicago's new favorites," she grumbled.

I stood in the doorway for a minute, hoping for a little more direction from Luc—what the hell was I supposed to do with paparazzi?—but got nothing until he shooed me toward the door.

"You've read your talking points, I hope," he said. "Go

forth and . . . Sentinelize." It wasn't until I was out of the room and on my way toward the stairs, when I heard words yelled behind me. "And no ass pictures, Sentinel!"

That, I could do.

Although the House had been all but empty a few minutes ago, the first floor was now sprinkled with vampires in Cadogan black, some with gadgets in their hands, all looking busy and supernaturally attractive, preparing for evenings among the humans or, like me, evenings in service to the House and its Master.

Some looked up as I passed, their expressions ranging from curiosity to outright disdain. I hadn't made the best impression on my fellow Novitiates, having challenged Ethan only a few days after my change. The near havoc I wreaked at their Commendation ceremony, in which I'd accidentally ignored Ethan's orders, didn't help. Ethan made me Sentinel at Commendation, giving me the historic duty of defending Cadogan House. But Lindsey was right—the position set me apart from the other vampires. My fellow guards had been supportive, but I knew the rest of the House still wondered— Was she loyal? Was she strong? Was she sleeping with Ethan?

(I know. That last one was disturbing to me, too. Seriously.)

I exited the gigantic stone-clad House through the front door, then took the sidewalk to the front gate, nodding at the two black-clad fairies who stood point. They were tall and lean, with long, straight hair pulled back tightly from their handsome, if angular, faces. Their uniforms were black shirts, cargo pants tucked neatly into black boots, and black-scabbarded swords. They had fraternally similar faces, so much so that I couldn't tell them apart. I didn't know if they were brothers, or twins, or even related. I didn't even know their names, and my polling the other Cadogan guards for information hadn't been successful. It seemed the RDI staff preferred to interact with vampires on a purely professional basis, if at all.

Lindsey had taken to calling the guards the "Twins." I'd

settled on Rob and Steve. I wasn't entirely sure which Rob and Steve were guarding the House tonight, but they nodded back at me, and I found the act, if cold, comfortingly familiar. The little I'd learned about the supernatural in the last two months made me glad these sword-wearing warriors were on our side . . . at least as long as we paid them to be.

"Press?" I asked them. One of them looked down at me, an angular eyebrow raised from his six feet plus. Even at five foot nine, I suddenly felt very, very short.

"Corner," he said, then turned his gaze back to the street before him. Having apparently lost his attention, I glanced down the street.

Sure enough, there they were. Given the size of the knot of them, I guessed a baker's dozen. Since paparazzi weren't rumored to be the most manageable of critters, the guards had done an impressive job of rounding them up. On the other hand, who wouldn't obey more than twelve collective feet of sullen, sword-bearing sups?

I headed down the sidewalk in their direction, planning to make a survey of the perimeter before moving back in for a sweep of the grounds. I wasn't sure I had the innate moxie to stare down a group of paparazzi, but I figured now was as good a time as any to test the confidence Ethan expected me to show Friday night. I kept my smile vaguely pleasant as I sauntered toward them, gazing at them beneath my long, straight bangs.

As I moved closer, the confidence got a little easier to fake. Although they wore the expressions of men hell-bent on getting the Next Great Shot, the smell of fear tingled the air. Maybe their proximity to the RDI guards, maybe their proximity to vampires. Ironic, wasn't it, that they were afraid of the people (*ahem*) that they were obsessively trying to capture on film?

When I was younger, and still well integrated into the Merit clan, I'd been photographed with my family at charity gatherings, sporting events, the razing or raising of important Chicago buildings. But the reporters were different this time around, and so was my role. I was the main dish, not just the cute kid being dragged around Chicago by social-climbing parents. As I neared them, they began calling my name, clamoring for my attention, for the perfect head shot.

Flashbulbs popped, the afterimages blinding to my nocturnally adjusted eyes. Calling up some of my newfound fake-it-till-you-make-it attitude, I tapped the fingers of my left hand against the handle of my sword, and reveled in the way their eyes tightened at the corners.

Like prey.

I nibbled the edge of my lip provocatively.

"Good evening, gentlemen."

The questions came so fast I could hardly differentiate them. "Merit, show us the sword!"

"Merit, Merit, over here!"

"Merit, how are things in Cadogan House tonight?"

"It's a beautiful spring night in Chicago," I said, smiling cannily, "and we're proud to be in the Windy City."

They asked questions. I kept to the talking points Luc had provided us last night; thank God I'd taken the time to look them over. Not that there was much to them—mostly blurbs about our love of Chicago and our desire to assimilate, to be part of the neighborhoods around us. Fortunately, those were the subjects of their questions. At least at first.

"Were you surprised to learn that the perpetrator of the park killings was a vampire?" a voice barked out. "Were you satisfied by the extradition of Celina Desaulniers?"

My smile flattened, and my heart thudded in my chest. That sounded like the kind of question Ethan and Luc feared. The kind Jamie was supposed to ask.

"No response?" the reporter asked, stepping to the front of the pack.

This time my heart nearly stopped altogether. It was a Breckenridge, but not the one I'd have expected to see. I guess everybody, vampires and humans alike, came back to Chicago eventually. "Nicholas?"

He looked the same, but older. More grave, somehow. Caesar-cut brown hair, blue eyes. The boy was gorgeous in a stoic kind of way. That lean, stoic form was currently wrapped in jeans, Dr. Martens, and a fitted gray T-shirt. He also wore a blank expression—no indication in his eyes that he knew me or that he was willing to acknowledge our shared history.

I'd often wondered what it would be like to see Nick again, if there'd be camaraderie or something more detached. The latter, apparently, given his businesslike posture, his opening volleys.

So much for the warm reunion.

Apparently undeterred, Nick kept going. "Was the extradition of Celina Desaulniers sufficient punishment given the heinous crimes she helped commit in Chicago? For the deaths of Jennifer Porter and Patricia Long?"

Since we were apparently playing dumb about our relationship, I gave back the same all-business, vaguely condescending stare. "Celina Desaulniers committed a terrible crime against Ms. Long and Ms. Porter," I said. I had been graciously allowed to keep my own attack secret. The fact that a Merit had become a vampire was common knowledge; the manner of my making was not, at least among humans.

"As a result of her role in their murders, she was punished. She gave up her life in the United States and her freedom for having taken part in those crimes."

My stomach curled at the omission, at the fact that I hadn't mentioned that Celina had been released and was, in fact, no longer serving out her sentence of imprisonment. But that little admission would invite a shitstorm of panic that I'd prefer to leave to Ethan and the other Masters.

I put on my most professional face. "If you have questions about the Houses' reactions to that punishment," I added, "I can direct you to our public relations staff."

Take that, Breckenridge.

He did, arching back an arrogant brow. "Is this what the citizens of Chicago have to expect from vampires living among us? Murder? Mayhem?"

"Vampires have been in Chicago for many years, Nick." Calling him by name was enough to invite curious stares among the other photographers. Some lowered their cameras, glanced between us, probably wondering at the dialogue. "And we've lived peacefully together for a very long time."

"So you say," Nick said. "But how do we know that all of the city's unsolved murders weren't perpetrated by vamps?"

"Judging all vampires based on the actions of a single bad apple? That's classy, Nick."

"You're all fanged."

"So that justifies the prejudice?"

He shrugged again. "If the shoe fits."

There was no mistaking the animosity in his voice. But what confused me was its source. Nick and I had broken off our high school relationship when we departed for our respective colleges—Yale's journalism program for Nicholas, NYU's English program for me. Our breakup hadn't been very dramatic, both of us having reached the conclusion that we made better friends than partners. Occasional telephone calls and e-mails kept us in contact, and we'd gone our separate directions with no bad blood between us. Or so I'd thought.

That wasn't the only strange thing. If vampires were taking hits from the Breckenridge corner, why was it Nick, not Jamie, throwing the punches? Something very odd was going on.

"Merit, Merit!"

I dragged my gaze away from Nicholas, from the bitterness in his eyes.

"Merit, any truth to the rumor that you're seeing Morgan Greer?"

Okay, now we were back on track. Justice be damned if there was sex to discuss.

"As Cadogan House Sentinel, I see Mr. Greer quite a bit. He's one of Chicago's Masters, as you all know."

They chuckled at the diversion, but pushed forward.

"How about a little romance, Merit? Are you two a hot item? That's what our sources say."

I smiled brightly at the reporter, a thin man with thick blond hair and a week's worth of stubble. "You tell me who your sources are," I said, "and I'll answer that question."

"Sorry, Merit. Can't reveal a source. But they're reliable. My word on it."

The gaggle of reporters chuckled at the exchange.

I grinned back. "Hate to burst your bubble, but I'm not paid to take your word on things."

The pocket of my suit coat vibrated—my cell phone. I wasn't thrilled to leave a mysteriously angry Breckenridge at my corner, especially among curious humans with notebooks and cameras, but neither did I want to talk to whoever might be calling me in front of those curious humans. Besides, I needed to move along to other parts of the grounds. There were blocks of Cadogan House fence yet to walk. The ringing phone offered me a handy excuse to step aside.

"Good night, gentlemen," I offered, and left them behind, still calling my name.

Slipping the buzzing cell phone from my pocket, I made a note to update Luc and Ethan on this latest Breckenridge development—right after I figured out what the hell was going on. Either we had an ignorant source who didn't know the difference between Brecks, or we had a bad source who didn't much care and was trying to lead us astray. I wasn't sure which was the worse possibility.

As I moved down the block, camera strobes still flashing behind me, I lifted the phone to my ear. The shouting began almost immediately.

I pressed a hand to my other ear. "Mallory? What's wrong?"

I managed to catch only a few words of her first volley— "Order," "Catcher," "magic," "Detroit," and what I guessed was the impetus for the phone call, the phrase "three months."

"Hon, I need you to slow down. I can't understand what you're saying."

The diatribe slowed, but she switched to a bevy of four-letter words that blistered even my jaded vampire ears.

"—and if that asshole thinks I'm going to spend three months in Detroit at some kind of internship, he is seriously mistaken. Seriously! I swear to God, Merit, I'm going postal on the next person who so much as mutters the word 'magic.'"

That Catcher was the "asshole" was easy enough to guess, but the rest of it was a morass. "I'm playing catch-up here, Mal—Catcher wants to send you to Michigan for three months?"

I heard rhythmic breathing, like she was practicing La-maze during a long contraction. "He talked to someone from the Order. Apparently, union or not, the Order doesn't have a local in Chicago, notwithstanding the fact that we're the third-freaking-biggest city in the country. Anyhoo, not your problem, that's some kind of historical crap, and it's part of the reason he got kicked out, so they want to send me to Detroit so I can train with some official sorcerer-type to avoid the temptation of publicly using the magic I don't know how to use in the first place. It's ridiculous, Merit! Ridiculous!"

I kept walking, trying to pay some attention to my sur-roundings as she continued the rant. Handling stuff like this would be so much easier if I didn't have to worry about whether trolls or orcs were going to jump out from behind every lamppost. Ooh—that made me pause. Were there orcs in Chicago?

"I have to leave in two days!" she said. "And this is the real punch in the junk—no return trips to Chicago, no trips out of Detroit at all—until the internship is done."

"I'm not sure girls technically have 'junk,'" I observed, "but I take your point. Catcher has a history with the Order. Can't he arrange something?"

Mallory snorted. "I wish. Long story short, Catcher lost his seniority—and everything else—when he opted to stay in Chicago. That's apparently why they kicked him out—because he wanted to stay here, and they didn't buy that the Order needed a sorcerer, much less a local, in Chicago. He's a little low on pull at the moment. You know, it's a bitch there's no part-time sorcerer school," Mallory said. "Magic vo-tech or something. Anything like that, hon?"

I smiled at the pause in the conversation, the intermittent mumbling that indicated he'd been standing there while she referred to him as an asshole. Given the workouts he'd been putting me through lately, I was happy to know he was taking some heat of his own. I mean, I understood the need to prepare me for the worst, especially since Celina had been released, but there's only so many times that a girl needs to squeak past the whistling blade of an antique samurai sword.

"Nope," she finally said.

"Huh," I said, half of my brain wondering about those details—the man was ornery and evasive whenever the Order came up—while the other half surveyed what looked like a gap in the hedge that lined the wrought-iron fence. I walked closer and picked at a couple of leaves that were barely visible in the beam of the overhead streetlight. Fortunately, upon my expert inspection, it looked like a browning spot in the greenery, not the work of a saboteur or would-be burglar. I made a note to tell . . . well, I had no idea whom to tell, but I bet we had some kind of gardener.

"Are you paying attention to me? I'm pretty much having a huge crisis here, Mer."

"Sorry, Mal. I'm on duty, making my rounds outside." I kept walking, surveying the dark, empty street. Not too much going on once you got past the dozen paparazzi. "The Order's like a union, right? So can't you file a grievance or something about this Detroit trip?"

"Hmm. Good question. Catch, can we grieve this?"

I heard mumbled conversation.

"Can't grieve this," Mallory finally reported back. "But I'm supposed to leave in two days! You need to get that cute butt back over here and comfort me. I mean, Detroit, Merit. Who spends three months in Detroit?"

"The million or so citizens of Detroit would be a prelim guess. And I can't come by right now. I'm working. Can I get a rain check until after shift?"

"I guess. And FYI, Darth Sullivan is putting a crimp in our friendship. I know you're living over there now, but you should still be at my beck and call."

I snorted. "Darth Sullivan would disagree, but I'll do what I can."

"I'm heading for the Chunky Monkey," Mal said. "Ben

and Jerry will hold me until you get here." She hung up before I could say goodbye, probably already two spoonfuls into a carton of ice cream. She'd be fine, I decided. At least until I could make it over there.

The rest of my shift passed by, thankfully, with no drama. While I was learning what I could, training when scheduled, and performing what felt like perfunctory guard duties, I had no illusions about my ability to handle the nasties that might come creeping out of the dark. Sure, I'd managed to stake Celina in the shoulder when she made her final stand against Ethan—but I'd been aiming for her heart. If something, or some*things*, gathered the strength and bravado to attack Cadogan House, me and my sword were hardly going to scare them off. I considered myself more of a first-warning unit. I might not be able to fend off any bad guys, but I could at least alert the rest of the crew—the vastly more experienced crew—to the problem.

And speaking of problems, although I knew I needed to report the latest Breckenridge developments—the fact that Nick was back in Chicago and that he'd camped out with the paparazzi at our gate—I'd spent enough time with Ethan and Luc discussing supernatural drama over the last couple of days. Besides, I had some questions for Nick, questions I couldn't ask in front of a bevy of reporters. Questions about Nick's newfound hostility. Ethan and I would be at the Breckenridge estate tomorrow night. If Nick was there, I'd have time to do a little investigating of my own.

It sounded like a good plan, a solid course of action for a newbie Sentinel. Either that or a pretty detailed way to continue avoiding Ethan.

"Win-win," I murmured with a smile.

To add a little more space between Darth Sullivan and me—and to repay Mallory for taking care of me during my own awkward supernatural transition—I got into my Volvo and drove back to Wicker Park to provide a little postshift BFF solace.

The brownstone was well lit as I drove up, even in the

early hours of the morning. I didn't bother ringing the door-
bell, but walked right in and headed for the kitchen. Which
smelled delicious.

"Chicken and rice," Mallory announced from her spot in
front of the stove, where she was spooning rice and sauce
onto a plate. She heaped a piece of roasted chicken on top of
the combo, then smiled at me. "I knew you'd want food."

"You're a goddess among women, Mallory Carmichael." I
took the plate to a stool at the kitchen island and tucked into
the food. The wicked fast vampire metabolism was great for
the waistline but awful for the appetite. It was a rare hour that
didn't involve my dreaming about grilled, roasted, or fried
beast. Sure, I needed blood to survive—I was a vampire, after
all—but like Mal had once said, blood was like another vita-
min. It was fulfilling in a very important way. Comforting—
like chicken soup for vampires. That it came from plastic bags
and was delivered to our door by a company uncreatively
named Blood4You didn't diminish the comfort, although it
wasn't much in the way of chic.

The chicken and rice, on the other hand, was a hunger
spot-hitter. It was a delicious recipe, and one of the first
meals that Mallory had cooked for us when we'd become
roommates three years ago. It was also better, or so I guessed,
than anything I could get in the Cadogan House cafeteria.

Catcher padded into the kitchen, barefoot and jeaned and
pulling on a T-shirt. The hem came down just in time to hide
the circular tattoo that I knew marked his abdomen. It was a
circle cut into quadrants, a graphical representation of the
organization of magic into the four Keys.

"Merit," he said, heading for the refrigerator. "I see you
managed to stay away for, what, all of twenty-four hours?"

I chewed a mouthful of chicken and rice, swallowed. "I'm
investigating disorderly sorcerers."

He humphed and grabbed a carton of milk, then chugged
directly from the cardboard spout. Mallory and I watched
him, the same grimace on both our faces. Sure, I did the same
thing with OJ, but he was a boy, and it was milk. That was
just gross.

I glanced over at her, and she met my gaze, rolled her eyes. "At least he's putting the toilet paper *on* the roll now. That's a big step. Love you, Catch."

Catcher grunted, but he was smirking as he did it. After closing the refrigerator door, he joined us, standing next to Mallory on her side of the kitchen island. "I assume Sullivan filled you in about Celina?"

"That she's probably on her way back to Chicago to take care of me? Yeah, he mentioned that."

"Celina's been released?" Mallory asked, casting a worried glance in Catcher's direction. "Seriously?"

He bobbed his head. "We're not issuing a press release or anything, but yes." Then he turned his gaze on me and scoured me with a look. "One wonders if vampires enjoy drama, since they just keep making more of it."

"*Celina* keeps making more of it," I clarified, pointing at him with my fork. "I was more than happy to keep her locked away in a damp British dungeon." I took another bite of chicken, my hunger apparently undiminished by the possibility that a narcissistic vampire was crossing the Atlantic to get me. On the other hand, might as well enjoy food while I still could.

"Now that we've covered that," I said, changing the subject, "someone wanna fill me in on the sorcery drama?"

"They're going to take me away," Mallory said.

"To Schaumburg," Catcher said dryly. "I'm taking her to Schaumburg."

"So not to Detroit, then?" I asked, glancing back and forth between them. It was a pretty big difference, Schaumburg being a suburb northwest of the city. It was thirty miles and an entire Great Lake closer to Chicago—and me—than Detroit.

Mallory crooked a thumb at Catcher. "This one made a phone call. Apparently, he hasn't lost all of his pull with the Order."

As if on cue, Catcher's expression clouded. "Given that it was phone *calls*, plural, before they'd even let Baumgartner near the phone, saying that I have pull vastly overstates my influence. Let's just say they've softened their position on keeping a resident sorcerer in the Chicago metro."

"Who's Baumgartner?" I asked.

"President of the 155." At my blank stare, Catcher clarified, "My former union, Local 155 of the Union of Amalgamated Sorcerers and Spellcasters."

I nearly choked on chicken, and when I was done with the coughing fit, asked, "The acronym for the Order of sorcerers is 'U-ASS'?"

"A, seriously appropriate," Mallory commented, giving Catcher a sideways grin. "B, explains why they call it 'the Order.'"

I nodded my agreement on both points.

"So, they're good with the benefits, shitty with the marketing," Catcher said. "The point is, she won't be spending three months in Detroit."

"Not that it isn't a lovely city," Mallory put in.

"Lovely city," I agreed, but just for form, as I'd never been there. "So this training is, what, magical classes and whatnot?"

"Whatnot," Catcher said. "No classes—just on-the-job training. She'll begin to utilize and manipulate the Keys, major and minor, so that she can understand her duties and obligations to the rest of the Order and, if they have a few spare minutes"—his voice went dry as toast—"how to harness and redistribute the power that is beginning to funnel its way through her body."

I looked at her, blinking, trying to imagine exactly how my blue-haired, blue-eyed, ad exec of a best friend—currently in a MISS BEHAVIN' T-shirt and skinny jeans—was going to manage to do that.

"Huh," was all I said.

"She'll live and breathe the power of it, learn to exercise the control." He paused contemplatively, staring off into space until Mallory touched his hand with the tips of her fingers. He turned and looked at her. "Sorcerers learn by practice, by actually funneling the power. No books, no classrooms, just doing it. She'll be put into a situation in

Schaumburg, and she'll handle it. The hard way—on her own, no nets."

I guessed "the way I had to do it" was coming next. The speech had the ring of old-school practitioner complaining about the way things had changed since *his* time, when he had to walk uphill both ways to get to school, etc., etc. Of course, I bet learning to funnel magic through Mal's slender frame took considerably more effort than hauling a couple of arithmetic books up a hill.

"Damn," I said, giving her a sympathetic look. "At least vampires get a desk reference." On the other hand, that's about all we got. Although Luc valued training, and I appreciated the effort, he and Ethan had had decades to gain experience before assuming their House positions. To play the part of Sentinel, I got two weeks, a sorcerer with an attitude, and a katana.

"So's I'm going to Schaumburg," Mal said, "where I'll get a little less practical experience than if I'd summered full-time in Detroit, but hopefully enough that I learn not to turn bad guys into piles of glitter because I inadvertently snapped my fingers."

As if to illustrate her point, she snapped them, a tiny blue spark jumping from her fingertips, the air suddenly stirring with the electricity of magic. Catcher closed his fingers around the spark, and when he opened them again, a glowing blue orb was centered in his palm. He lifted his hand, pursed his lips, and blew the orb away. It shattered into a crystalline glitter that peppered the air with sparkling magic before it dispersed and faded.

Then he turned to Mallory with a lurid look that made me happy, *super happy*, to be living in Cadogan House. "She's a nice funnel."

Oh, dear, sweet God, did I *not* need to hear about Mallory being a funnel. "So you're going to Schaumburg," I repeated, refocusing the conversation and taking another bite before I lost my appetite completely. "And you'll do your internship there. How long do you have to stay? How long will it take? Give me the deets."

"It'll be nightlies," Catcher said. "She'll spend most of her evenings in Schaumburg for a while. Since she's getting an exemption, we're not sure how long her practice will last. Special case, special rules. She'll stay, I assume, until she proves her worth."

Mallory and I shared a snarky glance about that one. "Sad thing is," she said, "he's serious."

Something occurred to me. "Oh, shit, Mal, what are you going to do about your job?"

Mallory's expression went uncharacteristically wan. She stretched up from the stool and grabbed a white envelope from atop a pile of mail that sat at one end of the island. She held it in front of me so I could read the addressee—McGettrick Combs.

"Resignation letter?" I asked. She nodded, then returned the envelope to the pile.

Catcher put his hand at the back of her neck, rubbed it. "We talked about this."

"I know," she said, nodding her head. "It's just a change." When she looked up at me, her eyes were bright with tears. Notwithstanding the discomfort of being witness to their more amorous adventures, I was glad Catcher was here for her, that she had someone who'd been through similar experiences, who could guide her through the process or just be there when she needed comforting.

"I'm sorry, Mallory," was all I could think to say, knowing how much she'd loved her job, how well suited for it she'd been, how much pride she'd taken when a commercial or print ad she'd conceptualized appeared in the *Trib* or on ABC-7.

She sniffed, nodded, and knuckled away the tears that had slipped beneath her lashes, before chuckling. "Hey, I'll get my union card, and think of all the doors that will open for me then."

"Absolutely, kiddo," Catcher said, leaning over to plant a kiss on her temple. "Absolutely."

"I don't want to bust the pro-union party here," I said, "but will those doors open into any bank vaults or some kind of salary?"

Catcher nodded. "Once she's completed her on-the-job, since the Order has finally realized they need someone on the ground in Chicago, she'll be on call." The middle part of that sentence had been spoken gruffly and with obvious bitterness. Typical Catcher, in other words.

"On call?" I asked, turning my gaze to Mallory, who smiled slyly.

"I'll be doing my own dispute handling, investigating, that kind of thing." She shrugged. "It's a job. I mean, it's not Cadogan–Hyde Park kind of money, but I'll manage. Speaking of Cadogan money, what's up on your end of things? How's life under the tutelage of Darth Sullivan?"

"Well," I began, "I've been roped into shenanigans."

Without preface, Catcher muttered a curse, then leaned over, slipped his wallet from his jeans, and pulled out a twenty-dollar bill, which he handed to Mallory.

She grinned down at it, then carefully folded it and tucked it into her shirt. "On behalf of Carmichael Savings and Loan, we appreciate your business."

At my arched eyebrows, she bobbed her head toward Catcher. "I voted shenanigans within the first twenty-four hours. Mr. Bell over here thought Darth Sullivan would let you get 'settled.'" She used air quotes for that last part.

"Damn. I wish I could have taken that bet," I said. I debated how much I could tell them about said ensuing shenanigans, but since Ethan would probably tell Catcher his plans, and Catcher would undoubtedly tell Mallory, I didn't think I was risking much.

"We'll be doing some reconnaissance work. Long story short, I'm going home."

Mallory arched an eyebrow. "What do you mean, going home?"

"I'll be hanging out with the Merit clan."

"Seriously?"

"Oh, yeah. I'm going to try to get close to an old friend.

According to Ethan, at least the part he's telling me, we're trying to keep prying human eyes away from some questionable vamp activities. God only knows what other secret motivations he's got."

"Does getting into your pants count as a secret motivation these days?"

I screwed up my face. "Ew."

Mal rolled her eyes, apparently not buying my disgust. "Whatever. You'd totally hit that if he weren't such an ass."

"And that's exactly his problem," I muttered.

"And speaking of hitting that," Mal added, perking up, "any word from Morgan? You guys have anything planned for the weekend?"

"Not really," I vaguely said, and left it at that. It was true that there wasn't much to report, but I also wasn't up for talking about it; being conflicted about the guy I was pseudo-dating wasn't helped by analyzing it to death.

I checked my watch. It was two hours until sunup. That gave me time to sneak back to Cadogan House, grab an obscenely long shower, and chillax a little before bed.

"I should go," I told them. I took my empty plate to the sink, deposited it and then glanced back. "When does the training start?"

"Sunday," Mallory said, rising from her stool. That gave her two full days to wreak pre-internship havoc, or at least enjoy some rowdy pre-internship rounds with Catcher.

"I'll walk you out," she said. Catcher followed us, a hand at Mallory's back. We reached the living room and, without another word, he sat down on the couch, crossed his ankles on the coffee table and slouched back, remote control in his hand. He flicked on the television and tuned it immediately to the Lifetime Channel.

Mallory and I stood there, heads cocked, watching this incredibly sexy, incredibly masculine man, whose eyes were glued to a made-for-TV movie. He slid us an annoyed glance, rolled his eyes, and turned back to the television.

"You know I love this shit," he said, then made a vague gesture at Mallory, "and she lives with me." That apparently being defense enough, he sniffed, settled the remote control in the crux between his legs, and crossed his arms behind his head.

"My life," Mallory said. "My love. The keeper of my heart."

"The keeper of your remote," I pointed out, then enveloped her in a hug. "I love you. Call me if you need to."

"I love you, too," she said, and when we'd released each other, nodded her head in Catcher's direction. "He's making dinner Saturday night, kind of a pre-training deal. I don't really need a going-away party anymore, but far be it from me to complain when someone tries to make dinner in my honor. We'll call it a not-going-that-far-away party. Come over, maybe bring Morgan?"

I offered back a sardonic look. "A not-going-that-far-away party?"

"Jeez," she said, rolling her eyes. "You're as stubborn as he is. Call it a kickoff party if that makes you feel better. I am a burgeoning sorceress. We haven't celebrated that yet, and I figure I'm due."

With that, we made our final goodbyes, and I headed back to my car. When I arrived back in Hyde Park, I parked outside the Cadogan gate, then moved through the House and back to my second-floor room.

I dropped off my keys and unbelted my sword, then glanced around. I'd planned on a long shower and a little reading in my pajamas before the sun hit the horizon. But since I'd been here nearly forty-eight hours and had hardly seen the other ninety-seven resident Cadogan vampires, I decided to opt for something considerably less geeky, and a lot more social. I flipped off the light in my room and headed for the stairs.

Noise leaked from Lindsey's room on the third floor, a cacophony of voices and television sounds. I knocked, and at Lindsey's invitation ("Get your ass in here, Sentinel"), pulled it open.

The tiny room, already crowded with furniture and Lindsey's expressive decor, was stuffed with vampires. I counted six, including Lindsey and Malik, who were reclining on her bed. Kelley and newbie vampire (and Lindsey's current paramour) Connor sat on the floor beside two vampires I didn't know. All six of them faced a small round television that sat atop Lindsey's bookshelf. On TV, thin people with strong accents berated the fashion choices of a large, flustered woman who wore a dress of eye-bruising colors but who was giving back as good as she was getting.

"Door," Kelley said without looking at me. I obeyed and closed it.

"Cop a squat, Sentinel," Lindsey directed, patting the bed beside her and shuffling farther from Malik, giving me room to sit between them. I stepped carefully among vampires and over a half-eaten box of pizza that made my stomach grumble in a way blood didn't, and climbed onto the bed. I had to go in headfirst, then carefully turn around, apologizing to Malik and Linds for kicks and pokes along the way. I heard grunts and moans, but assumed they were related to the show, which seemed to be heading for some kind of bitchfest climax.

"This is Margot and Katherine," Lindsey said, pointing at the unfamiliar vampires on the floor in turn. Margot, a strikingly gorgeous brunette with an angular crop of dark hair and bangs that curved into a point between amber-colored eyes, turned and offered a finger wave. Katherine, her light brown hair piled into a high knot, turned back and smiled.

"Merit," I said, waving back.

"They know who you are, hot shit. And you obviously know Connor and Kelley," Lindsey added when I'd settled myself, a pillow between my back and the wall, legs crossed at the ankles, tiny, glowing reality television show half a dozen feet away.

Connor glanced back and grinned. "Thank God you're here. I was the youngest person in the room by at least fifty years."

"Hate to break it to you, Sweet Tits," Lindsey said, "but you aren't a person anymore." She called for a piece of pizza, and the box was passed up. Eyes on the television, she grabbed a slice, then handed over the box. I settled it on my lap and tucked into a piece, pausing only long enough to make sure it was covered in meat. Bingo. While it was barely warm, and consisted of an offensive New York hybrid crust that could have used two more inches of dough and sauce and cheese, it was better than a kick in the face.

Malik leaned toward me. "You heard she's been released?"

In the two months that I'd been a Cadogan vampire, this was the first solo conversation I'd had with Malik. And while we were on the subject, it was also the first time I'd seen him in jeans and a polo shirt.

I swallowed a mouthful of Canadian bacon, cheese, and crust. "Yes," I whispered back. "Ethan told me yesterday."

He nodded, his expression inscrutable, then turned back to the television.

As first conversations went, it wasn't much. But I took it for concern, and decided I was satisfied with it.

A commercial came on and the room erupted in sound, Margot, Lindsey, Connor, Katherine, and Kelley rehashing what they'd seen, who was "winning," and who'd cry first when the results came in. I wasn't entirely sure what the contest was, much less the prize, but since vampires apparently delighted in human drama, I settled in and tried to catch up.

"We're rooting for the bitchy one," Lindsey explained, nibbling the crust on her pizza slice.

"I thought they were all bitchy," I noted.

After a few minutes of commercials, Malik began the process of getting off the bed.

"Is it me?" I asked lightly. "I can shower."

He chuckled as he took to his feet, the glow of the television glinting off the medal around his neck, and something else—a thin silver crucifix that dangled from a thin silver chain. So much for that myth.

"It's not you," Malik said. "I need to get back." He began to step between the vampires, who were completely unmoved by his effort not to step on them.

"Down in front!"

"Out of the way, vampire," Margot said, tossing a handful of popcorn in his direction. "Let's move it."

He waved them off good-naturedly, then disappeared out the door.

"What did he have to get back to?" I asked Lindsey.

"Hmm?" she absently asked, gaze on the television.

"Malik. He said he had to get back. What did he have to get back to?"

"Oh," Lindsey said. "His wife. She lives here with him. They've got a suite on your floor."

I blinked. "Malik's *married*?" It wasn't the "Malik" part that surprised me, but the "married" part. That a vampire was married seemed kind of odd. I mean, from what I'd seen so far, the vampire lifestyle was pretty comparable to dorm life. Living in a would-be vampire frat house didn't seem conducive to a long-term relationship.

"He's always been married," Lindsey said. "They were turned together." She glanced over at me. "You live down the hall from them. It's not real neighborly of you not to say hello."

"I'm not real neighborly," I admitted, recognizing that Malik was the only other vampire that I knew had a room on the second floor, and I'd only learned that four seconds ago. "We need a mixer," I decided.

Lindsey huffed. "What are we, sophomores? Mixers are excuses to get drunk and make out with people you hardly know." She slowly lowered her gaze to the back of Connor's head and smiled lasciviously. "On the other hand . . ."

"On the other hand, you'd break Luc's heart. Maybe let's skip the mixer for now."

"You're such a mommy."

I snorted. "Can I ground you?"

"*Unlikely*," she said, drawing out the word. "Now shut up and watch the bitchy humans."

I stayed until the show was done, until the pizza was done, until the vampires on the floor stood and stretched and said their goodbyes. I was glad I'd made the trip, glad I'd been able to spend time in the company of a Cadogan vampire other than the House's 394-year-old Master. I'd missed out on a lot of college socializing, more focused on reading and studying than was probably healthy, always assuming there'd be time for making friends later. And then graduation arrived, and I didn't know my classmates as well as I might have. I had a chance to do that over now—to invest in the people around me instead of losing myself in the intellectual details.

I rounded a corner to head for the stairs, so lost in my thoughts that I nearly forgot that Ethan, too, was a resident of the third floor.

But there he was.

He stood in the doorway of the apartment that had once been Amber's—his former Consort and the woman who'd betrayed him for Celina. He glanced up as I neared, but two burly men carrying a sizable chest of drawers stepped between us and broke the eye contact.

"Couple more loads," one said to Ethan in a thick Chicagoland accent as they hobbled down the hallway. "Then we're done."

"Thank you," he replied, half turning to watch them struggle under the weight of the furniture.

I wondered at the arrangements. Vampires could have managed the bulk much easier than the humans, and wouldn't have required Ethan's supervision at five o'clock in the morning. Humans or not, Ethan didn't look thrilled to be supervising them, and I also wondered why he hadn't let Helen coordinate.

Maybe, I realized, he needed this. Maybe this was his catharsis, his chance to clean the room, clear the air, and prepare for a changing of the lascivious guards.

I wanted to say something, to acknowledge the pain he probably felt, but had no idea how to say it, how to form words he wouldn't find insulting. Words he'd find too emotional. Too sentimental. Too human. I caught his gaze again, grudging resignation in it, before he looked away and slipped back inside the room.

I stood there for a moment, torn between following him

and trying to offer comfort, and letting it go, giving him back the same silence he'd given me, assuming the silence was what he needed. I pushed on toward the stairs, decision made, and dropped headfirst into bed just before Homer's "rosy-fingered Dawn" appeared, just as the horizon began to pinken. It was a little less rosy, I thought, when that dawn could fry you to ashes.

CHAPTER SEVEN

†HE BELLE OF †HE BALL

I woke suddenly, raps on the door jolting me from unconsciousness. I tried to shake off the dream I'd been having about moonlight over dark water, sat up, and rubbed my eyes.

The knock sounded again.

"Just a second." I untangled myself from the blankets I'd pulled up during the day and cast a glance at the alarm clock beside my bed. It was just after seven p.m., only an hour or so before the beginning of cocktails at the Breckenridge party. I swung my feet over the edge of the bed and onto the floor. A second to stand up, then I shuffled to the door, still, I realized, in yesterday's wrinkled shirt and suit pants.

I flipped the lock and opened it. Ethan stood in my doorway, tidy in suit pants and white button-up. His hair was pulled back, the Cadogan medal at his neck. Where I was rumpled, he was pristine, his eyes bright emerald green, alert. His expression was some cross between bemusement and disappointment, like he couldn't decide which emotion to choose.

"Long night, Sentinel?"

His voice was flat. It took me a moment to realize the conclusion he'd reached, that a rendezvous had kept me out late and prevented me from changing out of yesterday's uniform. His Sentinel, the woman he'd passed over to the Master of Navarre House to secure an alliance, was still in yesterday's clothes.

Of course, I hadn't seen Morgan in days. But Ethan didn't need to know that.

I hid my grin and answered back provocatively, "Yes. It was, actually." One eyebrow arched in disapproval, Ethan held out a black garment bag.

I reached out and took it. "What's this?"

"It's for this evening. Something a little more . . . apropos than your usual options."

I nearly snarked back—Ethan was not keen on my jeans-and-layered-T-shirts fashion sensibilities—but decided I appreciated the gesture more than I needed the last word. Tonight I was returning to the fold. Returning to Chicago's most elite social circle. This was my chance to don a dress and an attitude, to act like I belonged. To use my name as the entry ticket it truly was. But that name or not, that task would be a helluva lot easier in a nice dress than in anything I had in my closet at the moment.

So, "Thank you," I said.

He looked down and flicked up the cuff at his wrist, revealing a wide, silver watch. "You'll find shoes to match in your closet. I had Helen drop them off last night. As I'm sure you know, it's quite a drive to Loring Park, so we need to leave directly. Be downstairs in half an hour."

"Forty-five minutes," I countered, and at his raised eyebrow, offered, "I'm a girl."

His gaze went flat again. "I'm aware of that, Sentinel. Forty minutes."

I saluted crisply after he turned and walked down the hallway, then shut the door behind him. Curiosity getting the best of me, I went to the bed and spread the garment bag upon it, then clasped the zipper.

"Five bucks says it's black," I bet, and unzipped it.

I was right.

It was black taffeta, a cocktail dress with a fitted bodice and just-above-the-knees swingy skirt. The taffeta was pleated in well-constructed tucks, turning a classic little black dress into something much sassier.

Sassy or not, it was still fustier than my usual jeans and Pumas. It was the dress I'd successfully avoided wearing for ten years.

I pulled it from the bag and slipped it off the hanger, then held it up against my chest in front of the full-length mirror. I looked, at twenty-eight, almost exactly as I had at twenty-seven. But my straight hair was darker, my skin paler. Barring some ill-advised trip into the sun or a run-in with the wrong end of a katana or an aspen stake, I'd look the same as I did now—the twenty-seven years I'd owned when Ethan changed me—for the remainder of my life. For an eternity, if I managed to last that long. That, of course, would depend on how many enemies I made, and how much I was asked to sacrifice to Cadogan House.

To Ethan.

That thought in mind, I blew out a slow breath and offered a silent prayer for patience. The clock ticking, I spread the dress back on the bed and headed for the shower.

Maybe unsurprisingly, it took time for the water in the antique House to heat. I slipped into the claw-foot tub and pulled the ringed shower curtain around me, then dunked my head beneath the spray, relishing the heat. I missed daylight, being able to stand in the warmth of a spring day, my face tilted toward the sun, basking in the heat of it. I was relegated to fluorescent lights and moonglow now, but a hot shower was a surprisingly good substitute.

I stayed in the tub huddled beneath the water until the tiny bathroom was fogged with steam. Once out, I toweled off and turbaned my hair, then arranged my ensemble. The shoes Ethan had mentioned were in the closet, carefully wrapped in white tissue paper and nestled inside a glossy black box. I unwrapped them. They were evening pumps, an arrangement of spaghetti-thin straps atop three needle-sharp inches of heel.

I pulled them out by the straps and dangled them in the

air, giving them a once-over as they twirled. I used to dance *en pointe*, but during my grad school days, I'd gotten used to Converse and Puma, not Louboutin and Prada. I'd do Ethan a solid and wear them, but I truly hoped I wouldn't have to make a run for it at the Breckenridge estate.

I arranged undergarments, prepped and dried my hair, and applied makeup. Lip gloss. Mascara. Blush, since it was a special occasion. When my dark hair gleamed, I pulled it into a high ponytail, long bangs across my forehead, which I thought looked modern enough to match the kicky cocktail dress and heels.

I looked at myself in the mirror, pleasantly surprised at the result. I glowed beneath the makeup, my blue eyes a nice contrast to pale skin, my lips a bee-stung pink. When I was human, I'd been called "pretty," but I'd been too busy with books and library stacks, glasses and Chuck Taylors to play up my more feminine attributes. Ironically, now that I'd been made a predator, I'd become more alluring for it.

Satisfied that I'd done what I could, I went to the bureau and pulled out a small box of indigo velvet that I'd brought with me from Wicker Park. It held the Merit pearls, one of the first purchases my father had made with his newfound fortune, bought for my mother for their tenth anniversary. My sister, Charlotte, had worn them for her debut, and I'd worn them for mine. Someday, I would pass them to Mary Katherine and Olivia, Charlotte's daughters.

I fingered the silk-soft globes, then glanced over at the thin gold chain that lay across the bureau's top. Hanging from it was my own gold Cadogan medal, the thin, stamped disk bearing the Cadogan name, Cadogan's North American Vampire Registry number (4), and my name and position.

It was an interesting decision—should I accessorize according to the dictates of my father or my boss?

I dismissed both choices and picked a third—I opted to dress for Merit, Cadogan Sentinel. I wasn't going to the Brecks' because I had an urge to see my father, or out of some misdirected sense of family obligation. I was going because that's what I'd promised to do—to act in Cadogan's best interests.

Decision made, I fastened the medal around my neck, pulled on the dress and slid into the heels, arranging the straps. I filled a small clutch purse with necessities, then grabbed my sword. I was working, after all.

I checked the clock—two minutes to get downstairs. Since I'd run out of time for procrastination, I plucked my cell phone from the bureau, and as I left the room and shut the door behind me, dialed Morgan's number.

"Morgan Greer."

"Merit, um, well, Merit. 'Cause I only have the one name."

He chuckled. "For how long remains the question," he said, which I took as a compliment regarding my future Master status. "What are you up to?"

"Work," I quickly answered, unable and unwilling to give him more details than that. I had the sense that Morgan had questions about my relationship with Ethan, no need to fan those flames. But I could do one thing . . .

"Listen, Mallory starts her sorcery internship on Sunday, so we're having a kickoff dinner thing tomorrow night. Her and Catcher and me. Can you join us?"

There was brightness in his voice, relief at having been asked. "Absolutely. Wicker Park?"

"Yeah, I mean, unless you're eager to lunch in the Cadogan cafeteria. I hear it's chicken fingers and a Jell-O cup tomorrow."

"Wicker Park it is." He paused. "Merit?"

"Yeah?"

"I'm glad you called. Glad I get to see you."

"Me, too, Morgan."

"Good night, Mer."

"Good night."

Ethan was downstairs, golden hair shining as he adjusted the cuff of one starched sleeve. Vampires milled around him, all in their Cadogan black. But while he wore the same shade—

a crisp black suit and impeccable silver tie—he stood out. He was, as always, ridiculously handsome, easily outshining the immortals around him.

My heart tripping a bit at the sight of him, I clenched the banister harder, scabbard and purse in my free hand, and eased my way down the stairs in the stilts he'd called shoes.

I caught the hitch in his gaze when he saw me, the tiny flinch, the bare acknowledgment. His gaze went from incredulous to obviously appraising, eyebrow cocked as he looked me over, no doubt ensuring that I satisfied his mental checklist.

I reached the bottom of the stairs and stood in front of him.

Given the glow in his emerald eyes, I assumed that I passed.

"You're wearing your medal," he said.

I grazed the gold with my fingertips. "I wasn't sure if I should, if it was dressy enough?"

"You should. Consider it your dog tag."

"In case I get lost?"

"In case you're fried to ash and that sliver of gold is all that's left of you."

Vampire tact, I thought, left something to be desired.

Malik emerged from the hallway, dashing in his own Cadogan black (no tie), and handed Ethan a glossy black gift bag with handles of black satin rope. I couldn't see what was in it, but I knew what it held. Steel. A weapon. Because of the connection I'd made to my own katana—a tempering wrought by my sacrificing a few drops of blood to the blade—I could feel out steel, could sense the change in magical currents around someone who carried it.

"As you requested," Malik said, then bobbed his head in my direction. I smiled a little at the acknowledgment.

Bag in hand, Ethan nodded and began walking. Malik fell in step beside him. Assuming I was to follow, I did. We headed for the basement stairs.

"I'm not anticipating problems," Ethan told him. "Not tonight anyway."

Malik nodded. "The dailies are clean. Should Celina attempt to cross the border, she'll be flagged."

"Assuming she doesn't glamour the TSA," Ethan said.

And assuming she wasn't already here, I thought.

Ethan rounded the corner at the foot of the basement stairs, then walked toward a steel door, beside which was mounted a small keypad. This was the door to the garage, providing access to Cadogan's few coveted off-street parking spaces. I was nowhere near high enough in the ranks to get one.

Ethan and Malik stopped before the door and faced each other. Then I witnessed a surprising moment of ceremony.

Ethan held out his hand, and Malik took it. Hands clasped, and with gravity, Ethan said, "The House is given into your care."

Malik nodded. "I acknowledge my right and obligation to defend her, and await your return, Liege." Gently, Ethan cupped the back of Malik's head, leaned forward, and whispered something in his ear. Malik nodded, and the men separated. After another nod in my direction, Malik headed for the stairs again. Then Ethan punched in a code, and we were through the door.

"Is he Master while you're gone?" I asked.

"Only of the environs," Ethan answered as we walked steps to his sleek black Mercedes roadster, which was parked snugly between concrete support columns. "I remain Master of the House as an entity, of the vampires."

He opened the passenger door for me, and after I lowered myself onto the red and black leather upholstery, he closed the door and moved to his side of the car. He opened his door, placed the glossy black bag on the console between us, and climbed in. When he'd started the engine, he maneuvered the roadster through the columns and toward a ramp and security door that rose as he took the incline.

"The ceremony," he said, "is an anachronism of the influence of English feudalism on the vampires who formalized the House system."

I nodded. I'd learned from the *Canon* that the organization

of the Houses was feudal in origin, heavy on the liege-and-
vassal mentality, the sense that the Novitiate vampire owed a
duty to his liege and was obliged to believe in his liege lord's
paternal goodness.

Personally, I wasn't comfortable thinking about Ethan in
a paternal fashion.

"If the king left his castle," I offered, "he'd leave instructions for her defense with his successor."

"Precisely," Ethan said, swinging the car onto the street. He
reached between us, lifted the gift bag, and handed it to me.

I took it, but arched a brow in his direction. "What's this?"

"The sword needs to remain in the vehicle," he said. "We
will be spectacle enough without the accoutrements." Leave
it to Ethan to refer to three and a half feet of steel, leather,
and rayskin as "accoutrements."

"The bag," he said, "is a replacement. At least in some
way."

Curious, I peeked inside and pulled out the contents. The
bag held a black sheath, which held a blade—a thin, fierce
dagger, mother-of-pearl covering the tang.

"It's beautiful." I slipped the dagger from its cover and
held it up. It was an elegant and gleaming wedge of polished
steel, sharp on both edges.

We passed beneath a streetlight, and the reflection caught
the end of the pommel, revealing a flat disk of gold. It looked
like a smaller version of our Cadogan medals, this one also
bearing my position. CADOGAN SENTINEL, it read.

It was a dagger created for me. Personalized for me.
"Thank you," I said, thumbing the disk.

"There's one more item in the bag."

Brow arched, I reached in again and pulled out a holster—
two leather straps attached to a thin sheath.

No, not just a holster—a *thigh* holster.

I glanced down at my skirt, then over at Ethan. I really
wasn't eager to strap on a thigh holster, much less in front of
him. Maybe because I didn't want to flip up my skirt for my
boss. Maybe because a few-inches-long dagger wouldn't be
nearly as effective in a rumble as my katana. Not that I antic-

ipated an attack by society mavens, but stranger things had happened. Especially recently.

Besides, I was Ethan's only guard for the event, and I'd be damned if I was going to return to Cadogan House with a wounded Master in tow. Even if I lived through the attack, I would never live down the humiliation.

I sighed, knowing when I'd lost, deciding that the dagger would be better than nothing.

"Keep your eyes on the road," I ordered, then unfastened the buckles.

"I'm not going to look."

"Yeah, well, keep it that way."

He made a disdainful sound, but kept his gaze on the windshield. He also gripped the steering wheel a little harder. I enjoyed that crack in his facade probably more than I should have.

I was right-handed, so I slipped the poufy skirt of my dress up a little on the right side and extended my right hand, trying to figure out where I'd want the blade positioned if I needed to grab it in a hurry. I settled on a spot about midway up my thigh, the sheath just to the outside edge. I fastened the first buckle, then the second, and twisted a little in the seat to make sure it was secure.

The sheath had to be tight enough to stay taut when I pulled out the blade. That was the only way to ensure that I could release the knife quickly and safely. On the other hand, too tight and I'd cut off my own circulation. No one needed that, much less a vampire.

When I was satisfied it was secure, at least as sure as I could be in the front seat of a roadster speeding toward the suburbs, I inserted the blade. A tug brought the dagger out in a clean swipe, the holster still in place.

"Good enough," I concluded. I straightened my skirt again, then looked over at Ethan. We were coasting through relatively light traffic on the interstate, but his expression of blandness looked a little too bland. He was working very hard to look very uninterested.

Since we were heading into an enemy camp, I figured I'd

pique his interest—and give him the dutiful Sentinel update. "You'll never guess who was camped out on photographers' row last night," I said, baiting him.

"Jamie?" His voice was sardonic. I think he was kidding. Unfortunately, I wasn't.

"Nicholas."

His eyes widened. "Nicholas Breckenridge? At Cadogan House."

"Live and in person. He was on the corner with the paparazzi."

"And where was Jamie?"

"That was my question, too. I'm beginning to think, Sullivan, that there is no Jamie—I mean, I know there's a Jamie, but I'm not sure Jamie is the real threat here. At the very least, we don't have the entire story."

Ethan made a dry sound. "This wouldn't be the first time for that, as you're well aware. Wait—did you say last night? You saw Nick Breckenridge outside the House and you didn't tell anyone? Did you think to mention this to me? Or Luc? Or anyone else with authority to handle the situation?"

I ignored the near panic in his tone. "I'm mentioning it now," I pointed out. "He asked some pretty pointed questions about the Houses, about Celina. He wanted to know if we thought her punishment was sufficient."

"What did you tell him?"

"Party line," I said. "You guys were very timely with the talking points."

"Did you know he was back in Chicago?"

I shook my head. "I also didn't know that he was curious about us. It's like a disease working its way through that family."

"I suppose it's doubly fortuitous that we're heading to the Breck estate."

Or doubly troublesome, I thought. Double the number of would-be rabble-rousers in residence.

"Ethan, if the raves could cause us such a problem—negative attention and backlash—why are we focused on the story, whoever is writing it? Why are we driving to Loring Park, trying to work the press instead of trying to stop the raves?"

He was quiet for a moment until he asked gravely, "We aren't trying to stop them?"

That made me sit up a little straighter. I'd assumed, being House Sentinel, that if some kind of mission was going down I'd be a part of it. Clearly that wasn't the case.

"Oh," I said, not happy to discover there were secret plans afoot and I hadn't been included.

"Stopping the story isn't controversial, not for vampires anyway," Ethan said. "Stopping the raves is. Raves happen outside the House establishment, but that doesn't mean the Houses don't know they occur. And I have no authority over other Masters, over other Houses' vampires, any more than I do the city's Rogues."

Much to your own chagrin, I thought.

"Frankly, although plans are in the works, largely through your grandfather's efforts, it's unlikely we can put a stop to them completely. Your grandfather has excellent connections, strong mediating skills, and a loyal staff. But vampires, being vampires, will drink."

"And so we spin," I said.

"The first front is the press," he agreed. "It's not the only front, but it's the battle we fight tonight."

I blew out a breath, not eager for the skirmish—Merit versus the world she left behind.

"It's going to be fine," Ethan said, and I glanced over at him with surprise. Both that he'd read me so well and that he'd responded supportively.

"I hope so," I told him. "I'm not thrilled about the possibility of running into Nick again, and you know how I feel about my father."

"But not why," Ethan softly said. "Why the animosity? This breach between you?"

I frowned out the window, unsure how much I wanted to share with him. How much ammunition I wanted to give him.

"I wasn't the daughter my father wanted," I finally said.

Silence. Then, "I see. Are you close to Charlotte and Robert?"

"I wouldn't say there's animosity there, and we stay in touch, but they're not on speed dial." I didn't tell him that I hadn't talked to my siblings in a month. "We just don't have that much in common." Robert was preparing to take over my father's business; Charlotte was married to a physician and populating the world with tiny new Merits. Well, Mrs. Dr. Corkburger-Merits.

Oh, yeah. *Corkburger.*

"Do they share your animosity toward your father?"

"Not really," I told him, looking out the window. "I didn't acclimate well to the socializing. Charlotte and Robert did. We were all born into it, but they thrived. They're, I don't know, equipped for it. For that kind of lifestyle, that kind of attention, for the constant competition. I think because of that there was less friction between them and my father. Their relationship was, I don't know, easier?"

"And what did you do while they were enjoying the Merit advantage?"

I chuckled. "I spent a lot of time in libraries. I spent a lot of time with books. I mean, my home life was peaceful. My parents didn't fight. We had, materially, everything we needed. I was fortunate in many ways, and I realize that. But I was a dreamer, not much interested in the societal goodies." I laughed. "I'm a reader, not a fighter."

Ethan rolled his eyes at the admittedly lame joke. "And clearly not a comedian," he said, but there was a hint of a smile on his face. He guided the Mercedes off the freeway and onto a divided highway. I watched neighborhoods pass, some houses lit, others dark, human families engaged in the act of living.

I glanced over at him. "We're getting close. What's the plan?"

"Ingratiation and groundwork," he said, eyes scanning the road. "You reintroduce yourself to these people, let them know you're back and that you belong. That everything due to the Merits—the respect, the access, the approbation—is due to you as well. We determine what we can about this supposed story, Jamie's involvement, Nick's involvement." He shook his head. "Your news of Nick's visit muddies the water somewhat, and we need to know where we stand. And based on that information, if your father is there, we consider whether there are ways he can help."

My stomach twisted in unpleasant anticipation. I was more than willing to give up what was "due" to me as a Merit in order to avoid my father. But this was about access, about neutralizing a threat. I was a big enough girl to take one for the team.

"And we're the bribe?" I asked.

Ethan nodded. "Your father is an ambitious man, with ambitious goals for his business and his family. You provide him access to a certain segment of the population."

"A fanged segment," I added. "Let's not doubt his real interest: I'm delivering him a Master vampire."

"Whether it's one or both of us he wants to see, remember who you are. Neither a Master nor merely a Merit, but a powerful vampire in her own right."

We passed into rural, wooded acreages, a sign we were nearing our destination. We'd just turned onto a tree-lined road, dark in the absence of streetlights, when Ethan—without warning—slowed and pulled the Mercedes onto the shoulder. When the engine was off and the car silent, he flicked on the overhead light and looked at me.

I watched him, waiting, wondering why he'd stopped the car.

"Celina's release concerns me," he finally said.

"Concerns you?"

"As you know, in the past, the GP's focus has been the protection of Housed vampires and assimilation into human society. Ensuring our immortality."

I nodded. The precursor to the GP had been created in the aftermath of the First Clearing. Survival was the directive.

"And you're concerned that Celina's release signals what, a new era?"

Ethan paused, ran a hand through his hair, and finally nodded. "Humans will die. Vampires will die. I can't imagine any other end to the story."

He quieted again, and this time when he looked at me, his expression was different—full of determination. Motivational speech on its way, I assumed.

"We have reminded humans about our existence. Tonight, we remind them of our connections. We will need every advantage we can get, Merit. For whether her plans are long term, short term, some sort of minor insurrection, outright rebellion, the demand of political rights—something is coming."

"Something wicked."

Ethan nodded. "The thumbs have been pricked, at least proverbially."

I raised a hand to my neck, now healed and free of scars, once torn out by a vampire she'd convinced to kill me. "Not proverbially," I said. "Whatever spell she's 'conjuring,' she's already spilled blood, turned vampires against their Masters, convinced the GP—and treasonous or not, I'll admit I'm not impressed so far—that the death of humans is merely collateral damage."

He made a sound of agreement, but gripped the wheel again, thumbs tapping nervously against the leather wrap. Since we were still parked, I assumed there was more to it.

I looked over at him, tried to ferret out his motivation, some clue as to what else remained. "Why are you telling me this now?"

"I've talked to Malik and Luc," he said, almost defensively, as if I was questioning his adherence to his own chain of command.

"That's not what I asked you."

"You're Sentinel of my House."

Too easy an answer, I thought, and too quick a response. "Why, Ethan?"

"I don't know if I'm strong enough to say no to her."

This time, it took me a moment to respond. "To say no?"

Voice softer, words slower, he said, "If she tries to convince me to join her cause by using blood or glamour against me, I'm not sure that I can say no."

You could have heard a pin drop in the car. I stared forward, shocked at the admission, that he'd share this info—this *weakness*—with me. The girl he'd asked to be his Consort. The girl who'd refused him. The girl who'd witnessed, firsthand, his betrayal by Amber. The girl who'd seen the look on his face when Amber confessed her sin, her involvement in Celina's conspiracy.

The girl who'd felt the thrust of Celina's glamour, and powered through it. But so had he.

"You said no in the park," I reminded him. "When she confessed her involvement in the murders, when she wanted you on her side, you said no."

Ethan shook his head. "She wanted to be caught, to play martyr. That was hardly the extent of her glamour, the tools she's using against the GP."

"And Malik and Luc?"

"They aren't as strong as me." The unfortunate implication being that if Ethan was worried about his ability to withstand the glamour, Luc and Malik had little hope.

"Glamour," Ethan said, "is about convincing someone to do something they wouldn't ordinarily do. It's not like alcohol—Celina didn't lower the inhibitions of the GP members. She has controlled them."

Psychic manipulation, all but undetectable. Thank God the CIA hadn't gotten wind of that yet.

"And because the power is a psychic one, the only trace that she has used her power in this fashion is the magic that leaks when she performs it. Vampires who can glamour can convince the subjects of their glamour that they have an altogether different desire. It's easier, of course, on weaker minds, on those who could have been convinced with but a little pushing. It's harder on those with firmer minds. On those more used to finding their own paths."

Ethan looked at me and lifted his brows, as if willing me to understand.

"You think I repelled her glamour because I'm stubborn?"

"I think it is, perhaps, part of the reason."

The general absurdity of the conversation aside—debating

the metaphysics of vampire glamour—I got a kick out of his admission, and couldn't stop my grin. "So, you're saying my stubbornness is a blessing."

With a snort, he started the Mercedes and pulled it smoothly back onto the road. I guess I'd humored him out of his mood.

"You know, vampires are exhausting," I told him, parroting one of Catcher's favorite complaints.

"This time, Merit, I won't disagree with you."

CHAPTER EIGHT

PAPA DON'T PREACH

The Breckenridge estate, nestled in the Illinois country-side, was a massive would-be French château, modeled on Vanderbilt's Biltmore after one of the Breckenridge forefathers, swollen with profit, took a serendipitous trip to Asheville, North Carolina. Although the Breck estate didn't nearly rival the size of George Vanderbilt's home, the pale stone mansion was a massive asymmetrical homage, complete with pointy spires, chimneys, and high windows dotting the steeply pitched roof.

Ethan pulled the Mercedes down the lengthy drive that ran through the park-sized front lawn to the front door, where a white-gloved valet signaled him to stop.

When an attendant opened my door, I carefully stepped out, the blade and holster an unfamiliar weight on my thigh. As the Mercedes—my getaway vehicle—zipped away, I craned my neck to look upward at the house. It had been six or seven years since I'd been here. My stomach knotted, a combination of nerves from the thought of reentering a life I'd escaped at the first opportunity and the possibility of a confrontation with my father.

Gravel scratched as Ethan stepped beside me. We headed for the front door, Mrs. Breckenridge visible in the foyer through the open door in front of us, but before we stepped inside, Ethan stopped and put a hand at my elbow.

"We need an invitation," he quietly reminded me.

I'd forgotten. Unlike the bit about crucifixes and photographs, this vampire myth was actually true—we weren't to enter a home without an invitation. But this myth wasn't about magic or evil. It was, as so many other vampire issues were, about rules and regulations. About the vampire paradigm.

We waited a minute or so, long enough for Mrs. Breck to finish shaking hands and chatting up the couple that had arrived just before us. When they walked away, she looked up. I saw a blink of recognition as she realized that we were waiting outside. Her face lit up, and I hoped it was because she was pleased to see me darkening her doorway again.

She walked toward us as elegant and slender as Princess Grace, everything feminine despite having raised a brood of rowdy boys. Julia Breckenridge was a beautiful woman, tall and graceful in a simple champagne sheath, blond hair in a tidy knot at the back of her neck.

Ethan bowed slightly. "Madam. Ethan Sullivan, Master, Cadogan House. My companion and guard, Merit, Sentinel, Cadogan House. Upon your invitation"—he flicked the invitation I'd given to Luc from his pocket and held it between two long fingers before her, his proof of our legitimacy—"we seek admission to your home."

She held out her hand, and carefully, gracefully, Ethan lifted it, eyes on hers as he pressed his lips to her hand. Mrs. Breck, who'd probably dined with heads of state and movie stars, blushed, then smiled as Ethan released her hand.

"Upon this night," she said, "you and your companion may enter our home with our blessing."

Her answer was interesting, her invitation formal and specific to one night in the Breckenridge house, as if intended to limit our access.

"I had my people research the appropriate protocol," Mrs. Breck said, moving aside to allow us entry. When we were just inside the foyer, she reached up and cupped my face in her hands, the scent of warm jasmine rising from her wrists.

"Merit, darling, you look beautiful. I'm so glad you could join us tonight."

"Thank you. It's nice to see you again, Mrs. Breckenridge."

She placed a kiss on my right cheek, then turned to Ethan, a glimmer of feminine appreciation in her eyes. I could sympathize. He looked, as was his irritating way, good enough to bite.

"You must be Mr. Sullivan."

He smiled slowly, wolfishly. "Ethan, please, Mrs. Breckenridge."

"Ethan, then. And you'll call me Julia." She gazed at Ethan for a few seconds, a kind of vague expression of pleasure on her face, until a shortish, bald man with round spectacles approached us and popped her on the elbow with his clipboard.

"Guests, Julia. Guests."

Mrs. Breck—I hadn't called her Julia when I was running through her hallways as a child, and I wasn't going to start now—shook her head as if to clear it, then nodded at the man at her elbow.

"I'm sorry, but I'll have to excuse myself. It was lovely to meet you, Ethan, and it's lovely to see you again, Merit. Please enjoy the party." She indicated the way to the ballroom and then moved back to the door to greet a new cluster of guests.

I made a guess that the vacant expression on her face had been Ethan's doing. "Ah," I whispered as we walked away, "but can he charm the humans without resorting to glamour?"

"Jealous?"

"Not on your life."

We were just outside the ballroom when he stopped and looked at me. "It's a tradition."

I stopped, too, frowning as I tried to puzzle out the context. "Glamouring the host is a tradition? That explains why vampires were in hiding for so long."

"The blade. Your blade. The dagger I gave you. Malik researched the *Canon*. It's tradition for the Master to present a blade to the Sentinel of his House."

"Oh," I said, fingers pressing the spot on my dress that lay just above the blade. "Well. Thank you."

He nodded crisply, then adjusted his tie, all verve and smooth confidence. "A bit of advice?"

I blew out a breath and smoothed my skirt. "What?"

"Remember who, and what, you are."

That made me chuckle. He really had no idea the gauntlet he was about to walk.

"What?" he asked, sliding me a sideways glance.

"Fangs or not, we're still outsiders." I bobbed my head toward the ballroom doors. "They're sharks, waiting to circle. It's like *Gossip Girl* in there. That I come from money, and that we're vampires, doesn't guarantee us entrée."

But as if on cue, two tuxedoed doormen pushed open the doors for us. Literally, they gave us access. Symbolically, they gave us access. But the judging hadn't yet begun.

I took a breath and adopted my best grin of Merit-worthy entitlement, then glanced up at my companion.

He of the golden hair and green eyes surveyed the glittering party before us. "Then, Merit, Sentinel of my House, let's show them who we are."

His hand at my back, a frisson of heat slipping down my spine, we stepped inside.

The ballroom was awash in the light of crystal chandeliers. Beneath them in the glow stood all the people I remembered. The society matrons. The two-doctor families. The bitter wives. The charming, cheating husbands. The children who were fawned over solely because they'd been spawned by the wealthy.

Technically, I suppose that last group included me.

We found a spot on the edge of the room and made camp. That's where I began Ethan's education. I pointed out some of Chicago's old-money families—the O'Briens, the Porters, and the Johnsons, who'd made their money in commodities trading, pianos, and beef, respectively. The room was also sprinkled with new money—celebs, music magnates who made their home in the Windy City, Board of Trade members, and sports team presidents.

Some guests Ethan knew, some he asked questions about—their connections, their neighborhoods, the manner in which they'd made their fortunes. For the families he knew, I asked about their take on the supernatural: Did they have ties to our communities? Sons and daughters in the Houses? He was, unsurprisingly, well-informed, given his penchant for connections and strategies. Really, the entire conversation could have walked itself out of a Jane Austen novel, both of us rating and evaluating the matriarchs and patriarchs of Chicago's social elite.

Noticeably absent from the party was the remainder of the Breckenridge clan—Nicholas and his brothers and Michael Breckenridge, Sr., who was known in friendly circles as Papa Breck. I'm not saying I was thrilled at the idea of jumping into another Nick encounter, but if I wanted to learn more about this Nick/Jamie business, I would at least need to be in the same room with him again. The no-show thing was going to put the kibosh on my investigation.

I also saw neither hide nor hair of my father. Not that I looked too hard.

I did see a cluster of people my age, a knot of twenty-somethings in cocktail dresses and sharp suits, a couple of the guys with scarves draped around their collars. These, I supposed, were the people I would have been friends with had I chosen my siblings' paths.

"What do you think I'd have been like?" I asked him.

Ethan plucked two delicate flutes of champagne from the tray of a passing waiter and handed one to me. "At what?"

I sipped the champagne, which was cold and crisp and tasted like apples, then gestured to the crowd around us. "At this. If I'd skipped school in New York or Stanford, stayed in Illinois, met a boy, joined the auxiliary with my mother."

"You wouldn't be a Cadogan vampire," he said darkly.

"And you'd be missing out on my sparkling personality."

I made eye contact with another tuxedoed waiter, this one bearing food, and beckoned him closer with a crooked finger. I knew from the handful of galas I'd peeked into as a kid that the fare at charity events tended a little toward the weird side—foams of this and canapés of that. But what they lacked in homespun comfort they more than made up for in quantity.

The waiter reached us, watery blue eyes in the midst of a bored expression, and extended his tray and a handful of "B"-engraved cocktail napkins.

I reviewed the arrangement of hors d'oeuvres, which rested artistically on a bed of rock salt. One involved tiny pale cubes of something soaking in an endive cup. Another formed a cone of various pink layers. But for the endive, I had no clue what they were.

I looked up at the waiter, brows raised, seeking help.

"A napoleon of prawn and prawn mousse," he said, nodding down at the pink columns, "and tuna ceviche in endive."

Both weird seafood combinations, I thought, but, ever brave when it came to matters of *gastronomie*, I picked up one of each.

"You and food," Ethan muttered, with what I thought was amusement.

I bit into the endive. I was a little weirded out by the ceviche treatment, but I was accommodating a vampire-sized hunger that wasn't nearly as picky as I was. I raised my gaze from the appetizer as I noshed, pausing midbite at the realization that the cluster of twentysomethings across the room was staring at me. They talked among themselves and, some decision apparently made, one of them began walking toward us.

I finished my bite, then scarfed the shrimp napoleon, which was good but a little exotic for my junk-food-ruined palate. "Sharks, two o'clock."

Brows raised, Ethan cast a glance at the away team, then smiled at me, with teeth. "Humans, two o'clock," he corrected. "Time to do a little acting, Sentinel."

I sipped at my champagne, erasing the taste of whipped shellfish. "Is that a challenge, Sullivan?"

"If that's what it takes, Sentinel, then yes."

The brunette leader of the ensemble, her petite figure tucked into a sequined silver dress, approached, her entourage watching from across the room.

"Hi," she said, politely. "You're Merit, right?"

I nodded at her.

"I don't know if you remember me, but we were in the same cotillion class. I'm Jennifer Mortimer."

I picked back through my memories and tried to place her face. She looked vaguely familiar, but I'd spent most of my cotillion being humiliated by the fact that I'd been trussed up and stuffed into a billowing white gown in order to be paraded before Chicago's wealthy like a cow on parade. I hadn't paid much attention to the people around me.

But I faked it. "It's nice to see you again, Jennifer."

"Nick Breck was your escort, wasn't he? I mean, at our cotillion?"

Well, I had paid attention to him, so I nodded, then used my champagne glass to gesture at Ethan, whose expression had flattened at Jennifer's announcement. I guess I hadn't mentioned that part of our history. "Ethan Sullivan," I offered.

"A pleasure," Ethan said.

"Can I . . ." She half smiled, looked away uncomfortably, then twisted a ring on her right hand. "Could I . . . ask you a question?"

"Sure."

"I noticed earlier . . . with the appetizers . . ."

"We eat food," Ethan smoothly answered. He'd realized what she'd wanted to know before I did, which was funny, because that was one of the first questions I'd asked as a new vampire.

Jennifer blushed, but nodded. "Okay, sure. It's just, the blood thing, obviously, but we weren't sure about the rest, and, God, was that really rude of me?" She pressed a hand to her chest, grimaced. "Am I completely gauche?"

"It's no problem," I said. "Better to ask a question than assume the worst."

Her face brightened. "Okay, okay, great. Listen, one more thing."

I'm not sure what I expected—another question, sure, but not her next move. She slipped a thin business card from her bodice, and with manicured fingers that somehow worked under the weight of a gigantic marquis-cut diamond engagement ring, handed it to me.

This time when she spoke, her voice was all smooth confidence. "I know this is a little forward, but I did want to give you my card. I think you could benefit from representation."

"I'm sorry?" I glanced down at the card, which bore her name beneath the heading CHICAGO ARTS MANAGEMENT.

She was an *agent*.

I nearly dropped my glass.

Jennifer cast a cautious glance at Ethan, then back at me. "You've got a great look, a good family, and an interesting story. We could work that."

"I—uh—"

"I'm not sure about your experience or interests—modeling, acting, that kind of thing—but we could definitely find a niche for you."

"She'll call you," Ethan said, and Jennifer, all smiles and thank-yous, walked away. "I'm not surprised by anything anymore," he said.

"Seconded." I flipped up the card between two fingers, showed it to him. "What the hell just happened?"

"I believe, Sentinel, that you're being wooed." He laughed softly, and I enjoyed the sound of that laughter a little more than I should have. "That didn't take nearly as long as I thought it would."

"I'm amused that you thought it was inevitable."

"Yes, well." Another waiter approached, and this time Ethan picked a curl of endive from the tray. "Things have become decidedly less predictable since you came on staff. I believe I'm beginning to appreciate that."

"You appreciate having a chance to bolster your social connections."

"That helps," he admitted, biting into his endive. He chewed, then, his face contorted in displeasure, sipped his champagne. Glad I wasn't the only one.

Without warning, my main social connection suddenly appeared at my side and touched my elbow.

"We'll use Michael's office," my father said by way of greeting, then walked away, apparently confident that we'd follow. Ethan and I exchanged a glance, then did.

My father strutted through the halls of the Breck estate as if he'd traveled them a million times before, as if he were strolling through his own Oak Park mansion and not someone else's.

Papa Breck's office was located in a back corner of the first floor. It was full of furniture, books, globes, and framed maps, the detritus of wealth collected by the Breck family. It smelled comfortingly familiar, of cigars and ancient paper and cologne. It was Papa Breck's respite from the world, a secret sanctuary that Nicholas and I had only occasionally dared to violate. We'd spent a handful of rainy days in the office, hiding amidst the antiquities, pretending to be castaways on a nineteenth-century ship of the line, sprinting down the hall when we heard his father approaching.

The door closed behind us. I blinked my way out of the memory.

My father turned to us, hands in his pockets. He bobbed his head at me, then looked at Ethan. "Mr. Sullivan."

"Call me Ethan, please, Mr. Merit," Ethan said. They shook, the guy who made me, and the vampire who made me something else. That seemed fundamentally wrong.

Or maybe discomfortingly right.

"I read about your acquisition of the Indemnity National Building," Ethan said. "Congratulations. That's quite an achievement."

My father offered a manly head bob of acknowledgment, then slid a glance my way. "You've gained a Merit property of your own."

I nearly stepped forward to wipe that smug smile off my father's face, at least until I remembered my pretty party dress.

"Yes, well," Ethan said, a hint of dryness in his voice. "Vampirism does have its benefits."

My father made a sound of agreement, then looked at me over the top of his glasses. "Your mother informs me that you want to, to use your words, rebuild some relationships. Meet the right people." He used the same tone he'd adopted when, as a child, I'd finally made my way to his office to apologize for some presumed transgression.

"I've reconsidered your request to assist Robert."

He seemed to freeze for a moment, as if utterly shocked by the offer. Given our interaction the last time he'd asked me—I'd all but thrown him out of Mallory's house—maybe he was.

"What, exactly, did you have in mind in that regard?" he finally asked.

Let the acting begin, I thought, and prepared to lay out the script that Ethan and I had prepared—details that might be useful as Robert attempted to build connections among the city's supernatural population. A few words about that population (which was, but for the vampires, unknown to the populace), House finances, and our connections to the city administration—leaving out, of course, the fact that my grandfather was playing Ombud to the city. It would be enough, or so Ethan hoped, to make my father believe we were offering bites of a much larger apple.

But before I could speak, Ethan handed over the entire Red Delicious.

"Celina has been released by the Presidium."

I turned my head to stare at him. That was so *not* the plan.

I didn't think I could activate the mental connection between us—the telepathic link he'd initiated when I'd been Commended into the House—but the sarcasm was boiling me from the inside, so I had to try. *That's your "tidbit"??*

If he heard me, he ignored it.

And Ethan's gift was only the first surprise.

"When?" my father asked, his tone as bland as if we'd been discussing the weather. Apparently, the loosing of a would-be serial killer—a woman who'd arranged to have his daughter killed—wasn't any more interesting than the day's high temperature.

"Within the week," Ethan answered.

My father made a motion with his hand, and Ethan followed him to a group of chairs, where they sat down. I followed, but stayed standing behind Ethan.

"Why was she released?" my father asked.

Ethan covered the ground we'd already discussed. But unlike the surprise I'd shown, my father reacted with nods and sounds of understanding. There was a familiarity with sups and the workings of the Houses and the GP that surprised me. It wasn't so much that he had the information that was surprising—the Internet was chock-full of vamp facts. But he also seemed to understand the rules, the players, the connections.

The Ombud's office had a secret vampire employee, a source of information about the Houses. Maybe my father had one, too.

After Ethan finished his explanation, my father glanced at me.

"You've certainly piqued my curiosity," he said. "But why the change in attitude?"

Okay, so I'd been wrong to assume that if we offered information that might help Robert, my father wouldn't ask questions.

Go ahead, Ethan mentally prompted, and I delivered my lines.

"I'd like to become more involved in the family's social activities. Given my new position in the House, and the family's position, my becoming more involved could be, let's say, mutually beneficial."

My father leaned back, placed an elbow on the back of his chair, and tapped a bent knuckle against his chin. He could hardly have looked more skeptical. "Why now?"

"I'm in a different position now," I told him. "I have different responsibilities. Different abilities." I cast a glance toward Ethan. "Different connections. I'm old enough to understand that the Merit name makes certain things easier. For one, it makes alliances easier to forge." I touched the Cadogan medal at my neck. "And now there's an alliance that I can help build."

He watched me, evaluated in silence, then gave a single nod. "I'll assume for our purposes that you aren't lying to me. But that doesn't answer my question." He slid his gaze to Ethan. "Why now? Why tonight?"

Ethan smoothed the knee of his trousers with a swipe of his hand. The move was so casual, almost careless, that I knew it was forced. "The Breckenridges may be . . . dabbling in our world."

"Dabbling," my father repeated. "In what way?"

A moment of hesitation, and then Ethan decided—unilaterally, I might add—to trust my father. "We were informed that Jamie Breckenridge planned to publish a very damaging story."

"Damaging to vampires?"

Ethan bobbed his head. He was playing the story off, giving my father unemotional seeds of information, with no hint of the fear and concern that he'd shown me earlier.

"And if I assumed the content of the story is too . . . delicate to be shared here?"

"Then you would be correct," Ethan said. "I take it you aren't aware of anything in that regard?"

"I am not," my father said. "However, I'm assuming it's no coincidence that you've made the Breckenridge home your first social stop?"

"It was a coincidence, actually," Ethan responded. "But a fortuitous one."

My father arched dubious eyebrows. "Be that as it may, I take it you noticed that Julia is the only Breckenridge at home this evening?"

"I thought that odd," Ethan said.

"As did we all," my father agreed. "And we didn't understand the reason for it." Slowly, he lifted his gaze to me. "But now perhaps we do. Perhaps they are absent because of certain . . . *visitors* in their home."

His very gaze was an accusation, and an unearned one. Neither the story nor the Breckenridges' absence had anything to do with me. Well, nothing I'd done on purpose anyway. But he was willing, nevertheless, to assign blame.

Charming, Ethan telepathically commented.

I told you, I said back.

Ethan stood up. "I appreciate your time, Joshua. I trust the information we've shared will be held in confidence?"

"If you prefer," said my father, without bothering to rise. "I trust you'll be circumspect in your inquiries? While I understand that you have a concern, whatever it might be, these people—these families—are my friends. It wouldn't do for gossip to travel, for undue aspersions to be cast upon them."

Ethan had turned away from my father, and I saw the look of irritation cross his face, probably at the suggestion that his aspersions were "undue." Nevertheless, always the smooth player, he slipped his hands into his pockets, and when he turned back again, his expression was mild and politic once again. "Of course."

"I'm glad we understand each other," my father said, then checked his watch. That was our dismissal, so I moved toward the door, Ethan behind me.

"Remember," my father said, and we turned back. "Whatever this is, if it falls apart, it falls on you. Both of you."

It was a final blow. We walked into the hallway, and let him have the last word.

On the way back to the ballroom, Ethan and I paused in a window-lined corridor that linked the public and private portions of the house.

He stared out the windows, hands at his hips. "Your father . . ."

"Is a piece of work," I finished. "I know."

"He could help us . . . or crush us."

I glanced beside me, noticed that line of worry between his eyes, and offered the nearly four-hundred-year-old vampire a piece of advice. "And never forget, Ethan, that the choice is his to make."

He looked over at me, brow raised.

I turned away and looked out at the dark, sloping lawn. "Never forget that whatever boon he offers, whatever suggestion he makes, is calculated. He has the money and power to help or hurt a lot of people, but his reasons are usually his own, they're usually selfish, and they aren't easy to ferret out. He plays his pieces three or four moves ahead, without obvious outcomes. But never doubt they're there."

Ethan sighed, long and haggard. A dove cooed in the distance.

"Ms. Merit."

We both turned to find a woman at the portico door. She wore a simple black dress and white apron, thick-soled shoes on her feet. Her hair was in a neat bun. A housekeeper, maybe.

"Yes?" I asked.

She held out a piece of paper. "Mr. Nicholas asked me to give this to you."

I arched a brow, but walked to where she stood and took the paper. When I offered my thanks, she disappeared back through the doorway.

"Mr. Nicholas?" Ethan asked when we were alone again.

I ignored the question, and unfolded the note, which read:

Meet me at the castle. Now.

—NB

"What is it?" Ethan asked.

I glanced out the window, then back at him as I refolded the note and slipped it into my purse.

"An opportunity to make some connections of my own. I'll be back," I added, and before he could respond or express whatever doubts were pinching that line between his eyes again, I walked to the end of the hallway to the patio door.

The patio was brick in a carefully laid demilune form, which ended in an arc of stairs leading down to the lawn. I leaned against the brick banister and untied the straps of my shoes, then placed them and my purse on a step. The night was gloriously warm, white paper lanterns hanging from the flowering trees that dotted the back lawn. Relieved of the stilettos, I crept down to the lawn, the bricks cool beneath my feet, then stepped into the grass. I stood there for a quiet moment, eyes closed, reveling in the soft, cool carpet of green.

The Breckenridge estate was huge—hundreds of acres of land that had been carefully groomed and manicured to seem just this side of wild—the Brecks' primeval respite from the workaday world. The lawn led down to a wood that covered the back acres of the property, a carefully clipped trail winding through them.

I'd spent a lot of time on that trail as a child, chasing Nicholas through thick trees on summer days and through frosted, ice-tipped boughs on cold November mornings. I left the dresses and pinafores to Charlotte—I wanted running and fallen branches and fresh air, the outdoor fantasy world of a child with an expansive imagination and a constrictive home life.

But this time, when I reached the narrow dirt path, I had to push limbs from my face. I was taller than I had been the last time I'd traversed it; then I'd been short enough to skip beneath the boughs. Now branches crackled as I moved, until I made it to the clearing.

To the labyrinth.

The fence was low, only three or four feet tall, a delicate and rust-covered ring that ran for yards in both directions around the hedge maze Papa Breck had commissioned in the woods behind the house. The gate was ajar. He was here already, then.

The maze itself was simple, rings of concentric circles with dead ends and passageways along its length, a pattern I'd memorized many years ago. The web of boxwood had been our castle, defended by Nicholas and me against bands of marauders—usually his brothers. We'd used stick swords and cardboard shields, both of us fighting until his siblings grew bored and retreated back to the comfort of the main house. This had been our secret garden, our tiny kingdom of leaves.

I neared the glowing inner core of it, my footsteps nearly silent on the soft dirt path, the night silent but for the occasional rustling of trees or scampering in the undergrowth around me. And it was still silent when I met him in the middle.

CHAPTER NINE

THE SECRET GARDEN'S SECRETS

"I wondered how long it would take you to make it out here," Nicholas said, arms crossed over his chest as he looked at me. Two hurricane lamps cast a golden glow across his torso, which was currently covered by a Chicago Marathon T-shirt. He'd skipped the suit for a T-shirt, and he'd also skipped the suit pants for jeans.

I walked to the center of the circle and glanced up at him, my smile tenuous. "I'd nearly forgotten this was out here."

Nicholas made a sarcastic sound that bobbed his shoulders. "I doubt very much, Merit, that you'd forget about the castle."

Although a corner of his lip lifted as he said it, his expression sobered again quickly enough. He scanned my dress, then lifted his gaze to mine. "The vampires appear to have accomplished what your father was unable to do."

I stared at him for a second, unsure if he meant to insult me, or my father, or Ethan, although it felt like a shot at all three of us. I opted to ignore it, and walked around him to trace the perimeter of the circle that marked the inner core of the labyrinth. It was probably fifteen feet across, marked by facing gaps in the hedge that allowed entrance and egress, and curved wooden benches along the side walls that currently held the lamps.

"I didn't expect to find you outside Cadogan House," I admitted.

"I didn't expect to find you *inside* Cadogan House. Times change."

"People change?" I asked, glancing back over my shoulder.

His expression stayed the same. Blank, guarded.

I decided to start with niceties. "How have you been?"

"I'm more interested in how you've been. In the . . . *thing* you've become."

I lifted my brows. "The thing?"

"The vampire." He fairly spat out the word, as if the sound on his lips disgusted him. He looked away, glanced out at the woods. "People do change, apparently."

"Yes, they do," I agreed, but managed to keep my thoughts about his current attitude to myself. "I didn't know you were back in Chicago."

"I had business."

"You're back to stay?"

"We'll see."

More important question: "So you're working? In Chicago, I mean?"

His gaze shifted back to me, one dark eyebrow arched. "I'm not sure I'm comfortable discussing my plans with you."

It was my turn to arch an eyebrow. "You asked me to meet you out here, Nick, not the other way around. If you weren't comfortable discussing things with me, you probably should have let me stay in the house."

He looked at me for a long time. An intense time, those steel gray eyes fixed on mine, as if he could see through me to ferret out my intentions. I had to work not to shift my feet in the silence.

"I want to know why you're here," he finally said. "In my parents' home. In my family's home." Given the distrust in his voice, I guessed it wasn't a coincidence that Julia was the only Breckenridge at the party.

I clasped my hands behind my back, and looked at him. "It's time that I recall my family obligations."

He responded with a dry look. "I've known you for twenty

years, Merit. Family obligations aren't high on your priority list, especially when those obligations involve black-tie affairs. Try me again."

I didn't know what he was up to, but I wasn't about to spill all my secrets. "Tell me why you were outside Cadogan House."

He glanced up at me, his expression a challenge: Why should I answer your questions?

"Quid pro quo," I told him. "You answer mine, and I'll answer yours."

He wet his bottom lip while he silently considered the offer, then looked up at me. "I'm investigating," he said.

"You're writing a story?"

"I didn't say I was writing a story. I said I was investigating."

Okay, so he was investigating, but not in order to write a story—about vampires or otherwise. So what was he investigating? And if he had questions, why was he looking for answers in a knot of paparazzi outside the House, instead of using his own connections? More importantly, why Nick, and why not Jamie?

Nick stuffed his hands into his pockets and bobbed his head at me. "Quid pro quo. Why are you here?"

A second of consideration before I told him. "We're doing our own investigating."

"Of whom?"

"Not precisely who, but what. We're trying to keep our people safe." Not the whole truth, but true enough.

"From what?"

I shook my head. It was time to dig a little deeper. "Quid pro quo. While we're discussing the Brecks, what's the family been up to? How's Jamie these days?"

Nick's expression changed so suddenly I nearly took a step back. His jaw hardened, nostrils flaring, and his hands clenched into fists. For a second, I could have sworn I felt a brief pulse of magic—but then it was gone.

"Stay. Away. From Jamie," he bit out.

I frowned, trying to figure out where the anger had come

from. "I just asked how he was, Nick." Mostly to figure out if he's trying to sacrifice us to win props from Papa Breck, but Nick didn't need to know that. "Why do I need to stay away from him? What do you think I'm going to do?"

"He's my brother, Merit. Family history or not, *personal* history or not, I'll protect him."

I frowned at him, put my hands on my hips. "Are you under the impression that I'm going to harm your brother? Because I can tell you—promise you, in fact—that isn't the case."

"And vamps are known for their reliability, aren't they, Merit?"

That one stung, and widened my eyes. Not just animosity, not only some sense of fraternal protectiveness, but a thick, acrid prejudice. I just stared at him.

"I don't know what I'm supposed to say to that, Nick." My voice was quiet. Part shock, part dismay that a friendship had gone so awry.

Nick apparently wasn't sympathetic to that dismay; he nailed me with a glare that raised the hair on my neck. "If something happens to Jamie, I'm coming after you."

One final threatening look, then he turned away and disappeared through the opposite gap in the hedge.

I stared after him, tapped my fingers against my hip, trying to get a handle on what had just happened. Not only the fact that Nick wasn't writing a story (or so he said), but the sudden protectiveness for his formerly loafing youngest brother. What the hell was going on?

I blew out a breath and glanced around the labyrinth. The glow of the hurricane lamps wavered as the oil began to run out. The light fading, and with more questions than I'd arrived with, I started back through the boxwood.

Nick's anger, his distrust, made the walk back through the woods a little less sentimental—and a little scarier. Nocturnal or not, I wasn't thrilled to be wandering through the woods in the middle of the night. I carefully picked my way back through the trees, eyes and ears alert to the presence of creepy or crawly things that lived and thrived in the dark.

Suddenly, without warning, there was shuffling in the trees.

I froze, my head snapping to the side to catch the sound, heart pounding in my ears. . . . And the pique of interest by my vampire.

But the forest was silent again.

As quietly as I could, I slipped my hand beneath the hem of my dress and reached for my holstered blade. Ever so slowly, ever so quietly, I pulled out the dagger. I wasn't entirely sure what I was going to do with it, but having it in hand slowed my heart's percussion. I squinted into the darkness, trying to pierce the thicket of trees.

Something padded through the woods. An animal, four-legged by the sound of it. It was probably yards away, but close enough that I could hear the *pat-pat* of feet in the undergrowth.

I tightened sweaty fingers around the handle of the dagger.

But then, standing there in the dark, the blade in my hand, my heart pounding with the rush of fear and adrenaline, I remembered something Ethan had told me about our predatory natures: For better or worse, we were the top of the food chain.

Not humans.

Not animals.

Not the thing that roamed the woods beside me.

Vampires.

I was the predator, not the prey. So, in a voice that sounded a little too breathy to be my own, my eyes on the spot between the trees where I imagined it to be, I advised that animal in the dark, *"Run."*

A split second of silence before sudden movement, the sound of trampled earth and snapping twigs, feet moving away as the animal darted for safety.

Seconds later, the forest was quiet again, whatever thing had been there having sought safety in the other direction, away from the threat.

Away from *me*.

That was a handy skill, if a mildly disturbing one.

"Top of the food chain," I whispered, then resumed my trip back to the house, the dagger's handle now damp in my hand. I kept it there until I cleared the copse of trees, until I could see the welcoming glow of the house. When I hit the grass, I resheathed the blade, then ran the final yards full out. But like Lot's wife, I couldn't resist a final glimpse over my shoulder.

When I looked back, the woods were dense, bleak and unwelcoming, and sent a chill down my spine.

"Merit?" I reached the patio, looked up. Ethan stood at the top of the brick steps, hands in his pockets, head tilted to the side in curiosity.

I nodded, passed him by, and moved to the stash of accessories I'd left at the banister. The walk across dewy grass had cleansed the forest from my feet, and I slipped the heels back on.

Wordlessly, he walked to me, stood and watched as I shoed myself, collected my purse.

"Your meeting?" he asked.

I shook my head. "I'll tell you later." I glanced back one final time and took in the expanse of trees. Something flashed in the woods—eyes or light I couldn't tell—but I shuddered either way. "Let's get inside."

He looked at me and cast a glance back at the trees, but nodded and followed me back into the house.

Mrs. Breckenridge spoke, thanked the partygoers for attending. Volunteers were introduced, made polite speeches about the importance of the Harvest Coalition to the city of Chicago, and were applauded. Money was raised, numbers exchanged, and Ethan and I cut a swath through the wealthiest citizens in the Chicago metropolitan area. Just an average Friday night in the upper echelons.

When we'd done our parts and made our own contribution to the cause on Cadogan's behalf, Ethan signing a check with a flourish, we thanked Mrs. Breckenridge for the invite and escaped into the quiet of the Mercedes.

The interior of the car smelled like his cologne, clean and soapy. I hadn't noticed that before.

"And your meeting?" he asked when we were back on the road.

I frowned and crossed my arms over my chest. "Do you want the good news or the bad news?"

"I need both, unfortunately."

"There's a maze behind the house. He was waiting for me. Gave me some snark about becoming a vampire, then said he was waiting in front of Cadogan because he was investigating. Not working on a story," I clarified before Ethan could ask, "but investigating."

Ethan frowned. "Which indicates what about Jamie's supposed vampire story?"

"No clue," I said. "And now for the bad news—I asked about Jamie, a totally innocuous question, and he flew off the handle. Told me to stay away from Jamie. He seems to think we have it in for him."

"We?" Ethan asked.

"Vampires. He said something about how we aren't known for our reliability."

"Hmm," he said. "And how did you leave it?"

"Before he stormed off, he promised that if anything happened to Jamie, he'd come after me."

"These people you associate with are charming, Sentinel." His tone had gone back to chill, prissy. I hated that tone.

"They're the people you've asked me to associate with, Sullivan. Don't forget that. And speaking of which, why the change of plans? Since when does my father have full access to vampire secrets?"

"I opted for a last-minute change in strategy."

"Understatement," I muttered. "What exactly was that strategy supposed to accomplish?"

"I had a hunch. Your father is incredibly well connected, but lacks relationships among supernaturals. That's no doubt why he was eager to work with you, and eager to meet with me. However, his lack of connections doesn't mean he doesn't do his homework. Did anything about his reaction surprise you?"

"His total lack of surprise surprised me." I glanced over at him, an appreciative smile tilting one corner of my mouth. "Very sneaky, Sullivan. Without asking, you managed to get him to indicate that he's been paying very close attention to Celina's situation."

"I manage a redeemable idea now and again."

I made a sardonic sound.

"But you're right—it seems unlikely that anything we discussed came as a surprise."

"Tell him what you think you need to," I said, "as long as you know that if he thinks he can accomplish some end of his own, he'll use that information against us."

"I know, Merit. I'm canny enough to have taken his measure by now."

My stomach growled ominously, and I pressed a hand to it. I could feel the gnawing ache of hunger, and I wasn't about to risk a bout of bloodlust while strapped into a roadster with a man I already had issues with. I could admit that Ethan was a little bit delicious, but I wasn't eager to have my vampire aching for a taste.

"I need a break," I warned him. I glanced out the window and noted a freeway exit ahead of us, then tapped a finger against the glass. "There."

Leaning to the side to check out the exit, he arched a brow. "A break. A break for what?"

"I need food."

"You always need food."

"It's either food or blood, Ethan. And given that it's just me and you in this car right now, food would be considerably less complicated, don't you think?"

Ethan grumbled, but he seemed to get the larger point and aimed the Mercedes toward the exit, then coasted into the parking lot of a roadside hamburger joint. Given the hour— nearly three in the morning—we were one of only a few proud, late-night, burger-hungry scragglers in the lot.

He parked next to the building and glanced through the

driver's-side window at the tacky aluminum siding, the scrubby landscaping, and the marquee at the former Dairy Blitz (the marquee now reading only DA RY LITZ), which had clearly seen better days. I rolled down the window, and the smell of meat and potatoes and hot grease wafted through the car.

Oh, this was going to be good. I just knew it.

He turned to look at me, one eyebrow arched. "The Dary Litz, Sentinel?"

"You'll love it, Sullivan. Smell those fries! That batch is just for you."

"We just had a meal of ceviche and prawn parfait." There was a snicker in his voice that I appreciated.

"Seriously—we ate whipped shellfish, can you believe that? And you've made my point. Drive around."

He made some vague sound of disagreement, but not a very earnest one, before backing up the car and maneuvering it into the drive-through lane.

I scanned the illuminated menu, vacillating between a single or double bacon cheeseburger before deciding on the triple. It was sunlight or an aspen stake, not cholesterol, that would bring me down eventually anyway.

Ethan stared at the menu. "I have no idea what to do here."

"There's the proof positive you made the right decision by bringing me on staff."

I offered some suggestions and when he argued with me, ordered enough for both of us—burgers, fries, chocolate shakes, an extra order of onion rings. He paid with cash that he slipped from a long, thin leather folder in his interior jacket pocket.

When the Mercedes was full of vampires and fried food, he drove to the exit, then paused at the curb while I made a sleeve of the paper wrap around his burger. When I handed it to him, he stared at it for a moment, eyebrow arched, before taking a bite.

He made a vague sound of approval while he chewed.

"You know," I said, biting into an onion ring, "I feel like things would go a lot smoother for you if you'd just admit that I'm always right."

"I'm willing to give you 'right about food,' but that's as far as I can go."

"I'll take that," I said, grinning at him, my mood elevated by our escape from Nick and my father, and probably from the impact of greasy fast food on my serotonin level. Feeling no need for ladylike delicacy, I took a massive bite of my own bacon-laced burger, closing my eyes as I chewed. If there was anything for which I owed Ethan Sullivan thanks, it was the fact that I could eat what I wanted without gaining weight. Sure, I was hungry all the time, and had once nearly latched onto his carotid, but all in all it was a small price to pay. Life was a smorgasbord!

All that serotonin, that relief, probably motivated my next comment. "Thank you," I told him.

Wrapped burger in hand, he pulled onto the road again, and we resumed our journey back to Hyde Park. "For what?"

"For changing me."

He paused. "For changing you?"

"Yeah. I mean, I'm not saying there hasn't been an adjustment period—"

Ethan snorted as he reached into the box of onion rings perched between us. "That's rather an understatement, don't you think?"

"Give me a break, I'm trying to Gratefully Condescend."

Ethan snickered at the reference to the anachronistic *Canon* tradition—Grateful Condescension being the attitude I was supposed to adopt toward Ethan, my Liege. And not the kind of condescension I usually got from him—this was the old-school, Jane Austen version. The kind where you deferred to your betters and employed all the social niceties. Definitely not my bag.

"Thank you," I said, "because if I hadn't been changed, I couldn't eat this incredibly unhealthy food. I wouldn't be immortal. I'd be completely useless with a katana—and that's a skill every twenty-eight-year-old Chicagoan needs." At his flat smile, I nudged him gently, teasingly, with an elbow. "Right?"

He chuckled softly.

"And you wouldn't have me to harass. You wouldn't have my connections or my fabulous fashion sense."

"I chose that dress."

I blinked back surprise. The admission surprised me and kind of thrilled me, although I didn't admit it. I did point out that it wouldn't look nearly as good on him, and got a "hmph" for my trouble.

"Anyway, thank you."

"You're welcome, Sentinel."

"Were you gonna eat the rest of those fries?"

We noshed until we reached the House again. We took the long way around the building, avoiding the tangle of paparazzi outside the gate. Ethan waved his access card at the parking gate, a section of it sliding aside to allow him entry to the underground ramp. After he slid the Mercedes into his parking spot, we got out of the car, shut the doors behind us, and Ethan—despite the fact that the car was parked behind a ten-foot iron gate beneath a House of vampires in a garage accessible only by secret code—beeped the Mercedes' security system.

Halfway to the door, he stopped. "Thank you."

"For?"

"Because of your willingness to go home, and although we seem to have additional questions regarding Nicholas' involvement, we've made some inroads, and we know more now than we did before." He cleared his throat. "You did good today."

I grinned at him. "You like me. You really, really like me!"

"Don't overplay your hand, Sentinel."

I pulled open the basement door and waved him ahead with a hand. "Age before beauty."

Ethan hmphed, but I caught a glimpse of a smile. "Funny."

When I turned to walk to the Ops Room, figuring I should do my duty, check in, and let Luc know that I'd managed to keep Ethan alive during our jaunt off campus, Ethan stopped me with an arm.

"Where are you going?"

I arched an eyebrow at him. "I'm not up for an after party if that's what you're offering." At his flat stare, I explained. "I need to check my folder in the Ops Room."

He dropped my arm, then slipped his hands into his pockets. "You aren't excused yet," he said. "I'll wait."

Frowning, I turned and walked to the closed Ops Room doors. I had no idea what he was up to, and that wasn't the kind of mystery I enjoyed.

When I opened the door and slipped inside, I was greeted by catcalls that would have made a construction worker proud.

Juliet swiveled around in her chair to get a look, then winked at me. "Looking good, Sentinel."

"She's right," Lindsey said from her own station. "You clean up surprisingly well."

I rolled my eyes, but pinched the hem of my skirt and did a little curtsy, then plucked my folder from its hanger on the wall. There was a single piece of paper inside, a printout of a memo that Peter had e-mailed to Luc. The memo contained the names of the paparazzi who'd been assigned to cover Cadogan House, and the papers, Web sites, and magazines they pimped for.

I lifted my gaze, found Peter looking at me curiously. "That was quick work," I said, waving the paper at him.

"You'd be amazed what fangs will get you," he said. He gave me a blank look, then turned back to his computer, fingers flying across the keyboard.

He was a strange one.

"I assume your Liege and mine made it through the evening?" Luc asked.

"Healthy and hale," said a voice behind me. I glanced back. Ethan stood in the doorway, arms crossed over his chest.

"Shall we?" he asked.

I silently cursed the question, knowing exactly what the rest of the guards were going to think about it. Namely, they would imagine much more lascivious things on his agenda. His attraction to me notwithstanding, I knew better. I was a tool in Ethan's vampire toolbox, a pass card to be pulled out when he needed access.

"Sure," I said, after giving Lindsey a warning look. Her lips were pinched together, as if she was only just managing not to snark.

I slipped my folder back into its slot and, memo in hand, followed Ethan into the hallway, then up to the first floor. He took the hallway to the main staircase, then made the corner and took the stairs to the second floor. He paused in front of the doors that I knew led to the library, but hadn't yet had time to explore.

I stepped beside him. He slid me a glance. "You've not been inside?"

I shook my head.

He seemed gratified by my answer, an oddly satisfied smile on his face, and gripped the door handles with both hands. He twisted, pushed, and opened the doors. "Sentinel, your library."

CHAPTER TEN

YOU CAN TELL A LOT BY THE SIZE
OF A MAN'S LIBRARY

It was astonishing.

My mouth open in shock, I walked inside and turned in a slow circle to take it all in. The library was square, rising through the second and third floors. Three high-arched windows illuminated the room. An intricate railing of crimson wrought iron bounded the upper floor, which was accessible by a spiral staircase of the same crimson metal. Tables topped by brass lamps with green shades filled in the middle.

The walls—floor to ceiling—were lined in books. Big and small, leather-bound and paperback, all of them divided into sections—history, reference, vampire physiology, even a small group of fiction titles.

"Oh. My. God."

Ethan chuckled beside me. "And *now* we're even for the changing-you-without-consent issue."

I would have agreed to anything just to touch them, so I threw out an absent "Sure," walked to one of the shelves, and brushed my fingertips over the spines. The section was devoted to Western classics. Doyle was stacked between Dickens and Dumas, Carroll above and Eliot below.

I pulled a navy leather copy of *Bleak House* from its shelf. I opened the spine, paged past the vellum frontispiece, and checked the first rag-cut page. The print was tiny and pressed so deeply into the paper that you could feel the indentation of the letters. I whimpered happily, then closed the book again and slid it home.

"You're in thrall of the books," Ethan said, chuckling. "Had I known you'd be so easy to assuage, I'd have brought you to the library weeks ago."

I made a sound of agreement and pulled out a slim volume of Emily Dickinson's poetry. I thumbed through the pages until I found the poem I wanted, then read aloud, "I died for beauty, but was scarce adjusted in the tomb, when one who died for truth was lain in an adjoining room. He questioned softly why I failed? 'For beauty,' I replied. 'And I for truth— the two are one. We brethren are.'"

Gently, I closed the cover of the book and returned it home, then looked over at Ethan, who stood beside me, his expression thoughtful. "Did you die for beauty or truth?"

"I was a soldier," he said.

That surprised me, and didn't. The thought of Ethan warring—rather than politicking in a back room—surprised me. The thought of Ethan in the midst of war did not.

"Where?" I quietly asked him.

He paused in weighty silence, tension clear in the tilt of his chin, then gave me an obviously feigned light smile. "Sweden. A long time ago."

He'd been a vampire for 394 years; I did the historical math. "Thirty Years' War?"

He nodded. "Very good. I was seventeen when I fought for the first time. I made it to thirty before I was changed."

"You were changed in battle?"

Another nod, no elaboration. I took the hint. "I suppose I was changed in battle, in a manner of speaking."

Ethan pulled a book from the shelf before him and absently flipped through it. "You're referring to Celina's battle to control the Houses?"

"Such as it is." I leaned back against the bookshelves, arms crossed. "What do you think she ultimately wants, Ethan? Vampires controlling the world?"

He shook his head, shut his book and slid it back into place. "She wants whatever new world order puts her in power—whether in charge of vampires, or humans, or both." He angled his body, leaned an elbow on one of the shelves beside me, and propped his head on it, running long fingers through his hair. His other hand was canted on his hip. He looked, suddenly, very tired.

My heart clenched sympathetically.

"And what do you want, Merit?" He'd been looking down at the ground, but suddenly raised glass-green eyes to mine. The question was startling enough; the near-glow of his eyes was brutal.

My voice was soft. "What do you mean?"

"You hadn't planned it, but you're a member of an honorable House, in a unique position, a position of some power. You're strong. You have connections. If you could be in Celina's position, would you?"

Was he testing me? I searched his eyes. Did he mean to take my measure, to see if I could withstand the hunger for power that had overtaken Celina? Or was it simpler than that?

"You're assuming she went bad," I said, "that she'd been balanced as a human but lost some manner of control since her change. I'm not sure that's right. Maybe she was always bad, Ethan. Maybe she didn't get fed up, hasn't suddenly become an advocate for unified vampires. Maybe she's different from me, or from you."

His lips parted. "Are we different, Celina and I?"

I looked down and plucked nervously at my silk skirt. "Aren't you?"

When I looked up again, his own gaze was intimate and searching, maybe as he considered the question, weighed the balance of his own long life.

"Are you wondering if I'll betray you?" I asked him.

There was yearning in his gaze, in his expression. I don't

think he meant to kiss me, although the thought of it—maybe the want of it, maybe the fear of it—sped my pulse.

Sotto voce, he said, "There are things I want to tell you—about Cadogan, the House, the politics." He swallowed, as uncomfortable as I'd ever seen him. "There are things I need to tell you."

I lifted my brows, inviting him to speak.

He opened his mouth, then closed it again. "You're young, Merit. And I don't mean age—I was barely older than you when I was turned. You're a Novitiate vampire, and a new Novitiate at that. And yet, not even two months into your tutelage, you've seen the violence and maneuvering we're capable of."

He looked back at the books and smiled wistfully. "In that respect we aren't so very unlike humans after all."

There was silence in the cavernous room until he looked back at me again. When he did, his expression was somber. "Decisions are made . . ." He paused, seemed to gather his thoughts, then started again. "Decisions are made with an eye toward history, with an eye toward protecting our vampires, securing our Houses."

Ethan nodded at a wall of books across the room, a bank of yellowed volumes with red numbers on the spines.

"The complete *Canon*," he said, and I understood then why the *Canon* was delivered to Initiate vampires in *Desk Reference* form. There must have been fifteen or twenty volumes on each row, and there were multiple rows on multiple shelves.

"That's a lot of law," I told him, my gaze following the line of books.

"It's a lot of *history*," Ethan said. "Many, many centuries of it." He glanced back at me. "You're familiar with the origin of the House system, of the Clearings?"

I was. The *Desk Reference*, while apparently not offering the play-by-play that the complete collection provided, outlined the basic history of the House system, from its origins in Germany to the development of the French tribunal that, for the first time, collectively governed the vampires of Western

Europe, at least until the Presidium moved the convocation to England after the Napoleonic Wars. Both acts were attributable to the panic caused by the Clearings.

"Then you understand," he continued at my nod, "the importance of protecting vampires. Of building alliances."

I did understand, of course, having been handed to Morgan to secure a potential Navarre alliance. "The Breckenridges," I said. "I'd have considered them allies. I'd never have imagined that he'd talk to me that way. Not Nick. He called me a vampire—but it wasn't just a word, Ethan. It was a swear. A curse." I paused, lifted my gaze to Ethan. "He said he'd come after me."

"You know that you're protected?" he quietly asked, sincerely asked. "Being a Cadogan vampire. Living under my roof."

I appreciated the concern, but it wasn't that I feared Nick. It was that I regretted losing him to ignorance. To hatred. "The problem is," I said, "not only are they not allies— they're enemies."

Ethan's brow furrowed, that tiny line back between his eyebrows. And in his eyes—I don't know what it was, other than the heavy weight of something I was confident I'd prefer not knowing. I wasn't sure where his speech had been going, maybe just an acknowledgment of vampire history, but it felt like he wasn't sharing everything he might have. Something waited on the cusp.

Whatever it was, he shook it off, blanked his expression, and assumed the tone of Master vampire.

"I brought you here—the information is at your disposal. We know you're powerful. Support that power with knowledge. It wouldn't do for you to remain ignorant."

I squeezed my eyes shut at the strike. When I opened them again, he was headed for the door, his exit marked by the receding sound of his footsteps on the marble floor. The door opened and closed again, and then the room was quiet and still, a treasure box closed off to the greater world.

As I turned back to the books and scanned the shelves, I realized his pattern. Whenever he began to see me as something more than a liability or a weapon, whenever we spoke to each other without the barrier of rank and history between us, he backed away, more often than not insulting me to force the distance. I knew at least some of the reasons he backed away—including his general sense of my inferiority—and suspected others—the difference in our rank.

But there was something else there, something I couldn't identify. The fear in his eyes revealed it—he was afraid of something. Maybe something he wanted to tell me. Maybe something he *didn't* want to tell me.

I shook my head to clear the thought, then checked my watch. It was two hours until dawn, the bulk of my evening having been taken up by Ethan, Nick, and my father, so I took the opportunity to give the library the perusal of a former researcher.

The books were organized into fiction and nonfiction sections just like a traditional library, every section organized, every shelf impeccably clean. There must have been thousands of volumes in the room, and there was no way a collection that large could be maintained without a librarian. I looked around, but saw no sign of a circulation desk or administrator. I wonder who'd been lucky enough to get that assignment. And more importantly, I wondered why I hadn't been the obvious nominee. Books or a sword for an English lit student? Seemed like an easy call.

I searched the shelves for something readable and decided on a book of urban fantasy from the popular fiction shelf. I left the library after a geekily wistful goodbye, promising the stacks that I'd return when I had more time, then headed downstairs and toward the back of the House. I followed the long central hallway to the cafeteria area, where a handful of vampires munched on predawn snacks, their gazes lifting as I walked to the back door. I slipped outside to the brick patio that spanned the end of the House, then followed a path to the small formal garden. In the middle of the garden was a fountain illuminated by a dozen in-ground lights, and the light was just strong enough to read by. I picked a bench, curled my legs into the seat, and opened the book.

*   *   *

Time passed, the grounds quiet and empty around me. Since the night was waning, I dog-eared and closed the book and uncrossed my legs. As I stood, I glanced up at the back of the House. A figure stood at a window on the third floor, hands in pockets, facing the garden.

It was a window in Amber's former room, the Consort suite beside Ethan's, the rooms he'd cleaned out. She was gone, and so was the furniture; I couldn't imagine that anyone but him would be in the room, much less staring into the garden.

I stood there for a moment, book in my arms, watching his meditation. I wondered what he thought about. Did he mourn for her? Was he angry? Was he embarrassed that he hadn't predicted her betrayal? Or was he ruminating on the things that had happened tonight, worrying about Nicholas, Celina, and whatever war she might be leading us into?

The horizon began to purple. Since I had no urge to be caught in the sun, reduced to ashes because I'd been curled up with a paperback in the garden—or spying on my Master—I returned to the House, occasionally glancing up at the window, but he never changed position.

Peter Gabriel came to mind, his lyric about working just to survive. Ethan did that. Day in and day out, he kept watch over more than three hundred Cadogan vampires. We were a kind of kingdom, and he was the lord of the manor, the figurative and literal Master of the House. Our survival was a responsibility that fell upon his shoulders, and had since Peter Cadogan's death.

It was, I realized, a responsibility I trusted him with. Ethan's biggest fault, at least so far as I was aware, was his inability to separate that responsibility from everything else in this life.

Every*one* else in his life.

And so, on a night in late May, I found myself standing on the lawn of a Hyde Park mansion of vampires, staring up at the stone-framed visage of a boy in Armani, an enemy who'd become an ally. Ironic, I thought, that I'd given up one ally today, but gained another.

Ethan ran a hand through his hair.

"What are you thinking about?" I whispered up, knowing he couldn't hear me.

Where was a boom box when you needed one?

CHAPTER ELEVEN

IN WHICH OUR HEROINE IS SENT TO THE PRINCIPAL'S OFFICE

I woke with a start, sitting straight up in bed. The sun had finally set, allowing me the few hours of consciousness I'd be afforded each day during my first summer as a vampire. I wondered if life would be different in the winter, when we had hours and hours of darkness to enjoy.

On the other hand, we also had lake-effect snow to enjoy. That was going to make for a lot of cold, dark hours. I made a mental note to find a warm spot in the library.

I got up, showered, ponytailed my hair, and put on the training ensemble I'd been ordered to wear today. Although I wasn't officially on the clock, and had Mallory's not-going-that-far-away party and a follow-up date with Morgan to look forward to, the Cadogan guards and I were scheduled for a group training exercise so that we could learn to be better— or at least more efficiently violent—vampires.

The official workout uniform was a black mid-torso sports tank with crisscrossing straps and snug hip-waisted, yoga-type pants that reached mid-calf. Both, of course, in black, except for the stylized silver C on the upper left-hand side of the tank.

It might not have been a terribly interesting ensemble, but it covered a lot more skin than the outfit Catcher forced me to wear during his training sessions; sand volleyball players got to wear more clothing.

I slid on flip-flops for the walk downstairs, grabbed my sword, and shut the door behind me before making my way through the second floor to the main stairway, and then up to the third.

Lindsey's door was open, her room as loud as it had been two days ago, an episode of *South Park* now blaring from the tiny television.

"How do you sleep in here?" I asked her.

Lindsey, in the same outfit as me, her blond hair in a low ponytail, sat on the edge of her bed and pulled on tennis shoes. "When you're forced unconscious by the rising of the sun, it kinda takes care of itself."

"Good point."

"How was your date with Ethan last night?"

I should have known that was coming. "It wasn't a date."

"Whatevs. You're hot for teacher."

"We were in the library."

"*Oh*, nookie in the stacks. Figures you're the type to have that fantasy, grad school and all." Her feet clad in running shoes that had seen many, many better days, she hopped off the bed and grinned at me. "Let's go do some learnin'."

Downstairs in the Operations Room, Lindsey and I took a peek at our folders (empty) before filing toward the gigantic room at the end of the hall. This was the Sparring Room—the place where I challenged Ethan during my first trip to Cadogan House. It was high-ceilinged and boasted fighting mats and an arsenal of antique weaponry. The room was also ringed by a balcony, giving observers a firsthand view of the action below.

Today, thankfully, the balcony was empty. The room, however, was not. Guards milled about on the edges of the fighting mats, and a pissed-off-looking sorcerer stood in the middle in white martial arts–style pants, the circle tattoo blue-green across his abdomen. In his hands was the handle of his gleaming katana, overhead lights glinting from the pristine blade.

I was behind Lindsey and nearly stumbled into her when she stopped short and gave a low whistle in Catcher's direction. She glanced back at me. "Speaking of being hot for teacher. He's still dating Carmichael, right?"

"Very much so."

She muttered an expletive that drew a chuckle from Juliet and a low, possessive growl from Luc. "That is a damn shame."

"Can you at least pretend to be professional today?"

Lindsey stopped, glanced back at Luc. "You show me professional, and I'll show you professional."

Luc snorted, but his expression was gleeful. "Sweetheart, you wouldn't know professional if it bit you on the ass."

"I prefer my bites in other places."

"Is that an invitation?"

"If only you were so lucky, cowboy."

"Lucky? Hooking up with me would be the luckiest day of your life, Blondie."

"Oh, *please*." The word was spoken with such sarcasm that she stretched it into a couple of syllables.

Luc rolled his eyes. "All right, you've had your fun, now get that ass on the mat, if you can spare us a few minutes." He walked away before she could respond, moving around to wrangle other guards into position.

At the edge of the mats, as we peeled off our shoes, I gave her a sideways glance. "Torture isn't kind."

She gave an acknowledging nod, smiled back. "True. But it sure as hell is amusing."

When we were barefoot, we stepped onto the mats and did some perfunctory stretching, then moved back to the edge and stood in a line before Catcher. We descended to our knees and sat back in the *seiza* position, left hands on the handles of our swords, ready to listen.

When we were ready, Luc moved to stand beside Catcher, hands on his hips, and surveyed us.

"Ladies and . . . ladies," Luc said, "since the sexual harassment has already started, I assume you've recognized that we have a special guest. In two weeks, we'll be evaluating you on your katana skills, memory of the Katas, ability to execute the moves. In lieu of kicking each other's asses, enjoyable as that would be for me, Catcher Bell"—he inclined his head in Catcher's direction—"a former Keeper of the Keys, is going to show you how it's done. As Cadogan guards, and under my auspicious leadership, you are, of course, the best of the best, but he'll make you better."

"*Top Gun*," I whispered to Lindsey. We'd started pointing out Luc's ubiquitous pop culture references, having decided that because he cut his fangs in the Wild West, he'd been entranced by movies and television. You know, because living in a society of magically enhanced vampires didn't require enough willing suspension of disbelief.

"He's no longer a member of the Order," Luc told us, "but a civilian, so no need to salute him." Luc chuckled to himself, apparently amused by the throw-in. A couple of the guards laughed for effect, but mostly we groaned.

Lindsey leaned over. "You called it. Nice ass," she whispered, "but original, he ain't."

I was proud that Luc at least rated a "nice ass."

Catcher stepped forward, and the gravity of his gaze—which landed consecutively on each of us—shut down the snark immediately.

"You can jump," he said, "but you cannot fly. You live at night, because you cannot stand the sun. You are immortal, but a splinter of wood, carefully placed, will reduce you to ashes." The room went noticeably silent. He walked to the end of the line, began slowly pacing back. "You have been hunted. You have been exterminated. You have lived, hidden, for thousands of years. Because, like humans, like the rest of us, you have weaknesses."

He raised his katana, and I blinked as the blade caught the light, gleamed. He stopped in front of Peter. "But you fight with honor. You fight with steel."

He took another step, stopped in front of Juliet. "You are stronger."

Another step, and he was before Lindsey. "You are faster."

He paused before me. "You are more than you were."

My skin pebbled with goose bumps.

"Lesson number one," he said. "This is not *swordplay*. Call it that around me and risk the consequences. Lesson number two. You've been lucky so far—you've had peace for nearly a century, at least amongst the Houses, but that's gonna change. Celina's out, Celina's narcissistic, and Celina, maybe now, maybe later, will do damage if she can." Catcher tapped a finger against the side of his head. "That's the way she operates."

He lifted his katana, held it horizontally before him. "This is your weapon, your safety net, your life. This is not a toy, *capiche*?"

We nodded collectively.

Catcher turned, walked to another edge of the mat, and picked up the sheath for his katana. He sheathed the blade, then grabbed two *bokken*—wooden training swords that roughly echoed the shape and weight of the katanas—and came back again. He spun one *bokken* in his hand, as if adjusting to its weight. The second, he pointed at me. "Let's go, Sunshine."

Damn, I thought, not eager to be the focus of Catcher's lesson, especially in front of an audience, but I stood up and unbelted my own katana, then bowed respectfully before stepping into the middle of the mat. Catcher handed me the extra *bokken*.

"The next time we do this," he told the band of guards, who all looked a little too eager to watch me fight, "we do it blindfolded. Your senses are all good enough that you should be able to fend off an attack even without your visual acuity. But today"—Catcher bladed his body, one foot before the other, knees bent, both hands around the handle of his sword—"you may use your eyes. Standing position," he ordered, indicating that I could defend his attack without having to rise and act out the unsheathing of my sword.

I mirrored his stance, two sword lengths between us, *bokken* raised over our heads.

"First Kata," he said, just before striking down in front of me. My muscles clenched beneath the breeze of the slicing wood, but he didn't touch me. I responded with my own downward slice, my movements smooth and fluid. I was no Master, but I was comfortable enough with the Katas, the building blocks of katana sparring. It was the same idea as basic ballet positions—you learn the fundamentals, and the fundamentals give you the working knowledge necessary for more-complicated moves.

When we'd completed the first Kata, we went back to our starting position, then worked through the remaining six. He seemed generally pleased with my work, at one point stepping back and making me repeat the final three Katas against an invisible opponent to check my form. He was an exacting teacher, with comments about the angle of my spine, the placement of my fingers around the handle, whether my weight was appropriately distributed. When we were done, and after he'd made comments to the group, he turned back to me.

"Now we spar," he said, eyebrows arched in challenge.

My stomach sank. It was easy enough to hide multiple vampire personalities when I was wearing fancy clothes or walking around the block. It was going to be a lot harder in the middle of a sparring round when a wooden sword was being aimed at my head. That was just the kind of thing that got *her* attention.

I blew out a breath and bladed my body again, my sword before me. I wiggled my fingers, adjusting their positions on the blade, trying to keep my heart from racing in anticipation of the coming battle.

No. Correction: battles.

Between me and Catcher, and between me and *her*. The vampire inside.

"Ready. Set. Fight," Catcher said, and attacked.

He came at me with his arms raised, and brought the katana down in a clean, straight slice. I pivoted out of the way, bringing my own sword horizontal and swinging it around in a move that would have sliced his belly open. But for a human, Catcher was fast, not to mention nimble. He spun around in the air, his body at an angle, and avoided the slice of my *bokken*.

I was so impressed with the move—it looked like something Gene Kelly might have done, it was his brand of defying gravity—that I dropped my guard.

In that instant, he nailed me.

Catcher followed through with the spin, a full 360-degree turn, and brought his own *bokken*, the inertia of his body weight behind it, across my left arm.

Pain exploded. I threw out a curse and clenched my eyes against the pain.

"Never drop your guard," Catcher unrepentantly warned. I looked up, found him back in the starting position, *bokken* bladed. "And never take your eyes off an assailant." He bobbed his head at me. "You'll heal, and you'll probably have worse injuries than that when it's all said and done. Let's go again."

I muttered a choice curse about "my assailant," but bladed my body again and adjusted my grip on the handle of the *bokken*. My biceps throbbed, but I was a vampire; I'd heal. It was part of our genetic deal.

He may not have been a vampire, but he was good. I was fast and strong, but I didn't have either his natural knack or his experience at sparring. I was also injured. And I was trying, as hard as I could, to fight without *fighting*. To tamp down that coursing rush of adrenaline and anger that would bring *her* to the surface—in front of a crowd of combat-trained vampires. And loosing a half-formed vampire into the world, and in front of an audience, couldn't be a good thing.

But it was a tough line to walk.

As a newbie vamp, and a former grad student at that, I was still just reacting to whatever Catcher threw at me: spinning to get out of the way or slashing my own sword down when he failed to block rather than carrying out my own plan of attack. He was moving too quickly for me to both react defensively and take offensive strikes of my own, although I tried. I tried to analyze his moves, tried to watch for weaknesses.

The longer we sparred, the harder that analysis became. With each arc of my *bokken*, each slash and spin, my limbs loosened and my mind relaxed, and I began to fight back.

Unfortunately, the second I began to really fight back, to let the adrenaline rush me and let my body dance with the *bokken* in my hands, the vampire inside began to scream for release.

As I spun, *bokken* before me, she stretched through my limbs, and my eyes fluttered with the sensation of it, like warmth spilling through my veins as she moved. The warmth was fun enough—it was hard to come by in a vampiric body—but then she went a step too far.

Without warning, she pushed forward and took control, as if someone else had stepped inside my body. I watched events play out before me, but it was she that moved my arms, that prompted my sudden speed and agility. Speed and agility that were unmatched even by a sorcerer whose expertise, whose magical *raison d'être,* was weaponry.

She had little patience for the maneuverings of a human. Where I'd fought defensively, she advanced, slashing at Catcher and forcing him around and backward nearly to the other edge of the mat. It played out like a movie before me, as if I were sitting in a theater in my mind, watching the fight happen.

When my *bokken* grazed the side of Catcher's head, millimeters away from skull and scalp, the thought that I might have hurt him, and severely, pushed me—pushed Merit—back through. I blew out a breath as I spun away from another strike, forcing her back again.

When I'd sucked down oxygen and glanced back at him again, I found something unexpected in his eyes. Not reprobation.

Pride.

There was no fear that I'd nearly taken a swipe at his throat, no anger that I'd gone too far. Instead, his eyes shone with the thrill of a man in battle.

I think that look was almost worse. It thrilled her, that pride, that eagerness in his eyes.

It terrified me. I'd momentarily loosed her, and I'd nearly

concussed my training master. That math was pretty simple—the vampire was going to stay repressed.

Unfortunately, although repressing the vamp decreased the chance that Catcher would lose a vital appendage, it also decreased my ability to keep up with him. Just like Yeats predicted, things began to fall apart. The parts of my brain that had been focused on fighting back and keeping her down now also had to think about how close I'd come to taking his blood, to battering the man who was trying to prepare me for combat.

And expert in the Second Key or not, Catcher was tiring. He knew how to use the weapons, sure. How to and where to swing his *bokken* for maximum effect. But he was still human (or so I assumed), and I was a vampire. I had more endurance. What I didn't have—when I was struggling to keep myself together—was any skill at sparring. Which meant that even if he was tiring, I was getting worse. I endured his criticism, humiliating as it was. But the shots were harder to take.

Twice, he swung his *bokken* around in a kind of half-hearted arc. Twice, I got whapped with it. Once across my left arm—which still burned from the last contact—and once across the back of my calves—a shot that put me on my knees in front of my colleagues.

"Get up," Catcher said, motioning with the tip of his *bokken*. "And this time, at least try to move out of the way?"

"I *am* trying," I muttered, rising off my knees and blading my body again.

"You know," Catcher said, slicing forward with the *bokken* in a series of moves that backed me to the opposite side of the mat. "Celina isn't going to give you a chance to warm up. She isn't going to pull her punches. And she's not going to wait while you call for backup."

He half turned, then brought the *bokken* around in a sweeping move like a backhanded tennis shot.

"I'm doing," I said as I avoided one strike and tried to maneuver my way back to the near side of the room, "the best"—I swung my katana, but he stopped it with his own steel—"that I *can.*"

"That's *not good enough,*" he bellowed, and met my *bok-*

ken with a two-handed strike that whipped the wood from my sweaty hands. As if embarrassed by my clumsiness, the *bokken* flew, bounced on the mat once, twice, and finally came to a rolling stop.

The room went silent.

I risked a glance up. Catcher stood in front of me, *bokken* in one hand, skin damp from his exertions, bewilderment in his expression.

I wasn't interested in answering the question in his eyes, so I bent over, hands on my knees, my own breathing labored. I wiped sweaty bangs from my face.

"Pick it up," he directed, "and give it to Juliet."

I walked over to where the *bokken* lay, bent down and picked it up. Juliet stepped forward, and after a sympathetic glance, took it from my hand. Assuming I'd been dismissed, I turned away and rubbed sweat from my eyes.

But Catcher called my name, and I glanced back to meet his gaze once again. He searched my eyes, scanning my irises in a preternatural way I'd come to expect of the answer-seeking sorcerer. Seconds passed before his focus sharpened and he was looking at me again, instead of through me. "Is there anything you need to tell me?"

My pulse pounded in my ears. He had forgotten, apparently, that we'd broached the subject before, that I'd tried to talk to him about my malfunctioning vampire. I was more than happy to keep it that way. I shook my head.

I could tell he wasn't satisfied by that, but he looked at Juliet and prepared to fight.

Catcher worked Juliet through the same seven katas, her moves practiced and precise, the daintiness of her form belying her skill at wielding the lengthy weapon. When he was done with her, he asked us for critiques. The guards, at first with trepidation and then with confidence, offered their observations of her performance. Generally, folks were impressed, thinking that an enemy's underestimation of her slight form would work to her advantage.

Peter was also given a workout before Catcher called the

session to an end. He ended with a few parting comments and generally avoided eye contact with me, before shaking Luc's hand, pulling on a T-shirt, grabbing his weapons, and leaving the room.

I gathered my sword and stepped into my flip-flops, intent on catching a post-training shower. Lindsey walked over and put a hand on my arm as she toed into her shoes.

"You all right?" she asked.

"We'll see," I whispered back as Luc crooked his finger at me.

"Ethan's office," was all he said when I reached him. But given the irritation in his voice, that was plenty.

"Should I shower first? Or change?"

"Upstairs, Merit."

I nodded again. I wasn't entirely sure what I'd done to deserve a visit to the principal's office, but I was assuming my performance during training had something to do with it. Either they'd been impressed by the minute or two I'd allowed the vampire to take control, or they'd been unimpressed by the rest of it. Or, given the shots I'd taken and the fact that I'd actually *dropped* the *bokken*, actually offended by it. Either way, Catcher and Luc would have had questions, and I assumed those questions had been sent upstairs.

Scabbard in hand, I trotted up to the first floor and headed for Ethan's office, then knocked when I reached the closed door.

"In," he said.

I cracked the door and found him seated at his desk, hands clasped together on the desktop, gaze on me as I entered. That was a first. It was usually the paperwork that had his attention, not the vampire at the door.

I shut the door behind me and stood before him, stomach fluttering with nerves.

Ethan made me stand there for a good minute, maybe two, before speaking. "Word travels."

"Word?" I asked.

"Merit," he began, "you stand Sentinel for this House." He looked at me expectantly, eyebrows raised.

"That's what I hear," I dryly responded.

"My expectation," he continued without comment, "the expectation of this House, is that when you are asked to improve your skills, to strengthen your abilities, you do so. Upon request. Whenever you are asked, whether during your one-on-one training or in front of your colleagues."

He paused, apparently expecting an answer.

I just looked back at him. I could admit that I looked sloppy out there. But if they'd known the workout I was putting myself through, I guarantee they'd have been impressed.

"We've talked about this," he continued. "I need—*we* need—a functioning Sentinel in this House. We need a soldier, someone who will put out the effort that is required of her, whose dedication to this House does not falter, whose effort and attention are always given. We need a vampire who gives of herself, entirely, to this cause." He adjusted a silver stapler on his desk, aligning it with the silver tape dispenser it sat next to.

"I would have thought, given the fact that we'd trusted you with respect to the Breckenridges, the raves, that you understood this. That you wouldn't need an elementary lecture regarding the level of your effort."

I looked at him, managed not to offer up the bruise that had blossomed on my left arm—fading but not yet gone—as obvious evidence of my effort. Of my concerted exercise in self-control.

"Am I making myself clear?"

Standing there before him, sweaty in my workout gear, sheathed katana in my hand, I figured I had three choices. I could argue with him, tell him I'd worked my ass off (all evidence to the contrary), which would probably prompt questions I didn't want to answer. Or, I could come clean, tell him about my half-baked vampire problem, and wait to be handed over to the GP for handling.

No, thank you. I opted for choice number three.

"Liege," I acknowledged.

That was all I said. Although I had things to say about his own trust issues, I let him make his point, and I got to keep my secret.

Ethan looked at me for a long, quiet moment before lowering his eyes and scanning the documents on his desk. The knots in my shoulders loosened.

"Dismissed," he said, without glancing up again.

I let myself out.

Once upstairs again, I showered and donned clothes that were decidedly not within the Cadogan dress code—my favorite pair of jeans and a short-sleeved, long-waisted red top with an off-center scooped neck. I had a date with Morgan and a not-going-that-far-away party for Mallory to attend. The neck-revealing top was very appropriate for a date with the vampire boyfriend.

I applied gloss and mascara and blush, left my hair down around my shoulders, slipped into square-toed, red ballet flats, then grabbed my beeper and sword—both required accessories for House guards—and locked my room behind me. I walked down the second-floor hall and rounded the corner.

As I took the stairs, I lifted my gaze from the treads to the boy ascending the other side. It was Ethan, suit jacket over one arm.

His expression showed a kind of vague male interest, as if he hadn't yet recognized exactly whom he was checking out. Given the change from sweaty, post-workout Merit to pre-date Merit, not surprising that he didn't recognize me.

But as we passed, when he realized it was me, his eyes widened. And there was an incredibly satisfying hitch in his step.

I bit back a smile and kept walking. As I strolled through the first floor and out the front door, I probably looked unconcerned.

But I knew I'd always remember that little hitch.

————•—◦≡◇◈◇≡◦—•————

CHAPTER TWELVE

MERIT'S DEEP, DARK (72% COCOA) SECRET

It was nearly midnight when I made it to Wicker Park, but I got lucky, finding a corner grocery with its neon OPEN sign still blazing in the window. I grabbed a bottle of wine and a chocolate torte, my calorie-laden contribution to Mallory's not-going-that-far-away party.

On my way north, I tried to shrug off the job tension. It wasn't that I was the first girl to have boss issues, but how many bosses were four-hundred-year-old Master vampires or sword-wielding sorcerers? It didn't help that the same sword-wielding sorcerer was one-fourth of Mal's party.

Once in the 'hood, I opted to leave my sword in the car. Since I was off duty and off Cadogan House turf, it was unlikely that I'd need it and, more important, the act felt like a tiny rebellion. A wonderful rebellion. A rebellion I needed.

Mal opened the door as soon as I popped up the steps. "Hi, honey," she said. "Bad day at the office?"

I held up booze and chocolate.

"I'll take that as a yes," she said, holding open the door for me. When I was inside and the door was closed and locked behind us, I handed over the gifts.

"Chocolate and booze," she said. "You do know how to woo a girl. You've got mail, by the way." She bobbed her head toward the side table, then headed for the kitchen.

"Thanks," I mumbled after her, picking up the pile. Apparently the post office hadn't completely caught up with my change of address. I set aside magazines, interesting catalogs and bills, and dumped credit card offers addressed to "Merit, Vampire" into a pile for shredding. There was also a wedding invitation from a cousin and, at the bottom of the stack, a small crimson envelope.

I flipped it over. The envelope was blank but for my name and address, both written in elegant white calligraphy. I slid a finger beneath the flap and found a thick, cream-colored card tucked inside. I pulled it out. It bore a single phrase in the same calligraphy, this time in bloodred ink:

You are invited.

That was it. No event, no date, no time, and the back was completely blank. The card contained nothing but the phrase, as if the writer had forgotten, mid-invite, exactly what party she'd been inviting me to.

"Weird," I muttered. But the folks my parents hung out with could be a little flighty; maybe the printer was in a hurry, couldn't finish the stack. Whatever the reason, I stuffed the half-finished invite back into the pile, dropped the pile back on the table, and headed for the kitchen.

"So, my boss," I said, "is kind of an ass."

"Which boss did you mean?" Catcher stood at the stove, stirring something in a saucepan. He glanced back at me. "The asshole vampire or the asshole sorcerer?"

"Oh, I think the name applies pretty well to either." I took a seat at the kitchen island.

"Don't take Darth Sullivan personally," Mallory said, twisting a corkscrew into the wine like a seasoned expert. "And really don't take Catcher personally. He's full of shit."

"That's charming, Mallory," he said.

Mallory winked at me and filled three wineglasses. We clinked, and I took a sip. Not bad for a last-minute quick-stop find. "What's on the menu for dinner?"

"Salmon, asparagus, rice," Catcher said, "and probably too much talk about girly shit and vampires."

I appreciated the light mood. If he could leave our issues in the Sparring Room back in Cadogan House, I could, too. "You are aware that you're dating girly, right?" I asked. Mal may have loved soccer and the occult, but she was all girly-girl, from the blue hair to the patent leather flats.

Mal rolled her eyes. "Our Mr. Bell is in denial about certain issues."

"It's lotion, Mallory, for God's sake." Catcher used a long, flat spatula and the tips of his fingers to flip salmon in his sauté pan.

"Lotion?" I asked, crossing my legs on the island stool and prepping for some good drama. I could always appreciate being the audience for a domestic squabble that had nothing to do with me. And God knows Mal and Catcher were a constant source—I'd been able to give up TMZ completely, my need for gossip sated by Carmichael-Bell disputes.

"She has, like, fourteen kinds of lotion." He had trouble getting out the words, his shock and chagrin at Mallory's moisturizer stockpile apparently that intense.

Mallory waved her glass at me. "Tell him."

"Women moisturize," I reminded him. "Different lotions for different body parts, different scents for different occasions."

"Different thicknesses for different seasons," Mallory added. "It's pretty complicated, actually."

Catcher dumped a cutting board of trimmed asparagus into a steamer pot. "It's *lotion*. I'm pretty sure science has advanced to the point that you can buy a single bottle that will take care of all that."

"Missing the point," I said.

"He's missing the point," Mallory parroted. "You're totally missing the point."

Catcher snorted and turned to face us, arms crossed over a Marquette T-shirt. "You two would agree that the world is flat if it meant you could gang up on me."

Mallory bobbed her head. "True. That is true."

I nodded and grinned at Catcher. "That's what makes us awesome. A force of nature."

"What's bad about this conversation," Catcher said, pointing at Mallory as he stalked toward her, then waggling his finger between their bodies, "is that we're dating. You're supposed to side with me."

Mallory burst out laughing, just in time for Catcher to reach her and nab her glass of wine before Cabernet sloshed over the top. "Catch, you're a boy. I've known you for like a week." Two months, actually, but who was counting? "I've known Merit for years. I mean, the sex is great and all, but she's my BFF."

For the first time since I'd known Catcher, he was speechless. Oh, he sputtered a little, tried to get something out, but Mallory's pronouncement stopped him short. He looked to me for help. If I hadn't been amused, the desperation in his eyes would have moved me.

"You're the one that moved in, Slugger," I said with a shrug. "She's right. Maybe next time you should do a little of that famous Bell investigatory work before you sign up for the full ride."

"You two are impossible," he said, but wrapped his free arm around Mal's waist and pressed his lips to her temple. Just as I was visited by a pang of jealousy that tightened my stomach, I heard a car door shut outside.

"Morgan's here," I said, uncrossing my legs and bounding off my stool. I glanced back at both of them and pressed my hands together. "Please, for the love of God, have clothes on when I get back."

I smoothed my hair as I traveled the hallway, then pulled open the front door. He'd parked an SUV in front of the brownstone.

Correction, I thought, as Morgan popped out of the passenger side—Morgan's driver parked the SUV. I guess Morgan preferred to be chauffeured these days.

I stepped outside, hands on my hips as I waited for him on the stoop. He strode toward the house, dressed in jeans and a couple of layered T-shirts, a shamelessly happy grin on his face, a paper sleeve of flowers in his hand.

"Hello, Chicago's newest Master."

Morgan shook his head, grinned. "I come in peace," he said, and bounded up the stairs. He stood on the step below mine, which put us nearly at eye level. "Hello, beautiful."

I smiled down at him.

"In the interest of détente between our Houses," he said, leaning in and lowering his voice to a whisper, "and to celebrate this historic meeting of vampires, I'm going to kiss you."

"Fair enough."

He did, his lips soft and cool against mine, the length of his body warm as he pressed in. The kiss was sweet and very, very eager. He nipped at my lips, whispering my name as he did it, hinting at the depths of his desire. But before we'd gone further than propriety would have allowed, given that we were standing on the stoop in full view of the street, he pulled back.

"You look"—he shook his head as if in awe—"outstanding." He grinned up at me, dark blue eyes alight with pleasure . . . and what looked like pride.

"Thank you. You don't look half bad yourself. I mean, you're a vampire, but that's not really your fault."

Morgan clucked his tongue and leaned around me, gazing through the open door. "You should be affording me the Grateful Condescension I'm due. Is that salmon?"

I appreciated that the boy's love of food was nearly as big as mine. "That's what I hear."

"Sweet. Let's go in."

We made it as far as the hallway before he stopped me, before he sidled me against one of the few parts of the wall that weren't covered in Carmichael family photographs. Then he tucked his index finger into a belt loop on my jeans and tugged me closer.

He leaned in, smelling of bright, grassy cologne. It was kind of an odd smell on a night-dwelling vampire.

"I really didn't get a chance to say hello and good night properly," he murmured.

"I think you were gearing up for the salmon."

His voice was barely audible, a sultry rustling of sound. "Exactly. I got distracted, and I really don't think I gave it my best."

"In that case . . ." was all I got out before his lips found mine. This kiss was just as eager as his last had been, his mouth hungry and urgent, tongue teasing and insistent. His hands slid around my back, enveloping me in his arms and his spring-green scent. He sighed at the contact.

"Hey, did Morgan ever— Oh, dear God."

Morgan's head popped up, and we both looked to find Mallory just outside the kitchen door, hands over her eyes. She waved.

"Uh, hi, Morgan. Hi. Oh, God. Sorry," she sputtered, and immediately turned on her heel and walked back into the kitchen.

I grinned happily. "And *now* she knows what it feels like."

"Except we were actually clothed," Morgan pointed out, then looked back at me with a knowing smile. "But we could remedy that pretty easily."

"Yeah, getting naked to teach Mallory a lesson ain't real high on my priority list."

He barked out a laugh, leaning back with the force of it, our bodies still pressed together at the hips, then smiled down at me, eyes bright, grin wide. "I missed you, Mer."

I couldn't help it—my smile faltered, and I hated myself for it. I hated that I couldn't return that careless, joyous smile. I hated that I didn't—or maybe just didn't yet?—feel that same spark that lit Morgan's eyes. I wondered if it could grow, with time and with nearness. I wondered if I was being too hard on myself, expecting too much to think that I could fall for someone after just a few weeks. Maybe I needed more time. Maybe I was vastly overthinking it.

Morgan's smile dipped a bit at one corner. "Everything okay?"

"Yeah, I'm just . . . It's been a really long night." That was entirely true, so it was really only a lie of omission.

"Yeah?" He pushed a lock of hair behind my ear. "You wanna talk about it?"

"Nah, let's go get some food and make fun of Mallory and Catcher."

He closed his eyes, a tightness at the corners. I'd hurt him, by not telling him about my night, by not sharing more of myself with him, and I slapped myself mentally for it. But when he opened his eyes again, his expression was forgiving, a corner of his mouth tipped up into a smile. "You're going to have to help me out here, Merit. I can't be the only one doing this."

I gave him points for honesty, and for not saying that I owed it to him to try, given that Ethan had all but ordered our courtship. I half smiled back at him, simultaneously feeling a sense of relief, that at least he'd put the relationship issue out there, and a sense of foreboding, that I was going to be the one to bring that relationship down around us.

"I know," I said. "I know. I'm really about as good at relationships as I am at being a vampire. I'm kind of a smart but surprisingly inept girl." That was the entire truth.

Morgan laughed full out, then pressed a kiss to my forehead. "Come on, genius. Let's eat."

Dinner was ready by the time we made it into the kitchen, our fingers linked together as we walked. Morgan slipped his hand away and presented his bundle of red-tipped white tulips to Mallory. "Thanks for having me over."

"Oh, these are gorgeous." She enveloped him in a hug he didn't look like he was expecting, but seemed inordinately pleased by. "And you're welcome. We're glad you could come."

Mallory gave him a bright smile, and gave me a concealed thumbs-up, then set about finding a vase for the flowers while Morgan and Catcher said their manly hellos—consisting of a symbolic head bob from Catcher (of the "You're in my lair now" variety) and a responding nod from Morgan (of the "You are clearly the king of this castle" variety).

A vase in one hand and the flowers in the other, Mallory paused at the threshold of the kitchen. "Merit, do you need blood?"

I didn't even need to think about it. Although I hadn't had a run of overwhelming bloodlust since my first week as a vampire—the First Hunger that had led me to nearly plant my fangs in Ethan's neck, and a second bout of drinking roused by an unpleasant discussion with my father—I wasn't going to risk it, and tried to be preventative by drinking the *Canon*'s recommended pint every other day. Vampires were hardly the monsters we were made out to be in fairy tales and television shows. We were hardly different from humans, but for the genetic mutation, fangs, silvering eyes, and periodic penchant for blood.

What? I said *hardly* different.

"Yes, I need blood," I told her, petulant as a teenager reminded to take her vitamins, and snatched a bag of Blood4You Type A from the refrigerator. Although Mallory, as a now-former ad exec, found the name embarrassingly sophomoric, she appreciated not being my lunch.

I glanced back at Morgan, waved the bag at him. "Hungry?"

He moved closer to me, gaze surprisingly possessive, arms crossed over his chest, and leaned down. "You realize that we'd be sharing blood?"

"Is that a problem?"

His brow furrowed in confusion. "No, no. It's just . . ."

He paused, and I blinked. Did I miss something? I tried to flip mentally back through chapter three of the *Canon* ("Drink Me"), which discussed some of the etiquette of vampire drinking. Vampires could drink directly from humans or other vampires, and I'd witnessed firsthand the sensuality of it when Amber had been Ethan's beverage of choice. But the intimacy of drinking prepackaged blood in front of an audience escaped me. I'd seen Ethan do it just the other day.

On the other hand, Morgan was a Navarre vampire, prohibited from drinking blood directly from humans. The *Canon* didn't get into the emotions of it, but maybe even drinking from plastic assumed a greater importance when it was the only way you could share the act.

"Is that a problem?" I asked.

He must have reconciled my ignorance, as he finally smiled back. "Must be a House thing. Yeah, I'll take a pint. B if you have it."

There was a bag of B in the refrigerator, and I concluded his palate was more sensitive than mine if he could taste the difference in the coagulant qualities of a bag of blood. I was about to reach for two glasses when I realized that, in addition to the apparent philosophical differences, he might ingest differently, too.

My hand on the open cabinet door, I turned back to him. "How do you take it?"

"Just pour it into a glass." He frowned, scratched absently at his temple. "You know, maybe we need to have some kind of mixer. Get Cadogan and Navarre vamps together, get them talking. It seems like there's a lot we don't know about each other."

"I was just thinking that the other day, actually," I said, thinking Ethan would be thrilled at the opportunity to build rapport, and potentially an alliance, with the folks from Navarre.

I pulled down waffle-etched glasses from a cabinet and opened the plastic valves in the top of the bags, filling a glass for each of us. I handed one to Morgan, and took a sip of mine.

Morgan sipped from his own glass, eyes on me as he drank. His eyes didn't silver, but his predatory, seductive gaze left little doubt about his line of thinking. He drained the glass without taking a breath, chest heaving when he finally finished it.

And then, with the tip of his tongue, he grabbed a single drop that had caught on his upper lip.

"I win," he said, very softly.

It took Mallory's voice to drag my gaze away from his mouth. "All right, kids," she said from the dining room, "I think we're ready."

I took the final drink from my glass, put both our glasses into the sink, and accompanied Morgan into the dining room. His tulips were in the vase and the accessories of fancy dining—place mats, cloth napkins, silverware, and wine-glasses—lay on the table before each of the four chairs. Our plates were already laden with food—fillets of salmon, herb-sprinkled rice, and spears of steamed asparagus—larger portions for the calorie-sucks that were modern-day vampires.

Catcher and Mallory were already seated on two sides of the table. We took the remaining two chairs, then Morgan picked up his wineglass and raised it to both of them. "To good friends," he said.

"To vampires," Mallory said, clinking her glass against mine.

"No," Catcher said. "To Chicago."

Dinner was great. Good food, good conversation, good company. Catcher and Mallory were entertaining, as usual, and Morgan was charming, listening intently to Mallory's stories of my antics.

Of course, because I'd been a grad student the entire time that I'd known her, there weren't that many antics to report. There were, however, plenty of stories about my geekiness, including the tale of what she called my "Juilliard" stage.

"She'd been in the middle of some kind of musical obsession," Mallory began, grinning at me. She'd pushed back her plate and crossed her legs on her chair, clearly prepped for a lengthy tale. I pre-cut the last of my salmon into tiny bites, ready to intervene should things get dicey.

"She'd rented, like, every musical DVD she could find, from *Chicago* to *Oklahoma*. Girl could not get enough of the singing and dancing."

Morgan leaned forward. "Did she watch *Newsies*? Tell me she watched *Newsies*."

Mallory pursed her lips to bite back a laugh, then held up two fingers. "Twice."

"Do go on," Morgan said, giving me a sideways glance. "I'm fascinated."

"Well," Mallory said, lifting a hand to push blue hair behind her ear, "you know Merit used to dance—ballet—but she eventually came to her senses. And by the way, I don't know what kind of freaky shit vampires are into, but if at all possible, stay away from her feet."

"Mallory Carmichael!" My cheeks heated with a blush I'm sure was crimson red.

"What?" she asked with a nonchalant shrug. "You danced in toe shoes. It happens."

I put an elbow on the table, my forehead in my hand. This, I bet, is what my life would have been like had my sister Charlotte and I been closer—the kind of intimate humiliation that only siblings could provide. For better or for worse and, God willing, in sickness and in health, Mallory was a sister.

A hand caressed my back. Morgan leaned over, whispered in my ear, "It's okay, babe. I still like you."

I gave him a sardonic look. "That feeling is not mutual at the moment."

"Mmm-hmmm," he said, then turned back to Mallory. "So our former ballerina was hooked on musicals."

"Not so much the musicals, but the style." Mallory looked at me, made an apologetic face.

I waved her off. "Just put it out there."

"Keep in mind, she went to NYU, then Stanford, then lands back in Chicago. And our Merit loved the Big Apple. The Windy City is a little more akin to New York living than California was, but it's far from having a walkup in the Village. But Mer decides she can make up for it. With clothes. So this one winter, she starts wearing leggings, big floppy sweaters, and always a scarf. She never left the house without a scarf kind of"—Mallory waggled her arms in the air—"draped all around her. She had a pair of brown knee-high boots, wore them every day. It was this whole 'ballerina chic' thing." Mallory adjusted on her seat, leaned forward, and crooked a finger at Morgan and Catcher. They both leaned forward, obviously entranced. The girl knew how to work a crowd.

"There was a beret."

They both let out groans, sat up again. "How could you?" Morgan asked with a mock horror that was belied by the laugh that was threatening to escape him. "A beret, Merit? Really?"

"You will never give me shit again," Catcher said. "I own you now. I own your ass."

I plucked at a bite of salmon, chewed it with careful deliberation, then waved my fork at them. "You are all on my shit list. All of you."

Morgan sighed happily, drained the last of his glass of wine. "This is good," he said. "This is really helpful. What else do I need to know?"

"Oh, she has tons of secrets," Mallory confided, with a grin to me. "And I know all of them."

Morgan, one arm slung on the back of his chair, made a beckoning movement with his free hand. "Let's go. Keep 'em coming."

"Mallory," I warned, but she only laughed.

"Well, let's see. I bet you didn't tell him about the secret kitchen drawer. You should clean that out while you're over here."

Morgan sat up straight and slid a glance behind him at the kitchen door. "Secret kitchen drawer?" Then he looked back at me, winged up eyebrows.

My answer was quick and vehement. *"No."*

He slid back his chair.

"Morgan, no."

He was halfway to the kitchen before I was out of my chair, laughing as I rushed after him. "Morgan! Damn it, stop! She was kidding. There's no such thing."

By the time I made it to the kitchen, he was pulling drawers open left and right. I jumped on his back and wrapped my arms around his shoulders. "She was kidding! I swear."

I expected him to throw me off, but he laughed, pulled my legs around his waist, and kept searching.

"Merit, Merit, Merit. You're too quiet. So many secrets."

"She was kidding, Morgan." In a desperate attempt to keep my secret drawer, well, *secret*, I kissed the top curve of his ear. He paused and cocked his head to the side to give me better access. But after I put my chin on the top of his head and said, "Thank you," he started searching again.

"Hey! I thought you were going to stop!"

"Then you're naïve." He pulled open another drawer, froze. *"Holy shit."*

I sighed and slid down his back. "I can explain this."

He pulled out the drawer—a long, flat bay intended for silverware—as far as it would go, and stared into it. He gaped, mouth open, at its contents before turning his head to look at me. "Anything you want to say?"

I gnawed the edge of my lip. "My parents didn't let me have candy?"

Morgan reached in and grabbed a handful of the drawer's contents—South American chocolate bars, bags of chocolate-covered dried cherries, chocolate pastiches, chocolate buttons, chocolate stars, chocolate lollipops, chocolate shells, chocolate-covered gingerbread Christmas tree cookies, a white-chocolate-covered Twinkie, chocolate caramels, cocoa from a small-batch chocolatier and a foot-long Toblerone bar. He looked at me, tried not to laugh, and, for all that effort, made a strangled, hiccupped sound. "And so you're compensating for that?"

I crossed my arms. "Do you have a problem with my stash?"

He made that sound again. "No?"

"Quit laughing at me," I ordered, but I was grinning when I said it. Morgan redeposited his handful of chocolate, closed the drawer, grabbed my hips, and arranged my body between his and the island.

He looked down at me with an expression of mock gravity. "I'm not laughing at you, Mer. Chortling, maybe, but not laughing."

"Ha." I gave him a baleful look that even I knew was unconvincing.

"Um, not to get personal, but I saw that dessert you brought. Were you planning on sharing that, or was that just your portion?"

"HA," I repeated.

"It's a good thing you're not obsessive. Oh, wait," he said dryly, "yes, you are."

"Some people like wine. Some like cars. Some," I said,

tugging at the hem of his undoubtedly designer T-shirt, "like fantastically expensive clothes. I like chocolate."

"Yeah, Mer, I can see that. But the real question is, do you apply that passion to other areas of your life?"

"I have no idea what you're talking about."

"Liar," he said, closing his eyes and lowering his lips to mine. Our lips had just touched when the silence was broken.

"Would you please stop feeling up my Sentinel?"

CHAPTER THIRTEEN

THEY'LL EAT YOU ALIVE

Ethan, in black pants and a snug, long-sleeved black shirt, stood at the threshold of Mallory's kitchen, hands in his pockets. His hair was tied back, the casualness of the ensemble indicating he had plans that didn't involve negotiations or diplomacy. Mallory and Catcher stood just behind him.

Morgan's eyes snapped open, emotion tightening his features and, for a fraction of a second, silvering his eyes.

I was just kind of dumbfounded. Why was Ethan here?

"If you want me to court her properly, Sullivan, you're going to need to give us some time alone." The words and tone were for Ethan, but his gaze was on me.

"My apologies for the . . . interruption," he said, but he couldn't have sounded more sarcastic. In fact, he sounded plenty happy to interrupt.

It was a long, quiet, awkward moment before Morgan finally looked over at him. They exchanged manly nods, these two Masters, the two men who together controlled the fates of two-thirds of the vampires in Chicago. Two men who claimed a little too much authority over my time.

"I'm sorry to steal her away," Ethan said, "but we have Cadogan House business."

"Of course." Morgan turned back to me, and in full view

of God and the assorted houseguests, kissed me softly. "At least we got dinner."

I looked up into baleful eyes. "I'm sorry."

"Sure."

Uncomfortable silence fell again until Morgan offered, "I guess I should get going and leave you two to your . . . business." His tone was petulant, as if he wasn't entirely convinced Ethan was here for Cadogan-related reasons. God only knew why Ethan had decided to darken Mallory's door. If he needed me, why hadn't he just paged me?

"I'll walk you out," I said.

Ethan, Catcher, and Mallory turned to their sides in the hallway, allowing us egress from the kitchen. Morgan walked out, me behind, both of us ignoring Ethan as we passed him.

I walked him to the door and resumed my position on the stoop.

"It's not your fault," Morgan said, his eyes on the house. There was no doubt about that—it's not like I invited Ethan over—but I wondered if he really thought me truly blameless. I'm sure he mostly blamed Ethan, but Morgan had raised questions before about my relationship with my Master. This probably wasn't helping.

Whatever his thoughts, he shrugged off the gloom and gave me a cheery smile, then bobbed his head toward the brownstone. "I suppose being an omnipotent Master has its advantages: having people at your beck and call."

"Don't you have people at your beck and call?" I asked, reminding him that he was one of the Masters he'd been referring to.

"Well, I do *have* them, but I don't think I've officially becked or called them yet. And I suppose this is the price of dating the hot shit Cadogan Sentinel."

"I'm not sure about hot shit, but the Sentinel part is true enough." I cast my own dark glance at the doorway; Ethan and Catcher communed in the hall. "Although I have no idea what this is about."

"I'd like to know."

I looked back at him, hoping he wasn't about to pump me for information. That concern must have shown on my face; he shook his head. "I'm not going to ask, I'd just like to know." Then his tone went flat—Master vampire flat. He must have been practicing. "I hope that if it's something that affects us all, he'll fill us in."

Don't bet on that, I thought.

After we said our goodbyes, I shut the door behind me and found everyone still standing in the hallway. Catcher and Ethan were in identical poses—chests back, arms crossed, chins dropped. Warriors in concentration. This was serious, then, and not just a means for Ethan to further irritate me.

When I joined them, they expanded their semicircle to let me in.

"I've learned," Ethan began, "that a rave was held earlier tonight. We need to check it out. We also need to hope that we're the only ones who've heard about it."

How Ethan had learned about the rave, given that his usual source for such things was standing beside him, was an interesting question.

Catcher and I were apparently on the same wavelength. "How'd you find out?" he asked.

"Peter," Ethan said. "He received a tip." That made sense, I thought, since Peter was known for his contacts. "A friend of his, a bartender at a club in Naperville, heard two vampires discussing the fact that they'd received the text message announcing the rave."

"Alcohol loosens the lips of the fanged?" Catcher sardonically asked.

"Apparently so," Ethan agreed. "The bartender didn't recognize the vampires—they were likely drifter Rogues. By the time Peter heard from his source and contacted Luc, the rave was long since over."

"So we can't stop it?" I asked.

Ethan shook his head. "But we have an opportunity to investigate with significantly less political maneuvering than might be required if we were crashing the party." Ethan looked at Catcher. "And speaking of political maneuvering, can you join us?"

Catcher gave a single nod, then looked at me. "Is your sword in the car?"

I nodded. "Will I need it?"

"We'll know when we get there. I've got some gear stashed here, flashlights and whatnot." He glanced at Ethan. "Did you bring your sword?"

"No," he said. "I was out."

We all stood silently, waiting for Ethan to elaborate, but got nothing.

"Then I suppose I'll play vamp outfitter. And I need to call Chuck," he said, then whipped his cell phone out of his pocket and flipped it open. "We're supposed to be a diplomatic corps," he muttered, "not the Hardy Boys. And you can see how well that's working out for us."

Mallory rolled her eyes at the mini-tirade. I figured it wasn't the first time she'd heard it. "I'll get dinner cleaned up," she offered.

"Whoa, whoa, whoa," Catcher said, stopping her escape with a hand on her arm. "Sorry, kid, but you're coming with us."

"With us?" I repeated, Mallory and I sharing the same deer-in-the-headlights look. I knew he wanted to foster her learning, but I wasn't sure this was the time for that.

"She needs the experience," Catcher answered, his eyes on Mallory. "And I want you there with me. You're my partner, my asset. You can do it."

There was a tightness around her eyes, but she nodded.

"That's my girl," he murmured, and pressed his lips to her temple. Then he released her, put the cell up to his ear, and trotted down the hallway toward the back of the house. "Sullivan," he called out, "you owe me one big fuck of a favor. And Merit, you might want to change your shoes."

"Noted," Ethan replied. "On both counts."

Mallory and I looked down at my pretty ballet flats. Red or not, I probably didn't want to wear them to investigate a bloodletting.

"I'll grab a pair of boots or something," she said. "I know

you left some here." Although I undoubtedly had a better sense of where my remaining clothes were, Mal walked away, leaving me to babysit Ethan. Not that I could blame her for taking the out.

We stood there silently for a moment, both of us making every effort to avoid looking at each other. Ethan's gaze lifted to the photographs along the hallway wall, the same wall I'd been pressed up against a couple of hours ago.

"Why me?" I asked him.

He turned back to me, brow arched. "Excuse me?" His voice was frosty. Apparently, he was fully in Master and Commander mode. Lucky me.

"Why are you here? You knew that I had plans tonight; you saw me leave. Luc was at the House when I left, as were the rest of the guards. They're all more experienced than I am. You could have called one of them. Asked for their help." And given me a break, I silently added. Given me a chance to get over the training session, to have a break from Celina and my father and vampire drama. To just be me.

"Luc is busy protecting our vampires."

"Luc is your bodyguard. He swore an oath to protect *you*."

An irritated shake of his head. "You're in this already."

"Luc was there when you explained the raves, helped you plan for my involvement, and I'm sure you've brought him up to speed about what we learned so far. He knows everything that I know."

"Luc was busy."

"I was busy."

"Luc isn't you."

The words were quick, clipped, and completely dumbfounding. That was twice that he'd surprised me in the span of a few minutes.

Catcher was lumbering down the hall again before I could fathom a response, the mesh strap of a black canvas duffel bag in one hand, the black lacquer sheath of his katana in the other. "Your grandfather is now in the know," he said when he reached us, then glanced at Ethan. "If I'm going, that means we're doing this official-like. I'm looking into this on behalf of the Ombud's office and, therefore, on behalf of the city."

"So there will be no need to contact additional authorities," Ethan concluded, and they shared a knowing nod.

I heard Mallory's footsteps on the stairs. She appeared with an old pair of knee-high leather boots in her hands.

"In case there's, you know, *fluids*," she said, handing me the shoes, "I figured the taller the better."

"Good call."

My shoes in hand, I looked at Mallory, who then turned to look at Catcher, her brows lifted. There was stubbornness in the set of her jaw; clearly, she wasn't going to give in as easily as he might have wished.

"It will be good practice," he told her.

"I have weeks of training to accomplish practice, Catcher. I'm an ad exec—or was, anyway. I have no business running around Chicago in the middle of the night"—she flailed an arm nervously in the air—"cleaning up after vampires. No offense, Merit," she said, with a quick apologetic glance. I shrugged, knowing better than to argue.

Catcher rubbed his lips together, irritation obviously rising. That irritation was clear in the twitch in his jaw, and the tingle of magic that was beginning to rise, unseen but tangible, in the air. "I need a partner," he said. "A second opinion."

"Call Jeff."

In the years I'd known Mallory, I'm not sure I'd ever seen her this stubborn. Either she wasn't eager to visit the rave site, or she wasn't thrilled about the idea of testing whatever powers Catcher was expecting her to practice. I could sympathize on both counts.

Catcher rubbed his lips together, then dropped the bag on the floor. "Give us a minute?"

I nodded. "Come on," I said to Ethan, taking his hand and ignoring the small spark of contact that tingled my palm as I pulled him toward the front door.

He followed without comment and kept his hand in mine until we reached the front door, until I unlaced our fingers to grab my keys from the table.

The evening was cool when we stepped outside, the fresh air a relief. I sat down on the top step of the stoop and exchanged date shoes for work shoes, then walked to the car, grabbed my sword, and dropped off the flats. When I turned around again, Mallory and Catcher were on the stoop, locking the door behind them. She came down the sidewalk first and stopped when she got to me.

"You good?" I asked her.

When she rolled her eyes in irritation, I knew she'd be okay. "I love him, Merit, I swear to God I do, but he is seriously, *seriously*, an ass."

I looked around her at Catcher, who gave me a sly smile. He may have been an ass, but he knew how to work our girl out of her fear.

"He has his moments," I reminded her.

Ethan's car was too small for the four of us. Mine, being bright orange, wasn't exactly suitable for recon work, so we settled into Catcher's sedan, boys in the front, girls in the back, the katanas across my and Mallory's laps. Catcher drove south and east, and the car was silent until I spoke up.

"So, what should we expect?"

"Blood," Catcher and Ethan simultaneously answered. "Worst case," Catcher added, "the bodies that accompany it." He glanced over at Ethan. "If things are that bad, you know I'll have to call someone," Catcher said. "We can blur the jurisdictional boundaries, but I'll be obligated to report that."

"Understood," Ethan said quietly, probably imagining worst-case scenarios.

"Lovely," Mallory muttered, rubbing a hand nervously across her forehead. "That's lovely."

"No one should be there," Ethan said, a softness in his voice. "And given that vampires rarely drink their humans to death—"

"Present company excluded," I muttered, raising a hand to my neck.

"—it's unlikely we'll find bodies."

"Unlikely," Catcher said, "but not impossible. It's not like these particular vamps are big on following the rules. Let's just be prepared for the worst, hope for the best."

"And what am I truly capable of contributing to this mission?" Mallory asked. As if in answer, she closed her eyes, her angelic face calm, lips moving to the cadence of a mantra I couldn't hear. When she opened them again, she looked down at her palm.

I followed her gaze. A glowing orb of yellow light floated just above her hand, a soft, almost-matte ball of light that illuminated the backseat of the car.

"Nicely done," Catcher said, eyes flicking back to us in the rearview mirror. Ethan half turned in his seat, his own eyes widening at the sight of the orb in her hand.

"What is it?" I whispered to her, as if greater volume would dissipate the glow.

"It's . . ." Her hand shook, and the orb wavered. "It's the condensation of magic. The First Key. Power." Her fingers contracted, and the orb flattened into a plane of light and disappeared. Her hand still extended, she glanced over at me, this girl who could single-handedly channel magic into light, and I understood perfectly the expression on her face: *Who am I?*

"That's not all you are," Catcher quietly said, as if reading her thoughts. "And that's not why I brought you. You know better than that. And the First Key isn't only about channeling power into light. You know that, too."

She shrugged and looked out the side window.

It was funny, I thought, that we'd had similar conversations with our respective bosses as we adjusted to our powers. I wasn't sure if she was fortunate or not to be sleeping with the man who critiqued her.

"Boys," I muttered.

She glanced over at me, total agreement in her eyes.

We drove through residential neighborhoods, passing one span of houses or townhouses or townhouses-being-rehabbed after another. As was the way in Chicago, the tenor of the street changed every few blocks, from tidy condos with neatly trimmed hedges to run-down apartment buildings with rusting, half-hung gates.

We stopped in an industrial neighborhood near the Lake in front of a house—the single remaining residential building on the block—that had definitely seen better days.

It was the final remnant of what had likely once been a prosperous neighborhood, a remnant now surrounded by lots empty of everything but trash, scraggly brush, and industrial debris. The Queen Anne–style home, illuminated by the orange glow of a single overhead streetlamp, had probably been a princess in its time—a once-inviting porch flanked by fluted columns; a second-floor balcony; gingerbread brackets now rotting and hanging from their corners. Paint peeled in wide strips from the wood shingles, and random sprouts of grass pushed for life amidst a front yard tangled with discarded plastic.

Catcher's duffel bag rested on the seat between Mallory and me, and I handed it to him through the gap in the front seats. He unzipped it and pulled out four flashlights, then rezipped the bag and placed it between him and Ethan. He passed out the flashlights to the rest of us. "Let's go."

Katana in hand, I opened my door.

The scent hit when we stepped outside the car, flashlights and swords in hand. Blood—the iron tang of it. I took a sudden breath, the urge to drink in the scent nearly overwhelming. And even more problematic, because *she* stirred. Ethan stopped and turned to me, an eyebrow raised in question.

I swallowed down the craving and pushed down the vampire, glad I'd had blood earlier. I nodded at him. "I'm fine." The dilapidation and lingering odor of decay helped staunch the need. "I'm okay."

"What's wrong?" Mallory asked.

"Blood," Ethan somberly said, eyes on the house. "The smell of it remains."

Mallory handed Catcher's belted sword to Ethan, and we buckled our katanas around our waists.

The neighborhood was silent but for the breeze-blown crackle of a floating plastic bag and the faraway thunder of a freight train. Without comment, Catcher took the lead. He flipped on his flashlight, the circle of light bobbing before him as he crossed the street and walked toward the house. Ethan followed, then Mallory, then me.

We stood at the curb, the four of us in line. Stalling.

"Is anyone still in there?" Mallory asked, trepidation in her voice.

"No," Ethan and I answered simultaneously. The lack of sound—and thank God for predatory improvements in hearing—made that clear.

Catcher took another step forward, fisted hands on his hips, and scanned the house. "I'm in first," he said, exercising his Ombud authority, "then Ethan, Mallory, Merit. Be prepared to draw." He looked at Mallory. "Don't go in too far. Just keep your mind open like we talked about."

Mal nodded, seemed to firm her courage. I'd have squeezed her hand if I'd had any courage to offer. As it was, my right hand was sweating around the nubby barrel of the flashlight, the fingers of my left nervously tapping the handle of my sword.

Catcher started forward, and we followed in the order he'd set, Ethan and me with katanas at our sides. This time the sound of Ethan's voice in my head didn't surprise me.

You can control the craving?

I assured him I could, and asked, *What am I looking for?*

Evidence. An indication of House involvement. How many? Was there a struggle?

Our line of amateur investigators picked our way up the sidewalk over broken concrete, brown glass, and plastic soda bottles. The small porch at the front of the house creaked ominously when Catcher stepped onto it. After waiting to be sure it wouldn't collapse beneath him, we followed. I risked a glance through a slender, dirt-smeared window. The room was empty but for the skeletal remains of a massive chandelier, all but a handful of its crystals gone. It seemed an oddly appropriate symbol of the house's current condition.

Catcher pushed open the ancient door. The smell of dampness, decay, and blood spilled onto the sidewalk. I breathed through my mouth to avoid the temptation, however minimal, of the blood.

We trundled into what had once been a foyer and spun our flashlights around. There was rotting mahogany beneath our feet and flocked velvet wallpaper around us, marred by ripping peels, water stains, and slinking trickles of water. At the other end of the room, a gigantic stairway curved up to the second floor. Piles of wood and congealed paint cans were stashed in a corner, the rooms dotted here and there with threadbare pieces of heavy furniture. The building had been stripped of moldings, light fixtures gone, probably to be sold off. I didn't see any blood, although the smell of it hung in the air.

"Choose your adventure, vampires," Catcher advised in a whisper. "East or west?"

Ethan looked toward the rooms on the east side of the house, then toward the stairway in front of us. His head lifted as his gaze followed the rising staircase to the second floor.

"Up," he decided. "Merit, with me. Catcher, first floor."

"Done," Catcher responded. He turned to Mallory and tapped a finger against his right temple, then his chest, then his temple again.

Mallory nodded. Must have been some kind of secret sorcerer code. She squeezed my hand, then followed him to the left.

The two of us alone in the foyer, Ethan glanced at me. "Sentinel, what do you know?"

I lifted my own gaze to the stairway and closed my eyes. Vision gone, I let the sounds and scents surround me.

I'd felt the stirrings of magic before—when Celina had tested me, when Mallory and Catcher fought and at my Commendation, when I'd basked in the flow of it, the air thick with the lambent magic of dozens of vampires.

Here, there were no currents. If any magic remained in the house, it was minimal. Maybe a tingle here and there, but nothing strong enough for me to separate, identify.

The house was equally silent of living things, but for the downstairs movements of Mallory and Catcher, the steady sound of Ethan's heartbeat, and the disturbing scurry of tiny slithering things beneath our feet and in the walls.

I shivered, squeezing my eyes closed and forcing myself to ignore the ambient sound.

I focused on scent, imagined myself a predator, primed for the hunt (full though I may have been of salmon and asparagus). The tang of blood was obvious, in such quantity that it floated like a cloud of invisible smoke, flowing down the stairs and through the room, overlying the smells of mildew and standing water. I stood quietly for a moment, ensuring that I had control of myself to continue to investigate, ensuring that *she* was sufficiently locked down to preclude her mad rush to the second floor, to the blood.

In the silence, the quietness, I caught something else. Something above the mustiness and dust and blood.

Something animal.

I tilted my head, instincts piqued. Was it prey? Predator?

It was faint, but it was there—a trace of fur and musk. I opened my eyes, found Ethan eyeing me curiously. "Animals?"

He nodded. "Maybe animals. Maybe shifters who aren't skilled at masking their forms. Good catch."

He beckoned me with a hand and headed for the stairs. Fear and adrenaline making me unusually compliant, I followed without comment, but switched our positions at the landing. In appropriate Sentinel manner, I took point, keeping my body between his and whatever nasties hid in the dark. He stayed close behind as I used my flashlight to guide our way across the glass-strewn floor. Moonlight streamed through dirty windows, so we probably could have managed the exploration without the flashlights. But the tool in my hand was comforting. And since I was in the lead, I wasn't about to turn it off.

Typical of an older home, the upper floor contained a maze of small bedrooms. The smell of blood grew stronger as we passed through the rooms on the right side, the wooden floors creaking as we progressed, the beam of our flashlights occasionally illuminating an abandoned piece of furniture or a puddle of dirty liquid being fed from a rust-colored stain in the ceiling.

The faint smell of animal lingered, but it lay beneath the other scents in the room. If a shifter had been here, it was in passing. He, or she, hadn't been a key player.

We kept moving through the tiny bedrooms to the back of the house until we reached the room at the end of the line. I paused before entering it, the smell of blood suddenly blossoming into the hallway. Adrenaline pumping, I locked down my vampire and circled the beam of light around the room. Then froze.

"Ethan."

"I know," he said, stepping beside me. "I see it."

This was where they'd congregated. The floor was littered with random trash, soda cans, and candy wrappers. A mirrored bureau stood along one wall, our reflection warped by the effect of time on the mirror's silver backing.

Most importantly, three dirty, stained mattresses lay in various spots around the room. The blue-and-white ticking that covered them bore obvious bloodstains. Large bloodstains.

Ethan stepped around me and used the beam of his flashlight to survey the room, wall to wall, corner to corner. "Probably three humans," he concluded, "one for each mattress, one for each spill of blood. Maybe six vampires, two per person, one at a wrist, the other at the neck. No bodies, and no signs of struggle. Blood, yes, but not obscene quantities. They appear to have stopped themselves." There was relief in his voice. "No murders, but nor did the humans receive whatever benefits they imagined they'd get." His voice had turned dryer at the end; clearly not much of a fan of the would-be fanged.

"Benefits," I repeated, swinging the beam to where Ethan stood, free hand on his hip, gaze shifting between the two mattresses that lay closest together. "When we were in your office, you mentioned something about becoming a Renfield?"

"A human servant," he said. "Offering protection to a

vampire during daylight hours, perhaps interacting with humans on the vampire's behalf. But we haven't had Renfields for centuries. A human might also imagine they would be given the gift of immortality. But if a vampire was to make another"—he paused and kneeled down to inspect the middle mattress—"this is not the manner in which such act would occur."

I checked out the other mattress, the circle of blood upon it. "Ethan?"

"Yes, Merit?"

"If drinking is so problematic, so risky to humans, why allow it? Why not remove the risk and outlaw drinking altogether? Make everyone use the bagged stuff? Then there's no politics to allowing the raves. You could outright ban them."

Ethan was quiet long enough that I turned back to him, and found him staring at me with eyes of pure, melting quicksilver.

My lips parted, the breath stuttering out of me.

"Because, whatever the politics of it, we are vampires." Ethan parted his lips, showed me the needle-sharp tips of his fangs.

I was shocked to the core that he let me see him in full hunger, shocked and aroused by it, and when he tipped his head down, silvered eyes boring into me, I swallowed down a rise of lust so thick and swift it tripped my heart.

The sound of my heartbeat, the hollow thud of it, pounded in my ears.

Ethan held out a hand, palm up, an invitation.

Offer yourself, he whispered, his voice in my mind.

I gripped the handle of my katana. I knew what I wanted to do—step forward, arch my neck, and offer him access.

For a second, maybe two, I considered it. I let myself wonder what it might be like to let him bite. But my control, already weakened by the smell of blood, threatened to tip. If I let my fangs descend, if I let *her* take over, there was a good chance I'd end up sinking them into the long line of his neck, or letting him do the same to me.

And while I wasn't naïve enough to deny that I was curious, intrigued by the possibility, this was neither the time nor the place. I didn't want my first real experience in sharing blood to be here in the midst of industrial squalor, in a house where the trust of humans had so recently been violated.

So I fought for control, shaking my head clear. "Point made," I told him.

Ethan arched a brow as he snatched back his hand, clenching his fist as he regained his own control. He retracted his fangs, and his eyes cleared, fading from silver to emerald green. When he looked at me again, his expression was clinical.

My cheeks flushed with embarrassment.

It had all been a teaching point, then. Not about desire or bloodlust but an opportunity for Ethan to demonstrate his restraint. I felt ridiculously naïve.

"Our reaction to blood," Ethan matter-of-factly began, "is predatory. Instinctual. While we may need to seclude our habits, assimilate into the larger population of humans, we are still vampires. Suppression favors none of us."

I looked around the room at the peeling paint, balled-up newspapers, spare mattresses, and crimson dots scattered across the splintered hardwood floor.

"Suppression leads to this," I said.

"Yes, Sentinel."

I was Sentinel again. Things were back to normal.

We searched the room but found no indication of Houses or anything else that might identify the drinking vamps. They'd avoided leaving obvious evidence behind, which wasn't all that surprising for folks who would travel to a deserted house in exchange for a few illicit sips.

"We know humans were here," Ethan said, "that blood was taken. But that's it. Even if we called someone in, without more evidence of what went on, the only thing to come from further investigation would be bad press for us."

I assumed Ethan meant he wasn't willing to involve the CPD in the rave investigation. I didn't disagree with him, especially since Catcher was here on behalf of the Ombud's office. On the other hand, if Ethan was really that comfortable suppressing information, he probably wouldn't have bothered justifying it to me.

"I guess that makes sense," I said.

"The locus," Ethan suddenly said, and I frowned in confusion, thinking I'd missed something. But he hadn't been talking to me—Catcher and Mallory stood in the doorway behind us. They both looked fine, neither showing any signs of having been accosted by a loitering raver. Catcher's expression was back to his normal one—slightly bored. Mallory cast uncomfortable glances at the mattresses on the floor.

"Yeah," Catcher agreed, "it looks like the action went down here." He surveyed the room, then walked a loop around it, arms crossed over his chest, face pinched in concentration.

"Three humans?" he finally asked.

"That's what it looks like," Ethan confirmed. "Possibly six vampires, and who knows if there were observers. We found no evidence of Houses."

"Even if House vamps were involved," Catcher said, meeting Ethan in front of the center mattress, "it's unlikely they'd leave any noticeable evidence behind, especially since the Houses don't sanction this kind of conduct. Much less drinking, for most of them."

Ethan made a sound of agreement.

Silence fell as the men reviewed the dirty beds before them. They consulted quietly as they walked around, crouched before, and pointed over the mattresses. I looked back at Mallory, who shrugged in response, neither of us privy to their conversations.

Catcher finally stood again, then glanced back at Mallory. "Are you ready?" His voice was soft, careful.

She swallowed, then nodded.

I wasn't sure what she was going to do, but I felt for her, assuming Mal was about to dive headfirst into the supernatural pool. Having taken that dive as well, I knew the first step off the board was a little daunting.

She held out her right hand, palm up, and stared down at it.

"Look through it," Catcher whispered, but Mallory didn't waver.

The air in the room seemed to warm, to become thicker, an aftereffect of the magic that Mallory was funneling, of the magic that was beginning to warp the air above her hand.

"Breathe through it," Catcher said. I lifted my gaze from Mallory's hand to his eyes, and saw the sensuality there. Vampires could feel magic; we could sense its presence. But sorcerers' relationships with magic were something altogether different. Something altogether lustier, if the look in his eyes was any indication.

Mal's tongue darted out to wet her lips, but her blue eyes stayed focused on the shimmer above her hand.

"Bloodred," she suddenly said, her voice barely audible, eerily gravelly, "in the rise of the moon. And like the moon, they will rise and they will fall, these White City kings, and she will triumph. She will triumph, until he comes. Until he comes."

Silence. It was a prophecy of some kind, the same skill I'd seen Catcher perform in Cadogan House once before.

Ethan glanced over at Catcher. "Does that mean anything to you?"

Catcher shook his head ruefully. "I suppose we shouldn't deride the gift, but Nostradamus was easier to understand."

I glanced back at Mallory. Her eyes were still closed, sweat dampening her brow, her outstretched arm shaking with exertion.

"Guys," I said, "I think she's about had it."

They glanced back.

"Mallory," Catcher softly said.

She didn't respond.

"Mallory."

Her eyes snapped up, her biceps shaking.

"Let it go," he said.

She nodded, wet her lips, glanced down at her hand, and spread her fingers. The shimmer of air disappeared. After a second, Mal wiped at her forehead with the back of her wrist.

"Are you okay?"

She looked at me, nodded matter-of-factly. "Just hard work. Did I say anything helpful?"

I shrugged. "Not so much helpful as super-creepy."

"I think we've gotten everything we can get," Ethan said, "unless you've any other ideas?"

"Not much," Catcher answered. "Vague sense of fear, the suggestion of an animal." He looked between us. "I assume you got that?"

We both nodded.

"Nothing at all beyond that. Nothing else recognizable in the current, and I'm not sure the shifter was here when this happened. Maybe afterward. Either way, no sense that the media has discovered this place, at least not yet." Catcher looked around the room, hands on his hips. "Speaking of, should I call in a crew? Have the place stripped, cleaned?"

It hadn't occurred to me that the Ombud's office had the authority or manpower to erase the evidence. They referred to themselves as liaisons, go-betweens. I guess they were a little more proactive than that.

"You can do that?" I asked.

Catcher gave me a sardonic look. "You really don't talk to your grandfather very often."

"I talk to my grandfather plenty."

Catcher snorted and turned, led us from the room. "Not about the good stuff. The city of Chicago has been keeping the sups' existence under wraps since before the fire, Merit. And that's not because incidents don't happen. It's because the incidents are taken care of."

"And the city is none the wiser?"

He nodded. "That's the way it works. People weren't prepared to know. Still aren't, for some of the shenanigans vamps get into."

We headed to the stairs in the same order we'd entered the house.

"If they were prepared now," Mallory said, "we wouldn't

be here. I mean, I know you guys have pennants and bumper stickers and whatnot, but drinking in the dark in a dilapidated house doesn't exactly scream assimilation. And now there's that business with Tate."

That stopped both Ethan and me in the middle of the staircase.

"What business with Tate?" he asked.

Mallory gave Catcher a pointed look. "You didn't tell them?"

"Other business to attend to," Catcher responded, hitching a thumb at the second floor behind us. "One crisis at a time."

Catcher continued down the stairs. With no other choice, we followed, the silence thick enough to cut through. Ethan practically trotted down the staircase. When we reached the front door, then the porch, then the sidewalk, Ethan stopped, hands on his hips. Mallory made a low whistle of warning. I prepared for Ethan's outburst, predicting quietly, "And the shit will hit the fan in four . . . three . . . two . . ."

"What business with Tate?" Ethan repeated, an edge of anger in his voice.

I bit back a smile, glad Catcher was the one Ethan was about to light into. That made a nice change.

Catcher stopped and turned back to Ethan. "Tate's staff has been calling the office," he said. "He's been asking questions about vampire leadership, about the Houses, about the Sentinel."

Since I was the only Sentinel in town, I perked up. "About me?"

Catcher nodded. "The General Assembly agreed to forgo vamp management legislation this year in lieu of investigation, to ensure that nothing too prejudicial was passed. But that wasn't too hard a choice, since greater Illinois doesn't have to deal with vampires in their midst—all the Houses are in Chicago. The City Council's getting antsy, though. I know you and Grey talked to your aldermen"—Ethan nodded at this—"but the rest of the council has concerns. There's talk about zoning, about curfews, regulations."

"And what's Tate's position on that stuff?" I asked.

Catcher shrugged. "Who the hell knows what Tate thinks?"

"And he still hasn't come to any of us," Ethan muttered, eyes on the ground, brow furrowed. "He hasn't talked to Scott or Morgan or me."

"He's probably not ready to talk to you in person," Catcher said. "Maybe doing his groundwork before he sets up that meeting?"

"Or he's keeping his distance on purpose," Ethan muttered. He shook his head in reprobation, then glanced at me. "What does he want to know about Merit?"

"Likes, dislikes, favorite flowers," Mallory put in.

"So not helping," I whispered.

"I'm not kidding. I think he's totally crushing you."

I snorted in disbelief. "Yeah. The mayor of Chicago is crushing on me. That's likely." Unlike Ethan, I had met Tate, and though he'd seemed likable enough, there was no way he was crushing on me.

"He just wants information," Catcher said. "I think at this point it's a vague curiosity. And frankly, his interest could be related to her parentage, rather than her affiliation."

Ethan leaned toward me. "At least I know you aren't feeding Tate information, or you'd surely have ferreted that out."

I clenched my jaw at the insinuation, which he'd made before, that I was some kind of informational spigot between the House and Tate's office. I decided I'd been on the receiving end of one too many speeches and snarky comments today. I glanced at Catcher and asked the same favor he'd asked of us earlier. "Would you two give us a minute?"

Catcher looked between us, grinned cheekily. "Knock yourself out, kid. We'll be in the car."

I waited until the car doors were shut before I stepped forward, stopped within inches of Ethan's body. "Look. I know why you gave me that speech earlier today. I know you have an obligation to protect your vampires. But irrespective of the way that I was made, I have done everything that you've asked of me. I've taken training, I gave up my dissertation, I moved into the House, I got you in to see my father,

I got you into the Breckenridge house, and I've dated the man you asked me to." I pointed at the house behind us. "And even though I was supposed to get a few hours free from the drama of Cadogan House tonight with said man, I followed you here because you requested it. At some point, Ethan, you might consider giving me a little credit."

I didn't wait for him to answer, but turned on my heel and went to the car. I opened the back door, climbed inside, and slammed it shut behind me.

Catcher caught my gaze in the rearview mirror. "Feel better?"

"Is he still standing there with that dumbstruck expression on his face?"

There was a pause while he checked, then a chuckle. "Yes, he is."

"Then, yes, I feel better."

The car was quiet on the ride north to Wicker Park, Ethan pissed at Catcher for not sharing information about Tate within his preferred time frame (i.e., immediately), Mallory napping in the backseat, apparently worn out by her magical exertions, and Catcher humming along with an ABBA marathon he'd found on an a.m. radio station.

We reached the brownstone and said our goodbyes. Catcher reminded me that I was scheduled to practice with him first thing tomorrow evening, and Mallory and I teared up at her transition to Apprentice Sorceress, at the fact that my time with her for the next six weeks would be largely limited to phone calls. But I trusted Catcher, and given that Celina was on the loose, I was glad Mal would be learning more about her gifts, her skills, her ability to wield magic. The more protection she had, the better I felt, and I was pretty sure Catcher felt the same.

Since we'd arrived separately, Ethan and I drove our respective cars back to Cadogan House—him in the sleek Mercedes, me in my boxy Volvo. I parked the Volvo on the street, glad I'd completed my round of obligations for the night so I could have at least a few hours to myself. But he met me in the foyer, cream-colored envelope in his hand. I adjusted my own armfuls of stuff—mail, shoes, sword—and took it from him.

"This was messengered to you," he said.

I opened it up. Inside was an invitation to a gala at my parents' house the next night. I made a face. Tonight had been long enough; it didn't look like tomorrow would afford much relief.

"Lovely," I said, then showed him the invite.

He read it over, then nodded. "I'll arrange for a dress. You have katana training with Catcher tomorrow?" At my nod, he nodded back. "Then we'll leave shortly after."

"What's on the agenda?"

Ethan turned and began walking back toward his office. I followed him, at least as far as the staircase.

"The agenda," he said when we paused, "is to continue our investigations. Your father is aware that we are interested in a threat involving the Breckenridges. Given what I know of him, it's likely he'll have done some checking of his own."

"You planned it," I said, thinking of the seeds he'd planted with my father. "Told him just enough about the Breckenridges, about the danger facing us, to make him want to ask questions." Although I wasn't thrilled about the thought of going home, I could appreciate a good strategy when I heard one. "That's not bad, Sullivan."

He gave me a dry look before turning toward his office. "I appreciate the vote of confidence. Until dusk," he said, and walked away.

Once in my room, I dumped my sword and my pile of mail, then kicked off my shoes. I'd left my cell phone in my room, since I'd planned to spend the evening with the only people likely to call me, but found a voice mail waiting.

It was from Morgan. He said he was checking in, ensuring that I'd gotten home safely. But I could hear the questions in his voice—where I'd been, what I'd been doing, what had been important enough to motivate Ethan to pull in a few-months-old Sentinel for duty. I still wasn't sure I had an answer to the last one.

I checked the clock; it was nearly four in the morning. I guessed Morgan would still be awake, but after a moment of hesitation, I opted not to call him back. I didn't want to dance around issues, and I wasn't in the mood to deal with his less-than-veiled animosity toward Ethan. The night had been long enough, contentious enough, without that.

With dawn threatening, I stripped out of my date ensemble and got into pajamas, then washed my face, grabbed a Moleskine journal and a pen, and climbed into bed. I scribbled random notes as the sun rose—about vampires, the Houses, the philosophy of drinking—and fell asleep, pen in hand.

CHAPTER FOURTEEN

THE CENTER CANNOT HOLD

I woke happy, at least until I remembered what the evening had in store. I grumbled and grabbed the invitation to the party at my parents' house. This one was a gala for a teen mentoring program. It's not that the cause wasn't legitimate, but I always wondered about my father's motivations. His interest in making connections, in shaking hands, was at least as big as any interest he had in actually helping the organization.

Rising tides lift all boats, I thought, and put the invitation on the bed. I sat up and pushed the hair out of my eyes, then uncurled my legs and hit the floor. I didn't bother to shower, knowing I'd just get sweaty again during my training session, but changed into my Catcher-approved ensemble—bandeaux bra and barely there shorts, throwing a track jacket over the top so I'd be decent during the drive.

Just as I zipped up the jacket, there was a knock at the door. I opened it and found Helen in the hallway in a tidy tweed suit.

"Hello, dear," she said, holding out a royal blue garment bag emblazoned with the logo of a chic-chic store in the Loop. "I was just dropping off your gown."

I took the bag from her hands, the weight not as heavy as I'd have expected given the size of the bag. Her hands free, she pulled a small pink notebook from the pocket of her nubby pink suit jacket. Nodding, she read it over.

"Tonight is a black-tie event. The color theme is black and white," she read, then lifted her gaze to mine. "That helped my selection process, of course, but it took no small bit of finagling to obtain a gown this quickly. It was delivered moments ago."

It bothered me, more than it should have, that she'd picked out the dress. That Ethan hadn't picked out the dress.

That it bothered me was just wrong in so many ways.

"Thank you," I told her. "I appreciate the effort." More's the pity she couldn't have taken my place.

"Of course," Helen said. "I need to get back downstairs. Plenty of work to do. Do enjoy the party." She smiled and tucked the notebook back into her pocket. "And be careful with the dress. It was rather an investment."

I frowned down at the garment bag. "Define 'investment.'"

"Near twelve, actually."

"Twelve? *Twelve hundred dollars?*" I stared at the dress bag, horrified at the thought that I was going to be responsible for four figures of Cadogan investment.

Helen chuckled. "Twelve thousand dollars, dear." She dropped that bomb, then headed back down the hallway, completely missing my look of abject horror.

Ever so carefully, as if carrying the Gutenberg Bible, I laid the dress bag on my bed.

"Take two," I murmured, and unzipped the bag.

A soft sound escaped me.

It was black silk, a fabric so delicate I could barely feel it between my fingers. And it was, indeed, a ball gown. A square strapless bodice that dropped to a spill of the luscious, inky silk.

I wiped my hands on my shorts, pulled the dress from the bag and held it up against my chest, spinning just to watch the skirt move. And move it did. The silk flowed like black water, the fabric the darkest shade of black I'd ever seen. It wasn't the kind of black that you confused with navy in the dressing room. It was *black*. Moonless, midnight black. It was stunning.

My cell rang, and I hugged the dress to my body with my free hand, scanned the caller ID, and flipped it open.

"Oh, my God, you should see this dress I'm wearing tonight."

"Did you just say something complimentary about a dress? Where's my Merit? What have you done with her?"

"I'm serious, Mallory. It's amazing. Black silk, this ball gown thing." I stood in front of the mirror, half turned. "It's beautiful."

"Seriously, I'm totally weirded out by the girly nature of this conversation. And yet, it's kinda like you're growing up. Do you think Judy Blume made a book about adolescent vampires? *Are You There God, It's Me, Merit*?" Mallory snorted, obviously pleased with herself.

"Ha, ha, ha," I said, placing the dress carefully on top of the garment bag. "I got an invitation to a deal at my parents', so we're heading back to Oak Park in a bit."

"Oh, that's classy, vampire. Forget about your old friends now that you're all high society."

"I'm torn between two answers. First, the obvious one: I just saw you last night. Also acceptable: Were we friends? I thought I was using you for rent and gratuitous branding."

"My turn to laugh," she said, instead of actually laughing. "Seriously, I'm on the road, driving to Schaumburg, and I wanted to check on you. I assume you and Darth Sullivan got back to Cadogan okay?"

"We didn't get chased by raving vampires, so I'd call it a successful return trip."

"Was Morgan okay about having to leave last night?"

Phone pinched between shoulder and ear, I tightened my ponytail. "He probably wasn't thrilled about being replaced by Ethan, but I haven't had a chance to talk to him."

"What do you mean you haven't talked to him? He's practically your boyfriend."

I frowned at the disapproval in her voice. "He's not my boyfriend. We're still just . . . dating. Kind of."

"Okay, semantics, whatever, but don't you think you should have called him?"

I'm not sure if it was because I thought she was being nosy or because, on some level, I agreed with her, but the direction of the conversation bothered me. I tried laughing it off. "Are you lecturing me about my boyfriend choices?"

"I just . . . He's a great guy, Merit, and you guys seem to have a great time together. I just don't want you to pass that up for . . ."

"For?" I didn't need to prompt her, didn't need to ask it. I knew exactly what she meant, exactly whom she was referring to. And while I knew she cared about me as much as anyone did, the comment pricked. A lot.

"Merit," she said, my name apparently standing in for the one she didn't want to say aloud.

"Mallory, I'm really not in the mood for this right now."

"Because you have to run off and play with Ethan?"

We were doing this, I thought to myself. My best friend and I were actually going to have this argument.

"I'm doing what I have to do."

"He's manipulating you into spending time with him."

"That's not true, Mallory. He hardly even likes me. We're just trying to deal with this rave problem right now."

"Don't make excuses for him."

Ire rising, vampire rising, I kicked my closet door closed with enough force to rattle a silver-framed picture of Mallory and me that sat on the top of the bureau next to it. "You know I'm not Ethan's biggest fan, but let's face facts. I'd be in the ground if it wasn't for him. And for better or worse, he's my boss. I don't really have a lot of room to maneuver on this."

"Fine. Deal with Ethan on your own terms. But at least be honest about Morgan."

"What is *that* supposed to mean?"

"Merit, if you don't like Morgan, then fine, break it off. But don't lead him on. It's not fair. He's a good guy, and he deserves better than that."

I made a sound that was equal parts shock and hurt. "I'm leading him on? That's a really shitty thing to say."

"You need to make up your mind."

"And you need to mind your own business."

I heard the sharp intake of breath, knew that I'd hurt her. I immediately regretted it, but was too angry, too tired of having no control over my body, my life, my time, to apologize. She'd hurt me, and I slapped back.

"We need to end this conversation before we say something we're going to regret," I quietly said. "I've got enough to deal with, not to mention the fact that I have to be at my father's in a couple of hours."

"You know what, Merit, if your dating life isn't my business, then your daddy issues aren't, either."

I couldn't speak, couldn't fathom how to respond to that. And even if I'd wanted to, emotion tightened my throat.

"Maybe it's the genetics," she continued, apparently unwilling to abandon the argument. "Maybe it's the person he's asking you to be. We both have different lives now, bigger lives, than we did a few months ago. But the Merit I knew wouldn't push this boy away. Not this boy. Think about that."

The phone went dead.

The windshield wipers slapped against the glass as I drove, the summer night wet and humid, fast-moving clouds whipping through the sky below a darker, ominous mass that pulsed with branching threads of lightning. I parked directly in front of the architecturally austere building that held the gym where I trained with Catcher, and ran inside to avoid the falling rain.

Catcher was already there. He stood in the middle of the blue gymnastics mat that filled the training room, wearing a T-shirt and warm-up pants. His head was bowed, eyes closed, hands pressed together prayerfully.

"Take a seat," he said, without opening his eyes.

"Good evening to you, too, *sensei*."

He opened a single eye, and the look he gave me left no doubt about how unfunny he'd found the retort. "Take a seat, Merit." This time his words were biting.

I arched a brow back at him, but stripped off my track jacket and took a seat in one of the orange plastic chairs near the door.

Catcher remained in his pose of quiet concentration for a

few minutes, finally rolling his shoulders and opening his eyes.

"Done with meditation?" I lightly asked.

He didn't respond, but strode forcefully toward me, enough malevolence in his gaze to speed my heart.

"Is there a problem?" I asked him.

"Shut it."

"Excuse me?"

Shut. It." Catcher stepped before me, pulled a hand across his jaw, then put his hands on the arms of the chair. He leaned forward. His torso arched over mine, I hunched back into the chair.

"She is my top priority."

I didn't need to ask who "she" was. Obviously, Mal had called Catcher.

"She is unhappy." He paused, pale green eyes tracking back and forth across my face. "She's having a difficult time. And I get that you're having a difficult time, Merit. Jesus knows, we all get it. You had problems adjusting to the transition from human to vampire, and now you appear to have trouble remembering your humanity."

He leaned incrementally forward. My heart began to thud, warmth flowing through my body as anxiety and adrenaline pulled the vampire from slumber, pushed her closer to the surface.

Not now, I begged her. *Not now*. He'd see, he'd know, and he'd handle me. Nothing good could come from that. For a split second, I thought he knew, his brow knitting as he leaned over me. I closed my eyes, counted backward, tried to push her down even as I felt him above me, the bulk of his body perched over my chair, the faint sizzle of latent magic electrifying the air.

Slowly, one drop at a time, I felt her recede.

"She's having trouble adjusting, Merit, just like you did. And she was there for you. It's time for you to be there for her. Cut her a little slack. I know she said some . . . regrettable things. And believe me, she knows it."

I opened my eyes, kept my gaze on his T-shirt and nodded, a little.

With a creak of plastic, he straightened, took a step backward, and looked down at me, arms crossed. This time his expression bore a hint of sympathy. His voice was softer, too. "I know you're trying to help Ethan. Trying to get him access, trying to do your job. I get that. And maybe that's the problem here, maybe it isn't. Frankly, that's your business, not mine. But before you alienate everyone who cares about you, Mallory or Morgan or whoever, remember who you were before this happened, before you were changed. Try to find some balance. Try to find a place in your life for the things that mattered before he changed you." He started to turn away, but apparently thought better of it. "I know you have limited time today, but you better be willing to bust your ass. If you're going to stand Sentinel, then you will damn well be prepared for it."

I shook my head, irritated that he'd assumed it was a lack of effort, of trying, that kept me from being the fighter he wanted when, in fact, it was the opposite. "You don't get it," I told him.

His eyebrows lifted, surprise obvious on his face. "Then enlighten me."

I looked at him, and for a long, quiet moment I nearly did tell him. I nearly trusted him, trusted myself, enough to ask him about it, to tell him that I was broken—that my vampire was broken. Separate, somehow. But I couldn't bring myself to do it. I'd tried to broach the subject once; he'd shaken off my concern. So I shook my head, lowered it.

"I don't know what you know," he said, "or what you've seen, or what you think you've done. But I advise you to find someone you can trust, and spill those beans. *Capiche?*"

Silently, I nodded.

"Then let's get to work."

We did. He wouldn't allow me to spar, given what he'd deemed my subpar effort two days ago. It was a punishment in his eyes, but a moral victory for me, allowing me to put my effort into movement and speed rather than holding back the predatory instinct that threatened to overwhelm me. And besides—since we hadn't been sparring, and thus didn't risk damaging the blades, he let me practice with my katana.

We worked through the first seven Katas for nearly an hour. While the movements of each Kata lasted only a few seconds, Catcher made me repeat the steps—over and over and over again—until he was satisfied with my performance. Until the moves became rote, until my movements were mechanically precise, until I could move so quickly through them that the gestures were blurred by speed. That fast, the Katas lost some of their tradition, but they made up for it in dance. Unfortunately, as Catcher pointed out, if I needed to use a sword in a fight, it would likely be against a vampire who was moving as quickly as I was.

After he'd taught me the basic movements of a second set of Katas, these using only one hand on the sword, he released me.

"I'm seeing some improvement," he said, when we'd settled on the blue mat, a spread of katana-cleaning implements before us.

"Thanks," I told him, sliding a piece of rice paper along the sword's sharpened edge.

"The interesting question is, why don't I see the same kind of effort when you're sparring?"

I glanced over at him, saw that his gaze was still on his sword. He clearly didn't understand that I'd been working double time to help him. And I'd already decided not to tell him, so I didn't answer the question. We were silent for a moment, both of us wiping down our blades, me refusing to answer.

"No answer?" he finally asked.

I shook my head.

"You are as stubborn as she is, I swear to God."

Without comment, although I agreed, I slid my sword into its sheath.

CHAPTER FIFTEEN

I COULD HAVE DANCED ALL NIGHT

Back at the House, I showered and arranged undergarments, then slipped on my thigh holster and strappy heels. I opted for an updo tonight, twisting my hair into a knot at the back of my neck. All the basics accomplished, I slithered carefully into the dress. Short timing or not, the fit was exquisite. The dress was exquisite. Pale skin, dark hair, glossy lips, black dress. I looked like an exotic princess. A vampire princess.

But the lingering sting of my fight with Mallory lessened a little of the fairy tale.

As ready as I could be, I grabbed my clutch and scabbard and went downstairs, where Mallory's devil waited.

He stood in the foyer, hands in his pockets, lean body clad in a tuxedo. Black, crisply shouldered, a perfect bow tie at his neck. His hair was down, the gold of it straight around his face, highlighting cruelly perfect cheekbones, emerald eyes. He was almost too handsome, untouchably handsome, the face of a god—or something altogether more wicked.

"What's wrong?" he asked, without looking up.

I reached the first floor, shook my head. "I'd rather not talk about it."

That lifted his gaze, his lips parting infinitesimally as he took in the waterfall silk. "That's a lovely dress." His voice was soft, somehow that much more intensely masculine.

I nodded, ignoring the undertone. "Are we ready?"

Ethan tilted his head to the side. "Are you ready?"

"Let's just go."

Ethan paused, then nodded and headed for the stairs.

He let me be silent for most of the ride to Oak Park, which was considerably faster than the trip to the Breckenridge estate. But while he didn't talk, he kept turning to look at me, casting worried, surreptitious glances at my face, and a few more lascivious ones at other parts of my anatomy.

I noticed them, but ignored them. In the quiet of the car, my thoughts kept going back to my conversation with Mallory. Was I forgetting who I'd been, my life before Cadogan House? I'd known Mal for three years. Sure, we'd had a spat or two along the way. We'd been roommates, after all. But never something like this. Never an argument where we questioned the other's choices, where we questioned our roles in each other's lives. This was different. And it was, I feared, the harbinger of unfortunate things. Of the slow dissolution of a friendship already weakened by physical separation, new ties, supernatural disasters.

"What happened?"

Since Ethan's question was softly spoken and, I thought, sincere, I answered it. "Mallory and I had a fight." About you, I silently added, then said aloud, "Suffice it to say, she's not happy with the person, the vampire, I'm becoming."

"I see." He sounded as uncomfortable as you might expect a boy, even a four-hundred-year-old boy, to sound.

I skipped a responsive nod, fearful that the movement would trip the tears, smear my mascara, and leave track marks down my face.

I really, really wasn't in the mood for this. Not to go to Oak Park, to play dress-up, to be in the same room as my father, to pretend at being that girl.

"I need a motivational speech," I told him. "It's been a pretty awful night so far, and I'm fighting the urge to take a cab right back to Cadogan House and spend an intimate evening with a couple of deep-dish meat pies. I could use one of those 'Do it for Cadogan!' lectures you're so fond of."

He chuckled, and the sound of it was comforting somehow. "How about I tell you that you look radiant?"

The compliment was probably the best, and worst, thing he could have said. Coming from him, it felt weightier, more validating, than it should have. And that bothered me. A lot.

Scared me. A lot.

God, was Mal right? Was I sabotaging my relationship with Morgan for this man? Was I exchanging real friendships, real relationships, for the possibility of Ethan? I felt like I was spiraling around in some kind of vampire whirlpool, the remnants of my normal life draining away. God only knew what would be left of me.

"How about I remind you," he began, "that this is your opportunity to be someone else for a few hours. I understand, maybe better than I did before, that you're different from these people. But tonight you can leave the real Merit in Hyde Park. Tonight, you can play make-believe. You can be . . . the girl they weren't expecting."

The girl they weren't expecting. That had kind of a nice ring to it. "That's not bad," I told him. "And certainly better than the last speech you gave me."

He made a Master-vampire-worthy huff. "As Master of the House—"

"—it's your duty to give me the benefit of the doubt," I finished for him. "And to motivate me when you can." I glanced at him. "Challenge me, Ethan, if you need to. I understand a challenge; I can rise to it. But work from the assumption that I'm trying, that I'm doing my best." I glanced out the window. "That's what I need to hear."

He was quiet so long I thought I'd angered him. "You are so young," he finally said, poignancy in his voice. "Still so very human."

"I'm not sure if that's a compliment or an insult."

"Frankly, Merit, neither am I."

*　　*　　*

Twenty minutes later, we pulled into the circle drive in front of my parents' blocky Oak Park home. The house was a stylistic orphan, completely different from the Prairie-style, Wright-homage houses around it. But my parents had had enough sway over Chicago's political administration to get the plans approved. So here it sat, a rectangular box of pasty gray concrete in the middle of picturesque Oak Park.

Ethan stopped the Mercedes in front of the door and handed the keys to one of the ubiquitous valets that apparently haunted these kinds of galas.

"The architecture is . . . interesting," he said.

"It's atrocious," I replied. "But the food's usually pretty good."

I didn't bother knocking at the front door, nor did I wait to get an invitation into the house. Like it or not, this was my ancestral home; I figured I didn't need an invitation. More important, I hadn't bothered on my first trip back to the house shortly after I'd been changed. And here I was, the prodigal daughter, making her return.

Pennebaker, the butler, stood just inside the concrete-and-glass foyer, his skinny, stiff frame bowing at each passing guest. His nose lifted indignantly when I approached him.

"Peabody," I said in greeting. I loved faking him out.

"Pennebaker," he corrected in a growl. "Your father is currently in a meeting. Mrs. Merit and Mrs. Corkburger are entertaining the guests." He slid his steely gaze to Ethan and arched an eyebrow.

"This is Ethan Sullivan," I interjected. "My guest. He's welcome."

Pennebaker nodded dismissively, then looked back to the guests behind us.

That hurdle passed, I led Ethan away and began the trek toward the long concrete space at the back of the first floor where my parents entertained. Along the way, bare, angular hallways terminated in dead ends. Steel mesh blinds covered not windows but bare concrete walls. One stairway led to nothing but an alcove showcasing a single piece of modern art that would have been well suited to the living room of a maniacal serial killer. My parents called the design "thought-provoking," and claimed it was a challenge to the architectural mainstream, to people's expectations of what "stairways" and "windows" were supposed to be.

I called the design "contemporary psychopath." The space was packed with people in black-and-white clothing, and a jazz quintet provided a sound track from one of the room's corners. I glanced around, looking for targets. There were no Breckenridges in sight, and my father was equally absent. Not that that was a bad thing. But I found something just as interesting near the bank of windows that edged one side of the room.

"Prepare yourself," I warned him with a grin, and led him into the fray.

They stood together, my mother and sister, eyes scanning the crowd before them, heads together as they gossiped. And there was no doubt they gossiped. My mother was one of the ruling matrons of Chicago society, my sister an up-and-coming princess. Gossip was their bread and butter.

My mother wore a conservative gown of pale gold, a sheath and bolero jacket well suited for her trim frame. My sister, her hair as dark as mine, wore a pale blue sleeveless cocktail dress. Her hair was pulled back, a thin, glossy black headband keeping every dark strand in place. And in her arms, currently chewing on her tiny, pudgy fist, was one of the lights of my life. My niece, Olivia.

"Hi, Mom," I said.

My mother turned, frowned and touched fingers to my cheek. "You look thin. Are you eating?"

"More than I've ever eaten in my life. It's glorious." I gave Charlotte a half hug. "Mrs. Corkburger."

"If you think having my daughter in my arms will prevent me from swearing at you," Charlotte said, "you are sorely mistaken." Without batting an eyelash—and without explaining why she planned on swearing at me—she passed over my eighteen-month-old niece and the nubby burp cloth that rested on her shoulder.

"Mehw, mehw, mehw," Olivia gleefully sang, hands clapping as I took her in my arms. I was pretty sure she was singing my name. Olivia, having missed out on the dark-haired Merit gene, was as blond as her father, Major Corkburger, with a halo of curls around her angelic face and bright blue eyes. She was wearing her party best, a sleeveless pale blue dress the same color as Charlotte's, with a wide blue satin ribbon around the waist.

And by the way, yes. My brother-in-law's given name really was Major Corkburger. But for the fact that he was a blond-haired, blue-eyed former college quarterback, I'd have assumed he got the crap beat out of him in high school on a daily basis for that one. Nevertheless, I rarely failed to remind him that he was, in fact, a major Corkburger. I don't think he thought that was funny.

"Why are you going to swear at me?" I asked Charlotte, once I'd arranged Olivia and placed the cloth prophylactically on my shoulder.

"First things first," she said, eyes on Ethan. "We haven't been introduced."

"Oh. Mom, Charlotte, this is Ethan Sullivan."

"Mrs. Merit," Ethan said, kissing my mother's hand. "Mrs. Corkburger." He did the same to my sister, who nibbled the edge of her lip, one eyebrow arched in obvious pleasure.

"It is just . . . *lovely* to meet you," Charlotte intoned, then crossed her arms. "And how have you been treating my little sister?"

Ethan snuck a glance my way.

Don't look at me, I silently told him, assuming he could hear me. *This was your idea. You got yourself into it, so you can get yourself out.* I couldn't hold back a grin.

Ethan rolled his eyes, but seemed amused. "Merit is a very unique vampire. She has a certain . . ."

We all leaned forward a little, eager to catch the verdict.

". . . star quality."

He looked at me when he said it, a hint of pride in his emerald green eyes.

I was stunned enough that I couldn't quite manage to get out a thank-you, but there must have been sufficient shock in my eyes that he couldn't have missed it.

"You have a lovely home, Mrs. Merit," Ethan lied to my mother. She thanked him, and the conversation about the benefits and disadvantages of living in an architectural masterpiece began. I figured that gave me at least ten or fifteen minutes to catch up with Charlotte.

Charlotte looked at him with approval, then smiled smartly at me. "He is delish. Tell me you've hit that."

"Ugh. I have not 'hit that.' Nor do I plan to. He's trouble in a very pretty package."

Head tilted, she gave Ethan's body a complete scan. "Very pretty package indeed. I'm thinking he might be worth the trouble, little sister." She looked back at me, then frowned. "Now, what's going on with you and Daddy? You're fighting, and then you're a vampire, and then you're still fighting, and now, all of a sudden, you're here. At a party. In a *dress*."

"It's complicated," was my admittedly weak retort.

"You two need to sit down and hash some things out."

"I'm here, aren't I?" She didn't need to know exactly how much I'd dreaded it. "And as for the fighting, he's threatened to disinherit me twice in the last month."

"He threatens to disinherit everyone. You know how he is. You've known for twenty-eight years."

"He hasn't threatened Robert," I pointed out, my voice sounding every bit the petulant little sister.

"Well, obviously not Robert," Charlotte dryly agreed, reaching out to straighten the hem of Olivia's dress. "Dearest Robert can do no wrong. And speaking of family drama, did I get a phone call to tell me my baby sister was a vampire? No. I had to find out from Daddy." She flicked the tip of my ear with her thumb and index finger.

I guess that explained why she wanted to swear at me. "Hey!" I said, covering an ear with my non-baby-cradling hand. "That wasn't funny when I was twelve, and it's not funny now."

"Act your age, and I'll act mine," she said.

"I am acting my age."

"All evidence to the contrary," she muttered. "Just do me a favor, okay?"

"What?"

"Just try, for me? For better or worse, he's the only father you've got. And you're the only immortal Merit, as far as I'm aware anyway. I don't think Dearest Robert has acquired immortality yet, but that might only require a few dollars pressed into the right hands."

I smiled and relaxed a little. Charlotte and I weren't close, but I could appreciate her hands-on approach to sarcasm. And, of course, we shared a heady dose of sibling rivalry with Robert.

"About that immortality thing," she said. "Maybe now is the time for you and Daddy to mend some fences."

My eyes widened at the sudden seriousness in her voice.

"You'll be here longer than the rest of us," she said. "You'll be alive long after we're gone. After I'm gone. You'll watch my children and my grandchildren grow up. You'll watch them, and you'll watch over them. And that's your responsibility, Merit. I know you have duties to your House; I've learned enough in the last two months to understand that. But you're also a Merit, for better or for worse. You have the ability—you're the only one of us who does—to keep them safe."

She let out a haggard sigh, a motherly sigh, and settled serious eyes on her daughter, tugging again at her dress. I wasn't sure if it was a nervous movement, something to do with her hands, or just the simple comforting act of touching her child.

"There are crazy people in the world," she continued. "Being made a vampire certainly doesn't inoculate against crazy. They say—what was her name?"

No need to ask who she meant. "Celina."

"Celina. They say she's been confined, but how would we know that?"

She turned her gaze back on me, and I saw a mother's concern, and a mother's suspicion, in her eyes. She may have wondered if Celina had been released, but she didn't know. My father, apparently, had kept his word, and hadn't revealed what Ethan had told him.

I could have spilled the beans to Charlotte, told her things that would frighten her further, things that would impress upon her the need to keep her family close, to keep them safe.

Instead, I kept the burden in my hands. "It's taken care of," I said simply.

It wasn't, of course, taken care of. Celina was out there somewhere. She knew where I was, and she probably wasn't above going after my family to show how irritated she was with me. I assumed that's what I was to her—an irritation. An unfinished project.

But if I could swear two oaths to a stranger—in front of a House full of strangers—I could swear a silent one to Charlotte that I would watch over Olivia and her older brothers and sister, and if I stayed alive long enough, over their children. I could promise that I would stand Sentinel for the family that had given me my name, just as I would for the family I'd given a name for.

"It's taken care of," I repeated, meaning it, instilling my voice with the sincerity of belief that I'd take a stake myself before I'd let anything happen to Olivia.

She looked at me for a long, quiet time, then nodded, our understanding reached, the deal done. "P.S., that dress is foul."

Startled by both the abrupt change in conversation and the comment, I shifted Olivia's weight to the side to look down at my dress.

Charlotte shook her head. "Not yours. Lucy Cabot's." She pointed into the crowd at a woman draped in a polka-dotted tent of organza. "Horrendous. No, yours is lovely. I saw it at Fashion Week, can't remember who designed it. Badgley? I forget. Regardless, your stylist did good." She cast a sly glance back at Ethan, who was chatting up my mother. "And your accessories are fabulous."

"He's not my accessory," I reminded her. "He's my boss."

"He's fine, is what he is. He could sexually harass me any day."

I glanced down at the youngest Corkburger, who blinked wide blue eyes at me as she gnawed the end of her burp cloth. "Earmuffs, much?"

"Murf," Olivia said. I wasn't sure if that was gas or an attempt to mimic my words. I bet the latter. Olivia adored me.

"Honey," Charlotte said, "it's the twenty-first century. Vampires are chic, the Cubs have a pennant, and it's perfectly acceptable for a woman to find a man attractive. These are all things my daughter needs to know about."

"Especially the Cubs part," I said, waving the burp cloth at Olivia to her joyful cheers. She clapped her hands with the slow awkwardness and simple glee of a child.

"If you could live at Wright and Addison, you would," Charlotte predicted.

"That is true. I do love my Cubbies."

"And so often for naught." She smirked, then clapped her hands and held them out to Olivia, who bounced in my arms and leaned toward her mother, holding out her own hands. "It's been lovely catching up, sister, but I need to get this one home and into bed. Major's home with the rest of the troops. I just wanted to have a chance to say hi and let you visit your favorite niece."

"I love all your children equally," I protested, passing back the heavy, warm bundle of baby.

Charlotte snickered and balanced Olivia on her hip. "I'm going to be a good mommy and pretend that's true, whether it is or not. As long as you love my children more than Robert's, we're good." She leaned in, pressed a kiss against my cheek. "Night, little sister. And by the way, if you have the chance with Blondie, take it. Please. For me."

The lascivious look she cast in Ethan's direction when she pulled back left little doubt about what "chance" she meant me to take.

"Good night, Char. My love to Major. Good night, Livie."

"MEWH!" she cried, bouncing on her mother's hip. But the night had apparently taken its toll, and her blond head drooped to Charlotte's shoulder, her eyelids slowly closing. She fought it, I could tell, tried to keep her eyes open and her gaze on the dresses and partygoers around her. But when she popped a thumb into her mouth, I knew she was done. Her lids fell shut and this time stayed there.

Charlotte said her goodbyes to Ethan, managing not to wrap manicured fingers around his ass, and my mother excused herself to see to the rest of her guests.

"You're wearing a very serious expression," Ethan said, reaching my side again.

"I was reminded that I owe certain obligations to my family. That there are services I can provide."

"Because of your immortality?"

I nodded.

"It does impose a sense of obligation to one's family and friends," he agreed. "Just be careful that you don't give in to the guilt of it. That you have been given a gift, even if others cannot share in it, does not diminish its value. Live your life, Merit, the many years of it, and be grateful."

"Has that attitude worked for you?"

"Some days better than others," he admitted, then glanced at me. "I assume you'll need feeding soon?"

"I'm a girl, not a pet. But, realistically, yes. I pretty much always do." I pressed a hand to the thin black silk above my stomach. "Are you always hungry? I am *always* hungry."

"Did you eat breakfast?"

"I had part of a granola bar before training."

Ethan rolled his eyes. "That might explain something," he said, but beckoned a waitress in our direction. The young woman, who couldn't have been more than eighteen, was dressed, like all the waiters, in head-to-toe black. She was pale, and a flow of straight red hair spilled across her shoulders. When she reached us, she extended a square ceramic tray loaded with hors d'oeuvres toward Ethan.

"What have we got?" I asked, eyes scanning the platter. "I

hope there's something with bacon. Or prosciutto. I'd take anything cured or smoked."

"You're Ethan, right?"

I lifted my gaze from what looked like prosciutto-wrapped asparagus (score!) and found the waitress—her bright blue eyes big as saucers—gazing dreamily at Ethan.

"I am, yes," he answered.

"That's just . . . that's just . . . *great*," she said, her cheeks mottled with crimson. "Are you—you're like a Master vampire, right? The head of Cadogan House?"

"Um, yes. I am."

"That's just—*wow*."

We stood there for a moment, the waitress, lips parted, blinking doe eyes at Ethan, and Ethan, much to my amusement, shifting his feet uncomfortably.

"How about we'll just take that," he finally said, pulling the tray carefully from her outstretched hands. "And thank you for bringing it."

"Oh, no, thank you," she said, grinning dopily at him. "You're just . . . that's just . . . great," she said again, then turned to skip away through the crowd.

"I believe you have a fan," I told him, biting back a snicker.

He gave me a sardonic look, offered his tray. "Dinner?"

"Seriously. You have a fangirl. How bizarre. And, yes, thank you." I looked over the offerings, hand poised above the tray, and settled on a wooden-toothpick-staked cube of beef accompanied by a greenish sauce. As a vampire, I didn't care for the staked-meat analogy, but I wasn't going to turn down what was probably a choice cut.

"I'm not sure if your shock about my having a human fan is insulting or not."

"Much like everything else about me, it's endearing." I popped the beef into my mouth. It was delicious, so I scanned the tray, prepared for a second dive, and nabbed a pastry cup full of a spinach concoction.

It was also delicious. Say what you wanted about my

father—and I mean that literally: be my guest—but the man had good taste in caterers. You'd find no whipped shellfish at a Joshua Merit party.

"Would you like me to give you a few minutes with the tray?"

I glanced up at Ethan, my fingers poised over another beef cube, and grinned. "Could you, just? We'd really like to be alone right now."

"I think that means you've had enough," he said, turning away and setting the tray on a nearby side table.

"Did you just cut me off?"

"Come with me."

I arched a brow at him. "You can't order me around in my own house, Sullivan."

Ethan's gaze dropped to the medal at my neck. "This is hardly your house any longer, Sentinel."

I made a sound of disagreement, but when he turned and walked away, I followed. He strolled across the room like he owned it, like there was nothing unusual about a Master vampire sauntering through a crowd of Windy City bigwigs. Maybe, in this day and age, there wasn't. With those cheekbones, that sleek tux and the unmistakable air of power and entitlement, he looked like he belonged.

We reached a gap in the crowd, and Ethan stopped, turned, and held out a hand.

I stared at it blankly, then lifted my gaze to his. "Oh, no. This is not part of my assignment."

"You're a ballet dancer."

"*Was* a ballet dancer," I reminded him. I glanced around and saw the multitude of eyes on us, then leaned toward him. "I am not going to dance with you," I whispered, but fiercely. "Dancing is not part of my job description."

"It's one dance, Sentinel. And this is not a request; it's an order. If they see us dancing, perhaps they'll adjust to our presence a bit faster. Perhaps it will soften them up."

The excuse was hokey, but I could hear the mumbles of the people around us, who were wondering why I was standing there, why I hadn't yet accepted his hand.

I had the strangest sense of déjà vu.

On the other hand, I was at home, which meant a meeting with my father was imminent. My stomach was beginning to knot. I needed something to keep my mind off of it, and dancing with a ridiculously handsome, if often infuriating, Master vampire would probably do the trick.

"You owe me," I muttered, but took his hand, just as the quintet began to play "I Could Have Danced All Night."

I slid a glance to the members of the quintet, who grinned like they'd made their very first vampire joke. And maybe they had.

"Thank you," I mouthed to them, and they nodded back at me in unison.

"Your father hired comedians," Ethan commented, as he led me to a spot in the middle of the empty floor. He stopped and turned, and I placed my free hand on his shoulder. His free hand, the one that wasn't clutching mine, went to the back of my waist. He put pressure there, pulling me closer—not quite, but almost, against the line of his body. His body around mine, it was hard to avoid the scent of his cologne—clean, crisp, irritatingly delicious.

I swallowed. Maybe this hadn't been such a good idea. On the other hand, best thing to do was keep the mood light. "He has to pay people who have a sense of humor. Since he's lacking one," I added, when Ethan didn't laugh.

"I understood the joke, Merit," he quietly said, sparkling emerald eyes on me as we began to sway. "I didn't find it funny."

"Yes, well, your sense of humor leaves something to be desired."

Ethan spun me out and away, then pulled me back again. Stuck-up or not, I had to give him props—the boy could move.

"My sense of humor is perfectly well developed," he informed me when our bodies aligned again. "I merely have high standards."

"And yet you deign to dance with me."

"I'm dancing in a stately home with the owner's daughter,

who happens to be a powerful vampire." Ethan looked down at me, brow cocked. "A man could do worse."

"A man could do worse," I agreed. "But could a vampire?"

"If I find one, I'll ask him."

The response was corny enough that I laughed aloud, full and heartily, and had the odd, heart-clenching pleasure of watching him smile back, watching his green eyes shine with the delight of it.

No, I told myself, even as we danced, even as he smiled down at me, even as his hand at my waist, the warm weight of it, felt natural. I looked away, saw that the people around us watched us dance with obvious curiosity. But there was something else in their expressions—a kind of sweetness, like they were watching a couple's first wedding waltz.

I realized how it must look. Ethan, blond and handsome in his tuxedo, me in my black silk ball gown, two vampires— one of whom was the daughter of the host, a girl who'd disappeared from society only to reemerge with this handsome man on her arm—locked together, smiling as they shared a dance, the first couple to take the floor. If we'd actually been dating and had wanted to announce our relationship, we couldn't have staged it better.

My smile fell away. What had felt like a novelty—dancing with a vampire in my father's house—began to feel like a ridiculous theatrical production.

He must have seen the change in my expression; when I looked back at him, his smile had melted.

"We shouldn't be doing this."

"Why," he asked, "should we not be dancing?"

"It's not real."

"It could be."

I snapped my gaze up to meet his. There was desire in his eyes, and while I wasn't naïve enough to deny the chemistry between us, our relationship was complicated enough between Sentinel and Master. Dating wasn't going to make things easier.

"You think too much," Ethan quietly said, approbation in his voice.

I looked away at the couples finally beginning to join us on the dance floor. "You train me to think, Ethan. To always think, strategize, plan. To evaluate the consequences of my actions." I shook my head. "For what you're suggesting—no. There would be too many consequences."

Silence.

"Touché," he finally whispered.

I nodded almost imperceptibly, and took the point.

CHAPTER SIXTEEN

AN OFFER THEY CAN'T REFUSE

W e'd eaten, danced, and sipped champagne for nearly an hour, and still saw no sign of my father or the Breckenridges. It was hard to play Nancy Drew without evidence.

When I caught the interested rise of Ethan's brows, I looked automatically in the direction of his gaze, expecting to see Joshua Merit nearby.

But instead of my father, in the midst of a circle of laughing men, stood the mayor.

At thirty-six, Seth Tate was in the beginning of his second term. He'd named himself a reformer, but hadn't been able to produce the economic renaissance he'd promised when campaigning against the Potter political machine that had ruled Chicago before his election. He'd also given my grandfather his position as Ombud, thereby officially opening the city's administration and enforcement wings to Chicago's sups.

Tate was tall and surprisingly fit for a man who evaluated policy all day. He was also almost ridiculously handsome. He had the face of a rebellious angel—black hair, crystal blue eyes, perfect mouth—and a patented bad-boy brood that no doubt made him the fantasy of more than one woman in the Windy City. He'd been named "America's Sexiest Politician," his face splashed on the covers of more than one newsmagazine. Despite the press, Tate was still single, but it was rumored he'd installed mistresses in a sprinkling of Chicago-land neighborhoods. None, as far as I was aware, was a vampire. Although, having seen the voluptuous nymphs that ruled the segments of the Chicago River, it wouldn't have surprised me if he'd slipped one of them into his rotation.

I looked back at Ethan, his gaze on Tate, and saw a strange look of covetousness on his face. That's when the gears clicked into place.

I knew Ethan wanted access to my father and those of his ilk. Our attempt to keep the raves out of the press was a handy means toward building that connection. But the raves and the story aside, Ethan wanted access to Tate. Access that Tate hadn't, at least until now, been willing to provide.

"You should say hello to our young mayor," Ethan said.

"I've already said hello," I said. I'd met Tate twice before. That had been plenty.

"Yes," Ethan said. "I know that."

Slowly, I slid him a glance, my eyebrows raised. "You know that?"

Ethan sipped his champagne. "You know that Luc researches his guards, Merit, and that he did his background on you. I've reviewed that background, and I can read the *Tribune* as well as anyone."

I should have known. I should have known they'd have found the article, and I should have known Luc would have given it to Ethan.

I'd been home for a long weekend during my junior year at NYU. My parents got tickets to the Joffrey Ballet, and we'd run into Tate outside the theater, where a *Trib* reporter snapped a shot of Tate and me shaking hands. That's not the kind of thing that would have normally been picture-worthy, except for the fact that it almost perfectly mirrored a *Trib* picture of us from six years earlier. The first time around, I'd been fourteen with a bit part in a big ballet production. Tate had been a young alderman at the time, two years into law school. Probably to make inroads with my father, he'd delivered flowers to me after the performance. I'd still been in costume—leotard, tutu, pointe shoes and tights—and the photographer caught him in the middle of handing over a paper-wrapped bouquet of white roses. The *Trib* reporter who caught us at the Joffrey performance apparently liked the symbolism, and both shots ended up, side by side, on the local news page.

I suppose I couldn't fault Ethan for thinking ahead, for milking every drop of opportunity, but it stung to play middleman again.

"Humans are not the only political animals," I muttered.

Brows lifted, Ethan glanced over at me. "Is that a review of my tactics, Sentinel?"

Shaking my head, I looked back at the crowd and, surprisingly, found appraising blue eyes on me. I smiled slyly. "Why, no, Sullivan. If you have the perfect weapon, you might as well use it."

"Pardon me?"

"Let's see how well I can act, shall we?"

Before he could ask what I meant to do, I put on my brightest Merit-family smile, straightened my spine, and sauntered over to the mayor's throng.

His gaze following me as I moved, Tate nodded absently to those around him, then steered his way through the crowd and toward me, two men in stiff suits behind him. The entourage was not a turn-on, but I appreciated his decisiveness.

Tate didn't stop until he reached me, blue eyes sparkling, dimples perked at the corners of his mouth. Political upstart or not, he was undeniably attractive.

We met in the middle of the room, and I guessed, given his quick glance behind me, that Ethan had followed me.

"Ballerina," he whispered, taking the hands I held out to him.

"Mr. Mayor."

Tate squeezed my hands. When he leaned forward, pressing his lips to my cheek, a lock of soft dark hair—worn a little longer than generally thought appropriate by Chicago's more conservative voters—brushed my cheek. Tate smelled like lemon and sunshine and sugar, a weirdly ethereal combination for a city administrator, but delicious all the same.

"It's been too long," he whispered, and a shiver trickled up my spine. When he pulled back, I glanced behind me, saw enough fire in Ethan's emerald eyes to feel vindicated, and indicated him with a negligent hand.

"Ethan Sullivan, my . . . Master."

Tate was still smiling, but the smile didn't quite reach his eyes. He'd been excited to see me, for reasons lascivious or otherwise. He was clearly less excited to meet Ethan. Perhaps he *had* been avoiding encounters with the city's Masters. And here I'd gone and forced it. On the other hand, there's no way my father wouldn't have mentioned that we were planning to attend the party—that was information he wouldn't have been able to keep to himself. That was warning enough for Tate, I decided.

Ethan stepped forward, beside me, and Tate reached out a stiff hand.

"Ethan, glad to finally meet you."

Liar, liar, I thought, but watched the interaction with fascination.

They shook hands. "It's an honor to finally meet you, Mr. Mayor."

Tate took a step back, gave me an obvious perusal, the grin on his face softening a look that would have otherwise felt completely demeaning. (And, as it was, felt only forty to fifty percent demeaning. Bad boy or not, he was awfully pretty.)

"I haven't seen you in years," Tate said. "Not since the last *Tribune* picture." He smiled charmingly.

"I believe you're right."

He nodded. "I'd heard you moved back to Chicago to work on your doctorate. Your father was so proud of your academic accomplishments." That was news to me. "I was sorry to hear that you'd . . . halted your academic studies."

Tate slid a glance in Ethan's direction. Since I'd halted my studies only because Ethan had made me a vampire, the shot at Ethan was completely unsubtle and, frankly, a little surprising. Did Tate assume animosity between us? Or was he simply trying to create it, to drive a wedge?

While I admittedly enjoyed tweaking Ethan, I was still on his side, and I wasn't naïve enough to think that biting the hand that fed me was a good idea, even to flatter the mayor.

"I believe the immortality more than makes up for the diploma," I told Tate.

"Well," he said, not hiding his surprise. "I see. Apparently, even the mayor isn't always in the know." I appreciated that he took the hit, that he could recognize that his intel about the supposed animosity between me and Ethan, from whatever sources, hadn't been entirely correct.

Nor, to be honest, was it entirely incorrect.

"I wanted to thank you," I told him, changing the subject, "for the trust that you've put in my grandfather." I glanced around, thinking it best to limit what I said about my grandfather's position in mixed company—and in my father's house. As far as I knew, my father knew nothing about my grandfather's duties as the Ombud. I planned to keep it that way.

"Without getting into the details, given that this is neither the time nor the place for that kind of discussion," I prefaced, and Tate nodded his understanding, "he's glad he's able to stay busy, to help, and I'm glad to know I have someone in my corner. All of us are."

Tate nodded like you'd expect a campaigning politician might—seriousness and gravity in his expression. "We're on the same page there. You—all of you—deserve a voice in Chicago."

One of Tate's body men leaned toward him. The mayor listened for a moment, then nodded.

"I'm sorry to leave you," he told me, his lips curled into a melancholy smile, "but I need to get to a meeting." He reached a hand out to Ethan. "I'm glad we were finally able to connect. We should put aside some time to talk."

"That would be appreciated, Mr. Mayor," Ethan agreed, nodding.

Tate looked at me again, opened his mouth to speak, but then seemed to think better of it. He put his hands on my upper arms, leaned toward me, and pressed his lips against my cheek. Then he shifted, his lips at my ear. "When you can get away, get in touch. Call my office—they'll put you through, day or night."

The "day" part of that was superfluous, given my little sunlight problem. The rest of it—the fact that he'd requested a meeting from me, not Ethan, and the access he'd just granted—was surprising, but I nodded at him when he pulled back.

"Good evening," he said, with a half bow to both of us. One of his guards stepped before him and began to tunnel through the crowd. Tate followed into the space he'd made, a second guard behind him.

"He wants me to call him," I tattled, when the crowd had re-formed around us. "He told me to get in touch, anytime. That his office would put me through." I glanced up at Ethan. "What could that be about?"

Ethan frowned down at me. "I've no clue." He kept staring at me, one eyebrow arching into obvious disapproval.

"Why the long face?"

"Is there anyone who isn't infatuated with you?"

I smiled at him, with teeth. "If not, it's because you haven't assigned them to me yet. Mata Hari at your service. Would you like to add him to the list?"

"I don't appreciate your sarcasm."

"I don't appreciate being handed out like a party favor."

A muscle in his jaw ticked. "What would you like me to say to that?"

I opened my mouth to give an answer just as snarky as my question, but a silver tray appeared at my elbow, interrupting me. The tray held only a small white card. JOSHUA MERIT was printed in neat block letters across it.

My heart skipped a discomforting beat, those six square inches of cardstock eliciting the same sense of dreadful anticipation they had when I was a child. My father had wanted peace and quiet and perfection, and on those occasions when he sought an audience with me for some failing in one of those categories, this is how he'd done it.

I reached out and picked up the card, then glanced at Pennebaker, who'd delivered it.

"Your father will see you in his office," he said with a bob of his head, then disappeared into the crowd.

We stood silently for a moment, my gaze on the card in my hand.

"You're ready," Ethan said, and I understood that the statement was meant to be an affirmation.

"Ready enough," I said. I smoothed the silk at my waist, and led him away.

My father rose from a black-and-chrome Mies van der Rohe couch when we slid open the top-mounted, reclaimed-wood door. Where Papa Breck's office had been warm and masculine, my father's was cold. It fit right in with the rest of the house's ultramodern decor.

"Merit, Ethan," my father said, waving us inside with a hand. I heard the door slide shut behind us and assumed Pennebaker had attended to it.

Merit, I heard in my head, as I saw what Ethan had no doubt realized and meant to warn me about—that Nicholas and Papa Breck were standing in my father's office.

Nick was in jeans, a T-shirt, and a brown corduroy sports jacket. Papa Breck, a solidly large, barrel-chested man, was in a tuxedo. They stood together, bodies close and aligned, suspicious eyes on us as we entered.

I looked at Nick, tried to ferret out his mood, which didn't take long given the anger in his eyes, the tightness in his jaw. And when he looked from me to Ethan, took in the dress and the tuxedo, disappointment joined his other expressions. The others were confusing, but the disappointment stung.

Papa Breck nodded at me. That nod was apparently the only greeting he could spare for the (vampire) daughter of his best friend, for his son's former girlfriend. I hadn't seen Michael Breckenridge, Sr., in years, but I'd have expected more than a nod. Maybe words, some indication of the closeness of our families, the relationship that had existed between me and Nick. I'd practically been a member of that family, for all the summer vacations I'd spent at his house, running through the halls, through the grass, along the dirt-lined path to the labyrinth.

On the other hand, I suppose I should have considered myself fortunate, as he didn't even spare Ethan a nod.

"The Breckenridges have received information," my father said, "about a threat of violence against their son."

The surprise was evident in Ethan's expression. "A threat of violence?"

"Don't play coy," Nick muttered. "Don't pretend you don't know what we're talking about."

Ethan's jaw clenched, and he slipped his hands into his pockets. "I am afraid, Nicholas, that we have no idea what you're talking about. We do not threaten violence. We certainly have not issued a threat of violence against you."

"Not me," Nicholas said. "Jamie."

The room went silent, at least until I spoke up. "Someone threatened Jamie? What was the threat?" I asked. "And why would you think it came from us?"

Nick's gaze slowly shifted to mine, stubbornness in the set of his jaw.

"Tell me, Nick," I implored him. "I can guarantee you we haven't threatened Jamie. But even if we had, you lose nothing from telling us what you've heard. Either we made the threat, so we know what it is already, or we've been framed, and we need to figure out what the hell's going on."

Nick glanced back at his father, who nodded, then turned back to us. "Before we talked in the garden at my parents', we got a phone call at the house. Unlisted number. She said vampires were interested in Jamie."

She, Nick had said. The caller was female. Had it been Celina? Amber? Some other vamp who had it in for the Brecks, or who was itching to stir up trouble for Cadogan House?

"Today," Nick continued, "I got an e-mail. It had specifics—details about exactly how you planned to harm my brother."

Ethan frowned, clearly confused. "And why do we purportedly want to hurt Jamie?"

"The message didn't say," Nick answered, but the words were a little too quickly spoken to ring true. Maybe he knew about Jamie's story; maybe there was another reason he thought Jamie might be a target. And that wasn't the only problem with his evidence.

"How do you know the e-mail was from a Cadogan vamp?" I asked. "How do you know it wasn't just a hoax?"

"Give me a little credit, Merit. They gave me information to verify."

Ethan and I exchanged a glance. "What information?" he asked, caution in his tone.

Nick looked away, wet his lips, then looked up at me again. There was coldness in his eyes.

"There were details about you," he said, then turned that frigid gaze on Ethan. "And you. Together."

My cheeks flushed crimson. Ethan, apparently much less worried, made a soft, sardonic sound. "Rest assured, Nicholas, we have no plans to harm your brother. And I can most definitely assure you that you were not speaking with a Cadogan vampire. There is no 'together' where Merit and I are concerned."

Not that he hadn't considered it, I thought, remembering our dance.

"Oh?" Nick asked, as if feigning surprise. "Then you didn't share a moment in the library Friday night?" He turned his gaze to me. "I was told that you passed along the story of our meeting in the garden. That you informed your Master that I was 'coming for you.'"

This time, my cheeks paled. While his implication was wrong—our "moment" in the library had been completely platonic—the gossip part was true enough. Someone had been in the library. Had overheard our conversation. Someone was playing us.

And more important, someone was betraying Ethan. Again.

I didn't want to, but I made myself turn and check Ethan's expression. He stood frozen there beside me, jaw clenched, unmitigated fury on his face.

"We did not," he bit out, "nor have we ever issued a threat against Jamie or any other member of your family. That's not the way my House operates. If such a message was sent to you, it was not sent from a Cadogan vampire, and certainly not with my approval. If someone in my House has informed you otherwise, they are . . . *sorely* . . . mistaken."

Despite the gravity in Ethan's tone, Nick's responding shrug was careless. "I'm sorry, Sullivan. But that's not good enough."

Ethan's brows lifted. "Not good enough?"

"We're only asking you not to jump to conclusions," I told Nicholas. "That's all."

"Not jump to conclusions?" Nick took steps, closing the distance between us. I had to steel myself not to step back.

"How naïve are you, Merit? Or is that some kind of vampire denial talking?"

"Nicholas," Papa Breck said, but Nick shook his head.

"No," he spat out. "I told you that if you tried to harm him, I would come after you with everything I had. I will not stand by while vampires destroy my family, Merit."

"Nick, son," Papa Breck repeated, but Nicholas stayed where he was, inches away from me, staring down at me with eyes of furious electric blue.

"We did not issue a threat against Jamie, Nick."

"Do *not* lie to me, Merit." Nick leaned closer and whispered in a voice that I assumed was only for me, "They may give you a dress, and they may give you a sword, but I know who you are."

Oh, but I'd enjoy wiping that smirk from his face. I dropped my head, closed my eyes, and let the anger rise enough—just enough—to silver my eyes. I had to clench my fists to hold back the rest of it—to keep my fangs from descending, to keep the vampire asleep—and the fight of it kept me quiet for a moment. I was silent long enough to hear shuffling, the rest of the room growing increasingly nervous the longer I kept my head down.

I opened my eyes again and slowly lifted my head, gazing at Nick beneath half-hooded lashes. Predictably, his smile faded, his own eyes widening at the silver in mine. He swallowed, likely at the reminder that I wasn't just a girl he'd known in high school, and I wasn't to be bullied to satiate the anger that flowed from whatever prejudices darkened his soul.

"Nicholas," I began, my voice soft and low and lush, "I stand Sentinel for a House of three hundred and twenty vampires. I will not strike first, but he allows me to carry a weapon because I know how to use it. Because I will use it. I know my position, my obligation, and I will do what's necessary to protect them. Because you and I were friends once, I will warn you once. Step back."

Nick stood toe to toe with me, his body statue-still, until Papa Breck put a hand on his arm and whispered something in his ear. When Nick turned away, strode to the bar my father kept on a concrete table in one corner of the room, I'd have sworn I felt something in his wake. Something tingly, but I was distracted by the sudden sound of Ethan's voice in my head.

There is a traitor in my house, he silently said. *Again.*

My heart ached for him, for the betrayal he must have felt for the second time in only a few months, even if it was currently blanketed by a thick, righteous fury. *I know*, I said back, then promised, *I'll find him.*

Finally Nick stepped away from his father, a decision apparently made. "My father has decided to give you the benefit of the doubt. Assuming that you did not make a threat against Jamie, you have twenty-four hours to find out who did. If you don't contact us within twenty-four hours with a name and your assurances that the threat has been resolved, I will contact the mayor and inform him that Cadogan House made a threat against humans, against my family. That phone call will be followed by calls to the *Trib*, the *Sun-Times*, and every television station in the metro area. I may also have to tell them some other things I know. And then they'll be *raving* mad," he said, putting the emphasis on the word so we couldn't mistake his meaning.

"Your so-called celebrity," Nick continued, apparently not

yet done with his tirade, "is delicate, at best. There are plenty of people who think the congressional investigations were a joke, who think you constitute a legitimate threat to humans. There are plenty of people out there who think we'd all be better off if the vampire problem went away." Nick snapped his fingers ominously. "Poof."

I glanced at Ethan, watched his eyes turn glassy green, and guessed he was struggling to maintain his own control. Still, he managed to keep from silvering his eyes, from descending his fangs.

"I can't guarantee Jamie's safety from other parties," Ethan finally answered. "And I can't guarantee resolution of this issue in twenty-four hours, particularly when we will be unconscious for more than half of that time."

Nick's expression flattened. "Then I suggest you and your soldier here get your asses in gear."

Ethan looked down at the floor, then glanced up, but not at Nicholas. Instead, he focused his gaze on Papa Breck. "You should consider the possibility that if threats were made against Jamie, they were made for a reason. That he has stepped on one too many toes, or has involved himself in things that do not concern him. If we investigate this matter further, that information might come to light. Are you prepared for that? For answers you'd prefer to keep in-house?"

I'm not sure what information Ethan was referring to, or if he was merely bluffing. But I had to give him props—it was a good rebuttal.

Nick opened his mouth to counter Ethan, but his father held out a hand. "Nicholas," he warned, then turned to my father. "He's my son. I will protect him at all costs. Do we understand each other?"

"Clearly," my father answered.

"Twenty-four hours," Nick repeated, and began his stride toward the door.

I put a hand on Nick's arm to stop him. The contact didn't dissipate the menace in his glare.

"Is Jamie working right now?"

His lip curled. I figured he was seconds away from growling at me.

"I'm not going to hurt him, Nick. You're asking a lot from us, especially when we have nothing to do with any threat against your brother. If you want us to figure it out, give us something in return." When he continued to stare at me, I added, in a whisper, "Quid pro quo, Nick."

Nick wet his lips, then nodded. "Investments," he said. "Jamie's selling investments."

Bingo.

"Forward the e-mail to me," I told him. "Use my old address."

He looked at me for a moment before nodding, then went to the door, pushing it to the side with enough force to rattle the industrial hinges. Papa Breck followed him out, without even a glance in our direction.

When Pennebaker slid the door shut again, my father and I both looked at Ethan.

"Is there anything I can do?"

Ethan shook his head at my father's request. "Thank you, Joshua, but no. We'll handle this one internally. I'll call the Masters together. If we could just borrow your office for a few minutes longer?"

"Of course," he said, then left us alone.

"Forward the e-mail to me?" Ethan repeated, eyebrows lifted.

"Jeff Christopher," I reminded him, "in my grandfather's office. He's a computer whiz kid. He can help us, and he'll be thrilled to be asked."

There was doubt in Ethan's expression. "He's a shifter, right?"

I frowned back. "Yeah. Why?"

"As I'm sure you've discovered by now, shifters and vampires aren't exactly cozy."

"Sure, but isn't Gabriel Keene bringing his Pack to Chicago? This is the perfect opportunity to make inroads."

He considered the idea for a moment, then nodded. "Make the call."

Ethan massaged his forehead with the fingers of one hand, his gaze on the floor. "Jamie is not writing for the *Chicago World Weekly*; Jamie is selling investments. And although we believed we were the victims here, Nicholas believes that we've issued a threat against Jamie." He lifted his gaze to mine. "What do we learn from that?"

"There is no rave story," I concluded. "Or if there is, Nicholas doesn't know about it. He apparently knows about the raves, but that's a red herring." I shook my head. "No, someone's playing us against each other."

Ethan nodded his agreement. "A woman calls the Breckenridge house the day before we attend a party there and informs the Breckenridges of some vague threat. Nick asks you to meet him in the woods and raises this same issue. Today, before we arrive at another party, information regarding a more specific threat is sent directly to Nicholas."

"They discovered Nick was the point man," I said. "Whoever's behind this mess figured out he was the Breck to work through if they wanted to create chaos."

"Which is exactly what they've succeeded in doing," Ethan muttered. He crossed his arms and walked to one end of the office, then braced his hands on the back of a leather chair.

"Wait," I said. "The information about the story that first came from the Ombud's office—the stuff we talked about with Luc. How did they find out?"

"Anonymous tip," Ethan said. "The information was left at the office."

Damn, I thought. So much for that lead.

"Okay," I said, "then why Cadogan? And why the Breckenridges? We've been pitted against each other, although I have no clue why they'd put us together on the fight card."

"I'm aware of only one connection between us and them," he said, his gaze on me, intensity in his green eyes.

I put a hand to my chest. "Me? You think I'm the connection?"

"You're the only connection between our House and their family that I'm even aware of, Sentinel." Ethan crossed his arms over his chest. "And, unfortunately, I'm aware of only one enemy on your end."

There was a moment of silence as the pieces clicked into place.

"Nick said *she* called the House," I murmured, then lifted my gaze to Ethan. "Celina? You're thinking Celina?"

Ethan shrugged. "We have no evidence of that, of course, but would you consider it beyond her capabilities?"

"Creating chaos? Hardly. That's practically her calling card."

"Much to our chagrin. And this particular chaos has the added benefit of putting you right in the middle." Ethan shook his head. "That e-mail will have been sent by a Cadogan vampire. Someone who knows that I showed you the library—"

"More important," I interjected, "someone who knows what we said in the library, and someone who knows our social schedule. Someone who knows where we've been going, and who's set Nick up with bad information beforehand."

He stood up slowly, hands on his hips, and looked back at me, eyes wide. "What, precisely, are you suggesting?"

"There's only one group of vampires who know about the raves and Jamie's supposed story," I said. "Only one group who know about our excursions to visit the rich and famous."

I paused, wishing he'd reach the conclusion so I wouldn't have to say it aloud.

"Ethan, it had to be a guard."

CHAPTER SEVENTEEN

LOVE BÍTES

That declaration got as warm a reception as you might have imagined. Ethan turned away and immediately flipped open his cell phone, unwilling to engage in a discussion about the possibility that our current havoc was being wreaked by one of his own bodyguards.

One of my colleagues.

Ethan called the House, updating Malik and Luc about the threat but offering no information about my group of suspects. As if nothing was amiss, the guards were put into full investigation mode, their assignment to identify any and all information regarding the purported threat against Jamie.

I was also in full investigation mode, and I'll admit that my suspect list was pretty short. A woman had made the call to the Breckenridge house . . . and I'd seen Kelley arriving at Cadogan after spending the day somewhere else. Had she been the Cadogan vampire with a chip on her shoulder? The link to Celina?

Eager to solve the mystery, I borrowed the house phone and put in a call to the Ombud's office, updating my grandfather on the evening's revelations. I also talked to the man with the skills I needed.

"Jeff, I have a problem."

"I'm glad you've finally realized I'm your answer, Merit."

Okay, so the mood wasn't exactly light, but I couldn't help but smile at the comeback.

"Someone's using e-mail to make threats on behalf of Cadogan House," I told him, flipping open my cell and pulling up my e-mail client. Ever efficient, Nick had already forwarded the e-mail message.

> If it was us, we'd get a good solid aspen stake. But aspen's too good for you. Maybe quartering. The guts and appendages removed while you're still conscious so that you can *feel* the pain. Understand what it's like. Drowning? Hanging? A slow death at the tip of a sword, a slice from stem to stern, so that blood and gore and meat are all that's left of you?
>
> By the way, the youngest one gets it first.

I shivered as I read it, but appreciated that the author of this threat, unlike the last one I'd seen, hadn't tried to rhyme. I also wondered if Kelley was capable of that kind of violence. That kind of anger. Those questions unanswered, I asked Jeff for his e-mail address and sent the message on.

"Phew," he said after a moment, apparently having reviewed it. "That's a doozy."

It was a doozy. It was, however, notably empty of details about why, exactly, Jamie had been chosen. That he was a Breckenridge seemed to be the only knock against him.

"It is a doozy," I told him. "And we need to figure out who it came from. Can you work some of your mojo?"

"Easy breezy," Jeff absently said, the sound of furiously clicking keys in the background. "He's disguised the IP address—rudimentary stuff, but I'll have to do some backtracking. The e-mail addy is pretty generic, but being a representative of our fine city, I might be able to make a call."

"Call away," I told him, "but there's one small catch. I need the details on this as soon as you can get them." I checked the time on my cell—it was nearly midnight. "How's your schedule looking for the next few hours?"

"Flexible," he said. "Assuming the price is right."

I rolled my eyes. "Name your price."

Silence.

"Jeff?"

"Could I—can I get back to you on that? I'm kind of at a loss, and I want to make sure I take complete advantage of this situation. I mean, unless you're willing to give me two or three—"

"Jeff," I said, interrupting what was destined to become a very lascivious list. "Why don't you just give me a call when you've got something?"

"I'm your man. I mean, not literally or whatever, I know you and Morgan have kind of a thing going—although you're not officially *together*-together, right?"

"Jeff."

"Yo?"

"Get to work."

With our contacts on the trail of information that might mollify the Brecks, Ethan and I slipped out of my father's office and headed back through the crowd to the front door. The house was packed, and it took us a few minutes of squeezing through bodies and handshaking to make it to the other side. I think I managed a polite smile in the direction of the people I passed, but my mind was completely focused on a particular Breckenridge.

I didn't understand how he could think I was capable of the accusations he'd leveled against us. How could a childhood romance, a decades-long friendship, turn into something so ugly?

I nibbled the edge of my lip as we traversed the crowd, recalling scenes from my childhood. Nick had been my first kiss. We'd been in his father's library, me a girl of eight or nine, wearing a sleeveless party dress with an itchy crinoline petticoat. Nick had called me a "dumb girl" and kissed me because I'd dared him to, a quick peck on the lips that seemed to disgust him as much as it delighted me, albeit not as much as the fact that I'd beaten him at whatever game we'd been playing. As soon as he'd kissed me, he was off again, running out of his father's office and down the hallway. "Boys have cooties!" I'd yelled, Mary Janes clomping as I ran after him.

"Are you all right?"

I blinked and looked up. We'd reached the other end of the room. Ethan had stopped and was gazing at me curiously.

"Just thinking," I said. "I'm still in shock about Nick, about his father. About their attitude. We were friends. Good friends, Ethan, for a long time. I don't understand how it came to this. There was a time when Nick would have asked me, not accused me."

"The gift of immortality," Ethan dryly said, then glanced back at Chicago's rich and famous, who sipped champagne while the city buzzed around them. "Infinite opportunities for betrayal."

There were a bevy of his own stories behind that little aphorism, I guessed, but I couldn't see past my own.

Ethan shook his head as if to clear it, then put a hand at my back. "Let's go home," he said. I nodded, not even up to an argument that Cadogan wasn't "home."

We'd just moved into the foyer when Ethan stopped, his hand falling away. I glanced up.

Morgan stood just inside the door, arms crossed over worn jeans and a long-sleeved white T-shirt. A single brown curl draped rakishly across his forehead, and his blue eyes— accusing blue eyes—stared back at me.

I exhaled a curse, realizing what Morgan had seen. Me in a ball gown, Ethan in a tux, his hand at my back. The two of us together, in my parents' house, after I couldn't be bothered to return Morgan's phone calls. This was definitely not good.

"I believe someone has crashed your party, Sentinel," Ethan whispered.

I ignored him, and I'd just taken a step toward Morgan when I felt like I was falling through a tunnel. I had to touch Ethan's arm just to keep myself upright.

It was the telepathic connection Morgan and I had formed when he'd challenged Ethan at Cadogan House. The link was supposed to work only between vampire and Master, which might have been why the link with Morgan had such a strong effect. And why it seemed so wrong.

I'm sure you have an explanation, he silently said.

I wet my lips, uncurled my fingers from Ethan's arm, and forced my spine straight. "I'll meet you outside," I told Ethan. Without waiting for a response, I walked toward Morgan, forcing myself to keep my eyes on his.

"We need to talk," Morgan said aloud when I reached him, his gaze lifting to the man behind me, at least until that man slipped silently beside us and out the door.

"Come with me," I said, my voice flat.

We followed a concrete hallway to the back of the house, the walls still imprinted with the grain of their wooden forms. I picked a random door—a breach in the concrete—and opened it. Moonlight streamed through a small square window in the facing wall, providing a single beam of light in the otherwise pitch-black space. I stood quietly for a second, then two, and let my predatory eyes adjust to the darkness.

Morgan stepped into the room behind me.

"Why are you here?" I asked him.

There was a moment of silence before he met my gaze, one eyebrow raised in accusation. "Someone suggested I might see something interesting in Oak Park tonight, so here I am. You're busy working, I assume."

"I am working," I replied, my tone all business. "Who told you we'd be here?"

Morgan ignored the question. Instead he arched his eyebrows, and with a look that would have melted a lesser woman, raked his gaze across my body. Had waves of angry magic not radiated from him as he did it, I'd have called the move an invitation. But this was different. A verdict, I think, of my guilt.

He crossed arms over his chest. "Is that what he's dressing you in these days while you're . . . working?"

He made it sound like I was less a Sentinel than a call girl.

My voice was tight, words clipped, when I finally spoke. "I thought you knew me well enough to know that I wouldn't

be here, in my father's house, if there weren't a phenomenally good reason for it."

Morgan gave a strangled, mirthless half laugh. "I imagine
I can guess what the phenomenally good reason is. Or maybe
I should say, *who* the reason is."

"Cadogan House is the reason. I'm here because I'm
working. I can't explain why, but suffice it to say that if you
knew, you'd be sufficiently concerned and more supportive
than you're being now."

"Right, Merit. You blow me off, avoid me, and then turn
it around, blame me for being suspicious, for wanting some
answers. You haven't returned my phone calls and yet"—he
crossed his hands behind his head—"you're the victim here.
You should take Mallory's place at McGettrick, great as that
spin is." He nodded his head, then looked down at me. "Yeah,
I think that would really work out well for you."

"I'm sorry I didn't call you. Things have been a little
crazy."

"Oh, have they?" He released his hands, walked toward
me. He reached out a finger and traced his fingertip across
the top edge of my bodice. "I notice you aren't wearing your
sword, Sentinel." His voice was soft. Lush.

I wasn't buying it. "I'm armed, Morgan."

"Mmm-hmm." He lifted his eyes from my chest and met
my gaze. I could see the hurt in his face, but that hurt was
tempered by anger. Predatory anger. I'd seen him in the same
mode before, when he'd challenged Ethan at Cadogan House,
wrongly believing that Ethan had threatened Celina. That
Ethan had made a move after his own Master. Apparently this
was a theme for Morgan—the anger of a man who believed
another vamp was sniffing around his girl.

"If you have something to say," I told him, "maybe you
should just put it out there."

He stared at me for a long, long time, neither of us moving, but when he spoke, the words were softer, sadder, than
I'd expected. "Are you fucking him?"

A kiss in Mallory's hallway or not, we were hardly dating,
Morgan and me. He had no right to this kind of jealousy, and

certainly no basis for it. I was just about reaching the limit of my tolerance for ignorant men today. My anger rose, peppering my arms with goose bumps. I let it flow around me, working to keep the emotions off my face, the silver out of my eyes, the vampire asleep.

"You," I began, my voice low and on the edge of fury, "are being *incredibly* presumptuous. Ethan and I are not together, and you and I don't exactly have a commitment. You have no right to accuse me of being unfaithful, much less any basis."

"Ah," he said. "I see." He looked down at me, his expression flat. "So you two aren't together. Is that why you danced with him?"

I could have confessed that it was part of a plan to build relationships, to build connections. That it had been intended to get close to a reporter who had the power to make things very, very difficult for vampires, however unlikely that story seemed now.

But Morgan had a point. I'd had a choice. I could have walked away.

I could have set boundaries with Ethan, could have reminded him that we were at the party for information, not entertainment. I could have reminded him that I'd given up time with friends to do my job, and asked for a pass on the dance.

I hadn't done any of those things.

Maybe because he was my Master. Because I was duty-bound to accept his orders.

Or maybe because in some secret way, I wanted to say yes, as much as I'd wanted to tell him no, in spite of the discomfort that I felt around him. Despite the fact that he didn't trust me as much as I deserved.

But how could I admit that to Morgan, who'd gate-crashed my parents' party in order to catch me in the act of infidelity?

I couldn't, either to me or to him.

So I did the only other thing I could think of.

I took my exit.

"I don't need this," I told Morgan, sweeping up my skirt. I turned on my heel and headed for the door.

"Great," he called after me. "Walk away. That's mature, Merit. I appreciate that."

"I'm sure you can find your way out."

"Yeah, sorry to have interrupted your party. You and your boss have a great evening, *Sentinel*."

He spit it out like a curse. Maybe it was, but what right did he have to criticize? Ethan was my obligation. My duty. My burden. My *Liege*.

I knew it was immature. I knew it was childish and wrong, but I was pissed, and I couldn't help myself. I knew it was the one thing that as a Navarre vamp Morgan couldn't do. But it was the perfect line, the perfect exit, and I couldn't resist.

I glanced back at him, silk swirling around my legs, and, single eyebrow raised, gave him the haughtiest look I could muster.

"Bite me," I said, and walked away.

Ethan was outside, waiting beside the car in the gravel drive. His face was tilted up, eyes on the full moon that cast shadows against the house. He lowered his gaze as I began to cross the gravel.

"Ready?" he asked.

I nodded and followed him to the car.

The mood during the ride back to Hyde Park was even more somber than it had been on the ride to my parents'. I stared silently out the car window, replaying events. That was three times tonight that I'd managed to alienate people. Mallory. Catcher. Morgan. And for what? Or better yet, for whom? Was I pushing everyone else away in order to get closer to Ethan?

I glanced over at him, his gaze on the road, hands at ten and two on the steering wheel. His hair was tucked behind his ears, brow furrowed in concentration as he drove. I'd given up my life as a human for this man; not willingly, of course, but still. Was I giving up everything else? The things I'd brought with me across the transition—my home in Wicker Park? My best friend?

I sighed and turned back toward the window. Those questions, I guessed, weren't going to be answered tonight. I was hardly two months into my life as a vampire—and I still had an eternity of Ethan to go.

When we reached the House, Ethan parked the car, and we walked up from the basement together.

"What can I do?" I asked when we reached the first floor, not that I hadn't done enough already on behalf of Cadogan and its Master.

He frowned, then shook his head. "Keep me up to date about Jeff's progress with the e-mail. The Masters are investigating on their ends; I'm going to make some calls on my own until they arrive. In the meantime—" He paused, as if he was debating my skills, then finished, "Try the library. See what you can find."

I arched my eyebrows. "The library? What am I looking for?"

"You're the researcher, Sentinel. Figure that out."

Experienced enough to know that a ball gown wasn't appropriate research attire, I returned to my room to change, trading the silk for jeans and a short-sleeved black top. (A fusty suit wasn't, to my mind, research attire, either.) I was relieved, physically relieved, to hang the dress back in the closet, don jeans and pick up my katana. It felt right in my hand—comforting, as if I'd stepped out of a costume and back into my own skin. I stood in my room for a moment, left hand on the scabbard, right hand on the handle, just *breathing*.

When I was calmer and ready to face the world again, I grabbed a pen and a couple of notebooks, ready to begin my own brand of investigation.

The more I thought about it, the more I agreed with Ethan that Celina had a role in this. We didn't have much in the way of evidence, but this was totally her style—to sow discord, put the players in motion, and let the battle proceed on its own. I wasn't sure where Kelley fit in, or if she fit in at all, and I didn't exactly have the skills of a private investigator.

But I could research, study, peruse the library for information that might give us a clue—about Celina's plans, her connections, her history. Whether it would help us in the long run remained to be seen, but it was something proactive, something I had the skills to do.

And more important, it was something I could sink into, something that would keep my mind off other things. Off Morgan, and what seemed the inevitable end of that relationship. Off Ethan, and the attraction that, however ill-advised, lingered between us. Off Mallory.

I found the library quiet and empty—and this time, I double-checked—dropped my pens and notebooks on the table, and headed for the shelves.

CHAPTER EIGHTEEN

IN THE STACKS

"Late, isn't it?"

I blinked away black text and looked up, found Ethan walking toward my table. My immersion solution had worked—I hadn't even heard the library door open.

"Is it?" I flipped my wrist to check the time on my watch, but before I read the dial, he announced, "It's nearly three o'clock. You look to be engrossed."

Over an hour had passed, then, since we'd gone our separate ways. I'd been sitting in the chair with my sword poised beside me, Pumas discarded beneath the table, legs crossed, for most of that time.

I scratched my temple and glanced down at the book before me. "French Revolution," I told him.

Ethan looked confused and crossed his arms over his chest. "French Revolution? To what end are you researching the French Revolution?"

"Because we, *I*, will better understand who she is, what she's after, if we know where she came from."

"You mean Celina."

"Come here," I told him, flipping through a book to locate the passage I'd found earlier. When he reached the opposite side of the table, I turned the book toward him and tapped a finger against the relevant paragraph.

Frowning, he braced his hands on the table, leaned forward, and read aloud. "The Navarre family owned substantial holdings in the Burgundy region of France, including a château near Auxerre. On December 31, 1785, the oldest daughter, Marie Colette, was born." He glanced up. "That would be Celina."

I nodded. Celina Desaulniers, née Marie Collette Navarre. Vampires changed identities with some frequency, one burden of immortality being the fact that you outlived your name, your family. That tended to make humans a little suspicious; thus, the name changes.

Of course, Ethan had been a vampire for nearly two centuries before Celina had been a twinkle in her parents' aristocratic eyes, and she was a GP member. He'd probably long since memorized her name, date of birth, and hometown. But I thought the next few sentences, hidden away in this petite biography of a long-dead vampire, might be more interesting.

"Marie," he continued, "although born in France, was smuggled to England in 1789 to avoid the harshest persecutions of the Revolution. She became fluent in English and was considered highly intelligent and a rare beauty. She was raised as a foreign-born cousin of the Grenville family, which held the Dukedom of Buckingham. It was assumed that Miss Navarre would marry George Herbert, Viscount Penbridge, but the couple was never formally betrothed. George's family later announced his engagement to Miss Anne Dupree, of London, but George disappeared hours before the marriage was to have taken place."

Ethan made a sound of interest, looked up at me. "Shall we place any bets as to the disposition of poor George?"

"Unfortunately, that's unnecessary on all accounts. And we know what happened to Celina—she was made a vampire. But what's important is what happened to Anne." I waved a hand at him. "Skip to the footnote."

He frowned, but without taking his gaze away from the book, pulled out the chair in front of him. He settled himself into it, crossing one leg over the other, then arranged the book in his right hand, his left across his lap.

"George's body was found four days later," he continued. "The next day, Anne Dupree eloped with George's cousin, Edward." Ethan closed the book, placed it on the table, and frowned at me. "I assume you've taken me on a stroll through English social history for a reason?"

"Now you're ready for the punch line," I told him, and pulled from my stack a slim, leather-bound volume, this one providing biographical information about the current members of the Greenwich Presidium. I turned to the page I'd flagged and read aloud: "Harold Monmonth, holding the Presidium's fourth position and serving as Council Prelect, was born Edward Fitzwilliam Dupree in London, England, 1774." I lifted my gaze from the book, watched the connections form in his expression.

"So she and Edward, or Harold—what—plotted together? To have George killed?"

I closed the book, placed it on the table. "Do you remember what she said in the park, right before she attempted to fillet you? Something about humans being callous, about a human breaking her heart? Well, let me lay this out for you from a woman's perspective. You're living in a foreign country with your English cousins because you've been smuggled out of France. You're considered a rare beauty, cousin to a duke, and at the age of nineteen, you nab the first son of a viscount. That's our George. You want him, maybe you love him. You certainly love that you've managed to entice him. But just when you think you've sealed the deal, noble George tells you that he's fallen for the daughter of a London merchant. A merchant, Ethan. Someone Celina would have considered far, far beneath her. You don't bear any particular grudge toward Anne. You may even pity her for being less than what you are." I put my elbows on the table, leaned forward. "But you don't pity George. George, who could have had you, your beauty, your prestige, by his side. He throws you away for London trash." I lowered my voice. "Celina would never let that stand. And what if, conveniently, George has an older cousin, a thirty-year-old cousin, who has an attachment to our dear Anne, who is all of sixteen? You and Edward have a conversation. Mutual goals are discussed. Plans are made, and George's body is found in a London slum."

"Plans are made," Ethan repeated, nodding, "and two members of the Presidium have a murder between them. The Presidium that released Celina, despite what she'd done in Chicago."

I nodded back. "Why bother enthralling Presidium members with your glamour, or relying on your charms, as you put it, when you've got that kind of shared history? When you share a mutual belief in the disposability of humans?"

Ethan then looked down at the table, seemed to consider what he'd heard. A sigh, then he raised his gaze to mine again. "We could never prove this."

"I know. And I think this information shouldn't leave the House, not until we're more certain of who our friends are. But if we're trying to predict what she might do, where she might go, who her friends are, this is the best way to start. Well," I added, "this is the best way for *me* to start." I gazed across the table of books, open notebooks, uncapped pens— a treasure trove of information, waiting to be connected. "I know how to search an archive, Ethan. That's one skill I have no doubts about."

"It's unfortunate that your best source loathes you."

That made me smile. "Can you imagine the look on Celina's face if I called and asked her to sit down with me? Told her I wanted to interview her?"

He smirked. "She might appreciate the press." He glanced down at his watch. "And speaking of the press, the Masters should be here with the results of their inquiries within the hour."

It wasn't the best thing I'd heard all day, that I'd have to face down Morgan again, but I understood that it was necessary.

"I'd hoped to keep this contained, but we've clearly reached the point where the other Masters need to be brought on board." He cleared his throat, shuffled uncomfortably in his chair, then lifted ice green eyes to mine. "I won't ask what happened at your parents' house with Morgan, but I

need you there. Your position aside, you were a witness to the
meeting with the Breckenridges, to their accusations."

I nodded. I understood the need. And I gave him points for
diplomatically mentioning it. "I know."

He nodded, then picked up the small book of history
again, began flipping through the pages. I guessed he planned
to wait in the library until they arrived. I adjusted in my seat,
a little uncomfortable at the company, but once he was settled
in, and when I was reasonably confident that he intended to
read quietly, I turned back to my notes.

Minutes passed, peacefully. Ethan read or strategized or
planned or whatever he did on his side of the table, occasionally tapping at a BlackBerry he'd pulled from his pocket,
while I continued thumbing through the history books before
me, searching for additional information about Celina.

I was beginning a chapter on the Napoleonic Wars when I
felt Ethan's gaze. I kept my eyes downcast for a minute, then
two, before I gave in and lifted my eyes. His expression was
blank.

"What?"

"You're a scholar."

I turned back to my book. "We've talked about this before.
A few nights ago, if you'll recall."

"We've talked about your social discomfort, your love of
books. Not the fact that you've spent more time with a book
in your hand than you have with your Housemates."

Cadogan House was apparently full of spies. Someone
was reporting our activities to whoever had threatened Jamie,
and someone had apparently been reporting my activities to
Ethan.

I shrugged self-consciously. "I enjoy research. And given
the ignorance that you've repeatedly pointed out, I need it."

"I don't want to see you hide yourself away in this room."

"I do my job."

Ethan returned his gaze to his book. "I know."

The room was quiet again until he shuffled in his chair, the
wood squeaking as he adjusted. "These chairs aren't at all
comfortable."

"I didn't come down here for comfort." I looked up, gave him a predatory grin. "You're free to work in your office."

I didn't have that luxury. *Yet*.

"Yes, we're all agog at your studiousness."

I rolled my eyes, pricked by the accumulation of subtle insults. "I get that you have no confidence in my work ethic, Ethan, but if you're going to think up insults, could you do it somewhere else?"

His voice was flat, calm. "I have no doubts about your work ethic, Sentinel."

I pushed back my chair, then walked around the table to the pile of books at one end. I shuffled through the stack until I found the text I needed. "Could have fooled me," I muttered, flipping through to the index and tracing the alphabetical entries with a fingertip.

"I don't," he said lightly. "But you're so—what did you tell me once?" He glanced up, looked absently at the ceiling. "Ah, that I was easy to prick? Well, Sentinel, you and I have that in common."

I arched a brow. "So in the middle of a crisis, because you're angry at Celina and the Breckenridges, you've come down here to get a rise out of me? That's mature."

"You've missed my point completely."

"I didn't realize you had one," I muttered.

"I find it unfortunate," Ethan said, "that this is what your life would have been."

We avoided, usually, the issue of my dissertation. Of my looming doctorate. Of the fact that he'd had me pulled from the University of Chicago after he made me a vampire. It helped me, and therefore him vicariously, not to dwell on it. But for him to insult it, to insult what I'd done, managed a new level of pretension.

I looked up at him, palms flat on the table. "What is that supposed to mean?"

"It means you'd have finished your dissertation, secured a professorship at some East Coast liberal arts college, and then what? You'd buy yourself a cottage and update that box on wheels you call a car, and you'd spend most of your time in your tiny office nitpicking antiquated literary conceits."

I stood straight, crossed my arms over my chest, and had to take a moment in order to keep from snapping back at him. And I only did that because he was my boss.

Still, my tone was frosty. "Nitpicking antiquated literary conceits?"

His arched brows challenged me to respond.

"Ethan, it would have been a quiet life, I know that. But it would have been fulfilling." I looked down at my katana. "Maybe a little less adventurous, but fulfilling."

"A *little* less?"

His voice was so sarcastic it was nearly flabbergasting. I took it to be vampire arrogance that he couldn't believe the ordinary lives of human beings were in any way rewarding.

"Exciting things can happen in archives."

"Such as?"

Think, Merit, think. "I could unravel a literary mystery. Find a missing manuscript. Or, the archive could be haunted," I suggested, trying to think of something a little more in his area of expertise.

"That's quite a list, Sentinel."

"We can't all be soldiers turned Master vampires, Ethan." And thank God for that. One of him was plenty enough.

Ethan sat forward, linked his fingers on the table, and gazed at me. "My point, Sentinel, is this: Compared to this world, your new life, your human life would have been cloistered. It would have been a small life."

"It would have been a life of my choosing." Hoping to end that particular line of conversation, I closed the book I'd pretended to stare at. I picked it up, along with a couple of its companions, and walked them back to their shelves.

"It would have been a waste of you."

Thankfully, I was facing the bookshelf when he offered that little nugget, as I don't think he'd have appreciated the eye roll or mimicry. "You can stop plying me with compliments," I told him. "I've already gotten you in to see my father and the mayor."

"If you believe that sums up our interactions over the last week, you've missed the point."

When I heard the slide of his chair, I paused, hand on the spine of a book about French drinking customs. I pushed the book back in line with its comrades and said lightly, "And you've insulted me again, which means we're back on track."

I gathered up the next book in my stack, my eyes scanning the Dewey Decimal numbers on the shelves to locate its home.

In other words, I was trying very, very hard not to think about the sound of footsteps behind me, or the fact that they were moving closer.

Interesting that I hadn't yet moved out of his path.

"My point, Sentinel, is that you are more than a woman who hides in a library."

"Hmm," I nonchalantly said, sliding the final book into its home. I knew what was coming. I could hear it in his voice—the low, thick hum of it. I didn't know why he was trying, given his apparently conflicted feelings about me, but this was the prelude to seduction.

Footsteps, and then he was next to me, his body behind mine, his lips at the spot of skin just below my ear. I could feel the warmth of his breath against my neck. The smell of him—clean, soapy, almost discomfortingly familiar. As much as the want of it disturbed me, I wanted to sink back against him, let him envelop me.

Part of that, I knew, was vampire genetics, the fact that he'd changed me, some kind of evolutionary connection between Master and vampire.

But part of it was much, much simpler.

"Merit."

Part of it was boy and girl.

I shook my head. "No, thank you."

"Don't deny it. I want this. You want this."

He said the words, but the cant of them was wrong. Irritated. Not words of desire, but an accusation. As if we'd fought the attraction and hadn't been strong enough to resist it, and we were worse off for it.

But if Ethan fought it, he didn't resist. He leaned in, a hand at my waist, his body behind mine, and grazed his teeth along the sensitive skin of my neck. The breath shuddered out of me, my eyes rolling back, the vampire inside me thrilled by the innate dominance of the act. I tried to fight my way to the surface of the rising lust, and made the mistake of turning around, facing him. I'd been intent on giving him what-for, on sending him away, but he took full advantage of my shift in position.

Ethan pressed closer, one hand on each side of me, fingers gripping the shelves, framing my body with his, and stared down at me, eyes as green as cut emeralds. He raised a hand to my face, stroked my lip with his thumb. His eyes became quicksilver, a sure sign of his hunger. Of his arousal.

"Ethan," I said, a hesitation, but he shook his head, gaze dropping to my lips, then drifting shut. He leaned closer, his lips just touching mine. Teasing, hinting, but not quite kissing. My lids fell, and his hands were at my cheeks, fingers at my jaw, his breath staccato and rushed as his lips traced a trail, pressed kisses, against my closed eyes, my cheeks, everywhere but my lips.

"You are so much more than that."

It was the words that did me in, that sealed my fate. My core went liquid, body humming, limbs languid as he worked to arouse me, to incite me.

I opened my eyes and looked up at him as he pulled back, his eyes wide and intense and insanely green. He was so beautiful, his eyes on me, the desire clear, golden hair around his face, ridiculous cheekbones, mouth that would tempt a saint.

"*Merit*," he roughly said, then leaned his forehead against mine, asking for my consent, my permission.

I wasn't a saint.

My eyes wide, decision made and the repercussions be damned, I nodded.

CHAPTER NINETEEN

CRYING WOLF

His first move was the deadliest, a smile of boyish pleasure that transformed into the sexiest, most congratulatory grin I'd ever seen. It was a look of sheer predatory satisfaction, the look of a hunter who'd planned, schemed, and won his prize, who had the prey in his grasp.

How apropos, I thought.

"Be still," he whispered, then leaned in again, lids falling as he angled his head. I thought he'd kiss me, but this was just to tease, a prelude to whatever slate of activity he had in mind. He pressed a kiss to my jawline, then my chin, then nipped at my bottom lip, tugging it with his teeth.

When he released me, he stared at me again, rubbed his thumb across my cheekbone. He studied me, looked at me. This time, when his lashes fell, he kissed me fully, dipping his tongue into the cavern of my mouth.

He fisted his hands in the hair at the nape of my neck, teasing my tongue with his, willing me to engage, to fight back, to do anything but simply acquiesce.

I fisted my hands in the lapels of his coat, pulling him toward me, bringing the warmth of him, the smell of him, the taste of him, closer.

There was a moment of consideration before I decided I wasn't appalled enough by my actions to let him go.

Ethan.

It wasn't even a whisper, just the mental calling of his name, but he groaned triumphantly, sucked my tongue into his mouth, and tortured it with friction and the heat of his mouth.

I kissed him, let him kiss me, let him clutch my hips, curl his fingers into the fabric of my shirt, slide his hands around my waist and splay them against my back, pull me infinitesimally closer. He made a sound, a growl or purr, some predatory noise that rumbled in his throat, then said my name. And this time, it wasn't a question but a sound of victory, a claim on his prize.

He pressed in closer, fingers splayed and moving slowly upward. As he pressed against me, I felt the rise of his erection, the solidity of it against my stomach.

I cupped his face in my hands as we kissed in long, sensuous pulls and teasing bites, the thick golden silk of his hair falling around my fingers.

Until the knock at the library door.

Ethan shot away, one hand on his hip, one at his mouth, wiping away the evidence.

"Yes?" His voice was loud, a cannon shot in the otherwise empty room.

I brushed the back of my hand across my mouth.

The door opened, a body silhouetted in the doorway, and then Malik stepped inside. "They're here," he said, eyes on me, some shred of unspoken compassion there, then looked at Ethan. "Front parlor."

Ethan nodded. "Put them in my office. We'll be there in a moment." Without even so much as a second glance, Malik nodded and walked out again, the door closing with a heavy, slow *thush.*

I moved back to the table and kept my gaze on the notebooks and texts I began to gather up. My heart raced, the guilt I'd thrown back at Morgan now flooding my chest.

What had I done? What had I, *we*, been about to do?

"Merit."

"Don't." I finished stacking the notebooks, picked them up, grabbed my scabbarded katana, and held them to my chest like a shield. "Don't. That shouldn't have happened."

Ethan didn't respond until I began to move toward the door. He stopped me with a firm hand at my elbow. Even then, a single arched eyebrow was the only question I got.

"You gave me to him."

His eyes widened, instantaneously. He was surprised, then, that it mattered, that it mattered that Ethan had wanted me, for whatever his reasons, in spite of his doubts, and had still given me away. To Morgan. Who was waiting one floor below us.

I pulled my arm away and walked to the door. When I reached it, I stopped, turned, and looked back, seeing that stunned expression still on his face. "You made the decision," I told him. "You get to live with it."

After a moment of obvious shock, he shook his head. "We have visitors." His tone was steely. "Let's go."

Scabbard and paper in hand, I followed him out.

They were in the office when we arrived downstairs—Morgan, Scott Grey, and Noah Beck, all in chairs around Ethan's conference table. I hadn't seen Scott or Noah since the night I'd protected Ethan against a would-be sucker punch thrown by my future ex-boyfriend, one night before Celina attempted to kill Ethan. It seemed appropriate that we were meeting again under equally dramatic circumstances.

Scott was tall with dark brown hair, dressed in jeans and a Cubs T-shirt. He was a sports fan, so sportswear usually made up the uniform of Grey House, such as it was. Instead of the medals vampires from Navarre and Cadogan wore, Grey House vamps had jerseys.

Noah wore black cargo pants and a black thermal shirt, the only clothes I'd ever seen him in. Noah was shorter than Scott, which didn't say much given that Scott probably reached six foot four, but Noah was broader-shouldered. Noah clearly spent a lot of time in the weight room. And where Scott had a kind of frat-boy attractiveness, now sporting a little soul patch below his bottom lip, Noah was ruggedly handsome. His look was equally vampire rugged—brown hair around big blue eyes, sensuous lips, a few days' worth of stubble along his strong jaw.

Morgan was still in his jeans and T-shirt. He'd also kept the flat, pissed-off stare, which he leveled at me as soon I walked into the room.

I blushed, guilt riding high and warm on my cheekbones. Guilt, and a little fear. I'd done the very thing he'd dreaded. I'd given in to the temptation he'd predicted. Feared. And I'd bet money that I still carried the lingering scent of Ethan's cologne.

Luc and Malik stood point at either end of the table, both in Cadogan black. Ethan strode toward the table and took the seat at the head of it, Luc standing behind him.

I moved to the other end of the table, offering nods to Noah and Scott along the way. When Malik took his seat, I stood behind him.

"Gentlemen," Ethan said, "as I briefly mentioned earlier, we have a problem. We need a solution. And we need it quickly."

He laid out Nick's threat, the twenty-four-hour demand, and the research being conducted by Jeff. And then he got personal.

"We've been able to get this much information," he said, "because Merit agreed to return to her father's house, to revisit her family's circle of acquaintances on our behalf." He said the words to the group, but his gaze was on Morgan.

I closed my eyes, suddenly exhausted by Ethan Sullivan.

It was exoneration. He was trying, even after what had just transpired in the library, to give me an excuse to take to Morgan. To explain to Morgan that what seemed like impropriety— my appearing on Ethan's arm at a social function—was actually a duty he'd required of me, and a completely platonic one.

Arguably, it was a thoughtful thing to do—an attempt to mend the tear he'd rent by requiring me to accompany him to my father's.

On the other hand, it reeked of cowardice. He wanted me, that much was obvious, and this wasn't the first time he'd demonstrated it. But he kept passing me back to Morgan. He kept putting the effort into keeping Morgan and me together. That hinted at an abyss of emotional issues I knew I shouldn't dare to explore.

But I'd kissed him. I'd seen the look in his eyes—the desire, the triumph—of having accomplished me. Maybe Linds was right, that there was more beneath the surface of cool, calm, collected vampire. But what a risk . . .

I'd drifted into my thoughts, so when the sound of my name jolted me from them, I realized I was halfway to lifting fingers to my lips, touching the place where we'd connected. Covering, I tapped a finger against my chin, hoping it looked intellectual.

"Yes?" I asked Ethan, found all eyes on me. Morgan, in particular, looked to have lost a little fire, although he still looked suspicious.

"Do you have anything to add to my retelling?" Ethan asked. "Perhaps about the threat contained in the e-mail?"

I bobbed my head dutifully. "It's gory," I said. "Methods are mentioned, some new, some old school. But I didn't read anything in the e-mail that suggested a particular person, or vampire, was the would-be perpetrator."

Ethan surveyed the vampire heads of state. "Were any of you successful in discovering anything about this threat?"

Heads were shaken around the table.

"Black hole," Noah said. "I got nada."

"Ditto," Scott said.

Morgan leaned forward. "So what do we do now? It's two hours until dawn, and we'd only have, what, a handful of hours tomorrow night. That's not time for a full investigation, if we even knew who to start with."

"The e-mail may give us some direction yet tonight," Ethan reminded them. "We're waiting for the conclusion of that part of the investigation. At any rate, we need to reach some agreement before we separate. The first step, I think, is addressing the threat to the extent that we can. Both Merit and I have given the Breckenridges assurances that the threat does not derive from Cadogan House. Can you at least make the same promise?"

"The threat doesn't come from Grey," Scott flatly said. "As you know, not our style."

"It's not our style, either," Morgan said, his voice a little huffy. "Navarre vampires don't threaten humans."

Anymore, I thought, Ethan and I sharing a knowing glance.

"You know I can't make that kind of promise," Noah said. "I don't have that kind of authority on behalf of independent vampires. I'm just a delegate for informational purposes. That said, I don't know square one about the Breckenridge family, and I certainly haven't heard anything in the pipes. If vamps outside the Houses are involved in this, I'm not aware of it."

"Which is exactly why we have Houses," Morgan muttered, sitting back in his chair. "To prevent situations like this." He linked his hands behind his head, slid Ethan a glance. "So you've gotten assurances from Chicago's big three. You think that's gonna calm these people down?"

"Doubtful," Ethan said. "They're going to want specific information as to the threat, as to who made the phone call, as to who sent the e-mail."

"So if we don't figure it out, we're fucked," Morgan concluded. "He'll publish this story, and we're fucked. They'll restart the hearings, pass whatever shit legislation they've been considering, and lock us inside our Houses for the duration of the night."

"One step at a time," Ethan calmly said. "There's no need to jump to conclusions."

"Oh, don't pull that 'I'm the expert' Master bullshit on me, Sullivan. I'm not as old as you, but I'm not a newbie, either."

"Greer," Scott warned. Scott, I'd learned from my research, was a relatively new Master. But he still had more pull, more experience, than Morgan, and the tone of his voice was an obvious reminder of that fact. It was the first time I'd heard Scott pull rank, and that made it much more effective.

Morgan bit back whatever retort he had planned and sat back in his chair, eyes narrow, gaze on the table in front of him. Maybe I wasn't the only one who wasn't handling transitions well. Mine, from human to vampire. His, from Second to Master.

"We can offer assurances as to the Houses," Ethan said, recapping the deal we'd reached so far. "What else?"

"Actually," Scott said, "I've got a question." He glanced at Morgan. "While I mean no disrespect to you, we've got a new slate of raves, threats against us, someone spreading some nasty information about how manipulative we are. It's leading to this—our getting irritated with each other. What are the odds on Celina's involvement?"

Morgan's jaw clenched.

Ethan and I shared a glance. "I don't believe we have hard facts either way," he said, apparently deciding not to raise the circumstantial evidence we'd discovered in the library. "Although she has demonstrated that she's not above spreading discord among the Houses."

"And how much of that discord is personal, Sullivan?" Morgan sat forward, turned his head to Ethan. "Can you really be neutral about Celina?"

Ethan arched a single brow. "Neutral? About Celina? Have her actions to date suggested that she should be afforded neutrality?"

Agreed, I thought, given that the woman had tried to kill Ethan and had tried to have me killed. I had very specific, and very concrete, feelings about Celina Desaulniers. Neutrality wasn't even on the menu.

"Look," Noah said, "her previous acts notwithstanding, before we get too involved in personal vendetta, I'm with Greer. If we have no evidence either way, then let's leave out assigning blame to anyone in particular. The GP released her, so we'll be overstepping our bounds if we take too close a look—you know how that goes." I didn't, but the comment made me wonder. I added that to my library to-do list.

"So the only thing that focusing our attention on Celina is likely to accomplish is pissing off Greenwich or wasting our limited time on a direction we don't have the political capital to pursue." Noah shook his head, leaned back in his chair. "No. It's not that I think she's a saint, but without specifics, I say we keep the investigation open at this point."

Scott shrugged. "Definitely not a saint, but I agree. I threw it out there to test the waters. If we don't have evidence, we keep our focus broad."

"That's decided, then," Ethan said, but that line of worry was settled between his brows. The comments didn't suggest that Scott or Noah was blindly supportive of Celina, but they were going to have to be convinced of her guilt. That burden, apparently, lay on us.

"It comes back to the Breckenridges," Luc suggested. "There must be something we're missing. Why this family? Why now? If the perp had information on Jamie, and they're using it to get something out of the Brecks, why involve us? What's the connection between the Brecks and vamps? Why the animosity?"

Animosity.

That was the word that did it, that forced the puzzle pieces into place.

I thought about Nick's questions outside the House, then the labyrinth.

The tingle of magic, the hatred in his eyes.

The movement in the underbrush, and the animal that stared back at me through the trees.

The selfsame tingle I'd felt in Papa Breck's office.

The obvious prejudice, the hatred of vampires.

Circling the wagons around Jamie, protecting him.

"They aren't human," I said aloud, then glanced up, met Ethan's gaze.

"They aren't human?" Scott asked.

Ethan stared at me, and I saw the instant he understood. "The animosity. The distrust of vampires." He nodded. "You may very well be right."

"What are you saying?" Morgan asked.

Ethan, still looking at me, nodded, giving me the go-ahead to take the lead, to announce the conclusion. I looked around the room, met their gazes. "They're shifters. The Brecken-ridges are shifters."

That was why I'd felt the prickle of magic around Nick. He was a shifter. And unlike vampirism, being a shifter was hereditary, so he was a shifter like his father, like his brothers. All bound in loyalty to Gabriel Keene, the Apex, the alpha, of the North American Central Pack.

"The animal at the rave site," I said, remembering that tingle of animal and magic. "That must have been Nick."

Morgan's head snapped in my direction. "You went to a rave site?" He leaned forward, palms flat on the table, then turned his head toward Ethan. "You took her to a rave site? She's barely two months old, for Christ's sake."

"She had her sword."

"And I repeat, she's barely two months old. Are you trying to get her killed?"

"I made a decision based upon my knowledge of her skills."

"Jesus, Sullivan. I don't understand you."

Ethan pushed back his chair, stood up and leaned over the conference table, fingers splayed on the tabletop. "First of all, I would never put Merit in a situation I didn't think she was equipped to handle. Besides which, she was with me, as well as Catcher and Mallory Carmichael, who, as we've discussed, is coming into sufficient powers of her own to offer protection to those within her circle. I understand the Order is establishing a presence in Chicago solely to be able to capitalize on her skills."

That made me sit up a little straighter. Apparently, Mallory's trips to Schaumburg were a little more meaningful than I'd been led to believe.

He leaned down a little farther, skewered Morgan with a glance that would have sent me into a corner whimpering, tail between my legs, and arched an imperious brow.

"Second, I have said this to you once before, and this is the last time I'll say it. You need to remember your position.

I make no argument with the age or prestige of your House, Greer. But you have been a Master for less time than Merit has been a vampire, and you might recall that you owe your House to her, because your former Master saw fit to make an attempt on my life." He stopped talking, but the look in his eyes said plenty that he'd left unspoken—that if Morgan did challenge Ethan again, Ethan would see that he suffered the consequences of it.

The room fell heavily silent. After a minute of continuing to flay Morgan with that narrowed gaze—and Morgan staring back defiantly—Ethan slowly lifted green eyes to me, and I saw something different there.

Respect.

My stomach clenched with the force of that look, of being looked to as an equal by someone who'd previously seen me as something much less. We'd become a kind of team, a Cadogan duo united against our foes.

"Now," Ethan said, returning to his seat. "If they are shifters, how does that inform our investigation?"

"Maybe they're protecting the weaker member," Luc concluded. "They've been guarding Jamie, protecting Jamie, from this supposed threat against him. And from what I understand, that's unusual for the Brecks. Jamie had previously been the black sheep. The aimless one. Maybe that's why the Breckenridges were picked. Maybe someone knows something about Jamie, thought that made the family vulnerable." He frowned. "Jamie could have a magic glitch. Maybe he can't transform completely, maybe he can't shift at will. Something."

"If that's true, Papa Breck has a problem," Ethan concluded.

"And since Jamie's still alive, Papa Breck has a secret," Luc concluded.

I frowned at Luc. "What do you mean, since Jamie's still alive?"

"The Packs are strictly hierarchical," Noah explained. "The strongest members lead the Pack, the weaker members serve, or they're culled."

Culled. A politic way of suggesting the runts of the litter were put down. "That's . . . horrible," I said, my eyes wide.

"In human terms," Noah said, "Maybe. But they aren't human. They're ruled by different instincts, have different histories, different challenges in their histories." He shrugged a shoulder. "I'm not sure it's for us to judge."

"Killing off members of your society?" I shook my head. "I'm fairly comfortable judging that, regardless of their history. Natural selection is one thing, but this is eugenics, social Darwinism."

"Merit," Ethan said. There was gentle chastisement in his voice. "Neither the time nor the place."

I closed my mouth, accepted the criticism. I heard a disgusted sniff from Morgan's side of the table, assumed he'd disagreed either with the chastisement or with my obeying it.

"Putting aside the ethics," Ethan said, "Jamie is clearly still a part of the family. Either Gabriel doesn't know, or he knows and doesn't care."

"Jesus Christ," Scott said, scrubbing hands across his face. "It was bad enough when it was us against the *Trib* and the city of Chicago, but now we're gonna face off against the goddamned North American Central? Greer was right," he said, worry clear in his face. "We're fucked."

"Suggestions?" Ethan asked.

"Let me make a phone call," I said, figuring I already owed Jeff one favor. One more wasn't going to hurt.

Ethan looked at me for a moment, maybe deciding if he was willing to trust my judgment. He nodded. "Do it."

I volunteered to meet Jeff at the door of Cadogan House. I figured he'd appreciate the personal attention and be a little more comfortable in a House of vampires if he had his own personal guard and attendant. At least, that's how I explained it to him.

I stood in the doorway, arms crossed, waiting for the RDI guards to clear Jeff onto the property. He walked up wearing khakis and a long-sleeved, button-up shirt over his thin frame, the shirtsleeves rolled halfway to his elbows. His brown hair flopped as he bobbed up the sidewalk, hands in his pockets and a goofy grin on his face.

He hopped up the portico stairs and met me at the open door. There was a little more adoration in his eyes than I was comfortable with, but Jeff was doing us a big favor—particularly as a shifter, walking into a den of enemies—so I dealt.

"Hi, Merit."

I smiled at him. "It's about time you got here. Any news about the e-mail?"

"Yeah," he said, casting a worried glance inside the House. "But not here. Too many ears."

His answer didn't bode well, but I took the hint. "I appreciate your coming over here. And spending your evening sourcing an e-mail."

"That's why they call me the Champ."

I chuckled and moved aside to let him in the House. "Since when do they call you the Champ?"

He paused in the foyer as I closed the door behind us, and gave me a grin. "Remember how you and I are dating?"

"Right," I solemnly said. "How's that going, by the way?" I pointed the way toward Ethan's office and he fell in step beside me, surveying the House and the scattering of vampires.

"Well, they do call me the Champ. I mean, my work is suffering, though."

"Is it now?"

We reached the closed office door, and Jeff ran a hand through his hair. Nerves, I imagined, but he looked at me, laughed it off.

"Yeah, you tend to be a little . . . distracting. You know, with the hands. And always calling me, texting me." He looked over at me, and while he smiled, fear tightened his eyes, marked the air with an astringent tang.

"When we go in there, I'm your Sentinel, too."

This time he smiled, and I think a little of the tension went out of his shoulders.

"And you know what?" I asked him, clasping the door-knob.

He ran a hand through his hair again. "What?"

"You're my most favorite shifter."

Jeff rolled his eyes. "Not that I'm denying my manly appeal, but I'm the only shifter you know."

"Actually, Jeff, that's kind of our problem." I opened the door, and in we went.

CHAPTER TWENTY

THE RUNT OF THE LITTER

Although the rest of the vamps were still seated around the conference table, Luc had moved closer to the door and was leaning against the back of a leather chair when we walked in. I appreciated the move. This way, we could both escort Jeff to the table, give him protection from two sides. While Catcher had once assured me that Jeff could take care of himself, and having seen the depth of Nick's fury, I didn't doubt the shifter had it in him. But at twenty-one, he was younger, by far, than everyone else in the room, and the member of a group that wasn't high on the vamps' list of favorites right now. Even if there wasn't much of a risk that we'd have to break out the weaponry, this ensured that the Masters kept their manners.

"Thank you for agreeing to speak with us," Ethan said, standing and extending a hand as we moved to the table. "Especially on such short notice."

"No problem," Jeff lightly said, taking his hand. "Glad I can help, I guess." He sat down in an empty chair; I took the seat beside him.

Ethan smiled and turned back to the rest of the table. "I believe you know everyone here, but we'll do the introductions for form." He made the intros and the vampires responded graciously, probably because I gave everybody the evil eye, a warning against snarking back to our House guest.

Introductions complete, Jeff looked at Ethan, then me. "So, what do you want to know?"

"As you know," I began, "we're looking into a threat against Jamie Breckenridge that was supposedly made by Cadogan vampires. But we haven't been able to find anyone—any vampires—with a grudge against Jamie." I paused. "We believe that the Breckenridges are shifters."

"Oh," Jeff said, surprise in his expression. "Okay."

"What we're trying to figure out," I continued, "is whether another shifter might have a grudge against the family."

Jeff frowned. "I'm not following."

"Jamie's always been a little aimless, wouldn't you say, Merit?" Ethan asked.

I nodded. "I think that's fair."

"However, it seems the Breckenridge family is now circling around him. No one else, as far as I'm aware, knows that the Breckenridges are shifter in origin. The theory we're working from is that maybe they're circling for a reason. Maybe Jamie's weak, has some sort of magical problem. And maybe some members of the Pack want to do something about that."

Jeff shook his head. "I still don't—" Then he stopped, mouth falling open, shock and dismay and, worst of all, hurt, in his expression. He sat back in his chair, as if deflated by the question. "Wow."

The room went silent, gazes dropping guiltily to the table, the vamps unable to make eye contact.

A minute or two passed in silence. I wanted to reach out a hand, to touch him, both to comfort him and to reassure myself, but the move seemed patronizing. Instead, I looked up, caught Ethan's eye, that line of worry between his brows.

"No offense, but this is why shifters don't like vampires," Jeff quietly said, drawing our eyes back to him. "The rumor, the speculation. That you would actually ask me that to my face—do you kill off members of your Pack? That's insulting."

He looked at me. "I know you're new and maybe you don't know better," he said, then looked at Ethan and the rest of the vampires, "but the rest of you have been around. Surely you do."

None of them, to their credit, offered their ignorance as an excuse.

"Now," Jeff continued, sitting forward in the chair and putting his elbows on the table, "the fact that we don't exterminate members"—he gave us all a pointed look, suggesting he knew exactly which supernatural species did, and given the sword belted at my side, I thought he had a pretty good point—"doesn't mean we don't have intra-Pack struggles. Just because Jamie won't actually be taken out doesn't mean he wouldn't be bullied by stronger Pack members, that folks wouldn't use his weakness, whatever it is, against him or his family."

"Blackmail?" I asked.

"Or extortion. It's happened before. 'Give me what I want, and I'll ensure your kid's protected,' that kind of thing. Pack members who are already pretty far down in the ranks try to make themselves feel better. Part of where you stand is, well, you know, immutable. Every shifter has a primary form. The animal they change into. Shifters are born that way. The form a shifter takes, that doesn't change. You're born to it, and that affects your rank in the pack. But part of it is muscle, strength. And that strength determines what you do with your rank—do you sit back, let the Pack make decisions? Or do you try to have a role, try to influence Gabriel? The thing about blackmail, about the bullying, is that Pack members don't report that kind of thing to him."

"Because that's the kind of act that makes them seem that much weaker—not being able to handle their own problems?"

Jeff nodded at Scott. "Exactly. Gabriel is sovereign of the N.A. Central, the Pack as a whole, as a unit. He's not here to arbitrate family disputes or whatever. That's not his role."

Ethan held up a finger. "Unless they become Pack disputes."

Jeff nodded. "Sure. If they become Pack disputes. But that doesn't happen very often. That's the nature of the Pack. We take care of our own. You get enough Pack members riled up, we take care of it on our own."

Those words, spoken by a skinny twenty-one-year-old computer programmer, hovered uncomfortably in the air.

"Jeff," I asked, "do you know anything specific about a plan to harm Jamie, or any animosity toward the Brecks?"

"I didn't even know they were shifters until you told me. It's not like there's a list or radar or something. Remember, we're still kind of . . . in the closet, I guess. And while we're lumped into packs, there are only four packs in the U.S., and that's really just geography. We're born, not made like you, so we operate on more of a, I guess you'd say, family level."

"Like the Mafia," Scott suggested.

"We're not that bad," Jeff said.

Ethan looked around. "If Jamie, indeed, has some sort of magical injury, that information could be used to his detriment by other individuals inside the Pack. What can we extrapolate from that?"

"If it's true," Jeff put in, although I think the question had been meant for vampires, "and someone discovered it, they'd have found a trigger for the Breckenridges. Something that could completely set them off."

"Something that *has* set them off," Ethan darkly corrected.

"And if the owner of that information was a vampire," Luc said, fear in his expression, "that trigger could spark a war between us."

The room went silent.

Ethan sighed heavily, then looked around at the folks at the table. "As we've barely half an hour until dawn, if we have nothing else productive to contribute today, I'll contact RDI and ask that they supplement our investigation during the day. In the meantime, please canvass as best you can to determine if anyone has additional pertinent information. I suggest we meet here, an hour after sunset, to reconvene and share what we've learned. Any objections?"

"Best we can do on a short time frame," Scott said, pushing back his chair. Noah did the same. Scott and Noah nodded at Ethan, then went for the door. Morgan's exit was slower. He pushed back his chair, rose and waited until Noah and Scott were out the door, probably headed for cover as the sun threatened to peek above the horizon. Morgan looked at me, fury in his eyes, then shifted his gaze to Ethan. Morgan walked toward him, stopped within inches of his body, and whispered something that flattened Ethan's expression.

Without glancing back at me, Morgan walked away and out the office door, slamming it shut behind him.

Ethan, still standing at the head of the table, closed his eyes. "Someday, if he prepares for it, he could be a leader of vampires. God forbid that day comes before he is prepared."

"I think that day is here," Malik muttered to me. I nodded my agreement, but rued my impact on Morgan's interaction with the rest of the Masters. He'd been flummoxed by me, and yet had tried to be protective when I broached the rave topic. I didn't really know what to think about that.

"Jeff," Ethan said, "thank you again for venturing into Cadogan House. We appreciate the information more than we can say."

Jeff shrugged. "No problem. I'm happy to help correct the facts." But then he lowered his head, leaned toward me, and whispered, "About the other thing."

I glanced back at him. "Not here?"

He shook his head, and I nodded my agreement.

"I'll walk him out," I said aloud, then pushed back my chair. Jeff did the same.

"You're dismissed," Ethan said, walking back to his desk and picking up the handset of his phone. "I'll see you both tomorrow."

It wasn't until we were outside the House, halfway between the front door and the wrought-iron fence, that Jeff stopped me with a hand on my arm. He glanced around, gaze darting to and fro. He looked like he was casing the House.

"Avoiding the paparazzi," he explained, "and, no offense, but the guards—I'm not a fan."

We both glanced over to where they stood, dark and severe, at the Cadogan gate. As if on cue, they simultaneously glanced over their shoulders and regarded us.

"They're a little creepy," I agreed, then looked at Jeff. "What did you learn?"

"Okay," he said, both hands moving as he began to explain, "it took a few tries, but I managed to trace the e-mail address. The IP address was a non-starter, unfortunately. Way too many roundabouts, and even if I found an origin address, that's only going to give me a location, right? It's not going to tell me who sent the e-mail."

I blinked at him for a second. "I seriously have no clue what you just said."

He stopped talking and looked at me, then waved his hands before starting up again. "Doesn't matter. The e-mail address is the key. The e-mail to Nick was sent from a generic address. The kind you can set up for free on the Web. I managed to drill down into it, get the original setup data, but the info was fake. The name on the account was Vlad."

I rolled my eyes. "Points us in the right direction, I guess, but it's not very creative."

"Exactly what I thought, so I tried something else. Every time you set up one of these generic accounts, you have to enter another e-mail address. A place the company can send your password if you forget it or something like that."

"I assume the other e-mail address was fake, too?"

Jeff smiled. "Now you're getting it. I drilled down into six accounts—"

I interrupted him with a hand. "Wait. When you say 'drilled down,' you mean 'hacked,' right?"

Jeff had the grace to blush. It was charming, in its highly illegal way. "I'm totally white hat," he said, "not that you know what that means, but I am. It's all public service, when you think about it. And I'm a public servant, anyway."

I glanced up as he rationalized, suddenly realizing that the sky was beginning to pinken at the edges. "We need to hurry this up if at all possible, J, before I become considerably crispier. What did you find?"

His smile faded. Jeff looked around again, then pulled a folded piece of paper from his pocket. His expression dour, he handed it over.

"This is the chain I discovered," he said. "All the e-mails I could find, leading back to the origin e-mail at the bottom."

I unfolded the paper. I recognized nothing until I got to the very last name on the list. An e-mail address I'd seen before, the name giving it all away. I muttered a curse at the sight. "This is so not what I wanted to see."

"Yeah," he said. "I figure we're even on those favors now."

I stood on the portico for a moment after Jeff left, staring at the closed front door. Symbols were posted above the threshold, indications of the House's alliances. Unfortunately, given the results of Jeff's search, we were probably going to need those.

Even with only minutes left until dawn, I decided this wasn't something I could sit on. I headed for the basement stairs and the Ops Room. I'd guessed wrong about the would-be perpetrator; Kelley was cleared by Jeff's e-mail search. I couldn't say the same for the guard that actually sent it. Regardless, that guard fell under Luc's supervision, so I opted to start with him. Besides, no way was I taking this to Ethan without backup.

I pushed open the door and scanned the room, my heart thudding in my chest as I prepared to hand over the evidence of a colleague's betrayal. Even this close to dawn, the room buzzed with activity as vampires prepared to cede control over House security completely to RDI.

Lindsey and Kelley sat at their computer stations. Luc stood behind Lindsey's chair, his gaze on her monitor as she worked, but glanced back as I closed the door behind me.

"Sentinel," he said, straightening. "I didn't expect to see you back. What's up?"

"Where's Peter?"

Luc lifted his eyebrows. "Probably back in his room. He had the early shift. Why?"

I held out the e-mail. "Because he sent the threat."

The room went silent, Lindsey and Kelley turning, eyes wide, to face me.

"That's quite an accusation, Sentinel."

I glanced over at Lindsey. "Do you have a copy of the e-mail from Peter that had the paparazzi information on it?"

"Um, sure," she said. She looked confused, but opened a folder beside her computer station and pulled the printout from it, then spun in her chair and extended it to me. I grabbed it, then laid both pieces of paper flat on the conference table. Luc walked over, arms crossed defiantly over his chest.

I pointed to the first document. "This is the e-mail from Peter about the paparazzi."

Luc looked the e-mail over, a frown pulling his features. "Sure," he said. "He sent it to me from his Cadogan e-mail address. I printed it out."

"I know. I gave the e-mail with the threat against Jamie to Jeff Christopher. He traced it back through multiple addresses, all bogus. But at the end of the chain was this one." I pressed my finger onto the list Jeff had given me a few minutes ago and pointed at the final e-mail on the list— Peter's Cadogan e-mail address.

Silence for a moment, then unmitigated swearing.

"Son of a *bitch*." Luc looked up, jaw tight, nostrils flaring as he realized the betrayal. "He's been playing us. The whole time, playing us."

Luc put his palms flat on the table, head bowed. Then, without warning, he pulled back and punched a fist into the tabletop with a *crack* that split the air like thunder—and notched a fist-sized divot in the wood.

"Luc," Lindsey said. She popped up from her chair and wrapped an arm around his waist, her other hand on his shoulder. "Luc," she repeated, her voice softer.

I bit back a small smile; I was beginning to think that Lindsey protested too much about our intrepid guard captain.

"I know," he said, then looked up at me, his eyes blazing. "He's not in this alone. Not to turn against the House after all these years. If he's in this, it's because someone else is pulling the strings."

I thought of the "she" who'd left a message for Nick. "I know," I told him. "I think you're probably right about that."

"Would it be too much for me to ask that in addition to having this evidence, you have a sly plan to nail this little asshole?"

I smiled coyly. "Of course I have a sly plan. I am a Merit, after all."

Two minutes later we were on the first floor. Luc had Kelley deliver an update about the Breckenridge threat to Peter's room, confirming he was still in the House. We also alerted RDI, who were told to stop him in the event he tried to bolt.

Ethan's door was closed. Luc rapped knuckles against the door, but didn't wait for a response before opening it.

Ethan was behind his desk, flipping closed a laptop as if preparing for dawn himself. "Lucas?" he asked, brows furrowed at our entry.

I looked at Luc, who nodded, then made my request. "I need permission to kill two birds with one stone."

Ethan arched an eyebrow. "You need permission to kill fowl?"

"She's serious, Ethan." Luc's voice was quiet, severe, and it drew Ethan's eyes and put a look of surprise on his face. I was surprised, as well—I'm not sure I'd ever heard Luc refer to Ethan by his name.

They exchanged a look, then Ethan nodded and looked at me. "Sentinel?"

"It's Peter," I said. "He sent the threat to the Breckenridges."

I watched a bevy of emotions cross his face, from shock to denial to a fury that filled the air with an electric tingle, and narrowed his eyes into slits of glassy green . . . and then quicksilver.

"You have evidence of this, I assume?"

"He sent the e-mail," Luc said. "The message to Nick that threatened Jamie. It was routed through a lot of fake addresses, but originated in Peter's Cadogan address."

Ethan adjusted his jaw, and when he finally spoke, his voice was low, thick, and dangerous. "He sent a threatening e-mail to a shifter from this *House*?"

He stood up, then pushed back his chair with enough force that it continued to roll after he'd walked away toward the conference table at the other end of the room. I snapped my gaze to Luc, who shook his head. A warning, I assumed, not to interfere.

Ethan paced to the bar along the wall with the slinking intensity of a panther, grabbed a glass from the bar, and with a turn and windup of his torso, propelled it across the room. The glass flew, then crashed into the wall on the other side of the conference table. Glass fractured, shattered, and splintered to the ground.

"Liege," Luc said, quiet but stern.

"In my *House*," Ethan said, then turned back to us, hands on his hips. "In my goddamn *HOUSE*."

Luc nodded.

"Two traitors in my House, Lucas. In *Peter's* House. How? How is this possible? Is there anything I haven't given them? Anything they've lacked?" His gaze snapped to mine. "Sentinel?"

I dropped my gaze to the floor, unable to bear the pain and fury and betrayal in his. "No, Liege."

"Liege," Ethan muttered, the word rendered a joke.

"Merit has a plan," Luc put in.

Ethan looked at me, eyebrows raised, a bit of appreciative surprise in his expression. "Sentinel?"

"Killing two birds," I reminded him. "It's too late now, the sun's nearly up, but I think I know how we can confront him without risking the rest of the vampires in the House. We'll lure him out."

"And how will we accomplish that?"

"We offer Celina as bait."

His gaze went a little bit wicked, as if he fully condoned the manipulation. "Do what you have to do, Merit."

"That's permission?" I confirmed.

Ever so slowly, he raised his gaze to mine, then looked at me, this Master of vampires, emerald eyes glowing. "Nail him, Sentinel."

*　　*　　*

The plan set, and the sun glowing at the edge of the horizon, I returned to my room, and found my cell phone angry and blinking. Mallory had left four voice mails, each more consoling, slightly less angry, than the one before it. She seemed to have worked off some of her steam, but I couldn't say that mine had lessened. The vampire drama had focused my attention elsewhere, certainly, but it hadn't eliminated the dull current of anger. I just wasn't ready to talk to her.

And that wasn't the only thing waiting for me. I thought, at first, that the red paper on the floor of my room had slipped from the packet of mail I'd brought back from Mallory's house. But I knew there'd been no crimson envelope on the hardwood floor when I'd changed clothes a few hours ago.

It was the same envelope as the card sent to Mallory's, but this time it was addressed to me at Cadogan House. I picked it up, then lifted the heavy flap. No card inside this time, but there was something else. I upended the contents into my hand. Out came a rectangle of translucent red plastic about the size of a business card. It bore a single thin white line, the inscription RG, and a stylized *fleur-de-lis*.

The card in my hand, I went to the bed and sat down, then put the envelope on the comforter beside me. I flipped the card back and forth, held it up to the light, tried to read through to the reverse side. Nothing.

The envelopes had both been addressed to me—one at my old address, one at my new one. Someone had known where I'd lived and had discovered that I'd moved. Someone who wanted to give me random bits of paper and plastic? Were these supposed to be messages? Clues?

The sun rising, and my tolerance for mysteries having been exhausted for the day, I put the card on the nightstand beside my bed. I changed into pajamas—a long-sleeved, oversized Bears T-shirt—ensured that the shutter over the window was secure, and climbed into bed.

CHAPTER TWENTY-ONE

YOU GIVE BITE A BAD NAME

As it tends to do, the sun set again. Showered and dressed, I stood before the conference table in the Ops Room in my Cadogan black, katana belted and at the ready, preparing to, as Ethan had put it, nail my colleague.

Nailing Peter, of course, wasn't the hard part. The hard part was going to be convincing Peter to nail whomever he'd been in league with, whether the "she" from Nick's telephone call or someone else with insider information about the Breckenridges. The setup, of course, was easy. We'd send an e-mail to one of Peter's fake addresses in the guise of the person we suspected was guiding his hand—Celina—and ask him to meet her at their "usual" location. If he took the bait, we'd confirm that Celina was the manipulator behind the scenes. We'd follow him to the rendezvous spot and, from there, take him in.

"Or that's how it's supposed to go," I told the guards, my hands sweating as I explained the plan to the vampires around the conference table. This was, I guess, my first official op as Sentinel, and there were a million ways it could go wrong.

Among other potential problems, we'd gotten access to Peter's e-mails through the service providers; it wasn't like we'd hacked directly into his accounts. So, we had no clue if Celina set up meetings with him via e-mail or, if so, what address she used. But we had a pretty good clue. Jeff, being ever resourceful, spent some of the daylight hours scrubbing the Web for data that might help us, and managed to find a cached image of Peter's e-mail directory from a few weeks ago. Although we couldn't actually read the e-mails, we noticed that one addressee looked curiously familiar: Marie Collette.

Celina's human name.

More important, the e-mail was dated only a week before we'd met Celina at North Pond and Ethan had confronted her about her role in the park killings. Peter and Celina had communicated, and they'd done it just before she tried to kabob Ethan. Coincidence? Maybe. Likely not.

But even if Celina hadn't been the instigator for this newest betrayal, the fact that she and Peter had communicated increased the odds that he'd be curious enough to take the bait, especially since he'd been warned she would probably attempt to reenter Chicago. Either way, we could ensure that he was out of the House—and our vampires were out of danger—before we confronted him.

"Lindsey," Luc prompted when I'd finished my review.

She nodded. "Since Jeff couldn't get us into the existing 'Marie Collette' account, I've set up a new one using a different domain name. He's got at least six operative e-mail addresses, so it shouldn't come as a huge surprise that Celina's got more than one."

"We do what we can with what we've got," Luc said. "We just need to get him out the door. And the message?"

I clicked a button so the text displayed on the wall screen across from the conference table, then read aloud: "You've been compromised. Rendezvous point ASAP."

"We were afraid to pick a specific time since we weren't sure when he'd see the message," Juliet pointed out. "But assuming we've made the correct assumptions, and that Celina's behind this, it's not a bad plan."

Luc nodded, then looked at me. "It's your op, Sentinel. You ready?"

I thought of the betrayal in Ethan's eyes, and nodded, left hand on the handle of my katana. "Let's nail him."

*   *   *

Lindsey and Luc were in her SUV outside the House, an eye on Peter's own red sports car (which had been tagged by RDI with a tracking device), ready to follow Peter if he followed our plan. I stood beside the basement door, waiting impatiently for Juliet, who'd been assigned to drive both of us. Her vehicle, a black sedan, was apparently less noticeable than my orange Volvo, which Luc immediately vetoed as a surveillance car.

I heard footsteps on the stairs and stood straight, but it wasn't Juliet who appeared around the corner. Blond hair tied at the base of his neck, his body snugged into a short-sleeved black T-shirt and dark jeans, katana in a royal blue scabbard at his waist, he smiled just so, one corner of his mouth tipped up knowingly.

"Don't look so surprised, Sentinel," he said, moving past me to type numbers into the keypad. "I can't in good conscience allow you to have all the fun."

"Where's Juliet?" I asked.

Ethan opened the basement door and held it out for me.

"I'm still inside," Juliet said, her voice echoing through my tiny earpiece as Ethan and I walked to the Mercedes. "Kel and I are keeping an eye on the House while you four play vampire A-Team. And speaking of fun, numbnuts is still in his room and Kelley's got an eye out from the third-floor kitchen. Everybody else in position?"

"Car number one ready," Luc said. "And Blondie's here, looking pretty as always."

I bit back a smile at the curses that lit through the earpiece.

"Third floor ready," Kelley whispered.

"Car number two is ready," Ethan said, chirping the alarm on the Mercedes. We climbed inside and Ethan started the engine, adjusted his mirror, and headed for the ramp.

"Sending the e-mail in three, two, one, sent."

There was no sound but for the clank of the rising garage door and the hum of the Mercedes. Ethan pulled the car onto the street, this corner still dark and empty of paparazzi.

He sidled into a parallel spot and put the car in park. We waited.

It took thirty-seven minutes. Time enough for Peter to check his e-mail, grab his sword, and sprint to the red sports car, which was parked outside the House. Luc and Lindsey were in the least conspicuous of the vehicles, so they took off first, pulling onto the street a hundred yards or so behind Peter. When they were a couple of blocks ahead of us, we pulled out, all of us following the would-be saboteur, who drove east, then jumped onto Lake Shore Drive.

I glanced over at Ethan, who weaved through traffic to keep the vehicles ahead of us in sight. Peter flew north, apparently eager to see Celina, or whoever else he believed was meeting him. If it was Celina, I wondered if he was going of his own accord—because he loved her or believed in her or some indivisible bit of both—or because he'd been glamoured. Because Peter, for all his strength, couldn't overcome Celina's will.

"What are you going to do to him?" I asked Ethan, as we glided beside the Lake.

"Do to him?"

"When he confesses," I said, utter confidence that he would. "What will you do to him? What will be his punishment?"

"Excommunication," Ethan replied without hesitation. "He'll be banished from the House, his medal stripped. The same punishment ultimately received by Amber, albeit without her participation."

"What else?" I wondered, thinking excommunication was hardly sufficient for the betrayal.

"The *Canon* prescribes death for the betrayal of a House." Ethan had let Amber go, despite her betrayal; I wondered if Peter would be so lucky.

As if reading my mind, he offered, "Obviously, I don't subscribe to most of the more archaic punishments. Not that he doesn't deserve it."

I withheld judgment on that one.

We followed Lake Shore for miles, past the Pier and Oak Street Beach, then North Avenue Beach.

"Boss." Luc's voice echoed through our headsets. "He's taking the exit. Fullerton. Near North Pond."

Ethan's hands tightened on the wheel. North Pond, situated in a corner of Lincoln Park, was the place we'd enjoyed our previous Celina episode, her attempt on Ethan's life, her attempt to take control of Chicago's other Houses. I understood Ethan's hesitation. He'd nearly been stabbed, and I'd nearly committed vampiricide. That had been the finale in the bustle of our supernaturally busy weeks.

"The marina," Luc said, "he's heading to the harbor."

"Diversey Harbor," I added. "It's across Cannon from North Pond."

Ethan followed the SUV as it made a couple of right turns, but stopped before entering the harbor's parking lot.

"Keep going," I told Ethan. "Head him off at the other end of the lot."

Ethan nodded. We passed one entrance, then took a second, the lights on Peter's car the only thing moving in the lot. We parked the Mercedes, popped out, and rebelted our katanas. This time, Ethan skipped the noisy security check.

"We've got him," came Luc's whisper. "Linds is staying in the car in case he tries to run. I'm on foot. He's heading toward the boat launch. I'm going in, but I'll stay under cover until your mark."

"That's good," I whispered, as Ethan and I headed south again to the rendezvous point. "If we can corner him against the Lake, fewer escape routes."

"Do it," Ethan said.

Seconds of silence followed, seconds in which my heart thudded against my chest as Ethan and I trotted toward the launch.

"I'm in the car," Lindsey said. "Luc's in the trees to the south. He's here, looking around, obviously waiting for someone. He keeps checking his watch."

"Waiting for her?" Ethan whispered.

"Who would it surprise?" I wondered back. When we got

close enough to see him—a long figure before the dark void of the Lake—I stopped and put out a hand to stop Ethan.

"I'm first," I whispered. He glowered for a moment, but then relented with a nod. "Luc, let's keep him in the middle."

"Aye, aye, Sentinel."

I blew out a breath, then adjusted my grip on the katana and released the thumb guard. Three months ago, I'd been a grad student standing before a classroom of undergraduates. And today . . .

Today I stood Sentinel for a House of three hundred and twenty vampires. An old House. An honorable House. A House that had been betrayed by one of its own.

No, I mentally corrected—by another of its own.

Peter suddenly turned, katana out and poised in front of him. Behind him, the ramp angled down into the water.

"Who's there?" he called out.

Behind me, Ethan growled.

"Your colleagues," I called back. We stepped through the shadow of the trees into the overhead lights that illuminated the launch.

Peter's eyes widened, a breeze of magic floating through the air as his fear rose. "What are you doing here?"

"We'd ask you the same question, Novitiate." Ethan stepped beside me, his katana already loosed.

Rein it in, Sullivan, I mentally warned him. He must have heard me, as the katana dropped an inch.

"We know why you're here, Peter," I told him. "We know you sent the e-mail to the Breckenridges about the vampire threat, and we assume you gave the 'anonymous' information to the Ombud's office. It's not much of a stretch to assume that you've been feeding someone information about our social schedule."

Peter wet his lips.

"The question, Peter, is whether you want to cooperate or not."

"No," Ethan said. "The question is why." The words were softly spoken.

Peter's gaze flicked nervously from me to Ethan. "Liege."

"No," Ethan said, taking a step forward. "You have lost the right to call me, to call anyone, Liege. Peter Spencer, you have violated the *Canon* and the covenants of Cadogan House."

No longer just "Peter." Now "Peter Spencer." Peter had regained a last name. Not good.

"You can't do this," Peter said, a nervous laughter in his voice.

Ethan moved forward another step. I gripped the handle of my katana in my right hand.

"You have violated your responsibilities to your Master, your brethren, and your House, and you have broken your oaths as a Novitiate vampire."

"I acted in the best interest of vampires," Peter said, re-gripping his katana. "I acted when you wouldn't."

Ethan, I warned, pulling my own sword.

"You are, hereby—" Ethan reached out his hand toward Peter's neck. No, not his neck. His medal. Ethan reached for the symbol of Peter's soon-to-be-former membership in Cadogan House. His link to the rest of the Cadogan vampires.

"All right, stop!" Peter said, taking a step backward and out of Ethan's reach. "Stop." He looked around, then back at Ethan. "You don't get it, Sullivan. You don't understand what we need, what she can give us. We are *vampires*!" His voice rose, carried across the empty parking lot, across the Lake, then dropped again.

"They mock us. They are mortal, and weak, but they mock us. They would take away our rights. But we can't allow that."

"Who mocks us?" I asked. "Humans?"

Peter looked at me, frustration in his features. "Shifters. The pretenders."

And there was the vampire version of Nick's animosity, I thought. Born of some historic feud, and just as archaic.

"Ethan," Peter said, "Keene is bringing the shifters to Chicago. They are practically on their way. You can't let Cadogan House fall. Not to shifters, not to humans. You can't let us become some kind of amusement park vampire spectacle.

On the cover of magazines?" He spat out a curse. "We are better than that. We are *immortals*. We can control the night again, but we have to act."

How much of this paranoia, I silently asked Ethan, *is Peter, and how much is Celina's manipulation?*

I've no idea, he replied.

"The Houses need to be awakened," Peter said. "We let shifters escape the first time. During the Clearings, we let them avoid their responsibilities as supernaturals. They are our enemies, Ethan, and we have to remember that."

"We're at peace," Ethan said. "With humans, with shifters."

"We're in *denial*," Peter challenged. "And it's time for us to prepare."

"That's why the messages were sent? That's why the Breckenridges were targeted? To trigger a war between vampires and shifters?"

"They were targeted because they are weak." Peter's eyes glowed silver. "They were targeted to remind Keene who we are. What we are capable of. To remind him that Chicago is our city. Our town, and we won't let it go. Especially not to shifters. To *pretenders*."

As if he'd spoken his war cry, he attacked, katana raised. I muttered a curse and, as Ethan spun away, raised my own sword in attack. I executed a half turn, spinning as I sliced the katana upward. Peter, unfortunately, was older and a more experienced fighter. He moved, then brought the katana horizontally across my knees. I jumped, and for the first time as a vampire, took air, bounding in a flip that brought me down on Peter's other side.

Someone might have warned me I could do that, I mentally told Ethan, then sliced my katana down. Peter met my sword with his, the force vibrating the steel and my arm.

Unfortunately, that vibration also woke the vampire, like a hand on a shoulder waking someone from sleep. I huffed out a breath and pushed her back down, unwilling to lose control of this fight. I'd already seen how bad that could go, having stopped the *bokken* only millimeters from Catcher's head.

Peter and I clanged swords again and again and again as we sliced the katanas from side to side, me moving backward down the ramp as he pushed forward. The ribbed concrete was slick with water and algae, and I struggled to keep my footing as we moved. And worse—my head began to pound from the combined effort of fighting off his attacks, making my own advances, and trying to keep the vampire at bay.

"Celina will win," Peter said.

And there's my motivation, I thought. With a burst of energy that would have thrilled both Catcher and Aerobics Barbie—but which made the vampire that much more curious—I inched my way up the ramp, forcing Peter up and back with each slice and thrust of my sword. He turned to gain distance and I ran forward, katana in the air. I sliced down, but he turned on me, his own katana slicing upward.

"Celina is our future," he spit out again, then turned from me as the inertia forced us through the spins and away from each other. I pushed the sword beneath my right arm, but he rolled away from the thrust. I dropped my left hand away from the sword and spun around, raising the katana and bringing it around as I turned to face him again. I didn't land the strike, but Peter stumbled backward into Ethan, who caught him on the top of the head with the butt of his katana's handle.

"Celina is old news," Ethan said, voice flat, as Peter crumpled to the ground. As I lowered my sword, chest heaving from the exertion of the fight, Ethan crouched down and reached out his hand again.

"You are hereby excommunicated," he said, then ripped the medal from Peter's neck. Ethan stood again, pressed the medal to his lips, then tossed it into the Lake. Without comment, he pulled the cell phone from his pocket, punched in numbers, and raised it to his ear.

"Tell the Brecks," he said. "The threat has been contained."

—❖—◄◆►—❖—

CHAPTER TWENTY-TWO

GIVE PEACE A CHANCE

They debriefed via headset on the ride back to Cadogan House, but I stayed quiet, the pressure in my head forcing my silence. I rested my forehead against the cool glass of the passenger-side window and listened as they discussed the fight, the e-mail, events in Peter's history that might have triggered his defection to Celina's side. The loss of a loved one. A fight with a shifter. Celina's innate power.

The downpour of rain started just as Ethan pulled the Mercedes into the basement. Malik met us at the basement door.

"They're here," he said. "In the office. Breckenridges and Masters."

Ethan nodded, and we took the stairs to the first floor.

"You did good," he quietly said, as we rounded the corner toward his office.

I nodded my thanks. Luc met us in the hallway, having driven back to the House with Lindsey, just as Ethan pushed forward into his office.

The room was full of vampires and shifters.

Nick, in gray trousers and a slinky black polo, stood with his father just inside the door. He ignored me, but cast a dubious glance around the office. "I didn't know bloodsucking paid so well."

"Said the man who resorted to extortion to deal with his family problems," Ethan pointed out.

Headache or not, I bit back a grin. Who knew he had it in him?

"Have a seat, gentlemen," Ethan said, extending his hand toward the conference table. Scott, Noah, and Morgan were already there. After the Brecks made their way to the end of the room and took seats opposite the vampires, Ethan took his chair at the head of the table. Luc, Malik, and I followed, and stayed standing.

"Thank you all for agreeing to gather together," Ethan said. "As Malik has no doubt explained to you, we have identified and nullified the supposed threat against Jamie Breckenridge." He glanced at Papa Breck, whose features were pulled into a confused frown. "A vampire in our House fell under the influence of a supernatural with a less than stellar reputation. In so doing, he was convinced to issue a false threat against Jamie, while at the same time warning us of a threat by the Breckenridges against us." Ethan paused, then clasped his hands together on the table, interlacing his fingers. "His intent, we understand, was to foster animosity between vampires and shifters."

I had to give it to the Brecks. They didn't even blink an eyelash at the fact that they'd been outed.

"Thanks to the efforts of our guards corps and our Sentinel, we were able to detain the vampire," Ethan continued. "He has been excommunicated and is currently on his way to the U.K. for sentencing, as is our way. I want to stress that there is no indication that anyone, vampire or otherwise, Cadogan House or otherwise, intended to follow through with the threat against Jamie. Nevertheless, whether real or not, this threat has been neutralized."

"Who?" Nick asked. "Who made the threat, and who gave the order?"

Ethan arched an imperious eyebrow at Nick, who managed, impressively, to give back an equally stubborn look. "Sullivan, you can't think that I'm going to simply take your word on this and walk away. Not after what my family's been through."

"Then perhaps," Ethan said, "we could reach a compromise."

Silence, then, "I'm listening."

"The information regarding both the perpetrator and the individual we believe issued the orders is very precious to us." He linked his fingers together on the table, then glanced up at Nick. "That said, in the interest of goodwill between our respective organizations, we are willing to consider a trade. We will provide this information to you, upon your word that this information does not leave the room. That the information would not be provided to other shifters, other humans, advisors, officials, etc. Nor, of course, would it be provided to the press in any form."

Nick barked out a laugh and looked away before raising his gaze to Ethan's again. "I'm a journalist. Do you honestly expect me to agree to that?"

"I expect that if you agree to that, we will have no need to further investigate why the Breckenridges generally, and Jamie specifically, were targeted for this particular incident. We will have no reason," Ethan said, "to further investigate why your family was so eager to jump to young Jamie's defense."

Nick's nostrils flared. Clearly, even if we didn't know the details, something was amiss with Jamie. "Blackmail, Sullivan?"

Ethan smiled back at Nick, with teeth. "I learn from the best, Breckenridge."

There was silence in the room.

"Agreed," Papa Breck said into the silence, "on the terms you specified." When Nick opened his mouth to speak, Papa Breck silenced him with a finger. "We will close this down, Nicholas," he said. "We will close it down, and we will close it down tonight. We have lived peacefully in Chicago for three generations, and while I love you, I will not allow your pride as a journalist to bring that to an end. Family wins this one, not career." He returned his gaze to Ethan. "This is done."

Ethan nodded. "In that case, we are all witnesses to the terms of the agreement that we have reached."

There were nods around the room.

"Before we end this ridiculous lovefest," Nick said, sarcasm thick in his voice, "could we get to the meat of it? Who sent the e-mail?"

Ethan looked at him. "Peter," he said. "One of our House guards. As to the instigator, we have circumstantial evidence, albeit only circumstantial at this point, that the scheme itself was concocted by Celina."

"Celina?" Nick asked, eyes suddenly wide. I gave him points that he understood having Celina as an enemy was a cause for concern. "How did—"

"She was released," Ethan smoothly finished. "And in light of the fact that she has unfinished business"—he bobbed his head toward me—"we expect that she will return to Chicago. We have, however, no evidence that she bears any particular ill will toward your family. You appear to have been chosen because you were, let's say, strategically convenient."

"What evidence do you have that she's involved?" Scott asked, his head tilted curiously to the side.

"E-mails were sent from an address we believe to be her alias. And Peter confessed to the fact," he matter-of-factly added.

Scott made a low whistle. "This does not bode well. Not well at all."

The room went silent. Morgan, surprisingly, kept quiet, but a glance in his direction showed an abnormally pale cast to his cheeks. His eyes were wide, his gaze intense and centered on the tabletop in front of him, as if he contemplated grave things. I supposed more crimes perpetrated by your former Master, the vampire that made you, were pretty grave things to contemplate.

"Well," Papa Breck said, rising from his chair, "I believe that concludes this matter."

Nick interrupted the silence. "Wait—I want to say something."

We all looked in his direction.

"Chicago has three Houses," he said. "More than any other city in the United States. It is where vampires announced their existence to the world, and it is becoming the center of vampire activity in the United States. Chicago is the locus, the focus, of American vampires.

"I know about the raves," Nick continued, and the room went quiet enough to hear a pin drop. "Maybe you had an excuse before. When you were still in hiding, when vampires were myth and horror-movie fodder, maybe it was appropriate to pretend that raves were nothing more than the subject of some lonely human's overactive imagination. But things have changed. This is your city. The Presidium knows it. The vampires know it. The nymphs know it. The fairies know it.

"Shifters know it," he quietly, gravely, said, then lifted his blue eyes to mine. I don't know exactly what I saw there; I'm not sure I have words for the emotion. But it was bottomless— a well of experience, of life, of love and loss. A wealth of human history, or maybe shifter history, and a resulting world-weariness, in the depth of it.

Nick rose and stood before the table, hands on his hips. "Clean up your goddamned city, or someone else will do it for you."

With that pronouncement, he pushed back his chair and walked away. Papa Breck followed, the vampires silent until Luc had escorted them out of the room and the door was closed again.

Ethan put his palms flat on the table. "And with that," he said, "I believe we've brought this particular crisis to its resolution."

"I'm not sure how much resolution we've gotten," Scott said, pushing his own chair back, rising, and returning it to its spot at the conference table. "I wasn't ready to go a round with the *Trib* or with Tate, but this Celina news isn't exactly comforting, either. I mean, nice work in getting this thing wrapped up so quickly, but I'd rather Peter had acted on his own."

"Although I'd have preferred that Cadogan not serve as Celina's recruiting ground," Ethan darkly said, "I take your larger point. I would also propose that we stay in contact in the event that information regarding Celina's return to Chicago—or any future schemes—comes to light."

"Agreed," Scott said.

"Agreed," Noah said.

We all looked at Morgan. He still stared absently at the table, pain in his eyes. Maybe he'd finally taken to heart the truth about Celina—about the havoc she was apparently willing to wreak. That couldn't have been an easy pill to swallow.

"Agreed," he finally—and quietly—said.

Ethan rose and walked to the office door as the rest of the vampires did the same. He opened it, offered polite goodbyes to Noah, Scott, and Morgan, and when Luc, Malik, and I were left in the room, released us.

"I believe we've had enough drama for a few days," Ethan said. "Take the night, enjoy your evening. We'll speak at dusk tomorrow."

Luc, Malik, and I grinned at one another, smiled at Ethan.

"Thanks, Hoss," Luc said, and went for the door.

"What he said," I offered with a canny smile, and followed him out.

I made it around the corner of the hall before Morgan called my name. He stood in the foyer, hands in his pockets, some mix of anger and defeat in his expression and his stance.

"Can we talk?"

I nodded, my stomach suddenly knotted in anticipation of the coming battle. He opened the door, and I followed him out. Mist rose from the streets, a cool breeze blowing through Hyde Park.

"Why didn't you tell me?" he asked when we'd reached the sidewalk, his voice awkwardly loud in the quiet of the night. "About the threat, the story? You could have come to me with any of this. You could have told me when we were at your parents' house."

I looked around, realized any vampire near the front windows would be able to hear our conversation, and took his wrist. I led him down the sidewalk and through the gate, then to the street corner, which was empty of paparazzi. Maybe they melted in the rain like so many wicked witches.

"I was acting as Sentinel," I told him, when it seemed we were far enough from canny-eared vampires to afford some privacy. "This was Cadogan business."

Morgan crossed his arms. "It was *House* business. We all had a right to know."

"Right or not, that was Ethan's call, not mine."

"You stand Sentinel. You act in a manner that's best for your House. And what's best for your House is your determination, not Ethan's."

I didn't disagree with the sentiment in principle, but I wasn't about to admit that to Morgan.

"Even if it was my decision to make," I said, "it was *my* decision, not yours. I understand this is information you would have liked to have, but that's not my problem. I don't stand Sentinel for Navarre House."

"Oh, I think we're all *real* clear on that, Merit." His voice dripped with sarcasm. "It's pretty obvious where your loyalties lie."

I was tired of taking hits for the team, so I hit back. "And your loyalties didn't lie with Celina?"

A flush of crimson crossed his cheekbones.

"Look me in the eye and tell me your Master didn't make decisions that involved 'House business.' And if you knew anything, about what she's done or how completely off her rocker she is, you sure didn't share that with the rest of us."

He glowered. "I knew nothing that would have put anyone in danger. I did what I thought was best."

"And I did what I thought was best."

"Yeah, by acquiescing to Ethan."

I rolled my eyes. "Jesus, Morgan. He's the Master of my House. What do you want me to do? Start a rebellion? If you were having this conversation with one of your Novitiates about disobeying your orders, would you still suborn mutiny?"

Morgan shook his head. "This is completely different."

It was my turn to snort out disdain, and I threw up my hands, fueled by sheer irritation with the conversation. "How is that different?"

This time, he answered with fury, in loud, angry words. "Because it's *Ethan*, Merit—that's why!"

Thunder boomed in the distance, a bolt of spectacular lightning zigzagging its way across the sky.

I stared at him, felt the responsive trip of my own heart, and saw the sudden narrowing of his pupils. "He's my Master. And I know what you think. You've made clear what you think." It's what everyone thinks, I silently added. "But he's my Master, my boss, my employer. Period."

Morgan shook his head, looked away. "You're naïve."

I closed my eyes, put my hands on my hips, and tried counting to ten so as not to commit vampiricide here on the nice sidewalk the city of Chicago worked so hard to keep free of ash. "Do you not think I'm capable of judging for myself if I'm having a relationship with someone?"

He turned back to me again, and looked at me with eyes that pulsed, for a moment, silver at the edges. "Frankly, Merit, no."

I missed the subtext, the fact that he'd circled back around to us, and answered with sarcasm, irony. "What do you want me to say, since you aren't going to believe what I tell you? That I'm in love with him? That we're going to be married and start pumping out vampire children?"

"Vampires can't have children," was the only thing he said, and the flatness of his voice—and the fact that I hadn't yet considered the impact of the change on my becoming a mother—sucked the wind from my sails. Deflated, I looked at the ground, and when another peal of thunder rolled across Hyde Park, I wrapped my arms around myself.

"What are we doing, Merit?"

I blinked, looked up at him. "You were insulting me because you think I mishandled House business."

Morgan's expression didn't change, but his voice softened. "That's not what I meant." He uncrossed his arms, stuck his hands in his pockets. "I meant us. What are we doing?"

I found I couldn't answer him.

As if on cue, the rain began to fall again, began to pour in sheets, a silvery curtain that mirrored the emotional barrier between us. The rain came hard and fast, and soaked us in seconds.

I didn't have an answer for his question, and he didn't speak, so we stood there, silently together, our hair matted by water, raindrops trickling down our faces.

Drops clung to Morgan's lashes, and the shine of the water seemed to sharpen his already sculpted cheekbones. Hair plastered to his head, he looked, I thought, like an ancient warrior who'd been caught in a storm, maybe after the fall of some final enemy in battle.

Except, in this case, the last warrior standing looked . . . defeated.

Minutes passed while we stood there in the rain, silently facing each other.

"I don't know?" I finally said, trying to give the words the cant of apology.

Morgan closed his eyes, and when he opened them again, he wore an expression of grim resolution. "Do you want me?"

I swallowed, stared at him with eyes I knew were wide and remorseful, and hated myself for not being able to answer with all the conviction I knew he deserved, "My God, *yes*, I want you." I opened my mouth to give a pat response, then closed it again, deciding to honestly consider the question.

I wanted what most people wanted—love, companionship.

I wanted someone to touch. I wanted someone to touch me back.

I wanted someone to laugh with, someone who would laugh with me, laugh at me.

I wanted someone who looked and saw *me*. Not my power, not my position.

I wanted someone to say my name. To call out, "Merit," when it was time to go, or when we arrived. Someone who wanted to say to someone else, with pride, "I'm here with her. With Merit."

I wanted all those things. Indivisibly.

But I didn't want them from Morgan. Not now. Maybe it was too soon after my conversion to vampire to try a relationship; maybe it would never be the right time for us. I didn't know the why of it, but I knew I didn't feel the kind of emotions I ought to have.

I didn't want to fail him, but I couldn't lie to him. So I answered, quietly, "I want to want you."

It was as insulting a cop-out answer as I'd ever heard, and it had fallen from my own inconstant lips.

"Jesus Christ, Merit," he muttered. "Way to be equivocal." He shook his head, rain streaking down his face, and stared at the ground for what felt like an eternity. Then he lifted his gaze and blinked water from narrowed blue eyes.

"I deserve a better answer than that. Maybe you're not the one that can give it to me, but I deserve a better answer."

"Why would you want more from me? You don't even trust me."

"I could have trusted you, if you'd trusted me a little."

"You blackmailed me into dating you."

"Fine, Merit. Fine. Let's just call it what it is, right?" He gave me one last look of mild disgust, then turned away. I let him go, watched him walk down the sidewalk and through the rain until he disappeared into the mist of it.

I don't know how long I stood there in the middle of the street, rain streaming down my face, wondering what I'd done, how I'd managed to screw up the first potentially real relationship I'd had in years. But what could I do? I couldn't feign emotions I didn't feel, and I wasn't naïve enough to deny the connection between me and Ethan, even if we both regretted the attraction. Ethan had kissed me, had wanted to kiss me, and I had allowed it. Whatever I felt for Morgan, however much I enjoyed his company, the pull just wasn't the same.

Regrettably.

The rain slowed, then dissipated, mist clouding the neighborhood. I pushed the wet hair from my eyes and was preparing to turn back for the House when I heard it.

Click.

Click.

Click.

Click.

The sound of heels on concrete.

CHAPTER TWENTY-THREE

HIT ME WITH YOUR BEST SHOT

I turned quickly, but didn't need to change position to know what was coming. *Who* was coming. The goose bumps on my arms, the uncomfortable prickle at the back of my neck, were warning enough.

The scene played out like a Bogart film. She looked as glamorous as I'd ever seen her, lithe body tucked into a pair of black wide-legged pants and a black cap-sleeved top, her wavy black hair in soft curls across her shoulders. But while she might have channeled Katharine Hepburn aesthetically, I knew who she really was, the nihilistic core of her.

She strode toward me with feline grace, heels clicking on the wet asphalt, gleaming in the light of the overhead street-lamps.

I swallowed, fear and adrenaline tripping my heart into a quick, staccato beat, and gripped the scabbard at my side.

"I could have you before you unsheathed it," she warned.

I forced myself to keep my chin up, my body flexed and ready in case she moved. It took every ounce of strength I had not to recoil, not to take a step backward, not to run away. I couldn't have been less confident, there in the dark, the Cadogan gate a block away. So I bluffed.

"Maybe," I said, giving her a small smile. "Maybe not. What do you want?"

She tilted her head at me, tucking one hand around her side, one hip cocked. She had the look of a supermodel feigning confusion, or a mildly intrigued vampire. It was pretty much the same expression. "You haven't quite figured it out yet, have you?"

I arched a brow at her, and she chuckled in response, the sound low and throaty. "I don't think I'll tell you. I think I'll let you figure it out. But I'll enjoy it when the time comes." She suddenly snapped to attention, hands at her hips, chin thrust forward. A look of control and defiance. "And the time will come."

Celina did love to talk, to wax prophetic. Maybe she'd give me something I could use, something that would hint at her larger plans, something I could pass along to Ethan and Luc, so I asked the follow-up. "The time? For what?"

"You took Navarre from me. All of it, all of them, from me. Certainly, there are benefits—to take a House from a Master, a Presidium member, it's hardly done. That gained me no little bit of sympathy. So thank you, pet, for that. Nevertheless, Navarre was mine, bricks and mortar, blood and bone. You take from me, I take from you."

"Is that why you set Peter up?" I asked. "Because you're pissed that your plan to take over the Chicago Houses didn't quite pan out? You figured starting a world war between shifters and vampires was the next best thing?"

She smiled coyly. "Oh, I do like you, Merit. I like your . . . moxie. But the war wouldn't just be between shifters and vampires, would it? It was Cadogan House that threatened the Breckenridge boy. The war would be between Nicholas and Ethan. Between the old lover and the new, yes?"

I nearly growled at her.

"At any rate," she said, "two of Chicago's Houses would remain uninvolved. Untainted by the scandal. Grey House. Navarre House."

Celina reached up and fingered a thin gold chain around her neck. Moonlight glinted off the disk of gold that hung from it.

My stomach tightened.

It was a House medal. A shiny new pendant to replace the one taken from her by the GP.

"Where'd you get the medal, Celina?"

She smiled evilly and rubbed the medal like she expected a genie to pop out.

"Let's not be naïve, Merit. Where do you think I got it? Or perhaps I should ask, from whom?"

I suddenly had a little less sympathy for Navarre's new Master.

Celina may have kept her sway over his House, but I'd be damned if she poisoned mine. "You've made your play, Celina, twice now, and you lost. Learn your lesson—stay away from Cadogan House."

"Just the House, Merit? Or its Master as well?"

I felt the blush rise along my cheekbones.

She blinked at me, and her eyes—and smile—grew wide. She laughed with obvious delight. "Oh, I had no idea my luck would be that good. Are you sleeping with him, or just lusting after him? And let's not feign misunderstanding, Sentinel. I meant the one you want, not the one you have." She looked up, her expression thoughtful. "Or maybe the one you lost, if I learned anything from that last little scene."

"You're hallucinating," I said, but my stomach knotted. She'd been there, had watched Morgan and me fight. Had he set this up? Had he asked to talk to me outside in order to get me out here where she could find me?

Celina looked me over, head to toe, an appraisal. She'd kept her glamour in check, but I felt the slinky tendrils of it branching out, testing. "You're not his type, I hear. Ethan does prefer blondes." She cocked her head to the side. "Or redheads, I suppose. But I guess you know all about that. I hear you were a firsthand witness to his . . . prowess?" She looked at me thoughtfully, apparently expecting an honest appraisal.

She was right—I had been a witness to his "prowess," having inadvertently walked in while Ethan was servicing Amber. But I wasn't about to share that information with her. "I couldn't care less who or what he prefers."

"Mmm-hmm. Does that self-righteous anger keep you warm at night?"

I knew she was baiting me. Of course she was baiting me. Unfortunately, she'd picked the right bait, the conversation I was sick of having, the accusations I was sick of defending against. I could feel my blood begin to warm, the vampire I'd so carefully, cautiously, forced down peeking through, wondering at the worry, the adrenaline that woke her from sleep. My breathing quickened, and I knew my eyes had silvered. My fangs descended, and I let them.

I wouldn't fight her; I wasn't stupid. But Catcher had taught me about the benefits of bluffing. Assuming I could keep my vampire in check, I owed it to the impotent Presidium to see what happened when I played Celina's game.

I took a step forward, a step toward her, and ran the tip of my tongue across the tip of a needle-pointed canine. Vampire aggressive behavior. "Do you want to play, Celina? Do you want to know how strong I am? Do you want to see?"

She stared at me, magic flowing full force now, and I watched her eyes silver, like flipped coins catching the light. She took a step toward me, still eighteen or twenty feet between us.

"You're hardly worth his time, Sentinel. Why would you be worth mine?"

I took another step forward. "You came here, Celina. To find me."

"You'll never be as good as me."

There it was. The crack in the beguiling facade. Celina, beautiful and powerful and self-absorbed to a fault, was insecure.

I repeated the mantra. "You came here, Celina. To find me."

She stilled, glared at me beneath half-lidded eyes, shadows and moonlight sharpening the angles of her face. She took a breath, seemed to calm herself, and smiled. And then she fought back.

"I know who you are, Merit. I know about your family." She stepped forward. "I know about your sister."

I flinched, the words as effective as a slap across the face.

Another step, and this time she grinned. She knew she'd landed a blow.

"Yes," she said. "Best of all"—I could see the whites of her eyes and as if the cant of the words wasn't threat enough, the hatred in her gaze—"I know about that night on campus."

"Because you planned it," I reminded her, my breath coming faster, my heart beginning to thud again.

"Mmm-hmm," she said, tapping a red-manicured finger against her chest. "I had plans for you, I'll admit. But I wasn't the only one with plans."

My heart sped at the insinuation. "Who else had plans?"

"You know, I forget. But it's a pity you've had Peter extradited. He has so many interesting connections around town, don't you think?"

It was trickery, I reminded myself. She was behind it. She'd planned my attack, my death, to wreak havoc in the city. *She'd* planned it. But she wasn't the only one with knowledge, I reminded myself.

"I know about Anne Dupree, Celina. Did you and Edward have fun plotting and planning? Did George cry out when you beat him to death?"

Her smile faltered. "Bitch."

I was really beginning to dislike Navarre vampires. Thinking they had much arrogance in common, I used the phrase I'd used before on her apparent protégé. "Bite me, Celina."

She snapped her fangs at me. I flipped the thumb guard on my scabbard.

All right, that's it. "Bring it, dead girl."

She growled. I gripped the handle with my right hand, my heart thudding like a drum inside my chest.

Stupid, stupid, stupid, I thought, for baiting the crazy, but a little too late.

Moving so quickly that her body was a shiny black blur in the night, she advanced and kicked. She kicked with the force of a thundering freight train, and the unbelievable pain of it buckled my knees. I hit the ground, unable to catch a breath, unable to think or feel or react to anything but the crushing pain in my chest. A single kick shouldn't have hurt so much, but my God, did it. A screaming, ripping pain that made me wonder that I'd ever doubted Celina Desaulniers.

One hand braced to keep my face from hitting the ground, tears spilled over, and I gripped my chest with my free hand, to rip out the pain, to rip out the vise that was squeezing the air from my lungs. I struggled for breath, and a wave of pain, a morbid aftershock, convulsed my spine.

"Ethan did this to you."

I fought for air, looked up. She stood over me, hands on her hips.

I ground my fingers into the concrete, tunneled holes in the sidewalk, and tears pouring down my cheeks, watched her, hoping to God she wouldn't kick me again, wouldn't touch me again. Reminded myself—it was *her* plan. "No."

She bent down at the waist, put a fingertip beneath my chin, raised it up. I heard a growl, realized it was me, and when another shock rocked my body, realized that if she hit me again, I'd be completely unable to fight back.

One kick, and she'd brought me down, even after two months of training. She called my bluff, and had taken me down. Could I ever be as strong as she was? As fast? Maybe not. But I'd be damned if I'd crawl away like a wounded animal.

Then and there, I swore to myself that I would never be on my knees before her again.

Heaving for breath, I pushed my way up, one slow, devastating inch at a time, black fabric shredded around knees I'd bloodied when I fell to the ground. Celina watched, a predator enjoying the last licking sighs of a wounded animal.

Or maybe more accurately, alpha predator, enjoying her victory over a lesser female.

Slow, agonizing seconds later, I was standing.

Inhale.

Exhale.

I cradled my ribs with my right hand, lifted my eyes to hers.

Bright, nearly indigo blue, they fairly twinkled with pleasure in the moonlight. "He did this to you," she said. "Caused

this pain. If you weren't a vampire, if he hadn't made you—
if he'd taken you to the hospital instead of changing you,
converting you for his own purposes—you'd be in school.
You'd be with Mallory. Everything would be the same."

I shook my head, but something about that sounded right.
Was it right?

In the midst of the pain, the fact that he'd saved me from
her, from the killer she'd loosed on me, didn't cross my
mind.

"Confront him, Merit. See what you're made of."

I shook my head. Mutiny. Rebellion. He was my Master. I
couldn't fight him, wouldn't fight him. I'd already challenged
him once, my first week as a vampire, and I'd failed. I'd lost.

"He left you here for me to find. They both did."

My ribs screamed, probably broken. Maybe internal
bleeding. A punctured lung?

"All that effort," she said, "just to breathe. Imagine if it
had been a real fight, Sentinel. All that work, all that practice,
and what have you to show for it?" She cocked her head, as
if waiting for me to answer, but then offered, "He didn't prepare you for me, did he?"

"Fuck you," I managed to get out, gripping my side.

She arched a carefully shaped black eyebrow. "Don't direct your ire at me, Sentinel, for teaching the lesson you
needed. Blame Ethan. Your Master. The one who is supposed
to care for you. Prepare you. Protect you."

I ignored the words, but shook my head anyway, tried to
will myself to think, but it was becoming more difficult. The
pain was blurring the borders, forcing the reconciliation between whatever humanity was left, whatever predator lived
inside me. I didn't know what would happen if I let the vampire peek through, but I wasn't strong enough to hold her
back, not with the pain. The instinct was too strong, my de-
fenses too weak. I'd repressed her, and she was tired of being
relegated to some deep, dark corner of my psyche. I'd been a
vampire for nearly two months, but had managed to shield
myself in the remnants of my humanity.

No more, the vampire screamed.

"Don't fight it," Celina said, a tinge of lusty voyeurism in her voice.

The pain was too much, the night too long, my inhibitions too low. I stopped fighting it. I let it go.

I let her breathe.

I let her out.

She burst through my blood, the power of the vampire flowing through me, and as I kept my eyes on Celina, locked my limbs to keep from staggering back from the surge of it, I felt myself disassociate. I felt her move my body, stretch and test muscles inside my body—and sink into it.

Merit disappeared.

Morgan disappeared.

Mallory disappeared.

All the fear, the hurt, the resentment, of failing friends and lovers and teachers, of disappointing those I was supposed to care for, of ruining relationships. The discomfort of no longer knowing who I really was, what role I was supposed to play in this world—all of it disappeared.

For a moment, in its place, a vacuum. The undeniable appeal of nothingness, of the absence of hurt.

And then, the sensations I hadn't known I'd been waiting two months for.

The world accelerated, burst into music.

The night sang—voices and cars and gravel and screaming and laughter. Animals hunting, people chatting, fighting, fucking. A raven flew overhead. The night glowed—moonlight bringing everything into sharper relief.

The world was noisy—sounds and smells I'd apparently missed out on over the last two months, the senses of a predator.

I looked at Celina, and she smiled. Grinned victoriously.

"You've lost your humanity," she said. "You'll never get it back. And you can't defend yourself. You know who's to blame."

I meant to stay silent, to say nothing, but I heard myself answer her, ask her, "Ethan?"

A single nod, and, as if her task was accomplished, Celina

smoothed her shirt, turned, and walked into the shadows. Then she was gone.

The world exhaled.

I glanced back and saw, only yards away, the glow of the breach in the Cadogan gate.

He was there.

I took a step, ribs still screaming.

I wanted someone else to hurt.

I began walking. We began walking, the vampire and I, back to Cadogan House.

At the gate, the guards let me pass, but I could hear the whispers, could hear them talking, reporting me to the vampires inside.

The front lawn was empty, the door ajar. I took the steps slowly, one at a time, a hand on my ribs, the pain a little less, the healing begun, but still profound enough to bring tears to my eyes.

Inside, the House was silent, the few vampires frozen, staring as I moved between them, determined, my predatory eyes slitted against the harshness of electric lights.

Merit?

I heard his voice in my head.

Find me, I ordered, and stopped in the crossway between the stairs, the hallway, the parlors.

Down the hall, his office door opened. He stepped out, took one look at me, and moved forward.

"You did this to me."

I don't know if he heard me, but his expression didn't change. He reached me, stopped, and his eyes widened, and he searched my own. "Jesus Christ, Merit. What's happened to you?"

My sword whistled as I unsheathed it, and when I gripped it in both hands, I felt the circuit close. I closed my eyes, basking in the warmth of it.

"Merit!" This time, there was an order behind the words.

I opened my eyes, nearly flinched, wanted instinctively to bend to the will of my Master, my maker, but I fought it and through trembling limbs, I forced back the urge to yield.

"No," I heard myself say, my voice barely a whisper.

His eyes widened again, then flicked to something behind me. He shook his head, looked back at me. His voice low, intimate, insistent. "Come back from this, Merit. You don't want to fight me."

"I do," I heard, in a voice that was barely mine. "Find steel," she advised him.

We advised him.

He stood there for a long moment, silently, still, before nodding. Someone offered him a blade, a katana that glinted in the light. He took it, mirrored my stance—katana in both hands, body bladed.

"If the only way you'll come back from this is to be bloodied by it, then so be it."

He lunged.

It was easy to forget that he'd been a soldier. The perfectly cut Armani, pristine white shirts, and always shiny Italian shoes were more the workaday wrapping of a corporate CEO than of the leader of a band of three hundred and twenty vampires.

That was my mistake—forgetting who he was. Forgetting that he was head of Cadogan House for a reason, not just for his politics, not just for his age, but because he could fight, knew how to fight, because he knew how to swing a sword through the air.

He'd been a soldier, had learned to fight in the midst of a world war. She'd made me forget that.

He was amazing to watch, or would have been, had I not been on the receiving end of the slices and cuts, the kicks and turns that torqued his body nearly effortlessly. The lunges and blocks. He was so fast, so precise.

But the pain began to ease, and repressed for so long, held back by my human perceptions, misgivings fears, *she*—the vampire—began to fight back.

And she was faster.

I was faster.

My body knifed toward his, and I swung, used the katana

in my hands to slash, to force him to move, to spin, to slice his own sword in ways that looked comparatively awkward.

I don't know how long we fought, how long we chased each other in the midst of a circle of vampires on the first floor of Cadogan House, my hair wet and matted, tears streaking my face, bloodied hands and knees, broken ribs, the sleeves of my shirt in tatters from half a dozen near misses.

His arms were equally sliced, his twists and turns still not fast enough to avoid my parries. Where he'd once let me play the game, had moved in close enough to give me an opportunity to make contact before slipping away again, now he spun to save his skin; the expression on his face—blank, focused—told that story well enough. This wasn't play fighting. This was the real challenge, the fight I'd tried to bring to him months ago, the fight that he'd mocked. He owed me a fight, a real fight, in recognition of the fact that I hadn't asked to become a vampire but had acquiesced to this authority anyway because he'd asked it of me. This was less a challenge, I thought, than an acknowledgment. He was my Master, but I'd taken my oaths and he owed me a fight. A fair one, because I'd been willing to fight for him. To kill for him. To take a hit for him, if necessary.

"Merit."

I shrugged off the sound of my name and kept fighting, dodging, and swinging, smiling as I swung the blade at him, parried and countered, torqued my own body to stay out of the line of his honed steel.

"Merit."

I blocked his blow, and as he reoriented and rebalanced his body, I glanced behind me, just in time to see Mallory, my friend, my sister, hand outstretched, an orb of blue flame in her hand. She flicked, and it came toward me, and I was enveloped in flame.

The lights went out.

CHAPTER TWENTY-FOUR

CH . . . CH . . . CH . . . CH . . . CHANGES

A pale golden glow of light. The smell of lemon and comfort.

Then pain and cold and nausea. Waves of it.

Pain that clenched my stomach and a fever that flamed my cheeks, my skin so warm that the tears that slipped down my face left cold saline trails.

This was what I'd hardly remembered the first time it happened.

The change. I was going through the rest of it.

I'd sobbed at pain that racked me, seizing muscle, gnawing at my bones.

And at some point in the midst of that change, I'd opened silver eyes and sought out the nourishment I knew, in that instant, that I would kill for.

And in that instant, as if he'd been watching, waiting, a wrist was placed before me.

My body shook with cold, and I heard a growl, *my* growl, before I tried to move away. There was whispering. My name. An incantation.

Merit. Be still.

The wrist was put before me again.

Ethan's wrist. I looked up into his own silver eyes. He gazed down at me, a lock of blond across his forehead, hunger in his eyes. *It is offered. Willingly.*

I looked down, stared at the beads of vermilion that slowly, so slowly, traced twin trails down his forearm, across his skin.

"Merit."

I gripped his arm in my left hand, his hand in my right. His fingers curled around my thumb. Squeezed. His lashes fell.

I lifted his wrist, put my lips to his skin, and felt his echoing shudder of pleasure. Heard the earthy groan that accompanied it.

I closed my eyes.

Merit.

I drank.

The circuit closed.

When I came to, I was huddled in a ball, lying on my side in the cool, soft dark. I recognized the scent of it—I was at Mallory's house, in my old bedroom. Kicked out of Cadogan would have been my bet.

I blinked, gingerly touched my hand to my chest, the pain in my ribs now a dull ache. But the darkness—and the million sounds and scents that filled it—were suddenly choking, confining. I panicked. I choked back a sob, and in the thick darkness around me heard myself scream for light.

A golden glow lit the room. I blinked, adjusted to the light, and saw Ethan in the cushy armchair across from the bed, suit neatly pressed, legs crossed, his hand drawing back from the lamp that sat on the table beside the chair. "Better?"

My head swam, spun. I covered my mouth. Voice muffled, I warned him, "I think I'm gonna be sick."

He was up in a flash, putting a silver trash can from one corner of the room into my hands. Muscles contracted and my stomach heaved, but nothing came up. After minutes of retching, my stomach sore from it, I sat up, resting an elbow on the edge of the silver vessel, which was nestled between my crossed legs.

I risked a glance at Ethan. He stood silently at the end of the bed, arms crossed, legs braced, face completely blank.

After wiping the damp fringe of bangs from my face, I dared words. "How long was I out?"

"It's nearly dawn."

I nodded. Ethan reached into the interior pocket of his suit coat, pulled out a handkerchief, and offered it to me. Without meeting his eyes, I took it, dabbed at my eyes, my brow, then balled it into my hand. When the room stopped spinning, I set the can down on the floor, brought my knees up, wrapped my arms around them, and dropped my forehead.

Eyes closed, I heard the trash can being moved, the creak of the armchair, and lambent sounds of the city around me. I guess that predatory sense of hearing had finally come on-line. I concentrated to shut out the background noise, tried to turn it down to a level that would still allow me to function.

Some minutes later, when the screaming had softened to a dull roar, I opened my eyes again.

"When you went down we brought you here—just in case."

Of course, I thought. What else could they have done? I was lucky he hadn't reported me immediately to the Presidium, asked them to draw aspen and have me—as a danger to him, to the House, to the city—disposed of.

"What happened?"

Tears sprang to my eyes at the memory of the pain, and I shook my head against it. "Celina. She was outside the House. She wanted to test me." I shook my head. "One kick, Ethan. One kick, and I went down. I panicked, couldn't fight her." Tears spilled down my cheeks, which were warm from embarrassment. The warnings he'd given me in his office hadn't worked. I was a failure. "I panicked."

"She hurt you." His voice was soft. "Again."

"And again on purpose. I think she wanted me to let her out."

Silence, then, "Let her out?"

I looked over. He was sitting in the armchair, leaning forward, elbows on his knees, body language inviting candor.

"I'm not . . . I'm not normal," I finally confessed and felt some of the weight of it leave my shoulders. "Something went wrong when you made me."

He stared at me for a minute, unblinking, then said, with a strange kind of gravity, "Explain."

I took a breath, wiped a fallen tear from my cheek, and told him. I told him the vampire had somehow been separate from me, had a mind and will of her own, and had tried, time and again, to claim me. How, time after time, I'd fought her back down again, tried to keep her contained. And how, finally, the pain of Celina's single kick, her carefully crafted words, the doubt she'd sprouted in my mind, forced the vampire to the surface.

After a moment of silence, when he offered no response, I added, "I don't know what else to say."

I heard a choked sound, looked up, saw him with his elbows on his knees, head in his hands, blond hair spilling around them, his shoulders quaking.

"Are you laughing?"

"No. Not laughing," he assured me, then laughed uproariously.

Confused, I stared at him. "I don't get it."

He blew out a breath that puffed his cheeks, then ran his fingers through his hair.

"You attacked me. You attacked your Master, the one that made you, at least in part because the predator inside you was powerful enough to exist on its own—because the predator failed somehow to merge completely with your humanity. I'm not even sure how that's possible—biologically, genetically, metaphysically, magically."

He looked up at me, emerald eyes shining, and his voice went a little lower. "We knew you'd be powerful, Merit. This was a complete and total surprise." He gazed absently at the wall beside me, as if watching the replay of memories there.

"It's happened before, you said? When the vampire has . . . separated?"

I nodded sheepishly, wishing I'd spoken to him, to anyone, about this before today. When the fight and pain and humiliation I knew were probably in store could have been avoided.

"Since the beginning," I told him. "When you and I fought

the first time, when the First Hunger rose, when I met Celina, when I staked Celina, when I trained with Catcher, when I fought Peter. But I never . . . *really* let her out."

Brow furrowed, Ethan nodded. "That could tell us something—perhaps she, the vampire, was sick of being repressed, as it were. Perhaps she wanted airing out."

"I had that sense."

He was silent, then asked, tremulously, "What was it like?"

I looked up at him, found an expression of naked curiosity on his face. "It was like . . ." I frowned, picked at a thread in the blanket, trying to put it into words, then looked up again. "It was like breathing for the first time. Like . . . breathing in the world."

Ethan stared at me a long time, was quiet a long time, then offered softly, "I see."

He seemed to consider that for a long time. "You said Celina baited you, maybe tried to pull this reaction from you. How would she know?"

I offered my theory. "When I went to Red, Morgan's club, the first time, when she confronted me, I could feel that she was testing me. The same thing you'd done in your office after I told you about the confrontation. Maybe she had some sense of it there? Some sense that my chemistry was off?"

"Hmm."

I wrapped my arms around myself. "I guess I succumbed to her glamour this time?" She'd so easily swayed me, made me look for Ethan, made me blame him for my hurt and confusion. As much as I'd like to blame my alienation from Morgan and Mallory on Ethan, even I could admit that those things had nothing to do with him. They were about me.

"The stronger the mind," Ethan said, "the less susceptible the individual to glamour. You have withstood it before, from her, from me. But this time, you were in pain, and you've had some setbacks in your relationship with Mallory. I also assume your relationship with Morgan is not . . . at its strongest."

I nodded.

"Glamour can catch us in a weak moment. Not to change the subject, Merit, but while you were out, it looked as if you experienced a portion of the change again," he added. "The chills, the fevers. The pain."

Ethan, of course, knew what the change felt like.

He also understood now the thing that I'd finally figured out. That despite the three days I'd spent making the transition from human to vampire, it hadn't completely worked.

And I had a guess why that had been the case.

"I wasn't going through it again," I told him. "This was the first full time, the completion of it, anyway."

His gaze snapped to mine, a question in his eyes. And I answered it, offering the conclusion I'd reached. "I was drugged the first time I went through the change. After you bit me, drank me, fed me, you drugged me."

His expression blanked, eyes muting to forest green.

I continued, my gaze on his. "I know other vampires' changes were different from mine. I don't remember the things they remember. I was groggy when you sent me back to Mallory's house. It was because I hadn't fully shaken off whatever you'd given me. And whatever happened today, I remember more than I did the first time."

Including the fact that I'd taken his blood. That I had, for the first time, taken blood straight from another. I'd taken blood from Ethan, gripping his arm like it was the ballast that would anchor me to earth. I'd searched his silvered eyes as I drank, as I cried, as I shivered from the inescapable pleasure of it, of the whiskey-warm essence that still flowed through me, that healed the wounds he'd inflicted and erased the lingering pain of Celina's attack.

Erased the pain, but not the memories.

"You drugged me," I repeated, not a question.

He respected us both enough to nod—barely a nod, more a closing of the eyes in answer—but it was enough.

And then he stared at me for a long, quiet moment. This time it wasn't the House Master who stared back, but the man, the vampire. Not "Sullivan," not Liege, just Ethan and Merit.

"I didn't want you to feel it, Merit." His voice was soft. "You'd been attacked; you hadn't consented. I didn't want you to have to go through it. I didn't want you to have to remember it."

I searched his eyes and found that to be truth enough, if not the whole of it. "Be that as it may," I quietly said, "you took something from me. Luc told me once that the change, all three days of it, was like a hazing. Horrible, but important. A kind of bonding. Something I could share with the rest of the Novitiates. I didn't have that. And that's put distance between us."

His brows lifted, but he didn't deny it.

"I'm not like them," I continued. "And they know it. I'm separate enough from them already, Ethan, with the strength, my parents, our weird relationship. They don't see me the same way." I looked down, rubbed my sweaty palms across my thighs. "They didn't before, and they certainly won't after tonight. I'm no longer human, but I'm not like them, either. Not really. And I imagine you know what that's like well enough."

He looked away. We sat quietly together, gazes everywhere but on each other. Time passed, maybe minutes, before I looked at him and he looked away again, guilt in his eyes. Guilt, I assumed, for his forcing me to relive the experience, but also for precluding, however well-intentioned, the complete change the first time around.

Still, whatever the reason, there was nothing to be done about it now. Whatever his motivation, it was done, and we had more immediate problems.

"So what do we do now?"

He looked up, green eyes instantaneously widening. Surprise, maybe, that I wouldn't push the issue, that I would let it be. And what could I do? Blame him for trying to ease the transition? Berate him for the sin of omission?

Most important, wonder why he'd done it?

"About this, I've no idea," he finally said, his voice the flat tone of the Master vampire, whatever had passed between us fracturing again. "If it truly was related to your incomplete change and the process is now complete, we'll deal with your strength, assess it. As to Celina, this would have been an added bonus of her Breckenridge game. Start a war between shifters and vampires, manage to capitalize on the fact that the Sentinel of Cadogan House is biologically . . . unstable." He shook his head. "You can't give her too much credit for being organized, for orchestrating plans. The woman is a master manipulator, a composer of vampiric drama. She knows how to set the stage, arrange her Goldberg machine, then release the trigger and let the rest of us run the game on her behalf." He glanced back at me. "She'll keep doing it. Until she brings us to the brink of war, whether with humans or shifters. She'll keep doing it."

"As long as she's here, until we can put her away again, she'll keep doing it," I agreed. "And we can't put her away until the GP understands who she is, what she is."

"Merit, you should resign yourself to the fact that, like Harold, the rest of them fully understand who and what she is. And that they accept that fact."

I nodded and rubbed my arms.

Ethan sighed and returned to the armchair. He sat down again, crossing one leg over the other. "And why, in this particular scenario, did she send you back to me?"

"To finish you off? So you or Luc would finish me off?"

"If you'd killed me, I'd be out of the picture—a Master out of her way. It would be convenient for her if I was gone. If you weren't strong enough to best me, she may have imagined that whatever punishment I offered would keep you out of her way."

More silence while I avoided asking exactly what he had in mind re: punishment.

Ethan broke the silence. "So, Sentinel, what's the next question?"

"Identifying her allies," I finally said. "She must be staying somewhere, maybe had financial or other connections who got her back to Chicago. We need to figure out who she's working through, and why they're allowing her to do it." I looked over at him. "Blood? Fame? A position in whatever new world order she has in mind? Or are these people who've always been her allies?"

"You're thinking Navarre."

His tone was soft, unusually gentle, and he was right. I was thinking very discomforting thoughts about the current Master of Navarre, but without more proof I wasn't going to offer him up to Ethan as a sacrifice.

"I don't know."

"Perhaps we need to rethink your position."

I looked up at him. "How so?"

"To date, you're guarding the House *from* the House. Patrolling the premises, working with the House guards, studying the *Canon*. We've given you the roles and responsibilities that, historically, a Sentinel would have had. They'd have been tied to the castle, physically guarding it, but also advising the Master, the Second, the Guard Captain, on issues related to security, politics, maneuverings."

He shook his head. "The world is a vastly different place now. We're governed by a body situated a continent away, and we interact with vampires at a distance of thousands of miles. We're no longer merely defending our own ground, but trying to establish ourselves in the wider world." He looked up at me. "In this project, we've expanded your role, at least socially, to include a broader swath of the city. It's unclear what we'll reap from that strategy. Although we seem to have forestalled the immediate Breckenridge crisis, Nicholas remains a concern. His animosity is obvious, and I don't think we can assume that we've put that problem safely to bed."

"So what are you proposing?"

"I believe we need you on the streets, rather than guarding the grounds. Our best hope of countering Celina's insurgency plans may be grassroots tactics of our own." He rose and went for the door. "I need to speak with Luc, and we'll identify some strategies."

Of which, I guessed, they'd inform me at some later date.

"Ethan, what are we going to do about . . . what I did?"

"You'll be punished. There's no avoiding it." He answered

a little faster than made me comfortable. My stomach clenched, but not in surprise. The headline NOVITIATE VAMPIRE ATTACKS HER MASTER wasn't going to read well unless it was followed by LATER STRICTLY PUNISHED.

"I know," I told him. "For what it's worth, I'm sorry for it."

"Partly sorry," he said. "And partly glad we had it out. Perhaps it will . . . clear the air."

If he meant that it might clear the air between us, I doubted that, but I nodded anyway. "Am I out of Cadogan House?"

This question took longer for him to answer. More consideration, maybe, or more political evaluation. More strategy. He rubbed absently at his neck as he thought it out, but then shook his head. I wasn't sure whether I was relieved or not.

"You'll stay in Cadogan. Stay the day here, come back tomorrow night. See me first thing. But we'll adjust your duties, and you'll train—and not with Catcher this time. You need to be trained by a vampire, someone who understands the draw of the predator, who can help you control your— let's call it your predatory instinct."

"Who?"

He blinked. "Me, I suppose," was his answer, and then the door opened and closed, and he was gone.

I stared at the closed door for a moment.

"Fuck," was all I could think to say.

I knew who it was before the door opened, before she'd even knocked, from the cotton-candy brightness of her perfume in the hallway.

She peeked in, blue hair slipping through the crack between the door and jamb. "Is your head still spinning around?"

"Are you still trying to throw blue flaming shit at me?"

She winced and opened the door, then stepped inside the bedroom, hugging her arms. She was in pajamas, a shortish T-shirt and oversized cotton pants, white-painted toes peeking from beneath them. "I'm sorry. I'd just gotten back from Schaumburg. I was actually on my way to Cadogan when Luc called me, said you were in a bad way."

"Why were you on your way to Cadogan?"

Mallory leaned back against the doorjamb. There was a time—a few days ago—when she'd have plopped onto the bed beside me. We weren't there anymore, had lost that easy sense of comfort. "Catcher was going to meet me, and we were going to talk to Ethan. Catcher had some . . . concerns."

It wasn't difficult to translate the hesitation in her voice. "About me. He had concerns about me."

She held up a hand. "We were worried about you. Catcher thought you were holding back when you trained, thought something was up." She blew out a breath, ran a hand through her hair. "We had no idea you were some kind of freaky super vampire."

"Said the woman who can shoot fireballs from her palms."

She raised her eyes, looked at me. I saw something there—pain or worry—but it was tempered by her own reluctance to be candid with me. That made my stomach knot uncomfortably.

"This isn't easy for me either," she said.

I nodded, dropped my gaze, dropped my chin onto the upthrust pillow in my lap. "I know. And I know I bailed. I'm sorry."

"You bailed," she agreed, and pushed off the door. The bed dipped as she sat beside me, wiggled into a cross-legged position. "And I pushed you about this Morgan thing. It's just—"

"Mallory."

"No, Merit," she said. "Damn, just let me finish this for once. I want good things for you. I thought Morgan was one of those things. If he's not, then so be it. I just . . ."

"You think I'm in love with Ethan."

"Are you?"

A fair question. "I . . . No. Not like you think. Not like you and Catcher. It's stupid, I know. I have this thing, this idea. This bullshit 'Mr. Darcy' idea, about the one that changes his mind. That comes back for me. And I'll look up some night, and he'll be there in front of me. And he'll stare at me and say, 'It was you. It was always you.'"

She paused, then offered, so quietly, so gently, "Maybe the kind of guy worth your time is the kind of guy who's there from the beginning. Who wants you from the beginning."

"I know. I mean, intellectually, I understand that. It's just . . ."

Admit it, I thought to myself. Admit it and get it out there, and at least that way it won't be rolling around in your head anymore.

"I don't agree with him a lot of the time, *most* of the time, and he drives me crazy, but I get him. I know I drive him crazy, but I feel like he . . . like he gets me somehow, too. Appreciates something about me. I'm different, Mallory. I'm not like the rest of them. And I'm not like you anymore." I looked up at her and saw both sadness and acceptance in her eyes. I thought of what Lindsey had said, and parroted her words. "Ethan isn't like the rest of them, either. For all the strategy, the talk of alliances, he holds himself back from them."

"He holds himself back from you."

Not every time, I thought, and that was the payoff that kept me coming back for more.

"And you're holding yourself back from me, from Morgan."

"I know," I said again. "Look, about Morgan, there are other considerations. What you know isn't the entire story." What I knew wasn't the entire story either, but I wasn't sure I was ready to tell the rest of it, to tell Mallory about the lingering relationship between the current and former Masters of Navarre. "It doesn't matter. It's done anyway."

"Done?"

"Earlier. Before she found me. We ended it." Not that it truly mattered. He didn't trust me, had never trusted me. Maybe his own insecurities, maybe the rumors that seemed to follow me, maybe the sense that I'd never been really his.

Mallory interrupted my reverie and was, as usual, right on. "There is nothing we want quite as much as the thing we know we can't have."

I nodded, although I wasn't sure if she meant me or Morgan. "I know."

The room was silent for a minute. "You looked dead," she said.

I glanced back at her, saw tears brimming at her lashes. And yet I still couldn't reach back, the barrier still between us.

"I thought I'd killed you." She sniffed, swiped absently at a tear. "Catcher had to hold me up. The vampires freaked; I think they wanted to take us out. Ethan checked your pulse, said you were alive, and he was all bloodied up. Blood everywhere. You were, too, cuts and scratches on your arms, on your cheeks. You two beat the shit out of each other. Catcher picked you up, and someone brought Ethan a shirt, and everyone got in the car. I brought your sword." She pointed to the corner where it balanced on its pommel against the bedroom wall. It was back in the scabbard, cleaned, probably by Catcher, who'd have taken exquisite care of the blood-tempered blade.

"He carried you up here."

"Catcher?"

Mallory shook her head, then rubbed at her eyes and ran her hands through her hair, seemed to shake off the emotion.

"Ethan. He rode with us. They—the vampires, *your* vampires—followed him in another car."

My vampires. I'd become something else to her. A different kind of thing.

"Catcher said you needed to sleep it off, that you'd heal from it all."

I looked down at my arms, which were pale and pristine once again. I had healed, just like he'd predicted.

"So Ethan carried you up here, and Catcher took care of me, I guess, and Lindsey and Luc—we all waited downstairs." She glanced up at me. "You were unconscious the whole time?"

I looked back at her, my best friend, and I didn't tell her what I'd done.

That I'd gone through some part of the change again, and in the haze of it, the bloodlust of it, had taken blood from someone else.

His blood.

Ethan's.

And it had been like a homecoming.

I couldn't even begin to deal with that, to process it.

"I was out," I told her.

Mallory looked at me, but nodded, maybe not buying it completely, but not arguing the point. She sighed and leaned forward, enveloped me in a hug. "There's a reason they call it hopelessly romantic."

"And not rationally romantic?"

"Well-developed-thoughtly romantic."

I half chuckled and knuckled away my own tears. "That doesn't make any sense."

"Don't mock me." She squeezed, then let me go.

"You fireballed me. Knocked me out." Made me drink him, I thought, but didn't voice that aloud, being ill-equipped for the Freudian analysis that would follow the confession. "I'm entitled to mock a little."

"It's not fire. It's a way to transmit the magic. A kind of conduit." Mallory sighed and stood up. I hadn't noticed how tired she looked. Dark circles shadowed eyes already swollen from tears.

"As much as I'd like to continue this conversation, which is honestly not at all, dawn's nearly here. We both need sleep." She stood, went for the door and, hand on the door-knob, stood there for a moment. "We're going to change. This is going to change us both. There's no guarantee that we come out the end of it still liking each other."

My stomach clenched, but I nodded. "I know."

"We do the best we can."

"Yeah."

"Good night, Merit," she said, and flipped off the light, then shut the door behind her as she left.

I lay back, one hand under my head, one on my stomach, eyes on the ceiling. It hadn't been a particularly good night.

CHAPTER TWENTY-FIVE

THE KING AND I

The next night bloomed warm and clear. The house was quiet when I emerged downstairs, beeper and sword in hand. I nabbed a bottle of juice from Mallory's refrigerator, avoiding the last bag of blood, the drinking I'd done last night either satiating me fully or putting me off the taste completely.

Not that it had been horrible.

Because it hadn't been horrible.

And that was the thought that played over and over again in my head as I drove south again—just how unhorrible it had been.

My beeper sounded just as I pulled in front of the House. I unclipped it, found MTG @ U. NOW. BLRM scrolling on the display.

Charming. The entire House was being called to discuss my punishment, I presumed, given that the meeting was being held in the House's ballroom, rather than somewhere, I don't know, more intimate? Like Ethan's office? With only me and him in attendance?

Grumbling, I parked and closed up the car, thinking I wasn't exactly dressed for public humiliation in my leftover jeans and fitted black T-shirt. My Cadogan suit had been shredded; I wore the fanciest thing still in my closet at Mal's house. I had to pause outside the gate, not quite ready for the onslaught.

"Quite a show."

I looked up, found the RDI guards looking at me curiously. "Pardon me?"

"Last night," the one on the left offered. "You wreaked a good bit of havoc."

"Unintentionally," I dryly said, shifting my gaze back to the House. Normally I'd have been thrilled to get conversation out of the usually silent guards, but not on this topic.

"Good luck," said the one on the right.

I offered as appreciative a smile as I could muster, took a breath, and went for the door.

I could hear the sounds of the meeting as I climbed the stairs to the second-floor ballroom. The first floor had been quiet, but the echo of ambient vampire noise—conversations, coughing, shuffling—drifted down from the ballroom.

The doors were open when I reached it, a mass of Cadogan vampires inside. There were ninety-eight who resided in the House, and I guessed at least two-thirds of the group were here. Ethan, once again in his crisp black suit, stood alone on the short riser at the front of the room. Our gazes met and he held up a hand, silencing the vampires. Heads turned, eyes on me.

I swallowed, gripped the sword I still held in my hand, and walked inside. I couldn't bear to look at them, to see if their gazes were accusatory, insulted, fearful, so I kept my eyes on Ethan, the crowd parting around me as I walked through the room.

I didn't deny that, as Master, he needed to deal with me, to dole out punishment for what I'd done, for challenging him—for the second time—in his own House. But was the ceremony necessary? Was my humiliation in front of most of the vampires in the House necessary?

The final vampires separated, and I found consoling eyes in Lindsey, who offered a compassionate smile before turning to face Ethan. I walked to the riser, stood before him, and gazed up.

He looked back at me for a moment, expression carefully blank, before lifting his gaze to the crowd. He smiled at them, and I moved to the side so as not to block the view.

"Didn't we just do this?" he asked with a grin. The vampires laughed appreciatively. My cheeks blossomed with heat.

"I debated," he told them, "whether to offer a lengthy dissertation on why last night's events occurred. The biological and psychological precursors. The fact that Merit defended me against an attack by one of our own. And speaking of which, I regret to inform you that Peter is no longer a member of Cadogan House."

Vampires gasped, whispers trickling through the crowd.

"But most important," he said, "the attack by Celina Desaulniers that directly led to the incident here. I will preface my conclusions by advising you all to be aware of your surroundings. While it's possible that Celina has chosen a single target, she may have a vendetta against Cadogan vampires, Chicago vampires, Housed vampires in general. If you're away from the grounds, be careful. And if you hear anything with respect to her activities or her movement, contact me, Malik, or Luc immediately. I am not asking you to be spies. I am asking you to be careful, and not squander the immortality with which you've been gifted."

A rumbling of dissonant "Liege"s echoed through the room.

"And now to the matter at hand," he said, gaze falling on me again. "I am not sure what good it would do to tell you that I trust Merit. That despite the fact that she has challenged me twice, she has saved my life and provided invaluable services to this House."

I had to work to keep the shock from my face, that being quite an announcement to make to a roomful of vampires who'd seen what I'd done.

"You will make up your own minds. She is your sibling, and you must make up your own minds, reach your own conclusions, just as you would for any other member of this House. That said, it can be difficult to make up your minds when you hardly have an opportunity to see her."

Okay, I liked that first part, but I wasn't crazy about where this was going.

"It has been brought to my attention that it would be beneficial to host a House mixer of sorts, to allow you to meet each other socially, to get to know each other outside the bonds of work or duty."

Lindsey, I thought. The traitor. I gritted my teeth and slid a glance behind me to where she stood, grinning. She gave me a finger wave. I made a mental note to punk her as soon as I had the opportunity.

"Therefore," Ethan said, drawing my gaze again, "so that Merit can better appreciate the vampires she has sworn to protect, so that Merit can come to know you all as siblings, and you her, I have decided to name her Cadogan House . . . Social Chair."

I closed my eyes. It was a ridiculously mild punishment, I knew. But it was also completely humiliating.

"Of course, Helen and Merit can work together to plan functions that will be enjoyable for all parties."

Now that was just cruel. And he knew it, too, if the snarky cant of his words was any indication. I opened my eyes again, found him smiling with keen self-satisfaction, and bit back the curse that formed on my lips.

"Liege," I said, bobbing my head with Grateful Condescension.

Ethan lifted a dubious brow, crossed his arms as he scanned the crowd again. "I'm the first to admit it isn't the most . . . satisfying punishment."

Vampires chuckled.

"And I'm not able, at this point, to reveal details that I believe would sway your opinions, lead you to the same conclusions I've reached. But there are few I would trust with the duty of serving this House as Sentinel. And she is the only one I've appointed to that task. She'll remain in that position, and she'll remain here, in Cadogan House."

He grinned again, and this time gave them that look of wicked, boyish charm that probably incited adoration among his female subjects. "And she'll do what she can to ensure that, as they say, 'There ain't no party like a Cadogan party.'"

I couldn't help the dubious snort that escaped me, but the crowd, enamored as they were of their Master, hooted their agreement. When the loudest of the cheers had quieted, he announced that they were excused, and after a polite, unified "Liege," they filed from the room.

"The Constitution bans cruel and unusual punishment," I told him when he stepped down from the podium.

"What?" he innocently asked. "Getting you out of the library? I believe it's due time, Sentinel."

"Now that I'm a real, live vampire?"

"Something like that," he absently said, frowning as he pulled a cell phone from his pocket. He flipped it open, and as he scanned whatever text was displayed there, his expression blanked.

"Let's go," was all he said. I obediently followed.

Lindsey, a straggler at the back of the vampire crowd, winked at me as I passed. "You said you wanted a mixer," she whispered. "And I so told you he wanted you."

"Oh, you'll get what's coming to you, Blondie," I warned, index finger pointed in her direction, and followed Ethan out of the room.

He didn't speak, but tunneled through the vampires on the stairs to the first floor and then to the front door. Curious, katana still in hand, I followed him out to the portico.

A limousine was parked in front of the gate.

"Who is it?" I asked, standing just behind him.

"Gabriel," he said. "Gabriel Keene."

Head of the North American Central Pack.

Jeff had once referred to him as the most alpha of the alphas. When the limousine door opened, and he stepped booted feet onto the sidewalk, I understood why.

Gabriel was tall, broad-shouldered, intensely masculine. Thick, sun-streaked blond-brown hair reached his shoulders.

His confidence was obvious in the bearing of his shoulders, the swagger in his step. He wore snug jeans and biker boots and, even in the muggy spring night, a zipped-up leather driving jacket. He was handsome, almost fiercely so, amber eyes shining, almost drowsily powerful. This was a man who'd proven all he needed to prove and was now intent on action, on leading his people, protecting his people.

"There are more than three thousand shifters in the North American Central," Ethan whispered, eyes on the man, the shifter, before us. "And he's the Apex, the alpha, among them. The American Packs are autonomous, so he is, for all intents and purposes, their king. He's the political equivalent of Darius."

I nodded, kept my gaze on Gabriel.

Another person emerged from a limo, a lovely brunette, who moved to stand behind Gabriel, her delicate, wedding-ring-bound left hand resting on the gentle swell of an obvious pregnancy. She wore a fitted T-shirt and capris, her pink-tipped toes in flip-flops. Her sable hair was pulled back into a messy topknot, strands of it around her face. She wore no makeup, but didn't need it anyway. She was freshly pretty, pale green eyes in the midst of a rosy complexion, bee-stung lips curved into a gentle smile.

She was truly, simply, lovely.

I guessed this was Tonya, Gabriel's wife. The movement of his hand—he reached back, rested it on top of hers, linked their fingers together on her swollen belly, as if cradling his child—confirmed it.

"Sullivan," Gabriel said, when they'd walked up the sidewalk, stood before us.

Ethan nodded. "Keene. This is Merit. She stands Sentinel."

A grin quirked one corner of Gabriel's mouth. "I know who she is."

As if presenting his vulnerabilities for my inspection, he pivoted so that Tonya stood beside him, not behind him. Symbolic, I thought, and very un-vampirelike, this elevation of family.

"This is Tonya." Their fingers still linked, he rubbed a thumb across her belly. "And Connor."

I smiled at her. "It's nice to meet you."

Her voice was dulcet soft, the slightest hint of a southern accent trickling through. "Lovely to meet you, Merit."

When I glanced back at Gabriel, he was staring at me with eyes I'd swore swirled blue and green, the entirety of earth and existence contained there. Just like Nick's. I stared at them, at the hypnotic ebb and flow of them, and I suddenly understood the differences between us.

Vampires were creatures of evening, of frost, of moonlight-tipped architecture, and empty, dark streets.

Shifters were creatures of earth, of sunlight, of sun-scorched savannahs and knee-deep grass.

We flew; they ran.

We analyzed; they acted.

We drank; they devoured.

Not enemies, but not the same.

I couldn't, *was unable*, to argue with that kind of knowledge. "Sir," I said, my voice hardly a whisper, my gaze still on his eyes.

He laughed, full and throaty, and I blinked, the spell broken. But he apparently wasn't finished with me. He leaned down and whispered, "No need for formalities, Kitten. We're practically family, you and I, the drama notwithstanding." He leaned back, brow knitted, and gazed into my eyes. I had the sense he was looking through me, past me, into some future I couldn't discern. The air tingled, magic flowing around us. "We lose them, don't we, always?"

I had no idea what that cryptic message meant, or how to respond, so I stayed quiet, let him look through me. Suddenly, the air cleared, and he straightened again. "Fuck it. What can we do but do it, right?"

Gabriel turned back to Tonya, squeezed her hand, the question apparently rhetorical. When he turned around again, he looked at Ethan.

"We'll be back. The Pack is convening, and we plan to

meet in Chicago. I'm sure you'd heard the rumors, but out of respect for you and your people I wanted to give you a heads-up. I also understand that there's been some drama lately, and I apologize for that."

He waited until Ethan cautiously nodded before continuing. "And I want to talk to you about a certain arrangement for our conference, if you have time." He turned his gaze to me. "Security-related arrangement."

I could practically hear the wheels turning in Ethan's head as he considered just how useful I might be. "Of course," he responded.

Gabriel nodded, regarded Ethan, then glanced at me again. I could see evaluation in his eyes, but of what I didn't know.

"I'll be in touch," he said, then turned. His hand at the small of Tonya's back, they walked back to the car. They climbed in, the limousine door closed again, and they were off.

"What did he say?"

I glanced at Ethan. He looked at me, his head just tilted to the side, obviously curious. Unfortunately, even if I'd wanted to tattle to the nosy little vampire, Gabriel's comments had been completely obtuse, so I could hardly fill him in. "Something about our being family, me and him?"

Ethan arched a brow. "Family? Meaning what?"

I shrugged. "I just report the facts."

We stood there quietly for a moment, the bulk of the House behind us, a dark summer evening before us. Whatever he thought about, he didn't share. I wondered at Gabriel's comment, about the inevitability of loss.

I knew it was coming, knew it waited for me, that the green-eyed devil beside me would most likely be involved in it. But, there being nothing I could do about it today, I shook off the feeling and turned back to the door, leaving him there behind me.

A few minutes later, in my room, I found it lying on the hardwood floor. Another crimson envelope, the same heavy stock, identical to the other. I picked it up and opened it, and just as I had the first time, pulled out an ivory card. The front bore the phrase that had been on the first card: YOU ARE IN-VITED.

But this time, when I flipped the card over, there were details about the party:

Buckingham Fountain.

Midnight.

I stared down at the card in my hand for a full minute, before stuffing it back into the envelope and checking my watch. It was eleven-forty.

I grabbed my sword, and went for the door. I'd solved one mystery. Might as well see what other trouble I could get into.

Read on for a sneak peek
at the next book in
Chloe Neill's *New York Times* bestselling
Chicagoland Vampires series,

Twice Bitten

Available now wherever books
and e-books are sold.

CHAPTER ONE

JOIN THE CLUB

Early June
Chicago, Illinois

It was the beginning of Route 66, the spot where "America's Main Street" began to traverse the United States. Buckingham Fountain, the heart of Grant Park, was named for the brother of the woman who donated the fountain to the city of Chicago. By day, the fountain's main jet shot one hundred fifty feet into the air, a tower of water between the expanse of Lake Michigan and the expanse of downtown Chicago.

But it was late now, and the jets had been turned off for the night. The park was officially closed, but that didn't stop a handful of stragglers from walking around the fountain or perching on the steps that led down to Lake Shore Drive to take in the view of the dark and gleaming waters of Lake Michigan.

I checked my watch. It was eight minutes after midnight. I was here because someone had been leaving me anonymous notes. The first ones mentioned invitations. The last one had invited me to the fountain at midnight, which meant the mysterious someone was eight minutes late.

I had no clue who had invited me or why, but I was curious enough to make the drive downtown from my home in

Hyde Park. I was also cautious enough to show up with a weapon—a short pearl-handled dagger that was strapped beneath my suit jacket on my left side. The dagger had been a gift from Master vampire Ethan Sullivan to me, the Sentinel of his House of vampires.

I probably didn't look the part of the stereotypical vampire, as the Cadogan House uniform—a slim-fit, well-tailored black pantsuit—wasn't exactly the stuff of horror movies. My long, straight, dark hair was pulled into its usual high ponytail, dark bangs across my forehead. I'd donned a pair of black Mary Jane–style heels which, my preference for Pumas notwithstanding, looked pretty good with the suit. My beeper was clipped to my waist in case of House emergencies.

As House Sentinel, I usually carried a katana, thirty-odd inches of honed steel. But for this meeting, I'd left my katana at home, thinking the sight of a bloodred scabbard strapped to my side might inspire a bit too much attention from human eyes. I was, after all, in the park after hours. The members of the Chicago Police Department were going to be curious enough about that; a three-foot-long samurai sword wasn't going to instill much confidence that I was here only for introductions and conversation.

And speaking of introductions . . .

"I wasn't sure you'd come," a voice suddenly said from behind me.

I turned, my eyes widening at the vampire who'd addressed me. "Noah?"

More specifically, it was Noah Beck, leader of Chicago's Rogue vampires—the ones not tied to a particular House.

Noah was bulky—broad shoulders topping a muscular frame. His brown hair stood up in spiky whorls. His eyes were blue, and tonight his jaw bore a trace of stubble. Noah wasn't cover-model handsome, but with the build, strong jaw, and slightly crooked nose, he could fill the leading role in an action movie with no problems. He was dressed, as he usually was, in unrelieved black: black cargo pants, black boots, and a snug, ribbed black T-shirt to replace the long-sleeved version he'd worn in cooler weather.

"You asked to meet me?"

"I did," he said.

When a few seconds passed without elaboration, I tilted my head at him. "Why not just call me and ask for a meeting?" Or better yet, I thought, why not call Ethan? He was usually more than willing to send me into the arms of needy vampires.

Noah crossed his arms over his chest, his expression so serious that his down-thrust chin nearly touched his shirt. "Because you belong to Sullivan, and this meeting isn't about him. It's about you. If I'd signed those notes, I figured you would've felt obligated to tell him about the meet."

"I belong to *Cadogan House*," I clarified, making it known that I didn't, contrary to popular opinion, belong to Ethan. Not that I hadn't considered it. "That means I can't guarantee I won't spill whatever you tell me," I added, letting a small smile curl my lips. "But that depends on *what* you tell me."

Noah uncrossed his arms, slipped a hand into one of his pants pockets, and pulled out a thin red card. Holding the card between two fingers, he extended it toward me.

I knew what it would say before I took it from him. It would bear the initials "RG" and the white stamp of a flowerlike fleur-de-lis. An identical card had been left in my room in Cadogan House, but I still didn't know what it meant.

"What's 'RG'?" I asked him, returning the card.

Noah took it, slipping it back into his pocket. Then he looked around, crooked a finger at me, and began walking toward the Lake. Eyebrows raised, I followed him. That was when the history lesson began.

"The French Revolution was a crucial time for European vampires," he said as we walked down the steps that led from the park to the street below. "When the Reign of Terror struck, vampires got caught up in the hysteria—not unlike humans. But when the vampires began to turn over their fellow Novitiates and Masters to the military, when they were guillotined in the street, the members of the Conseil Rouge, the council that governed vampires before the Greenwich Presidium took power, began to panic."

"That was the Second Clearing, right?" I asked. "French vampires squealed about their friends to ensure their own safety. Unfortunately, the vamps they turned over to the mobs were executed."

Noah nodded. "Exactly. Conseil vampires were old, well established. They enjoyed their immortality, and they weren't eager to become mob victims. So they organized a group of vampires to protect them. Vampires willing to take aspen for them."

"A vampire Secret Service?"

"That's not a bad analogy," he agreed. "The vampires who were asked to serve named themselves the Red Guard."

Hence the RG. "And since you gave me the card, I'm guessing you're one yourself?"

"A card-carrying member, quite literally."

We crossed the street to the lawn in front of the Lake, then walked across grass to the concrete shoreline. When we stopped, I glanced over at Noah, wondering why I was getting the history lesson and the details on his secret life. "Okay, interesting history lesson, but what does all this have to do with me?"

"Impatient, are you?"

I cocked an eyebrow. "I agreed to a secret midnight meeting you didn't want my Master to know about. You're actually getting profound restraint."

Noah smiled back slowly, wolfishly, his lips gradually spreading to reveal straight white teeth—and needle-sharp fangs.

"Why, Merit, I'm surprised you haven't guessed yet. I'm here to recruit you."

It was a full minute before he spoke again. In the meantime, we stood in silence, the two of us staring out at the Lake and the bobbing lights of sailboats near the shore. I'm not sure what he was thinking about, but I was contemplating his offer.

"Things have changed since the RG was founded," Noah finally said, his voice booming in the darkness. "We make sure the Presidium doesn't overstep its authority, like a check and balance on the power of the GP. We also ensure the balance of power between Masters and Novitiates stays relatively stable. Sometimes we investigate. On rare occasions, we clean up."

So, to summarize, Noah wanted me to join an organization whose main goal was keeping Master vampires and GP members from having too much power, or from using that power indiscriminately; an organization whose members spied on their Masters.

I blew out a slow breath, something tightening in my stomach.

I didn't know Ethan's position on the Red Guard, but I had no doubt he would see my joining them as the betrayal of all betrayals. Serving as a Red Guard would pit me directly against Ethan, charging me, a Novitiate vampire, with watching and judging him. Ethan and I didn't have an easy relationship; our interactions were an uncomfortable tug-of-war between our being confidants and colleagues. But this went far beyond our usual brand of mutual irritation.

In fact, it was *exactly* the kind of thing Ethan already feared I'd do—spy on the House. He may not have known about the RG invite, but he knew my grandfather, Chuck Merit, served as a supernatural liaison to the city of Chicago, and he knew my family—the Merits (yes, Merit is my *last* name)—was connected to Seth Tate, mayor of Chicago. Those ties were close enough to concern him. Involvement in something like this would be the icing on the conniption-fit cake.

And that begged an interesting question. "Why me?" I asked Noah. "I'm only two months old, and I'm not exactly warrior material."

"You fit our profile," he said. "You were made a vampire without consent; maybe because of that, you seem to have a different kind of relationship with your Master. You're a child of wealth, but you've seen its abuses. As Sentinel, you're becoming a soldier, but you've been a scholar. You've sworn your oaths to Ethan, but you're skeptical enough not to blindly follow directions."

It was a list of traits that probably made Ethan nervous on

a daily basis. But Noah seemed convinced they were just the kind of things he was looking for.

"And what is it, exactly, that I'd be doing?"

"At this point, we'd like a latent player. You'd remain in Cadogan House, stand Sentinel, and stay in communication with your partner."

I lifted my eyebrows. "My partner?"

"We work in pairs," Noah said, then bobbed his head at something behind me. "Right on cue."

I glanced back, just as the vampire reached us at the shoreline. He was well suited to spying; even with my improved hearing, I hadn't heard him approach. This vamp was tall and lean, with longish auburn hair that just reached his shoulders, blue eyes set beneath long brows, and a chiseled chin. He wore a short-sleeved shirt with a collar, the bottom tucked into his jeans. Tattoos ringed each bicep—a flying angel on one arm, a slinking devil on the other.

I wondered what he was conflicted about.

The newcomer nodded curtly at me, then looked at Noah.

"Merit, Sentinel, Cadogan House," Noah said to him, then glanced at me. "Jonah, Guard Captain, Grey House."

"Guard Captain?" I asked aloud, shocked to the core that the Captain of Scott Grey's own House guards was also a member of the Red Guard. A vampire in a position of trust, whose purpose in the House was to guard the Master, to keep him safe, moonlighting for an organization with an inherent distrust of Masterdom? I guessed it wasn't the kind of thing Scott Grey would be thrilled to learn.

And seriously—was I channeling Ethan Sullivan or what?

"If you accept our offer," Noah said, "Jonah will be your partner."

I looked over at Jonah and found his gaze already on me, his brow furrowed. There was curiosity—but also disdain—in his eyes. He apparently wasn't too impressed with what he'd seen so far of the Cadogan Sentinel.

But since I wasn't interested in going to war with Ethan and thus had no plans to become Jonah's partner, I managed not to care.

I shook my head at Noah. "It's too much to ask."

"I understand your reticence," he said. "I know what it means to take the oaths to your House. I've taken them, too. But for better or worse, Celina's been released. I'd lay short odds on our futures being decidedly more violent than our recent past."

"Not great odds," I solemnly agreed. We'd put an end to the killing spree of Celina Desaulniers, former Navarre House Master. We'd promised the city of Chicago that she was tucked away in a European dungeon, serving time for arranging those murders, but the GP had put Celina back into circulation. She no longer had control of Navarre House, and she blamed me for that inconvenience. She'd come back to Chicago annoyed about her incarceration and eager for a fight.

Noah smiled sadly, as if he understood the direction of my thoughts. "The sorcerers have already predicted that war will come," he said. "We're afraid that's inevitable. Too many vampires have too much pent-up animosity toward humans to keep peace forever—and vice versa—and Celina has done a bang-up job of rousing them. She plays an unfortunately good martyr."

"And that doesn't even touch the shifter issue," Jonah pointed out. "Shape-shifters and vampires have a long, bloody history, but that's not stopping the Packs from heading to Chicago." He glanced at me. "Word is, they're meeting this week. That fit with what you've heard?"

I debated whether I should answer, thus giving away a precious bit of Cadogan House–gleaned information, but I opted to tell him. It's not like the info would be kept under wraps for long. "Yes. We've heard they'll be here within the week."

"Reps of all four Packs in Chicago," Noah muttered, eyes on the ground. "That's like the Hatfields moving in with the McCoys. A centuries-old feud, and the warring parties camping out in the same city. It reeks of trouble." He sighed. "Look, I'm just asking you to consider it. The only thing we'd ask of you now is a commitment to remain in Cadogan House on standby until . . ."

Until, he'd said, as if he believed a coming conflict was inevitable.

"You'd remain latent until we can't keep the peace any longer. At that point, you'd have to be prepared to join us full-time. You'd have to be prepared to leave the House."

I'm sure there was shock in my expression. "You'd want me to leave Cadogan House without a Sentinel in the middle of a war?"

"Think a little more broadly," Jonah put in. "You'd be offering your services, your skills, to all vampires, irrespective of their House affiliation. The RG would offer you a chance to stand for all vampires, not just Masters."

Not for just Ethan, he meant. I'd no longer be Ethan's Sentinel, his vampire. Instead, I'd be a vampire who stood apart from the Houses, from the Masters, from the Presidium, in order to keep the universe of vampires safe . . . and keep Celina and her rabble-rousers at bay.

I wasn't sure what I thought about the request or the RG. "I need time to process this," I told them.

Noah nodded. "This is a serious decision, and it deserves serious consideration. It's about your willingness to step outside your House to ensure all vampires are well protected."

"How can I reach you?" I asked, and wondered whether that question alone meant I'd crossed a line I wouldn't be able to step back from.

"I'm in the phone book, listed as a security consultant. In the meantime, we haven't spoken, and you've never met Jonah. Tell no one—friends, relatives, colleagues. But consider this, Merit: Who needs a Sentinel more? The vampires of Cadogan House, who have a corps of trained guards and a powerful Master at the helm . . . or the rest of us?"

With that, he and Jonah turned and walked away, fading into the darkness of the night.

Also available in the
Chicagoland Vampires series from
New York Times bestselling author

CHLOE NEILL

SOME GIRLS BITE
FRIDAY NIGHT BITES
TWICE BITTEN
HARD BITTEN
DRINK DEEP
BITING COLD
HOUSE RULES
BITING BAD
WILD THINGS

"These books are wonderful entertainment."
—#1 *New York Times* bestselling author Charlaine Harris

Available wherever books are sold or
at penguin.com

facebook.com/ProjectParanormalBooks